French Quarter Saints

French Quarter Saints

JOHN R. GREENE

gatekeeper press
Columbus, Ohio

The views and opinions expressed in this book are solely those of the author and do not reflect the views or opinions of Gatekeeper Press. Gatekeeper Press is not to be held responsible for and expressly disclaims responsibility of the content herein.

FRENCH QUARTER SAINTS

Published by **Gatekeeper Press**
2167 Stringtown Rd, Suite 109
Columbus, OH 43123-2989
www.GatekeeperPress.com

The editorial work for this book is entirely the product of the author. Gatekeeper Press did not participate in and is not responsible for any aspect of these elements.

Cover Illustration by Michelle Derbes Lynch

Library of Congress Control Number: 2022934978

ISBN (paperback): 9781662926426
eISBN: 9781662926433

For Patti

TABLE
OF CONTENTS

1

WHEN YOU LEAST EXPECT IT

April 5, 1972

"You lost your JOB! GAWD! Dat's CRAZY! Whadda'ya mean? How could ya be so STOOPID? How we gonna pay da bills? "

George Santos felt his neck muscles bunch as he cringed. He'd been married to Gloria for 18 of his 36 years, and knew what was coming next. A double chin appeared as he scrunched his head further down towards his shoulders. He made the effort to explain.

"I tried to tell you, dear. I couldn't take it anymore! That little shit kept trying to tell me how to do my job. I've been selling furniture for 15 years, and I'm a damned good salesman. No way I'm going to let a wet-behind-the-ears kid make me change my style. I don't care if he does have a degree from Tulane."

"Tulane, Schmoolane," Gloria responded, "ya get your ASS back there and BEG for ya job back. My father was right about ya. Ya'll never amount to no good! JEESUS GAWD!"

Gloria, a true, New Orleans Yat, used words like "Dawlin'" and "Gawd". Like, *"You should'a seen her outfit, dawlin'. Jeesus Gawd! It looked like she used a shoe hawn to squeeze into dem pants!"* When she'd been a younger woman, she'd been quite a looker in a Jayne Mansfieldesque type of way, but time, and gravity, had begun to blur everything but her voice. Right now, the timber and pitch of her voice was insistent.

George saw that, like a slow-moving, Mississippi River distributary, this discussion was going to curve back into familiar territory that had been covered time and time again in their 18 years of marital bliss. He wondered for the millionth time whether things would have been different had they had children, and, remembering the sadness this lack had occasioned, turned towards the door.

"You're right, dear. I don't know what I was thinking. I'll go back there right now and ask for my old job back."

"Ya DAMN right, ya gonna go back there!" Gloria fumed at him as he walked out the door.

George walked out of their shotgun house, down the porch step, and got into his car. It was springtime in New Orleans. His car was a pale, off-yellow, Ford Mustang that he had bought slightly used about 6 years back, before he'd gotten gray at the temples. He'd bought it the day after he'd made a big commission selling an entire house's worth of furniture to some wealthy person from Uptown. Now, he smiled to himself as he remembered Gloria's look of surprise and pride when he'd brought her outside to see the new car. But his smile turned to a grimace as he thought about what he was going to have to do to get his job back.

Oh well.

He drove down Gentilly Boulevard to Broad Street, and then to Tulane Avenue where the furniture store was located. When he'd been a child, most of the neighborhoods had been peopled with workers and their families. Almost everyone had been able to feel the tide of progress coming to lift all of their boats to a better future.

Now, in 1972, the neighborhoods seemed drastically different. They had changed in feeling, going from promising to abandoned. Places where neighbors had once sat on their front stoops in the humid New Orleans heat now stood empty, with only the beelike hum of hundreds of window-unit air conditioners. Many of the neighborhood businesses had been closed, their windows boarded up. The neighborhood theaters now advertised "XXX-rated" movies. He looked at a marquee as he drove by and saw that the movie currently playing was titled *Clusterf**ked*. "Can't be much of a plot to that one," he chuckled to himself.

The further he went down Tulane Avenue, the seedier the neighborhoods seemed. Bail bondsmen, pawn shops, and "head" shops had taken the place of the old mom-and-pop grocery stores, drug stores, and hardware stores. After all of them, he finally saw the neon sign for Forstahl Furniture. In the low, late afternoon light, the two "F's" lit up in a hot pink first, to be followed by the rest of the two words in a light neon blue. He'd always thought the neon sign was kind of pretty in a gaudy way.

George practiced what he was going to say as he parked the Mustang in the parking lot.

Speaking to himself quietly, he said, "Simon, I want to apologize for flying off the handle like that. I've decided to follow your advice and change the way I approach customers."

He walked up to the front door, opened it, and almost ran into Simon Patrick, the young manager he needed to speak to.

"What the hell are you doing back here, Santos?" Simon barked before George could say anything.

"I, er, I..."

"I told you you're fired, Santos. I don't want to see you back here again!"

"But, Simon, I mean, Mr. Patrick, sir, I wanted to apologize for flying off the handle," George stammered.

"Fine! Apology accepted. Now, get out." Simon stood there, raised to his full 5'7", and folded his arms.

"But...my job..." George said.

"You don't *have* a job here anymore, Santos! We're going to bring in some new blood with a better attitude. Go on, get out!"

"Uh...uh...." George wanted to say more, but it seemed that his brain had shut down and the only noises that would come out were completely incoherent.

Simon turned George around and steadily guided him out the front door. Once he was out, Simon pulled a key out of his pocket and deliberately locked it behind him. He then turned around and walked purposely to the back of the store, soon to be lost among the headboards, dressers, and mirrors.

George stood on the sidewalk in front of the store and stared into the glass door for a couple of minutes more. *Shit. What am I going to do now?*

Slowly, he turned and walked back to his car. A black and white Pontiac Parisienne blew its horn at a pedestrian who was stumbling across the street in a drunken stupor, but George barely noticed. He walked back to the Mustang, climbed in, and sat there with a simmering anger rising in his breast.

"Screw that son of a bitch," he thought, and then he started the car, put it into first gear, popped the clutch, and laid a good bit of rubber down on the parking lot, leaving a lot of acrid, blue smoke hanging in the air.

His thoughts as he retraced his steps were entirely different than the ones that had passed through his mind on the way to the furniture store. *What am I going to tell Gloria?* The more he thought about the possible explanations, however, the more he realized that there was nothing he'd be able to say that would make the situation better. Gloria would be pissed, no doubt about it. She would make his life miserable for some time to come—at least until he got another job. The car slowed markedly as he turned onto Jonquill Street, where they lived.

A blue and white New Orleans police car was parked in front of his house as he pulled into the small, double concrete strips that served as his driveway. His house had been built in the early 1920s. It had a low-pitched roof over the front porch, supported by four brick and concrete columns, and the red bricks created a solid base for the more slender concrete columns, which were painted white. The edge of the porch roof jutted out to the top of the three concrete steps leading up to the porch. Above the porch roof was a small, circular, stained glass window which looked out on the street like a Cyclops on Mardi Gras.

George walked up his porch steps and reached for the doorknob. It opened quickly, just as his hand touched it. Standing there in the doorway was his best friend, Sonny LaCoure, who'd gotten a job with the police in 1965, and loved it. George had known Sonny since their grade school days at St. Joseph's Catholic School. They'd served as each other's best men at their respective weddings. Sonny's marriage had lasted just 6 years, and he'd remained a confirmed bachelor since the divorce.

"Hi, Sonny, what brings you here tonight?" George asked.

"Um, I, well, George—" Sonny managed to get out before Gloria's voice took over.

"George, it's best dat ya know. I'm leavin' ya." Gloria glanced quickly at Sonny, and then back to George. "Jeezus Gawd knows I've tried hard to stay wit' ya, but ya don't fulfill me. I have emotional needs, ya know!" She paused, took a breath, and reached out to grasp George's hand. "Ya used to be da best. So attentive. So caring. But dat was a long time ago. Now, I think ya love ya Dixie beer more than ya love me."

George felt all of the air leave his lungs. Spots began to swim before his eyes, and sounds seemed as if they were coming from a long way away.

"But...Gloria...dear...I don't understand."

"Dat's exactly right, George. Ya don't understand. Ya haven't understood for yeahs. All ya do is go to work, come home, open a beer, sit on da couch, and watch da boob tube. Ya never pay attention to my wants, to my needs." Gloria stood in the living room of the shotgun house with two big suitcases next to her. She was wearing her black and white, swirly-striped dress that she usually wore to wedding receptions, and had on a bit too much makeup and perfume.

She continued to complain, "Ya remembah da time I wanned to go to da Ladies Auxiliary dance at church? I axed ya if ya'd take me an' ya said ya didn't wanna go. Ya even called dem 'crazy old bats!' An' my mom and 'em were membahs! An' anudda time, ya remembah when I wanned to go see dat movie, Docta Jivago? Ya tol' me dat ya didn't wanna see a stoopid movie about a bunch a crazy Russkies." Gloria was just beginning to hit her stride. It was plain to all involved that there were many different, flagrant episodes she'd cover, all related to George's failure to perform his husbandly duties.

"But...but..." George's mind was beginning to congeal around a thought, "Sonny, what are you doing here?"

"Er, George...I—" Sonny began.

"Me and Sonny are startin' a new life together!" Gloria said, her voice loud and hard-edged as she let go of George's hand. "He fulfills my emotional needs. Ya can stay right here with ya Dixie and ya tv. We're moving to da Nort' Shore. We're gonna start a new life dere, an' ya better not do anything to mess it up, mister!"

"Sonny!?" George strangled out as he looked at his old friend.

Sonny gazed at George like a big sheepdog that had eaten three of the four hot dogs his owner had prepared for supper. "I'm sorry, George," he said in a low, quiet voice. He picked up the two suitcases and walked past George onto the porch. Then, he walked down the porch steps to the curb, and put the suitcases down on the street as he fumbled in his pocket for the keys to the police car to open the trunk.

George felt as if he were paralyzed. "Take care of yaself, dawlin'," Gloria whispered as she walked up to him and gave him a peck on his cheek. Then, she walked firmly out the door, down the porch, and onto the street. She waited at the front passenger door of the police car for a few moments, looking at Sonny, who suddenly realized what he was supposed to do and quickly walked over and opened the door for her. He walked around the cruiser, opened the driver's side door, climbed in... and the blue and white police car disappeared slowly down the street.

2

FROM THE ASHES

April 5, 1972

George closed the door, walked into his living room, and collapsed onto the couch. Things had happened fast. He couldn't focus on a particular thought before another would take its place. When he lowered his hands from the sides of his head, he simply stared at them as he rested his forearms on his knees. It was then that he saw the letter on the coffee table in front of the couch. He picked it up and read.

Dear George,

By the time you read this, I will be gone. I have decided to seek my happiness with Sonny. We are going to move to the North Shore and start a new life. I know this probably comes as a surprise to you, but I've been thinking about this for a long time. I need more in my life. I don't want to spend the rest of my life with someone who I love, but am not in love with. Tonight, when you told me that you quit your job, I knew it was time for me to act. Please don't think bad of me or Sonny. I wish you all the luck in your future.

Sincerely,

Gloria

P.S. I have taken the money we had in our savings account to help me begin my new life. Also, I have taken $765.00 from the checking account.

*I know that doesn't leave you much to pay bills with, but you should have
thought more about money before you quit your job. G."*

George stared at the letter for a full half-minute after he'd finished
reading it. Then, he crumpled up the paper, threw it at the television
set, and yelled, "JESUS CHRIST!" He jumped up, kicking over the
coffee table, and ran to the dining room, where he began punching the
wall rhythmically, repeating the word "Fuck!" over and over with each
blow as the tears began to stream down his face. His whole world had
turned upside down.

Finally, he stopped hitting the wall when his knuckles were skinned
and sore. He'd made several cracks in the plaster, including one that
made it possible to see the wooden slats underneath.

George walked into the kitchen wondering what he was going to
do for the umpteenth time. Then, suddenly, he realized what his path
forward would be. "That's it," he whispered to himself. He opened up
the cabinet beneath the porcelain sink, reached in, and pulled out a
bottle of Sir Malcolm Scotch. Then, he reached into the cabinet above
the sink and got a large glass tumbler. "That's it. That's all that's left
to do," he mumbled again as the glass filled with the honey-colored
scotch. He raised the glass to his lips and took a large swallow before he
placed the glass on the kitchen table and walked towards the front of
the house, entering the bedroom. He opened the drawer in the bedside
table and took out a pad of paper and a pen.

Walking back into the kitchen, he put the pad on the table, sat down,
took another long draw of his drink, and focused on the ballpoint pen.
It had a blue base and a white body, with writing on the body. The
writing said, "New Orleans Police Force: New Orleans' Finest." When
George read this, he took the pen and threw it into the corner of the
room and buried his head in his hands again. A couple of minutes later,
he lifted his head, walked to the corner of the kitchen where the pen

lay on the black and white tile floor, picked it up, and returned to the kitchen table. He sat down, took another swig of his drink, and began to write:

Dear Gloria,

I don't know what to say. I thought that we would be together forever. I'm sorry if I've disappointed you. I should have been a better provider. I should have made something of myself. Instead, I'm just a pathetic loser. By the time you read this, I will have jumped off the Mississippi River Bridge. I wish you and Sonny luck in your new life. Try not to think too badly of me.

Love,

George

Tears streaked down George's face as he read, and reread, his letter. He downed the remaining scotch in two big gulps, folded the letter, and laid it on the kitchen table. Then, he took his wallet out of his back pocket, opened it, and looked inside. He had a total of $56—two twenties, one ten, and six ones. He stared at the bills as if willing them to speak to him, and then he got up and walked towards the front door with a slightly unsteady gait.

When he reached the front door, he stopped and turned back towards the house for a moment, as if to tell it goodbye, but then he turned back around, opened the door, and walked out onto the porch. The full moon was rising over the Theard's house next door. It cast cold shadows on the front lawn. Down the street, he heard the neighborhood children playing Kick the Can, their shrieks of laughter serving as a terrible counterpoint to the sadness and despair that filled his heart.

He walked down the porch steps, got into his Mustang, and backed out into the street.

He drove down Jonquil Street to Franklin Avenue and turned left without realizing where he was going. The houses on Franklin Avenue were much nicer than the ones on the back streets, reflecting the way that much of New Orleans had been developed. The larger homes were on the main streets, and homes and lots became smaller as one progressed away from the thoroughfares. He continued down Franklin to St. Claude, where he took a right. As he crossed Esplanade Avenue and St. Claude became N. Rampart, he realized he was on the edge of the French Quarter. On the spur of the moment, he turned left onto St. Ann Street. Almost immediately, he found a parking place on the street, and it occurred to him that this was the luckiest thing that had happened all day. He bumped the car behind him just slightly as he parallel-parked the Mustang.

George had grown up in New Orleans, and he'd been coming down to the Quarter (Gloria always pronounced it "Da Quahtahs") since he'd been a child. As he'd gotten older, he'd even spent some time in the strip clubs and dives on Bourbon Street. But, like many inhabitants of famous tourist destinations around the world, he rarely took the time and effort to go visit the most famous destination in his own town. As he climbed out of the car to do so tonight, a light rain began. It cooled the air, and gave a luster of even greater age to the street and buildings nearby. This part of the French Quarter was dark, mainly occupied by homeowners and renters. A streetlight put out a circle of warm light that seemed surrounded by a soft darkness, as if both dark and light had agreed to make peace in this ancient place.

George tripped and nearly fell as he stepped from the street onto the sidewalk. Like many of the sidewalks in the constantly subsiding city of New Orleans, it was uneven and, in places, the concrete was broken by large cracks. George could see the light of Bourbon Street towards the river, but he didn't feel like being around lights and crowds in the last hours of his life. He turned left on Dauphine St., and turned left again on Dumaine Street, moving back towards N. Rampart.

Just as he turned onto Dumaine Street, he saw the shadow of a person turn into an alleyway a short distance ahead of him. A blue sign, illuminated by a flickering gas lamp, was hanging over the dark hole that was the alleyway. The sign read simply, *Astro's*. George walked up to the alleyway and looked down its dark length. There wasn't much to see—just two brick walls that went back as far as he could see, and a subtle blueish light spilling out of the wall to the left about 50 feet down the alley.

George made his decision. As he approached the door toward the end of the alleyway, he began to feel rather than hear the rhythmic pounding of a drum. *Maybe it's one of those hippie bars.* He saw the blue light came from a small, blue neon *Astro's* sign hanging over the open door. He got to the doorway and looked in. It was the smallest bar he had ever seen in his life. The entire bar was lit with a cool, dim light, and the room was about twenty feet long, ending at a brick wall. It was about eight feet wide. The bar itself was about two feet wide and ran the length of the room. Behind the bar, there was enough room for just one person to tend bar, with bottles of liquor stacked on shelves vertically against a brick wall. There were stools in front of the bar, and another brick wall about two feet from the stools. Sitting near the middle of the bar was a person with long hair. The light was too dim for George to be sure, but he believed it was a woman. Behind the bar was a tall, dark-skinned black man with the largest Afro that George had ever seen. He wore dark glasses, even in the dim light. George wondered if the man was blind as he cautiously walked in and sat down three stools from the door.

"Hey, man," the bartender said in a smooth, deep voice, "what'll you have?"

"Uh, scotch, I guess," George responded.

"You got any preference?" the bartender asked.

"I guess Sir Malcolm," George replied.

"Holy shit, man!" The woman's voice reminded him of Suzanne Pleshette. "That's rot gut! If you're going to drink scotch, why don't you drink some real scotch? Give him some Laphroaig, JC!"

George turned away from the bartender with the large Afro and looked down the bar towards the woman who'd spoken these words. Her voice had been low and melodious, but had still carried over the slow, rhythmic bass beat that served as background noise in the bar. In the dim light, George could see that her face was slightly angular, but pretty. He turned back towards the barkeep and said, "Sure. Give me some Laphroaig, please."

"The smell from hell coming up," JC said, confusing George. The bartender then reached behind himself with one hand, without looking, and grabbed a bottle and then a glass. He set both down on the bar, pulled the cork out of the bottle, and began pouring a generous dose of the liquor. When the glass was half-full, he pushed it towards George and said, "Laphroaig is always drunk neat."

George took the glass and lifted it to his nose. "Jesus Christ! This smells like smoke!"

"He's taking your name in vain, JC!" the woman said. "Go ahead, man, drink it up."

It took George about three seconds to remember why he was there. Then, he lifted up the glass and took a big gulp. The peaty scotch filled his mouth with its smoky flavor and tickled his nose. He set the glass down quickly and sneezed.

"Bless you," JC said in his smooth voice.

The woman picked up her beer and walked over to the stool next to George. She was smiling as she sat down. "So, tell me, what do you think?" she asked.

"It's great," George managed to whisper back, "a little smoky, but great!" His voice began to return and he took another large sip of the scotch, held the glass up in the air looking through it for a few seconds, and then took another large swallow, finishing the glass.

"I'd like another, please," he told JC.

"Sure thing, my man!" he replied, and poured George another half-glass.

George took another big sip before he turned towards the woman and asked, "Whass your name?"

"Inanna," JC replied, "but most folks around here call her Anna."

Now that Anna was closer to him, George could see she was of an indeterminate age. Not old, but not young, either. He guessed her to be around 38 or so. He thought she'd be about 5'6" tall when she stood. She was olive-complected, slight of build, and had eyes with just the hint of an oriental flavor. Her hair was dark, but in the dim light, he couldn't tell what color it was. Same thing went for her eyes. She was altogether a very attractive woman.

George took another strong pull from his drink, shook his head, and set the glass down on the bar before saying, "My name is George."

"Well, well, George," said Anna, "it sure looks like you're in a hell of a rush to get a buzz on."

"Lost m'job," George mumbled.

"Ouch," Anna replied.

"An' my wife," George continued, staring at the nearly empty glass.

JC looked at George with a calm gaze. He picked up the bottle and filled the glass to near the top. "This one's on the house," he said quietly.

"Th...thanks, but I-I'm not finissshhhed. She ran off with my best friend, and took our money, too. There, thass it." And George took yet another swallow.

"That's a bummer," Anna said as she laid a hand on George's shoulder.

Just then, the quiet of the bar was interrupted by two young, long-haired men coming in the door. It was easy to tell they were identical twins, as they even wore the same type of faded jeans and faded jean work shirts.

"Hey! Whass happening, Anna, JC!" they both chimed loudly at about the same time.

"Slow down, dudes!" Anna said. "Take it easy. George here just told us that he's lost his job, his money, and his wife tonight. Show some respect!"

"Whoa! Sorry, man," they both replied. They walked up to George and both offered their hands.

George shook the first one's hand. "George," he said. The first twin replied that his name was Caz, and George repeated the handshake and introduction with the second twin, who gave his name as Paul. George found himself in the center of a small circle framed by JC across the bar, and Anna, Caz, and Paul on his side. He took another long swallow of the scotch.

Suddenly, George staggered to his feet. He looked around at the kind strangers. They were so nice. They cared about him. It almost made him weep. "I've gotta go now. How much I owe you?" he slurred, turning towards JC.

"I told you, man, it's on the house," JC replied in his smooth, soft voice, and so George began to weave his way towards the door.

"Hold on a minute, George," Anna said. "Where are you going to?"

"I'm gonna go jump off the bridge," he slurred.

"Oh, hell! You aren't in any condition to drive. Why don't you let me and the boys take you up there so you don't kill somebody? Come on, boys, give me a hand with him!" And with that, Anna put one of George's arms around her shoulder and began to steer him out of the bar.

JC gave George a brilliant smile and said, "Peace."

George found it difficult to hold his head still, but managed to smile back at JC and flash him a returning peace sign with the hand not held by Anna.

They walked out of the door and into the alleyway. A thick fog had enveloped the world. George, even if he could have seen well, couldn't have seen much at all. Just a cool mist caressing his face as Anna guided him to his car. For a brief second, he wondered how Anna knew which car was his, but she opened the passenger door for him and he didn't question it. He just slumped into the passenger seat as she walked around the car and got into the driver's seat.

"How about some keys?" she asked.

He mumbled, "Sorry," pulled the keys out of his pocket, and handed them to Anna.

An old, wood-paneled station wagon pulled up alongside the parked Mustang. It was so gaily painted that it seemed to banish the darkness and fog. A large, orange sun was painted on the hood, with tendrils of red, blue, green, and white coming out of it and swirling in different patterns on the sides and the roof. The word "SUNSHINE" was painted on the hood close to the windshield. George could almost swear that the colors were moving, but a small, rational part of his mind told him that it was the alcohol overload he'd gotten.

Caz, or Paul, rolled down the passenger-side window. "Y'all ready?" he asked.

"Let's go," Anna replied, and she started the Mustang's engine. As she pulled out of the parking spot, she looked over at George and said, "Put your seat belt on. It wouldn't do for you to get killed on your way to committing suicide." George sheepishly complied.

They went down N. Rampart Street and made their way to Loyola, then onto the Pontchartrain Expressway. The fog had enveloped the night so thoroughly that it seemed to George that they were flying through the air. Streetlights looked like moons shining through thin clouds. Curiously, there were no other cars on the streets.

"Are you sure you want to go through with this?" Anna asked. "I've found that most people who say they want to commit suicide are really looking for someone to pay attention to their problems."

"Yesss," George slurred, and then he hiccupped. "There's nothing leffft to do. It's really nice of you to drive me there. Here, let me pay you something." With that, he reached into his back pocket and pulled out his wallet. He unfolded it, reached in, and pulled out all of his cash. He held the cash in his hand, looking at the $20 dollar bill that was on the outside. The face on the bill was that of Andrew Jackson, but it looked to George like Andrew had a huge Afro. He picked up the bill with his other hand and raised it to eye-level, trying to hold his head still enough to focus. Sure enough, Andrew Jackson's hard-edged face was there, but with a gigantic Afro. And as George looked at the bill, Andrew gave him a large wink. George closed his eyes and shook his head. When he opened them again, he saw a normal $20 bill. He looked across the car towards Anna, who was humming a tune as she drove, and so he turned his head and looked out the passenger window. They were climbing up the bridge. The fog was dense, and what lights could be seen were muted by the cottony fog. There were still no cars in sight, except for the station wagon that followed close behind them. When they had reached the top of the bridge, both cars pulled in close to the guard rail.

Anna reached down and turned off the key. She looked towards George and said, "OK, George. This is it. The top of the Mississippi River Bridge. This is where you meet your destiny."

George looked at her in the dim light and thought to himself that she really was very pretty. "Thanksss'a'lot," he said, and then he opened the passenger door. He slowly got out of the seat, and using his right hand, he held on to the roof to steady himself. He shuffled to the nearby railing and, placing both hands on it, looked down. The fog was swirling and spinning in the bridge lights. It seemed almost solid, like sand swirling as it went down an hourglass. He leaned further down until his chest rested on the railing and watched the fog perform a ballet below. His feelings of despair and sorrow seemed increasingly distant as an appreciation of the performance of fog and light grew in him.

"Hey, you!" Anna yelled from the driver's seat. The noise startled him and made him move up and forward. He was too close to the railing, though, and, overbalanced, he began to tip forward. His impetus picked up and he began to fall over the rail in earnest.

"Whoooaaa! Hellllp!" he screamed as his body toppled over the rail and his feet left the ground. His right hand and arm slipped between the rail and the bridge and his body described a perfect 360-degree circle that left him dangling feet-first over the river below, with the railing caught in the bend of his elbow. "Hellllp!" he screamed again.

Before he could fill his lungs with breath enough to get out another scream, the twins were standing over him and reaching down to grab his arm and shoulder, and then his torso, and they lifted him back up over the railing.

"Hey, take it easy, buddy!" Caz (or Paul) said. "You're all good now!" George clung to the pair as they eased him back into the passenger's seat of the Mustang. Once he was in, they closed the door and walked back to their station wagon.

"So, you decided to give it another crack," Anna said cheerily. "Good."

George sat and shivered. He suddenly felt very sober.

The Mustang pulled away from the rail and made a U-turn on the bridge, followed by the station wagon. There were still no cars to be seen. As they began descending the bridge towards the city, the fog began to thin and the lights of Canal Street became visible, as did the lights of the various neighborhoods stretching up and down the river, as well as those towards Lake Pontchartrain. Anna retraced their path back to St. Ann Street. The same parking place was available and she quickly parked the car. Then, she got out, walked to the passenger side of the car, opened the door, and helped George out. He accepted her hand and they walked around the corner to the same alleyway on Dumaine Street. This time, the door to Astro's was closed. Anna went past Astro's to a door at the end of the alleyway, produced a key from her purse, and opened it.

They walked through the doorway with Anna in the lead. It opened into a courtyard. The courtyard was lit by gas lamps on posts, and it was surrounded by brick walls that were overtopped along the far side by an old, decrepit-looking, wooden porch. A second story also made of brick ran along three sides of the courtyard above the brick walls, and a two-story red brick wall held the door through which they had entered. At different places along the brick walls, and in the structures above, there were various doors, as well as some small windows that looked out on the courtyard. The areas between the downstairs doorways had lush garden beds. Different plants—including small palms, elephant ears, and palmetto—gave the gardens a jungle-like effect. Large sandstone flagstones surfaced the courtyard, and in the far corner stood a small, independent, two-story brick structure with carefully bricked, small holes all around it.

"Come on, George." Anna tugged on George's hand and led him to a door in the middle of the back wall. She opened the door and revealed a large bedroom that was lit by several candles. In the middle of the far wall, there was a huge, four-posted tester bed. The canopy of the bed showed a richly colored embroidery, and was carefully drawn along each bedpost by a golden-tassled, dark velvet rope. Anna led George into the room and closed the door behind them. She took his hand again, and led him to the side of the bed.

"You know, George," she said, "there's something about you that I like. You've really had a hard time of it tonight, losing your job and your wife. I don't blame you for wanting to kill yourself—although it's not something that would enter my mind. Anyway, you came through a close call, and now you've decided to give life another chance. That's something that I can completely approve of, for to me, life is beautiful."

With that, Anna reached down, took the bottom of her blouse in her hands, and pulled it up and over her head. In the warm, yellow light of the candles, George could see that she was, indeed, beautiful. Her hair, which was a dark, reddish blonde, framed her bright green eyes. Her full lips curled in a slight smile. She had high cheekbones and a slightly angular chin which gave her a defiant look. Her breasts were small and high, with beautifully pert, pink aureoles and nipples. She shook her head, and her hair fluffed and rested down on her slim shoulders. Arching one eyebrow, she pulled down the covers of the bed and sat down. She kicked off her shoes, unbuttoned her pants, and pulled them off one leg at a time, all the while looking an invitation at George.

George's mind raced as he stood over Anna. So many things had happened over the last eight hours. He had lost his job, Gloria, and almost his life. He had consumed more alcohol at once than he had drunk since he'd been freshly out of high school. The world was spinning faster than he could keep up with. He stood there weaving back and forth as he looked down on Anna, who seemed to shine in the warm light, sitting there before him. Then, he vomited over her beautiful breasts and fell down, passed out on the bed.

3
A DOOR OPENS

April 6, 1972

The first things George saw when he opened his eyes were several enormous, hand-hewn beams that spanned the high ceiling. White plaster filled the spaces between the beams. In the center of the ceiling, a dusty crystal chandelier hung from a plaster medallion. It took him a moment to remember the gist of what had happened the night before, and he groaned when he did. George's head felt as if it were full of spiky cotton. When he turned his head to the left or right, he could feel a throbbing pain behind his temples. The tester bedposts stood like sentries keeping the world at bay, and he wondered where the embroidered canopy had gone. He leaned up on one arm and looked around the room. Several pieces of old furniture lined the walls of the room, the most notable being a very large chifferobe that must have been 10 feet tall and 6 feet wide. Carved into the door was a bundle of wheat stalks arranged around a bunch of grapes. The piece, like all of the other furniture in the room, was covered in dust and looked to be very old.

Near the far corner of the room, George saw a large, white, 6-paneled door. He assumed it was a door to the bathroom, and wondered if Anna was in there. When he threw the covers off, he saw that he was clean, but naked. And he groaned again as he remembered vomiting on Anna. He looked, but could find no trace of the embarrassing episode when he got out of the bed. The slightly uneven wooden floor was pleasantly cool on his bare feet. He walked to the door and rapped it lightly with his knuckles.

"Anna, are you in there?" he asked, his voice husky with a hangover.

There was no reply, so he opened the door. The bathroom was spartan. There was an old, cast iron, clawfoot tub along one wall, with a towel hanging on a bar above it, a toilet against the far wall, and a small, white marble pedestal sink on the other wall. The floor was tiled with black and white ceramic tiles which were cool to the touch. Above the sink, an old, frameless mirror was hung on the wall. The mirror had a small crack in the lower right corner. A simple fixture with a bare bulb came out of the wall over the mirror.

After doing his business, George turned on the water to the tub and was pleasantly surprised to find that the hot water worked. He took the drain plug, which was attached to the faucet by a small metal ball chain, and shoved it in the drain. When the tub was full, he climbed in and submersed his entire body under the warm water. A half-used bar of soap was sitting on a metal soap dish attached to the far back of the tub. He used this to wash thoroughly, and then, after pulling the chained plug, he stood, grabbed the towel, and dried himself. He looked for but couldn't find anything like a toothbrush or toothpaste, so he rinsed his mouth well from the faucet in the pedestal sink. Finally, he looked in the mirror.

His familiar face stared back at him. There was no sign of the evening's traumatic events other than his bloodshot eyes. Even his headache had subsided to the point that he felt only a muted pain in his temples. As he was looking at his reflection in the old mirror, though, there came a soft knocking at the main door.

George startled, and then walked out of the bathroom to the outside door. He slowly opened it, hiding his nakedness, and peered out. There was a man sitting in a wheelchair, and he had George's clothes folded in his lap. The man appeared to be in his 20s. He was wearing a pair of cut-off blue jeans and no shirt. He was ruddy-faced and had long, full, curly blond hair that framed his face and hung down below his shoulders. He also had a long, full, curly reddish blonde beard. George was struck by how much he resembled a lion. That resemblance was belied by the thin legs that stuck out from the man's shorts; they were the legs of a person who had been in a wheelchair for a long time.

"Er...hello," George said to the man.

"Hey, man," the man in the wheelchair responded. "My name is Jim. Anna asked me to get these to you. I'd almost given up on anybody being in there." Saying this, he held the clothes out to George in a slightly clumsy manner. George sensed that the man's debility had affected more than his legs.

"Thank you, Jim. George," George replied as he took his clothes. "Do you know what time it is?"

"It's just past 10. Anna told me to knock on the door and wake you up if you slept past 10. Are you hungry?

"I'm starving," George said. "Give me a minute to put my clothes on and I'll be right out."

"Far out, man," was Jim's reply.

It only took George a couple of minutes to throw his clothes on. The courtyard gardens appeared as they had the night before when he stepped outside. If anything, the foliage and flowers appeared even more luxuriant. Mandevilla and Bougainvilla twined up several metal arbors that stood at the rear of the garden beds and crawled up along the brick walls. In the light, he could also see several small citrus trees, and a fig tree. Jim had wheeled his wheelchair into the shade of a crepe myrtle. He smiled as George walked up to him.

"Nice place, huh?" Jim asked.

"It's beautiful," George said as he turned to take in the entire courtyard. "How old is it? Do you know?"

"Not much of the Quarter that was left after the Great Fire of 1788," Jim replied. "However, this was built just afterwards in 1789. That wall there—" and here, Jim raised his right arm with his slightly curled hand in the direction of the standing wall that contained the door to the alleyway, "was built before the fire. It's what's left of a building that was destroyed. No one knows exactly how old it is, but I'll bet it was built before 1750. Are you ready to eat something?"

"Yes, please." George rubbed his stomach and added, "I'm really hungry. Is there a particular place you're thinking of going to?"

"Yes." Jim smiled. "To that door over there by the pigeonnier." Here, he pointed his hand towards the small building with the carefully bricked holes. "Mama Zulie lives there. She'll have something to eat for you."

George hesitated for a moment, and then asked, "Hey, Jim, do you know where Anna went?"

Jim smiled at him again. "Don't we all wish we knew? You mind?" And with this, Jim gestured again with his chin towards the handles of the wheelchair.

"Not at all," George said as he got behind the chair and pushed it towards the door Jim had singled out. The sand-colored flagstones were uneven, like all old flooring surfaces in New Orleans, and the wheels of the chair made a "shishing" noise like that of passing fine-grit sandpaper over wood.

The door opened as they drew closer to the pigeonnier, and a large, tall, dark-skinned, black man backed out. He turned and glanced angrily at the two of them for an instant, and then turned his attention back towards the doorway he was backing away from.

A woman came after him, though they heard her before they saw her. "Non, non, I will not go out with you. Jamais!" This was what she said, though it sounded more like, "I weel not go out wiss you!" because of her thick, French accent.

The speaker was an attractive, older black woman with skin the color of chocolate milk. With each word, she poked the much taller man in the chest with her index finger. He nearly tripped over an uneven flagstone, backing away from her anger.

"You will regret this decision, Erzulie!" the tall man boomed. With that, he turned away from the woman and walked quickly past George and Jim. As he drew nearer to them, he glared with a decidedly unfriendly visage. George took a half-step back, pulling Jim's wheelchair with him to give the man as much space as possible. The man quickly walked out the courtyard door and disappeared down the alley.

George turned his attention back to the feisty woman. She had a smooth, youthful face belied by her curly silver hair, which formed a halo around her head. She was small, no more than 5 feet tall with delicate hands and feet. There was a necklace of precious amber around her neck, and her hands sported rings of turquoise, lapis lazuli, and fire opal. She looked at George and Jim, and broke into a wide smile that revealed lustrous teeth as white as pearls .

"Bonjour, mon pauvre petit! Hallo, Jim! How are you today?"

"Hi, Mama Zulie," Jim replied cheerily, "this is George. Another one of Anna's projects. He just got up and could really use some food. I told him you could probably help him."

"Mais, oui, but of course!" she replied. "Please come into my home. I've got some wonderful sugar cakes that make a delicious breakfast!"

"Thank you," George and Jim said at the same time, and then George pushed Jim's wheelchair up and over the threshold into Mama Zulie's apartment. The apartment was larger than the one George had spent the night in. The door led into a living room with gaily colored walls. Many different types of wooden masks were mounted on the different walls—some plain, and some colored even more brightly than the walls. Two closed doors led to other parts of the apartment, and a narrow hallway led into what appeared to be the kitchen. It was down this hallway that Mama Zulie disappeared for a moment, only to return with a plate full of cakes and confections. She set this down on a table that appeared to be made of rosewood and motioned George to a chair. George pushed Jim's wheelchair up to the table and took the seat that had been offered to him. They both grabbed a cake and began to eat.

"Now, my dears, would you like some champagne with your cakes?" Mama Zulie asked.

George's stomach did a flip-flop and he drew his head in towards his shoulders. "No thank you, ma'am," he said, looking askance at Jim.

Jim returned his look, smiled, and shrugged his shoulders.

"Tsk, tsk. That is the trouble with you young people," Mama Zulie said. "No sense of adventure. No sense of joie de vivre! Ah, when I was young, it was cakes and champagne all day, every day. Now, everyone is, how do you say, nose to the groundstone. Where is your sense of adventure? Where is your sense of fun?"

"OK, Mama Zulie, you've talked us into it," Jim told him, smiling as he shrugged again at George.

"Bon, C'est bon!" Mama Zulie bustled back to the kitchen and then returned bearing a bottle of champagne. She set down two glasses in front of the men and poured them full of the sparkling drink. Jim was able to slide his hand under the glass and hold the stem between his second and third fingers, keeping the glass in his cupped hand and raising it, a little clumsily, up to drink.

George thought to himself, *When in Rome...* and reached for his glass. The champagne was cold and excellent. They each had several pastries washed down with the sparkling wine. "So, what are you young men going to do next?" Mama Zulie asked.

George replied, "Mama Zulie, that's the second time you've referred to me as young. I'll bet you're not much older than me."

"Ah, mon cher, you are a true gentleman. You would be very surprised to know how old I am, but I am grateful for your kind words."

"Anna asked me to take George for a ride to the Lakefront," Jim interjected.

"Well, then, let me not interfere with your plans for the day," Mama Zulie said.

George and Jim had finished with their sweets and their champagne by now, and so Mama Zulie began to clean up the table. She prepared to take the sweets and the bottle of champagne back to the kitchen area, but George rose from the table and, on impulse, grabbed her hand, bent over, and kissed it. "Thank you for the delicious breakfast, Mama Zulie. It was good to meet you."

She smiled first at George, then at Jim, and said, "Mon pauvre petit, Jim. Your friend is a true gentleman and is welcome in my home anytime. He is very handsome, also."

George felt himself blush as Jim laughed out loud.

After taking their leave of Mama Zulie, George pushed Jim out into the courtyard.

"What do you say, George? Do you have any other plans today, or would you like to go to the Lakefront?"

George stopped pushing the chair suddenly. "Excuse me, but I need to think for a minute." He sat down on a bench in the shade of the crepe myrtle tree. He thought for a moment about work, but since he didn't have a job at the moment, he certainly didn't have to be anywhere for that. Then, he thought about Gloria and Sonny. He felt a gnawing pit in his stomach, and unconsciously raised his hand to his mouth and began worrying a fingernail. Gloria didn't want him around anymore, so, other than sheer force of habit, there was no real reason for him to go back home right now. He raised his head up and looked at Jim, who was sitting patiently and looking at him with a bemused expression.

"Why not? I haven't been to the Lakefront in forever. Let's go."

"Out-a-sight!" Jim replied. "But first, how about some smoke?" He reached down inside his shorts and pulled up a clear baggie that was half filled with what had to be marijuana. Then, he reached into his pocket and pulled out a small, ceramic pipe. He carefully placed the baggie in his lap and put the pipe into the baggie. It was plain that he'd done this many, many times before, as he was able to successfully fill and extricate the pipe without spilling any of the green herb. He reached the pipe towards George and said, "Here, hold this for me."

George had heard about marijuana, and, like most in his generation, he'd considered it the potent drug of choice for jazz musicians and degenerate youth. But the experience of the last day, and the kindness that had been shown to him by Anna and her friends, had increased his vulnerability to the point that he was now able to accept what was happening as—sort of—normal. He took the pipe and looked down at the filled bowl. He could see signs of a scorched copper screen in the bowl, even through the pungent herb.

Jim reached into his other pocket and produced a silver Zippo lighter. He expertly held it in one cupped hand and used the back heel of his other palm to flip the top of the lighter. He then used the same technique to bring the heel of his palm to turn the striker, twisting his wrist as he did so. A spark struck, and a flame appeared over the lighter's wick. Jim held the lighter in his left hand, and reached his right hand towards George.

"Please, sir," he said with exaggerated formality, and took the pipe from George's hand. He raised the pipe to his lips and, carefully, placed the flame above the bowl. He turned his head slightly sideways, and George was struck by his ability to keep the flames from both his long hair and his beard. Jim puffed a couple of times. The flame sucked down into the bowl of the pipe with each puff. Tendrils of blue smoke surrounded the pipe and a red ember grew in the bowl. Then, Jim inhaled a large breath and held it, sitting up straight in his chair. Still holding his breath, he offered the pipe to George.

George shook his head and said, "No thanks, I don't do drugs."

Jim released his breath, exhaling a large amount of smoke, and said, "This isn't a drug. It's Mother Nature. Think about it. Nothing is done to herb but to dry it, and you don't even have to do that. There's no processing, distilling, or adding or subtracting. If it wasn't illegal, it would be free. You can't get freer than Mother Nature. Here, don't put it down if you've never tried it." And he held the pipe out to George again.

George took the pipe in his hand. He looked down at it, still smoking, and looked again at Jim. Then, he gave a wry grin, shook his head slightly, and raised the pipe to his lips. He took a big puff and breathed the herb into his lungs. It felt like the smoke expanded after it went in, and he was suddenly coughing out the pungent smoke as his eyes filled with tears. He held the pipe back out to Jim.

"Whoa, cowboy!" Jim said with a laugh. "You've got to take smaller hits when you start or you'll choke yourself!" He took another hit and gave the pipe back to George. This time, George was careful to take a small puff and not to breathe it in as deeply. When he released his breath, he was struck by how the smoke reminded him of burning leaves in the autumn—a smell he had always loved.

They passed the pipe back and forth several more times, until the pipe was finished. Then, Jim took the pipe, turned it over, and tapped it repeatedly on the metal of his armrest, launching a small flurry of ashes onto the flagstones. He looked at George. "Well, how do you feel?"

"I feel fine. I don't think that stuff works for me," George replied. He didn't really feel any different than he had before he'd smoked the marijuana.

"You ready to head out to the Lakefront?"

"Sure, let's go."

Jim pulled out a pack of Marlboro Red filtered cigarettes, opened the box, and shook it so that one of the cigarettes protruded a bit more than the others. He raised the box to his lips and pulled the cigarette out in his mouth. Then, he held the box out towards George. George shook his head. Smoking cigarettes was one habit he'd never acquired, and he didn't want to start now. After Jim had lit the cigarette with his Zippo, George moved to the back of the wheelchair and proceeded to push Jim to the alley, on through the door that the angry man had left open.

"Let's take my car," Jim said.

"You can drive?!" George asked, surprised.

"Just watch me," Jim said with a smile. "Head left on Dumaine."

Just a short distance from the mouth of the alleyway, Jim pointed to an old, gray 1964 Buick Skylark. "There she is," he said.

George stopped as he came to the front of the car, a bit confused as to how to get Jim's wheelchair down the sharp curb. Jim came to his rescue.

"George, take me down back-first," he said. "It's easier to hold the back up. Let the back wheels down slowly and leave the front wheels on the sidewalk. Then, after the back wheels are down, put your foot on the metal tipping lever in the back to raise the front wheels, and back the chair up till they're over the street. Keep your foot on the lever and slowly lower the front wheels down."

George followed the instructions and soon had Jim at his front, driver's side door. Jim reached out, opened the door, and, after telling George to stand back, wheeled his chair to the seat, removed his chair's armrest, and pushed himself as close as he could to the car seat. He locked his wheels and, using his arms, pushed his body up out of the wheelchair and onto the car seat. He then lifted his legs into the car. George was astounded at how readily Jim was able to maneuver himself, and on Jim's direction, he got the wheelchair folded around into the back seat, and then climbed into the front passenger seat. The car, although old, was spotless on the inside. There was a single lever which was connected to a Rube Goldberg looking series of levels and rods which allowed Jim to push the gas and brake pedals—down for gas and forward for brake. Jim started the car and, with a glance at his rear view mirror, pulled out into the street.

They made their way to Rampart Street, and then towards Canal Street. When they reached it, George looked left and saw the buildings and storefronts that had been there for generations. George remembered riding the streetcar down Canal Street. They'd removed the streetcars from the Canal line in 1963. George had thought it was a shame then, and he felt the same way about it now. There was something that was timeless, almost magical, about riding a streetcar, even in the sweltering New Orleans heat and humidity. Riding a bus just wasn't the same.

Jim took a right to head towards Lake Pontchartrain.

"You from around here, Jim?" George asked.

"Born and raised in Lakeview," Jim replied. "How about you?"

"I'm a Gentilly boy, myself," George replied with a grin. "If you don't mind my asking, what happened to put you in a chair?"

"Too young, too many beers, and too fast a car," Jim said. "My girlfriend had just broken up with me. I was twenty, and it really bummed me out. I had a souped-up '56 Ford at the time. We'd gone out to watch the submarine races at the Lakefront, and things went from bad to worse. After I dropped her off, I went by Pat's bar over by Metairie Road—"

"Yeah, I know the place," George said.

"Well, I bought myself a couple of six-packs and went out to West Grunch Road. Just sat there drinking beers as fast as I could get them down. After about ten of them, I decided to head out to Little Woods to sit on the levee and look out over the camps. I was too drunk to drive, and too pissed off to drive slowly. Anyway, when I came to, I was in Charity Hospital—strapped to a bed. They told me I'd been there for 2 weeks. I couldn't remember a thing. They said that my heart had stopped three times. After I found out I was a quadriplegic, I wished it had stopped. I spent almost six months in Charity, followed by another year and a half in rehab. When they cut me loose, I was a real mess, and as time passed, I grew even more bitter and angry. Booze, pills, heroin... I did 'em all and sank further and further into myself. One day, I decided that I'd had enough of dragging my dead ass around this planet and that I was going to end it. I went down to the Quarter to get drunk one last time... and then I met Anna. She had the same effect on me that I can see she's had on you. That was about three years ago."

George stared straight ahead. "Damn," he said.

"So, tell me, George, how did you happen to become one of Anna's projects?" Jim asked with a quick glance.

"Well... it's kind of a long story, but not as dramatic as yours. You see, I lost my job yesterday. I work...*worked*...at Forstahl's Furniture store. Been selling furniture for 18 years. Anyway, they've got this new manager, a young kid with a degree from Tulane. He didn't like my sales technique with customers and kept trying to tell me how to do my job. I mean, I've been doing it for 18 years! So, I told him that I'd had it with him and I quit. When I got home, my wife Gloria told me that I was nuts to quit, that I'd better go get my job back. I tried, but he wouldn't give me my job back. When I got home, I found Gloria leaving with my best friend, Sonny. She told me that I didn't fulfill her 'emotional needs.' Then, I found out she'd about cleaned out our savings and checking accounts. It didn't seem that I had much to live for, so I decided to jump off the bridge and end it all. I found Astro's and stopped for a last drink, and that's where I met Anna, JC, and Caz and Paul...."

"Oh, so you've met the twins?" Jim smiled as he drove.

"Oh, yes," George responded. "They were very nice. Saved me when I fell off the bridge. Tell me, are they from around here? They don't seem local. Hey, it sure is taking a lot of time to get to the Lakefront. Have we reached the cemeteries yet?"

They pulled up to a red light on Jefferson Davis Avenue, and Jim looked over at George and said, "You know, George, I think that you're high."

George began to deny it, and then stopped for a long moment and suddenly broke into laughter. Jim joined in.

"Holy shit!" George swore. "I must be."

4
THE BAITED HOOK

April 7, 1972

"Bless me, Father, for I have sinned. It has been one month since my last confession. I've taken the Lord's name in vain several times. I've lied. I've had sexual thoughts. For these and all other sins, I am heartily sorry."

Morgan Sanborne—the 35-year-old scion of an old, aristocratic New Orleans family and a rising city councilman—kneeled in the confessional as he uttered these words. He was dressed in khaki pants, a light blue shirt, a gray tweed sports coat, and penny loafers without socks. He heard the priest's admonition to say five "Our Fathers", five "Hail Marys," and to make a sincere act of contrition, and go and sin no more. Crossing himself, he stepped out of the confessional with his head bowed. He loved the way he felt after confession. Free and clean.

As he walked up towards the altar, he almost bumped into an attractive young woman rising from the kneeler.

Wow. Get a load of this broad! Morgan thought as he swiveled his head to watch her pass.

Having purged himself of his sins, Morgan walked out of the church and climbed into his brand new, blue-gray Mercedes Benz SL. He pulled out of the St. James parking lot, cutting in front of a car in a manner that caused it to put on its brakes and blow its horn. "Screw you!" he muttered as he gunned the engine.

Morgan drove his Mercedes down Claiborne Avenue, which turned into Jefferson Highway. The scenery changed from residential houses with largish lots on through to smaller, tighter residential neighborhoods before, finally, giving way to commercial buildings and businesses. He passed by the Water Works, where they took water from the mighty Mississippi, filtered and chlorinated it, and piped it throughout the city via a series of variably aged pipes for consumption. A little further down Jefferson Highway, he passed by the Oschner Hospital, where Dr. John Oschner had recently performed the first heart transplant in the Gulf South. Jefferson Highway followed the path of the Mississippi River as it rolled in broad, snaky curves on its way to the Gulf of Mexico, and when he reached Causeway Boulevard, Morgan turned right and made his way to West Metairie Boulevard, at which point he turned left. The road began as two one-way roads separated by a block of tidy, residential homes. After several blocks, the homes gave way to a large, drainage canal which ran between the two separate roads. The water level in the canal was fairly low, and Morgan saw several groups of young boys with buckets and dip nets at different places along the canal. He smiled to himself as he watched one group swarm to the water's edge, plunge their net into the water, and then raise it with a soft-shelled turtle in the pouch of the net. He wondered what the boys did with the turtles, even as the scene passed into his rear view mirror.

When he reached David Drive, he made a right turn and headed north towards Lake Pontchartrain. He thought about the meeting he was going to. The cryptic message he'd received from Mr. Mara had read, "Meet the Baron at the Old Jefferson Downs racetrack, in front of the grandstand." He wondered what a baron was doing at that old wreck of a racetrack. Jefferson Downs had been severely damaged by Hurricane Betsy, and its large, overgrown footprint had been abandoned to derelicts and druggies, teenagers in search of adventure, and young boys with pellet guns who were on rabbit-hunting expeditions.

He'd first heard about Mr. Mara several days ago when his neighbor, Michael Riley, had walked over on Saturday afternoon and asked if he could speak to Morgan for a moment. He'd carried a manila folder in his hand. Riley was a prominent attorney—the son, and grandson, of prominent, New Orleans attorneys—and he looked the part. Six-foot-three-inches tall, lean, and with silver hair and a patrician face. Morgan had invited him onto the porch for a drink. He'd called his wife, Sylva, through the front door and, after she had come out and greeted Riley, asked her to fix both of them a vodka tonic. When she'd returned with the drinks, he'd motioned Riley to a large, white wicker chair with a red cushion, and lowered himself into its twin.

Morgan had taken a sip of his vodka, looked over the glass, and asked, "Well, Michael, what can I do for you?"

"It's a bit of a long story, Morgan," Riley had replied with a southern drawl. "We received a letter yesterday from a Mr. Mara, the owner of Mara Industries, of Bombay, India."

Morgan had said nothing, only nodding his head for Riley to continue.

"Mara's letter came with a Letter of Credit issued by Crescent Bank to the tune of fifty million dollars."

Morgan had let out a long, low whistle. "That's not chump change!"

"No, it's not. I'll get to the point. It seems that Mr. Mara is aware of you and your position on the City Council. He is interested in acquiring a specific piece of property for development. It's in the French Quarter. He has detailed plans on how he would like to develop the property, and he would like you to spearhead the project here. He's specifically asked us to serve as an intermediary and deliver this letter to you." Here, Riley had opened the manila folder and produced a sealed envelope—one with "Morgan Sanborne" written on the outside in a spidery hand. Riley had held the envelope out to Morgan, who'd accepted it and set it down on a side table, next to his drink. The two men had then begun discussing local and neighborhood affairs as they'd finished their drinks. Upon finishing, they'd stood up and shook hands, and Riley had begun walking down the porch stairs. At the bottom, he'd turned and said, "I've done my job, Morgan, but if there are any opportunities that arise from this, I'd appreciate your consideration."

"Absolutely, Michael," Morgan had replied, "any legal work will be done by your firm, you've got my word on it." Riley had saluted and then walked down the sidewalk towards the street, at which point Morgan had picked up the envelope, opened it, and begun to read. As he'd read the letter, a smile had appeared on his lips.

His reverie broken, he glanced in his rear view mirror as he turned onto the long driveway of the defunct racetrack. As he did so, he remembered his first interaction with Mr. Mara. The letter had instructed him to call at 9 a.m. on Monday morning, Bombay time. This meant that Morgan had been forced to call around 10:30 on Sunday night. He'd called collect, as stated in the letter. The call had been quickly accepted by a woman speaking English with an Indian accent. She'd placed him on hold for a few moments, and then a very old man's voice had come on the line. "Hello, Mr. Sanborne," the man had said. The voice had been dry, and Morgan had imagined that the owner of the voice was at least a hundred years old.

"Mr. Mara?" he'd questioned, even as an unreasoned feeling that he was missing something important had made the hairs on the back of his neck stand up.

"Indeed, Mr. Sanborne. Thank you for calling. I presume you have read the letter and are aware of my desire to purchase and develop the property in question."

Morgan had swallowed, though it wasn't like him to feel nervous speaking to someone. "Er... yes, sir."

"I trust that you are up to the job?"

"Yes, sir. In my capacity as a city councilman, I am able to, shall we say, foresee problems that may arise and deal with them before they can impact such a project. I can promise you that I'm the best man for the job."

"Very good, Mr. Sanborne. I am not used to being disappointed," the man spoke in a dry hiss. "Now, please follow these instructions...."

What followed had been a long discussion, really more like a lecture, where Morgan had taken more notes than he'd taken since being a student at Tulane. When it had been done, Mara had asked, "Now, Mr. Sanborne, do you understand what is required of you?"

"Yes, Sir, Mr. Mara," Morgan had replied, glad that this particular ordeal was nearing an end.

"Do not disappoint me, Mr. Sanborne. "

Morgan had felt his heart tighten in his chest and a light sweat had appeared on his forehead. His hand had reached up as if to loosen his collar, but he'd been wearing his pajamas.

"I will not disappoint you, Mr. Mara," Morgan had said with conviction.

"Good. I bid you goodbye." And, with that, the connection had been broken.

Morgan had looked at the phone in his hand for a moment, then hung up. It had taken a while for him to go to sleep that night, and his dreams had been a procession of chaotic scenes which left him with a sense of dread upon waking.

That had been several days ago, and now he was on his way to meet Mr. Mara's contact. The intervening days had helped calm Morgan's uneasy feelings, and the promise of a large amount of money lifted his spirits as he drove.

He found the entrance to the track blocked by a chain link fence, but the gate across the road was open about three feet, so he parked his car at the entrance and walked through the gate. As he walked down the shell roadbed, he was surprised to see how much nature had reclaimed in seven short years. There were small trees and bushes overgrowing the road, such that he could only see in a few feet on either side. He rounded a bend and came across the circular dirt track, with its inner metal ring and the decrepit grandstands. The grandstands had once been capable of holding several thousand spectators, but were now in shambles. The roof was partially collapsed, and most of the glass panes which patrons had looked through to watch their favorites were broken. Debris was everywhere. As Morgan looked around, he saw a large, brown rat scurry over some debris and hurry into a hole created by some rotten timbers with asphalt shingles still attached.

He walked along the dirt track until he came to a stop in front of the dilapidated grandstands. He stood there for a moment, with his hands on his hips. A noise like some jungle beast rumbling deep in its throat reached him, and he suddenly saw a black Camaro come from the side of the grandstands and entered the track. The engine noise from the car grew louder as it came closer, rising and falling with an almost breath-like pulse. The Camaro pulled up alongside of him and the engine stopped.

A tall black man glided out of the driver's seat. To Morgan's mind, he almost uncoiled out of the car, like a large snake. He took a step towards Morgan, piercing him with intense eyes and a scowl. "Monsieur Sanborne?" he rumbled.

"Yes, I'm Morgan Sanborne. May I ask your name?"

"You can call me Baron."

"All right, Baron. I received a message from Mr. Mara to meet you here. Can you tell me what it's about? I'm a busy man."

"Don't think, Mr. Sanborne, that your time is worth more than mine... or Mr. Mara's," the large man replied, leaning toward Morgan. His intense eyes held Morgan's and his scowl intensified.

A crow began to caw. For an instant, Morgan had a vision of the baron being as tall and menacing as a mountain leaning over him. Then, Morgan felt a sharp pain in his chest, and sweat began beading on his forehead. His right hand instinctively raised, palm outward, as if to ward off a threat. He broke off his gaze into the baron's eyes, glanced at the ground, and said, "No... no, Baron. I would never waste your or Mr. Mara's time."

"Very wise of you, Monsieur Sanborne," the baron replied. "Now, I will tell you what is expected of you. We wish to build a series of apartment buildings in the French Quarter. These buildings must be built in a certain style... in a certain order, a certain configuration. We will build these buildings within the square block that is bounded by St. Ann Street, Burgundy Street, Dauphine Street, and Dumaine Street. You will purchase all properties within this square block. Price is no object. Do not haggle, as time is more valuable than money. I suspect that most of the properties will be easy to acquire. You may have problems with one particular parcel, however. If you do find yourself to have, er... difficulties, then contact me or Mr. Mara for direction.

"Once the property is acquired, it is Mr. Mara's intention to build five condominiums. Four of these condominiums will be seven stories tall. They will be placed on the corners of the property and each will face a different cardinal direction. A ten-story condominium will be built at the center point of the property. It will be positioned so that none of its walls face in a cardinal direction, but at a 45-degree angle, so that each side faces between the four, surrounding condominiums. Do you have any questions?"

Morgan swallowed, wiped his hand across his forehead, and said, "Mr. Mara described the project exactly as you say. But, I do have a couple of questions. When you say that money is no object, what does that mean?"

The baron looked down on Morgan and said, "Just exactly that, Monsieur. You will pay whatever it takes to acquire the properties."

Morgan thought quickly, and then asked, "Once the property is acquired, do you have someone in mind to head the team responsible for building the condominiums?"

The baron gave a low, sonorous chuckle. "Do not worry, Monsieur Sanborne. You will have many opportunities to make money on this project. Mr. Mara does not wish to be involved in the day to day decisions. He has informed me that he has already discussed your reward for overseeing this with you. "

Morgan thought back to the discussion with the mysterious Mr. Mara. He would indeed have opportunities to make money on this deal. More money than he had made on any other deal that he'd been involved with, in fact. This Mara fellow must be made of money, the way he planned on throwing it around. Morgan smiled and said, "You are right, Baron. Mr. Mara is being more than generous with me. I will work diligently to acquire the properties he is interested in. I will purchase all of the properties in the name of Mara Industries, as instructed, and will keep detailed records of all expenditures. Do I need to keep you informed of my progress?"

The baron looked coldly at Morgan. "You will consider me the intermediary between yourself and Mr. Mara." He reached into his coat pocket and pulled out a card, which he handed to Morgan. "Here is a phone number where I can be reached. Do not hesitate to contact me if you have any needs. If you encounter major problems, contact Mr. Mara directly at the phone number that you already have."

"Very well, Baron, I will keep you informed of my progress." And, with this, Morgan stuck out his hand. The baron looked down at Morgan's hand, and then back up at him before turning abruptly and coiling himself back into the black Camaro. The engine started with a roar, and the tires spit sand as it took off around the track and disappeared down the lane it had come from.

Morgan stood there watching the Camaro retreat. His hand had dropped to his side when the baron had climbed back into the car. Now, he held it up, looked at it, and then shook his head and muttered, "Asshole!" before he began walking back to his Mercedes.

5
___

A PLAN CONCEIVED

April 7, 1972

Morgan left Metairie and began driving back towards New Orleans. He had a meeting to attend, and he thought as he drove, *My time is important, too.* The meeting was downtown at the International Trade Mart, and he didn't have much time to get there. When he arrived at the foot of Canal Street, he got out of his car, tossed his keys to the parking attendant, and walked in the door. He rode the elevator to the 33rd floor and walked into the "Top of the Mart"—a revolving cocktail bar that overlooked the Mississippi River and New Orleans. At 1 p.m. on a Friday, the bar was getting crowded with businessmen, geologists, petroleum land men, salesmen, secretaries, high-priced call girls, and politicians. Morgan's usual table was against the glass, offering a beautiful view of the Crescent City. He walked around the bar shaking hands, slapping backs, laughing, and telling a few stories. After he'd made his rounds, he walked up to his usual table. Sitting around it were three people. Stan Boyle, who worked for Morgan as his sometimes driver, handyman, and helper; Brenda Ayotte, his secretary of three years and his lover for the last two of them; and Robert Cochran, a private investigator who Morgan had hired after Mr. Mara's phone call.

"Hi, everybody," Morgan greeted the seated group. The two men nodded, as they were each taking a sip of their drinks.

"Hi, Morgan," Brenda said a little breathlessly. She was petite, with dark hair, an olive complexion, and a nice figure. He took a seat next to her, turned to the waiter who had just come up, and said, "I'll have a Brandy and Benedictine." Then, turning back to the table, he said, "OK, now tell me some good news. Robert, what do you have?"

"Well, Mr. Sanborne, I've got the information on almost all of the property owners of the blocks you requested. That end of the Quarter has been running down for a long time, and most of the owners should be ready to sell, but one group of buildings on Dumaine Street near Burgundy is hard to get solid information on. I've run the title, and it's the damnedest thing I've ever seen. It looks like the buildings have been owned by the same family for the last 175 years. The first owner was a Monsieur Jaques Charles D'Or. Through time, there's always been someone named D'Or who's been the owner on record. Other than title information, however, there are no current records on the present Mr. D'Or. Since information was hard to get, I started staking out the location. There's a bar on the property called Astro's, and there's a lot of weirdos who go in and out. From what I can tell, it's a bunch of musicians and hippies. Blacks and whites. God knows what they're doing in there, but I can almost guarantee that there's some illegal activity happening."

"Really? Is that all you've got?" Morgan asked incredulously. "You're going to have to do better than this! I want to get all of the properties as soon as I can, and I do mean all of them!" Brenda was rubbing the inside of his leg with her bare foot, which distracted him for a moment and his voice began to rise. Morgan reminded himself that it wouldn't do for the people at the lounge to see him lose his temper, so in a lower voice, he said, "I want you to get me the information on all of the property owners of that square block by Monday." He then turned his attention to Stan. "Stan, I want you to get with Sam Wilson and get him started working up offers to buy those properties. Tell him to call me about the particulars. I want to get this project sealed up quickly!"

Both Robert and Stan were fast to reply, "Yes, sir!"

"All right," Morgan continued, "go start getting it done! Let's all meet here next Friday at 4 o'clock." Robert and Stan stood, said their goodbyes, and left. Morgan turned to Brenda and said, "Now, where were we?"

"Oh, I know," she cooed, and began rubbing his leg higher.

One week later, the four were at the same table. Morgan turned to the two men and said, "Bring me up to date."

Stan began by telling Morgan that offers had gone out to all of the property owners in the square block, with the exception of the D'Or property. He continued, "We haven't heard back from any of them, but we're offering well over the going price, so I would expect that we'll start hearing back this week. Sam Wilson said that he'll keep you apprised of progress."

"Good." Morgan turned to Robert next. "So, Robert, what is the word on the D'Or property?"

The look on Robert's face told Morgan all he needed to know, but he began anyway. "Well, Mr. Sanborne, the city has no information on J. C. D'Or. No birth certificate or voter registration, no current address, nothing. Taxes are paid with money orders, hand-delivered to City Hall. Whoever this D'Or is, he's really good at staying under the radar. I did go into the bar, Astro's, and found out that the bartender, a black guy, is named JC. I think that's a coincidence."

Morgan sat silently. He was pissed off. Morgan remembered the phone call from the mysterious Mr. Mara. Mr. Mara was evidently fabulously rich. He wanted to buy this particular block of the French Quarter, knock down the decrepit buildings, and build a bunch of high-end condominiums. He had offered to let Morgan in as a one-quarter owner, provided that Morgan was able to execute the purchase of all of the properties in the block. The fact that Morgan was a city councilman, and therefore couldn't officially be seen to be working on a large development that would eventually come before him in his official duties, bothered him not a whit. It was the way business had been done in New Orleans since the city had been founded. *You scratch my back, and I'll scratch yours.* In this fashion, most of the wealth of the city had been kept corralled by a small number of families over a large number of years.

The waiter arrived with Morgan's B&B. He took a long sip and let his anger subside before saying anything. "Ahhhhh," he sighed, "the perfect way to start a Friday afternoon! Now, Stan, I want you to help Robert here find me the lever I need to get those people out of the houses on Dumaine Street. I think the first place you should start is identifying everyone who goes there. Then use our contacts at NOPD to run a sheet on them and see if there are any outstanding warrants. If not, we might need to catch one of those hippies and plant some drugs on them to give us probable cause to raid the place. One way or another, I want that Mr. D'Or, wherever he is, to beg me to buy his property by the time this is done. Maybe I'll give him fifty percent of what the other owners get. Now, do you have any questions?"

"No, sir," Stan said, sitting up straighter.

"Good. Now, Brenda, I want you to be available to assist both Robert and Stan in this effort. We don't know how much effort it's going to take, so it's possible you might have to take one for the team. You're young and pretty, and it shouldn't be hard for you to get cozy with one of those assholes in that place. You'll be our spy on the inside. Just like Mata-Hari."

"Sure, Morgan," Brenda agreed as she began rubbing her bare foot up Morgan's leg, "it'll be fun."

At that moment, a waiter came up with a tray carrying a beige telephone. "A call for you, sir."

"Excuse me," Morgan said as he took the telephone and raised the handset to his ear. "Hello," he said, and then quickly covered the microphone with his hand and mouthed "my wife" to Brenda.

"Hello, Sylva, how's it going? Yes, I'm here meeting with my fellow councilmen. Chuck sends his regards. It's that T-shirt shop issue again. Looks like things are settling for all-out war between the vendors and the residents, and we're trying to figure out how to make everybody happy, but I'm afraid it's going to take a long time. .... No, don't wait supper on me. .... Yes, give the kids a kiss. I'll try and be home before then, but it's looking like midnight is more realistic. Here, he gave Brenda a strategic look and a wink, and she moved her foot a little higher up his leg. OK. .... Love you, too. Bye."

"Now, where was I...? Oh, yeah. *Mata-Hari*. Brenda, you're going to need to dress the part of a hippie. I'm sure you can manage that."

"Oh, yes, Morgan. I've got some of the cutest peanut jeans, and—"

"Fine, good," Morgan interrupted her. "Now, I'm going to go fishing this weekend down in Grand Isle. I'm leaving tomorrow morning. Brenda, I want you to meet me down there at the usual place. Stan, Robert, I want y'all to get to work. Brenda, check out the bar two weeks from Saturday. By then, I want y'all to either have the goods on some of the folks there, or to have identified the best target to serve as a patsy. Got it?"

"Got it!"

"Yes, sir!"

"Then, what are you waiting for? Get going!"

The two men rose simultaneously. They each nodded to Brenda and then left the bar silently.

Brenda looked longingly at Morgan. "What 'cha wanna do now, honey?"

"I want to finish my drink in peace," Morgan said as he smiled coldly. He caught the eye of a prominent attorney, a married deacon of his church who was sitting two tables away and chatting up an attractive blonde, and he raised his glass in salute. The attorney reciprocated the gesture, glancing approvingly at Brenda sitting there with her full lips in a pout.

"Now, Brenda, I'm just joking. Why don't we go to your apartment for some quality time?" he suggested as he reached under the table and stroked her thigh.

"OK, now you're talking!" Brenda said, and soon they'd both stood and headed to the elevator. Inside, she reached up and put her hand around his neck, pulling his head down to give him a long, deep kiss.

"You'd better watch it, or you'll get it right here," he whispered in her ear.

"Ooooooh, I'd like that," she whispered back with a smile. Then, the bell chimed as the elevator reached the lobby. They both straightened up, and walked out through the lobby and up to the parking attendant's desk. Morgan held out his ticket to the young man, who retrieved the Mercedes in short order. Morgan pulled a $5 bill from his wallet and tipped him.

"Thank you, sir!" he said.

"You're such a generous tipper, Morgan," Brenda said admiringly as she climbed into the car.

"Buying people is expensive," Morgan replied, "especially if you want them to stay bought." They drove down Canal and took a left at St. Charles. As luck would have it, they were stuck behind a streetcar for a few minutes, but Morgan took a right on Poydras Street as the streetcar continued towards the Garden District. They drove down Poydras and could soon see the cranes constructing the New Orleans Superdome. It was an impressive skeletal structure that was being billed as the "Ninth Wonder of the World." Morgan had made a great deal of money on the initial land deal, and even more on bribes for construction of the "greatest building ever constructed." He smiled at the memory as he continued down Poydras to the interstate ramp. He got up to speed on the interstate and glanced over at Brenda. She was looking out the passenger window.

In a few minutes, they were passing the cemeteries with their various ornate mausoleums. She looked at them and told Morgan, "Those are the creepiest things in New Orleans. Can you imagine? It's like being buried in a house."

They continued onto I-10 West and got off at the Bonnable Boulevard exit. They stayed on the service road, crossed Bonnable, and were soon at the Atlantis Apartments, the "swinging" place for "with it" singles in New Orleans. The complex was known as a happening place, and many stewardesses, pilots, and successful young businessmen made it their home. Brenda had a one-bedroom apartment on the second floor of the complex, close to the swimming pool.

Just before pulling into the complex, Morgan had a thought. "You want to get a drink first?" he asked, having already made the decision not to turn, but to remain on the service road towards Causeway Boulevard. As he rounded the sweeping turn, a large propeller airplane, a Constellation, became evident atop a square building off the right side of the service road. He pulled into the parking lot, parked, and he and Brenda walked into the boxy building below the airplane. The inside of the bar was dark, and there were only a few persons sitting at tables or on the bar. Morgan and Brenda walked up to the bar, and the bartender approached and asked, "Can I get you something?"

Morgan replied, "Yeah, I'd like a B&B, and my lady here would like a stinger."

In a very short time, the bartender placed the two drinks in front of Morgan and Brenda. Morgan raised his glass towards her and said, "Here's to the prettiest secretary in New Orleans!"

Brenda raised her glass and clinked it with his. "Only New Orleans?" she asked petulantly, though with a smile.

"I'm not sure—I've got to see what you've got," he replied.

"Oh, you'll see, all right!" she cooed.

They drank their drinks, and Brenda told Morgan about the latest scuttlebutt at the apartment complex. Morgan looked at Brenda after finishing his drink and said, "Drink up, girl. We've got things to do!" He followed this up with a leer and a wink.

She laughed, swallowed the last of her drink, and said, "Beat you to the car!"

"Thanks, Billy!" Morgan said as he waved a ten dollar bill at the bartender and laid it on the bar. He got up and followed Brenda out of the bar and into his car.

They left the parking lot and made the loop down Veterans Memorial Boulevard, back to the Atlantis Apartments. As they were about to pull into a parking spot, though, Brenda suddenly spotted a brown and beige Rolls Royce leaving the area. "Look, Morgan, there goes Allen Toussaint!" she said excitedly. "He lives here, too!"

"Big fucking deal!" Morgan replied between tight lips. "Who gives a shit? Now, come on and let's get up to your apartment. I haven't got all night." He opened his door and began walking up to the entryway without looking back. Brenda, looking disappointed, followed him into the entranceway and on to the elevator. Getting out on the second floor, they turned left and soon arrived at apartment 240, Brenda's home. She inserted her key, turned the lock, and walked inside with Morgan close behind her. Once in, he slammed the door shut and grabbed her from behind. Before she could say anything, he had her dress unzipped and was working on her brassiere.

"Wait a minute, honey. Let me help," she said.

Morgan responded by guiding her into the bedroom, pushing her onto the bed, and jumping on top of her.

6

THE ANCIENT DARKNESS

April 3, 1972

The modern high-rise that pierced the dusty, hazy Bombay sky was built on top of soil that had been molded and shaped into bricks, plowed as farmland, served as a site for funerary ceremonies, and trenched and dug, mounded and carried away for generation after generation for thousands of years. This part of India had served as the home for modern humans, or their predecessors, for over a million years. People had gathered into camps and villages in the area for over 10,000 years. So, despite the modern architecture and building materials, a feeling of ancient weight came over anyone standing at the high-rise's base and looking upward.

That was the first impression that Raj Patel had when he exited the cab in front of the Mara Building and looked up at its 55 stories. He mentally chanted, *Sri Vishnu, Sri Vishnu, Sri Vishnu,* before he shook his head and laughed at himself internally for being so superstitious. He'd been offered a great job working for Mara Industries as a personal secretary to Mr. Mara himself. He remembered telling his parents about the job, bursting with pride at the importance of his duties (as well as his munificent pay). Today was to be his first day on the job, so it was best not to be late. He turned and paid the cabby, and then walked up the steps into the glass doors of the high-rise. A guard stood behind a small counter and asked for identification. He presented his picture ID to the guard and told him it was his first day on the job.

The guard was unsmiling while he inspected the ID, comparing it to a paper with a written list of names. He moved his finger down the list until he said, "Ah, Mr. Patel. Welcome aboard." He flashed Raj a smile and handed him back his ID card. "You must report to the 30th floor, room 3040, to get your official identification card for Mara Industries. The elevators are down this corridor."

"Thank you," Raj told the guard, and walked down the corridor towards the elevator. He pressed the *up* button and, when the door opened, entered. After he'd pushed the button for the 30th floor, the door closed and the elevator began to rise rapidly. There was no one else in the elevator, but the buttons lit for each floor the elevator passed. At the 22nd floor, the lights in the elevator went out and Raj was surrounded with the most intense darkness he had ever experienced. At the same time, the elevator began a free-fall descent. Raj dropped his briefcase and threw out his hands as he felt his feet beginning to leave the floor. A scream choked in his throat. Then, as suddenly as it had begun, the lights came on and the elevator resumed its rapid rise. Raj fell to his knees and began to pick up his papers from the briefcase, which had opened when he'd dropped it. He was still on his knees when the elevator reached the 30th floor and the doors opened. No one was waiting for the elevator, so Raj quickly picked up his briefcase and stepped out. He closed his briefcase and leaned against the wall as his heart pounded in his chest. Still, he could see no one walking down the hallway. After regaining his composure, he began to look for room 3040. When he reached it, he opened the door and looked inside. A severe-looking woman dressed in a red sari sat behind a desk in the small room. There was a door on the wall to her left. Her graying hair was drawn back in a bun, and she looked up at him and said, "Yes?"

"Excuse me, I am Raj Patel. I am here to report for work. I was hired to be Mr. Mara's personal secretary."

She peered at him with a frown. "You are two minutes late. Mr. Mara demands punctuality from all of his employees."

"I am sorry. You see, the elevator malfunctioned. In fact, I thought I was going to fall to my doom," he said with a self-deprecating smile.

"I am sure it did. Just see to it that you fall to your doom on your own time, not Mr. Mara's. I am Mrs. Srithalam. May I see your identification, please?"

Raj produced the same ID he had given to the guard downstairs. Mrs. Srithalam held it up to her face and carefully inspected it. When she was done, she handed it back to him and said, "Follow me." She rose and walked through the door in the left wall. Raj followed her into a large room filled with filing cabinets. The fluorescent lights gave off an insect-like hum as the two of them walked single-file through the space between the cabinets. The far corner of the room had a large desk with an electric typewriter and a large, electric laminating machine. A white screen hung on the wall. When they reached the screen, Mrs. Srithalam told Raj, "Stand there." She went to the desk and opened the drawer, removing a large, Polaroid camera. Then, she stood about five feet from Raj, who was standing in front of the screen, and raised the camera to her face. Raj looked into the lens, which seemed to be faceted like a primeval eye. He smiled and the flash went off, slightly blinding him for a moment.

Mrs. Srithalam pulled the tab and picture out of the Polaroid, and waited silently for 60 seconds. Then, she peeled the cover off of the picture. There were four exact copies of Raj Patel smiling at the camera. She took the picture to the desk, opened a different drawer, and removed a pair of scissors, a small jar of rubber cement, and a white card with the Mara logo—a black circle with a small white dot in the center. She put the card into the typewriter and expertly typed

Raj's name and company position. Then, she cut one of the pictures of Raj, dabbed it with rubber cement, and placed it on the card. Once done, she took the card and laminated it in the laminating machine. She next opened another drawer and removed a red ribbon that had piercing studs on each end. She pushed the studs through the laminated card, capped them, and handed the ribbon to Raj.

"Wear this at all times when you are in the building," she told Raj. "Now, report to Mr. Mara on the 55th floor."

"Thank you, Mrs. Srithalam!" Raj placed both his hands together in the traditional Hindu manner and bowed.

Mrs. Srithalam grimaced and shook her head at Raj. "Go, now," she said.

Raj retraced his steps back through Mrs. Srithalam's office, into the hallway, and back to the elevators. But he paused before he pushed the up button. His harrowing experience on his last elevator ride made him wonder if he should find the stairway and climb to the 55th floor. *It will make me even later, which is not good on a first day*, he thought, and pressed the button. The elevator arrived, and he took it to the 55th floor with no further issues. The elevator doors opened to reveal the walls of a corridor painted black. A thin, white line was painted midway between the floor and ceiling, horizontal to the floor. The lighting was dim enough to make Raj stop once he exited the elevator, in order to let his eyes adjust.

His heart was beating fast as he began to walk down the hallway. There were no doors, windows, or any other distinguishing marks— only black walls with the thin white line, white ceiling, and white-tiled floor. The hallway ended at a set of large, double doors with ornate, dark brass handles. When Raj reached the doors, he looked closely at the handles and saw that they were made of dozens of differently sized skulls carefully crafted so their grinning jaws faced outwards. *Sri Vishnu, Sri Vishnu, Sri Vishnu*, Raj thought to himself as he reached for a handle. The door opened silently. Raj hesitated before he walked into the room. It was even darker than the hallway, and it took a moment for his eyes to accommodate the decreased light. The room was enormous. There were no windows, and everything was black—the floors, walls, and ceiling. There were thousands of glowing points in the floors, walls, and ceiling that looked for all the world like stars, and this was what provided the limited light in the room.

Raj was awestruck. He stood there with his briefcase in his right hand and his mouth agape as he looked around. He could just make out the outline of a large, tall desk in the far back of the room. Then, he heard a voice that made him tremble with fear. The voice whispered his name, and sounded ancient and dry, like the rough wings of thousands of insects or the rustling of dead, dry corn husks.

"Come in, Mr. Patel."

Raj's heart was pounding so hard that he felt sure it would jump into his mouth. His knees felt weak and watery. "Th...thank you, sir," he said.

The voice whispered again, "Come in and sit down, Mr. Patel."

Raj walked slowly towards the desk. When he got closer, he saw that there was a low chair in front of it. Behind the desk, a large, high-backed chair was turned so its back was facing the desk, and whoever sat in it—presumably Mr. Mara—was facing the back wall. Raj reached the chair and sank into it like an astronaut who had forgotten the pull of gravity. *Sri Vishnu, Sri Vishnu....*

"An interesting conceit, Mr. Patel," the dry voice whispered as the chair began to turn, "as humans can never understand that the universe doesn't revolve around them. Vishnu wouldn't give a rodent's eyelash about the fate of any individual human. Yet, you continue with your conceit that your miserable existence is the most important thing in the universe." As he finished speaking, the chair finished turning, and Raj could make out the speaker.

Mr. Mara was to ancient as ancient was to old. Even in the dim light, Raj could see he was completely bald. His nose was almost nonexistent, giving his face a cadaverous, skull-like quality. His eyes were enormous. They appeared to be totally black and recessed into his skull. His mouth was set in a rictus, with large, sharp teeth for tearing flesh. He began to rise from the chair in a fluid motion that resembled the continuous reconstitution of individual, sharp-skinned beetles.

Raj was speechless, paralyzed by fear as Mr. Mara moved slowly closer to him. His eyes were the only part of his body that still seemed to be under his control. Mr. Mara moved inexorably towards Raj, as a snake would move towards a small, defenseless bird. Finally, Raj was looking up at Mr. Mara. He was so tall, and smelled of desert dust. Mr. Mara loomed over Raj and the wings of thousands of insects whispered, "You'll do, Mr. Patel. You'll do quite well."

Raj could feel his bowels give way as Mr. Mara leaned down. The first, piercing bites loosened his tongue, and he screamed and screamed until the final darkness came.

The policeman found the body in one of Bombay's many small alleyways. "Uggh!" the cop grunted upon seeing the condition of the body, "the rats got this one."

His partner was writing in his notebook and asked, "Should we try to see what caused this poor buggar's death?"

"No use," the first policeman said. "There's hardly enough left here to tell."

"Any identification?"

"Not that I can find. Better call the morgue to collect the body. Poor guy. I hope he was dead before all those rats got to him."

7

A PEAK THROUGH THE VEIL

April 6, 1972

George and Jim arrived at the Lakefront just as the sun reached its zenith. They drove past the West End with its marina and restaurants, and down past the Mardi Gras fountain. Eventually, Jim pulled into a parking place near one of the small picnic pavilions. There were a group of people in the pavilion, and George got out of the car and brought Jim's wheelchair up to the driver's side door. Jim got out of the car and into the chair as quick as a cat, and looked up at George and gave him a wink. George wheeled Jim up to the pavilion feeling nervous and uncomfortable. *It must be obvious that I'm stoned*, he thought, and the thought made him even more nervous and uncomfortable.

A booming voice called out, "Hey, George! Good to see you, man!"—this followed by another similar voice booming out, "Jim, what's happening my man?"

George was pleasantly surprised to see Caz and Paul walk up to them. They all exchanged greetings, and Jim told George, "Why don't you wheel me up to the pavilion so you can meet the crew?"

The so-called crew consisted of about a dozen men and women of various ages, sizes, and shapes. They ranged in age from their early 20s through their mid-30s. It seemed to George that some of the people would be taken as "hippies" while others looked middle-class normal. The one thing that all of them shared were smiles on their faces. Jim introduced George to the crew to a general chiming of "Hi" and "Hello."

Then, one of the twins said, "We've been waiting for you to start, Jim."

"OK, do you have the teams picked yet?" Jim asked.

"Yep, you're on my team," the same twin replied.

"What about George—whose team is he on?" Jim looked over at George.

"Wait, wait...what are y'all going to do?" George asked, concerned.

"Death soccer!" both twins responded at the same time, evil-looking grins on their faces.

"Death soccer! I think I'll pass," George said. "I'm too old for that kind of stuff."

"OK, OK, we'll take it easy on you this time," Jim said with a smile, "but you watch how it's done, George, and next time, you're on my team."

With that, the crew split into two teams and walked out into the grassy area between the levee and the street. There were several pine trees dotting the area, and it appeared they'd be silent obstacles to the game about to be played. A tall, attractive, blond-haired woman with beautiful brown eyes had the soccer ball. George thought she had the kindest eyes he had ever seen. She gave the ball to Jim, who wheeled himself into the middle of the field with the ball on his lap.

"OK, folks. Here it is. Those two trees over there are one goal, and the two trees closest to Tim over there are the other goal. Now, we're going to play the same rules as always. I'll start off the game from the middle of the field—everyone get by their respective goals."

Both teams withdrew from the middle of the pitch and stood near their goals. Jim wheeled his chair so that he could see both sides. He held the ball between his cupped hands, looked both left and right, and said loudly, "Get ready, get set, GO!" And, with that, he threw the ball far up into the air.

Both teams raced towards the ball as it began dropping in its arc, the players screaming like banshees.

"Get it! Get it!" "Look out!" "Kick that thing!" people hollered.

The ball hit the ground at the same time the people reached the spot and a melee of feet kicking at the ball, other people's legs, and the wheels of Jim's chair made for a blur of activity. The thuds and thwacks of feet kicking the ball and other things were punctuated by screams of pain and laughter.

"Ow!" "Shit!" "Kick that fucker!"

People kept kicking the ball and each other, laughing like hell. The ball shot out of the melee, followed by most of the people. A couple of them were on the ground, rubbing one leg or another and laughing so hard that they couldn't breathe. The laughter slowed the pursuit of the ball as first one, then another of the teammates collapsed onto the ground doubled-over with laughter. Jim's wheelchair was toppled over in the process, and he lay there bellowing, "Somebody, get me up! Get the ball! Whoooooeeeeee!"

One of the twins was racing along kicking the ball with the other twin in hot pursuit and a gang of people trailing farther behind. The first twin attempted a mighty kick at the ball, but it hit a small bump on the ground and hopped up before he could connect, causing the kick to completely miss. The kicker's feet left the ground on the miss and he went horizontal, like a spear, hitting the ground with his feet and then with his torso, causing him to let out a loud *"ooooofff."* The trailing twin started laughing so hard that he became unable to run, and stood there doubled-up with laughter—so much so that a rope of drool fell from his lips. The following gang passed up the two twins, and the kicking, hollering, and laughing melee continued until one lucky kick sent the ball through the tree goal. Then, everyone collapsed on the ground laughing. Soon, they were at it again... with similar results.

George couldn't help but laugh at the spectacle of death soccer. It looked like it was a lot of fun. Certainly, every one of the players had laughed till they were out of breath. They played about nine or ten rounds with similar results. After the final round, Jim wheeled his chair up to the bench where George was sitting. "Well, George, what do you think?" he asked.

"That's one of the funniest things I've ever seen in my life," George replied with a laugh. "How do y'all keep from killing each other?"

"The basic rule is to kick the shit out of everything, but not so hard as to cause damage—except to the ball!" Jim laughed, and then he rubbed his elbow, which was red and still had some grass on it.

All of the participants came back to the pavilion eventually—some still laughing, but all smiling. Jim reached into his shorts and pulled out the baggie and the pipe. "Luckily, none of you suckers broke this when you dumped me out of my chair!" he said, pretending to be angry. He filled the pipe and held it out in his hand. "Let's give thanks to Mother Nature for this day and our friendship."

Everyone came close together in a huddle around Jim and murmured their appreciation. Then, Jim lit the pipe and passed it around. By the time it had reached all but the last three of the assembled crew, it was in need of being filled again, which was done by the woman who'd been holding the soccer ball. George politely took a small hit when it was passed to him, and then he passed it along. This ritual continued for about ten minutes before Jim put away the pipe. Several people went to their cars and came back with ice chests filled with fried chicken, potato salad, soft drinks, and beer. They spread a red-and-white checkered tablecloth on the picnic table provided in the pavilion, and all ate and drank their fill.

As he sat there with a drumstick in one hand and a can of Dixie beer in his other, George looked at the people around him and drifted into thought. *These kids aren't anything like I thought they were. They seem kind and considerate... even religious in a different kind of way. Not that Gloria would approve of them. No, she would see the long hair, the patched jeans, the marijuana use, and not see anything else. I don't think she can see people who are different from her and not find them bad in some way.* Despite his conclusion, he himself felt saddened at the thought of Gloria.

George's thoughts were interrupted by the blond-haired girl, whose name was Kris. She spoke up to say, "How about another story, Caz?"

"Yeah!" "Far out!" "Oh Boy!" came the chorus of the assembled crew.

Caz stood up from the bench he'd been sitting on, climbed up, and sat down on the picnic table with his feet on the bench.

"All right, are you ready for this?" he asked.

He was greeted with a chorus of affirmative noises.

"OK, then. I want you to imagine this Lakefront as it was 2,400 years ago. The area we're sitting on would have been an endless, waving field of Rosseau cane, grading to Spartina marsh grass. The Mississippi River would have had a maturely developed levee, and would have been in about the area where Metairie Road is now, moving from west to east. Picture it, everyone. The sky is filled with ducks, geese, cormorants, pelicans, and that most special of southeastern birds, the Roseate Spoonbill. The hum of mosquitos is thick in the humid, still, evening air. The clouds are golden and pink within a baby blue sky as the sun is setting. The schools of mullets and pogies are thick and suddenly ripped by the slashing strikes of the predatory speckled trout and redfish. The water reflects the glorious colors of the sky and earth with small, undulating ripples distorting the reflections.

"Just a mile or two away, the entrance to an old crevasse splay provides a bit of high land. This waterway, later to be called Bayou Choupique—and even later, Bayou St. Jean—continues inland for several miles till it melts into a backwater swamp near the Mississippi River levee. The high land at the intersection of the lake and the bayou is covered in live oaks, with gray Spanish Moss hiding dark green leaves with its gray drapery. There, on that bit of high land, are several huts, or houses, consisting of planted poles that are woven with palmetto leaves, and smeared with clay that's dried to a tannish color. The roofs of the houses are made of thatch. Several wisps of smoke rise up through the trees from fires that burn, both outside of these structures and inside. The sides of the bayou are gray and white with the cast-off shells of oysters and clams that serve as a staple of these people's diets. The laughter of several children splashing and playing in the water rises with the smoke. Two women can be seen watching the children, both of them young. Their hair is dark and slick with grease, held back from their faces by twine wrapped around their heads. They each wear a short skirt made of palmetto leaves, held by the same type of twine. Their names are Wa-Hee-La and Wa-Too-Ka. A cypress dugout is being poled down the bayou towards them as they stand there watching the children play.

"In that dugout stands a tall, well-built man. He poles the dugout with a skilled ease that comes from years of experience. His hair is black, like the women's, but only in a small topknot. The rest of his head is shaven smooth. His body glistens with a combination of sweat and grease as his muscles ripple with the effort of poling. When he gets close enough, he calls out to the women.

"'Wa-Hee-La, Wa-Too-Ka...come and see what I have!'

"The two women look at the children who are safely playing in the shallow water and walk up the bank towards the young man.

"'Quit teasing us, Mo-Gu-To,' says Wa-Hee-La. 'We are tired of making pots and came out to watch the children play. Now, you come and try to distract us.'

"The dugout comes to rest on the bank, near the village, and Mo-Gu-To steps out. He holds a rawhide thong in his hand, with something dangling from the loop as he walks towards the two women. When he gets closer, it becomes clear that the object that tied to the loop is a long, thin, quartz crystal. None of them have seen anything like it in the past. Each woman comes up to the necklace and reaches their hands out to feel the crystal, murmuring in amazement. Finally, Wa-Too-Ka says, 'Is it the air made hard, or frozen water made warm? Where did you get this Mo-Gu-To?'

"'From the Moskata people who traded for it farther up Great Father of Waters,' he says, bringing the crystal up closer to his face and looking at it.

"'What did you give for it?'

"'Three otter pelts.'

"'It is truly beautiful, Mo-Gu-To,' Wa-Hee-La says. 'You must show it to Grandfather.' And with that, the three young people walk up to the largest of the thatched dwellings. Outside of the round hut, an elderly woman is kneeling on the ground. She's rubbing her hands together, making ropes of clay which she will then coil to make a base and then the walls of a ceramic pot. Her hair is gray and she has many small wrinkles around her eyes and mouth.

"'Hello, Grandmother,' Mo-Gu-To says respectfully. 'May we disturb Grandfather? We have something to show him.'

"The woman gives a partially toothed grin to the young people. Without pausing in her efforts, she replies, 'As long as it's not another one of your jokes!', and with that, she calls out, 'Old man! The young people wish to speak with you.'

"A thin man with a gray topknot, slightly bent with age, steps out of the dark hut. 'Why do you bother me, old woman? I was resting.'

"Mo-Gu-To and the young women step up to the old man, and Mo-Gu-To says, 'Grandfather, look at what I have traded for!' And he holds out the rawhide thong with the crystal. The old man takes the thong from the young man and looks at the crystal. He holds it up in the air, and then puts it close to his eye and looks through the crystal at the surrounding village.

"Finally, he says, 'I have seen this before. It is called *Frozen Water that is not Cold*. When I was a young man, some traders came down the Father of Great Waters and had one of these. My friend, Too-Shu-Mah, traded him skins for it and brought it to our village. It was a powerful thing, and brought great calamity to the village. That night, it was very windy, and an ember caught one of the houses on fire. The wind spread the fire very quickly. Soon, the entire village was burned. My advice, Mo-Gu-To, is to throw this thing away as quickly as you can!'

"Mo-Gu-To can feel his cheeks burning. 'I cannot do this thing, Grandfather. If this object has great power, I would like to use it to help our people.' He bows to the old man and turns and walks away. The two women, concern on their faces, bow to the old man, as well, and follow Mo-Gu-To.

"As they reach the edge of the small village, Wa-Hee-La calls out, 'Wait, Mo-Gu-To, we must talk!' Both women walk up to the man. 'You should listen to Grandfather. He is wise, and knows many more things than you.'

"'I know that he is wise,' is the answer, 'but I believe that I can use the power in this object to help our people.'

"'What do you plan to do?' Wa-Too-Ka asks.

"'I will pray to the Great Spirit and ask our ancestors to guide me,' he replies, and walks out along the levee, moving towards the great river.

"Darkness comes over the little village as the wind begins to freshen from the Northeast. Low clouds scud across the face of the full moon, and the wisps of Spanish moss dance fitfully in tune to the wind. Mo-Gu-To sits alone in the trees along the bayou's edge, listening to the wind rustling in the branches and leaves. As the night draws on, the wind begins to rise out of the East and the fast-moving clouds grow closer together, until they hide the moon and sky entirely. The water begins to rise in the bayou, slowly at first, and then, as the night progresses, more rapidly. Mo-Gu-To recognizes the signs. The dreaded Ur-i-Kan, the eater of all, is coming. He knows that he has no time to lose.

"He runs back to the village to warn the others. 'Wake up! Wake up!' he calls when he reaches the houses. "Wake up! Ur-i-Kan is coming! Wake up!"

"The residents of the village come out of their huts and see the waters rising. Almost as one, they begin to gather special belongings and to climb the great oak trees. These trees have survived many storms over the years, and their height and strength are the villagers' only hope in times like these. The wind begins to gain more strength, and begins to whine through the branches. Mo-Gu-To feels that the wind has shifted direction and is coming directly from the North. Water begins to lap at the houses as the waves break over the top of the bayou's edge. It is getting difficult to walk in the wind. Mo-Gu-To knows what he has to do. He wades to the edge of the bayou, lifts the rawhide thong with the crystal off of his neck with both hands, and screams into the wind, 'Great Spirit! Forgive me for my impertinence! Please spare us!' And, with those words, he throws the crystal out onto the submerged shell bank. Then, he turns and runs to one of the great oaks, and climbs as high as he dares.

"The rest of the night, the wind howls and screams, but the water does not go very much higher. As time passes, the wind shifts to come out of the Northwest, and finally the Southwest, and the gusts decrease in frequency and intensity. By mid-morning, the village houses still stand, albeit with a good deal of damage to their roofs and some walls. All of the live oak trees have withstood the storm, and the villagers climb down and begin to assess the damage.

"Mo-Gu-To searches until he finds Grandfather. Then, he walks up to him, kneels in the shallow water that still covers the village ground, and lays his head against Grandfather's knee. 'Please forgive me, Grandfather. I did not listen. It will not happen again.'

"Grandfather looks down at the young man kneeling before him. He then looks around at the assembled villagers before gazing back down at the young man and, laying his hand upon Mo-Gu-To'shead, says,

'There is no shame in learning. You will not make the same mistake again. We are all grateful. You did well to warn us of Ur-i-Kan.'"

With a start, George suddenly realized that he'd been so captivated by Caz's story, he had forgotten where he was. He looked around and saw that the story had had the same effect on the others. Some had tears in their eyes, and others looked as if they had just woken up from a dream. Paul was looking on proudly at his brother, and Jim had his usual, amused smile on his face.

"Far Fucking Out!" "What a story!" The exclamations of amazement and praise from the friends floated in the air like the smell of Oleander on a warm, Summer's night.

George noticed that evening had come to the Lakefront. The clouds were beginning to turn pink and the sky was a powder blue. The friends began to say their goodbyes and leave. Caz and Paul shook George's hand before leaving with a small group of other folks. Kris left with the twins, and gave George a hug and a kiss on his cheek in parting. Finally, George and Jim were the only people remaining in the shelter.

Jim looked at George and said, "You ready to head back?"

"Sure," George said, "I'd like that."

He helped Jim to the car door and loaded up the wheelchair after Jim had slipped behind the steering wheel. He noticed some oyster shells that lay on the ground as he opened the passenger side door and climbed in.

As they were driving back to the French Quarter, George spoke to Jim.

"That was some story that Caz told. It was so real, almost like it was a memory."

"Well, you know, George, there are some places in the world where memories lie resident in the very being of the place. New Orleans is one of those places. You're from here. Think about it. How many times have you found yourself in some neighborhood or other in the city and felt the history of that neighborhood? The Ninth Ward, Gentilly,

Little Woods, Treme, Uptown, Downtown, the Quarter... all of those neighborhoods are pregnant with history. Just physically being in them causes the memories to rise in one way or another. Either in an appreciation of a subtle nuance of the physical imagery of the place, or a detailed historic memory...like the one that Caz tapped into when he told his story."

"Wait a minute," George interjected, "you sound like a philosopher now. All those big words.... Are you telling me that the story Caz told really happened? How can that be? There's no way that the story would have made it down through time. All of the participants are long gone."

Jim laughed. "I may look dumb, but I'm not. That's exactly what I'm trying to tell you. There's more here than meets the eye. Caz was tapping into a memory associated with the place we were in today. Time, and the things that happened in the past, are connected to, and spring from, a never-ending present. Think of it like a long millipede with an infinite number of legs. Each leg represents a moment in time. There are some who can perceive the entirety of the temporal millipede, and 'sample' memories from along its length."

"I don't know about that, Jim," George said disbelievingly. "Maybe it was just a good story."

"Well, you'll just have to believe what you believe," Jim said with his characteristically amused smile, "because we're back."

George looked around and saw that they were indeed back in the Quarter, and Jim parked in the same place the car had been in earlier—an almost unbelievable occurrence. George was going to say something about it, too, when Jim asked, "Would you mind getting my chair out of the back seat?"

"Sure." George got out of the car and retrieved the wheelchair. After Jim had gotten into it, George pushed it down the street toward the alleyway with the "Astro's" sign over it. The sun was setting and the pastel colors of the different houses in the area glowed with a palpable warmth.

8

ASTRO'S AND ALLEN

April 6, 1972

They stood in front of the alleyway and savored the sight of evening in the French Quarter. The warm sun cast shadows along the street—both blurring and illuminating in the contrast between bright light and dark shadow. George noticed that there was no one else within sight. *If it weren't for the cars parked along the street*, he thought, *I could be here anytime within the last 150 years.* As he had this thought, he heard the clip-clop of a horse's hooves and saw a horse-drawn carriage turn onto the street.

Startled, George snapped out of his reverie and heard the carriage driver announce to his fares, "And here we have the D'Or building. It was built in 1789 and was the home of Jacques D'Or. D'Or was a wealthy, free black merchant in early New Orleans history and owned all or part of five ocean-going ships. He was one of the primary sponsors of the Carondolet Canal, which extended the navigable waterway of Bayou St. Jean to the back edge of New Orleans at that time. Starting in 1794, the canal was a vital part of New Orleans' trading scene, and remained the primary trading route into New Orleans from Lake Pontchartrain until the completion of the New Basin Canal in the 1830s...." Still speaking, the carriage driver's voice dwindled to silence in the distance while the ringing of the horseshoes on the street could still be heard.

"You see what I mean?" Jim asked, looking up at George. "We're in one of those places where the past and the present blend. It's easy to see what was happening here many years ago. People's voices, children laughing and squealing at play, the singsong sound of a peddler offering to mend pots and pans, a living neighborhood with all of the joy, grief, despair, and uplifting hope that it can bring."

"I think I'm beginning to understand, Jim," George replied. "How about we go to Astro's for a drink?"

"Excellent idea, my man! Spoken like a true New Orleanian!" And, with that, George pushed Jim's wheelchair down the alleyway to Astro's.

The door to Astro's stood open, and the diffuse evening light bled into the bar. They could see one person sitting at the bar, as well as JC, who was drying a glass with a white towel. He was wearing his signature, dark sunglasses. "Hello, gentlemen, welcome, welcome!" he said. "How have you been, Jim? George?"

Jim grinned up at JC and announced, "We've been to the Lakefront for a rousing game of Death Soccer and a picnic. Now, we're feeling like having a nice, quiet evening's drink in good company."

George just nodded his head.

"Well, I'm glad you've come here. You know you're always welcome in my establishment. George, let me introduce you to an old friend of mine. This is Allen."

A tall, thin black man stood up from the barstool and walked slowly but purposefully over to Jim and George. "Hello, George," he said in a low, easy voice, "it's good to meet you." He had a short Afro and was wearing a gold-colored, Daishiki-type shirt over a pair of plum-colored slacks. "Hi, Jim. Good to see you again, man."

George looked up at the tall, slim man with his mouth agape. "You're Allen Toussaint!" he finally strangled out.

"Guilty as charged!" Allen said softly, and then he laughed in a controlled and friendly way.

"I love your music!" George said. "I've been dancing to it for years! 'Java,' 'A Certain Girl,' 'Fortune Teller,' 'Holy Cow,' 'Working in a Coal Mine,' 'Brickyard Blues!' I love them all! It's a real honor, Mr. Toussaint!"

Allen Toussaint just laughed an easy laugh again and said, "Why don't you just call me Allen, George?" JC and Jim couldn't help but giggle at George's star-struck outburst.

"Thanks, Mr... er... Allen," George responded, and stuck out his hand. Allen grasped it in a loose handshake that shifted until they grasped each other's thumbs.

Jim interjected, "Now that the introductions are over, what's been happening, Allen?"

"You know, writing and playing, playing and writing," Allen responded. "I've had a bit of writer's cramp and wanted to come over and drink from the spring. A visit to JC has always refreshed my feelings of creativity. Being here makes me feel like I'm in a cocoon of friendship and love. That's my muse for my music. Friendship and love are what make life worthwhile. To me, it's the difference between existing and living."

"Amen," JC said in a deep voice.

"Amen," Jim and George echoed.

"Tell you what, fellows," Allen said, "I've got a gig tomorrow night on the *President*. It's a special, Friday-night cruise. If y'all would like to come, I'll comp you."

"Oh, yeah!" Jim and George both agreed enthusiastically.

"I'll leave your names with the boat. Just come on up and give the guard your names, and you'll be my guests!"

"Far out!" Jim said. George was too happy to say anything, and just kept nodding his head.

"Groovy! I'll see you cats later. JC, I hope to see you soon. Later, everybody."

Allen shook hands with JC, Jim, and George, and walked smoothly out the door. George looked at JC and said, "I'm going to need a drink. Allen Toussaint! Can you imagine that?"

JC laughed a loud, friendly laugh as he opened their two beers and said, "I've known Allen since he was a child. He was always precocious... an intelligent, loving child who's become a brilliant, loving man."

"I'll drink to that!" Jim held out his drink in both of his cupped hands and clinked bottles with George and echoed the sentiment.

JC smiled at both of them and said, "Amen!" Then, he asked, "George, how are you feeling today? Last night, you were pretty low, but you seem to be feeling better now."

"Thanks to you and all of the nice folks I've met here, I'm feeling better. Last night, I couldn't see any reason to keep on living. Everything I had done and lived for, for the last twenty years, had been thrown out of the window. I guess the shock of losing Gloria, my job, our savings... well, it seemed like everything left me with nothing to live for. Last night and today, first with Anna and later with Jim here, and you, and the twins, too, has let me see that life keeps on and that there can always be something new and worthwhile just around the corner. I don't know if this feeling will last, but I'm feeling a lot more optimistic than I was when I met you. There was something funny, though. Last night, when Anna was driving me to the bridge to jump, I could swear that I saw your face on a twenty dollar bill. I guess I was pretty well drunk."

"Now, that's a good one!" JC laughed out loud. "My face on a twenty! I guess that I wouldn't have to worry about money anymore if it was me on the twenty dollar bill! No, sir!" He laughed again. Jim looked at JC for a moment before he joined in the laughter.

George sat talking with Jim and JC long enough to drink two Dixies. They talked and laughed about the day's adventures, but George suddenly fell into thought, and Jim asked, "What's up, George?"

"It just occurred to me that I don't want to go back to my house. The place I've lived in for the last twelve years."

"That's not a problem, man!" Jim reached out and touched George's arm. "You're welcome to stay here. You can stay in the upstairs apartment."

"You sure?" George asked.

JC replied, "Seeing that I own this cluster of buildings, Jim's offer is good. We talked a bit about it this morning before you woke up. You see, George, we like you. You've got a good heart, and that's what counts here."

George couldn't help being surprised. "Wow! Thanks! That's really nice of you, JC... and you, Jim. Are you sure?"

Jim laughed and tipped his beer towards George. "Long as you don't act like an asshole, George!" And they all laughed.

George then said, "I guess I need to go back home and get some things if I'm going to stay here."

"Sounds like a plan to me," Jim said. "I'll head on back and do some reading. I got a book the other day that I've been dying to read. Your apartment is close to Mama Zulie's. Go into the doorway next to hers, climb up the stairs, and it's the first door on the right."

"All right. Do you need me to give you a hand, Jim?"

"No, thanks, I've made it to this point in life, so I think I can handle it," Jim said wryly.

"Sorry, no disrespect intended. Well, I'll see you later, JC. Jim, when do you want to get together to go to the concert tomorrow?"

"Let's say a little before 7, or so."

"All right. Goodnight, y'all."

"Peace, George," JC responded.

"See ya!" was Jim's reply.

George stepped out of Astro's and made his way to the street. The shadows of the evening had melded and merged into the dim light of dusk. He walked around the block to where his car was parked and got in. After pulling out into the street, he made his way back to his house in Gentilly. But as he got closer to his home, he could feel the world beginning to close in on him. It was almost like having a weight put on his shoulders. He began to hunch over the steering wheel, and his foot pressed more lightly on the gas pedal. By the time he turned onto his block, the car was only travelling at about ten miles an hour or so. He slowly pulled up into the drive and got out of his car.

He was moving like a sleepwalker as he shuffled down the concrete walkway and up the steps to his front porch. He put the key in the lock upside-down first, and then turned it over and inserted it so that he could turn the latch. He pushed the door open and saw the house just as he'd left it the night before. Lights were still on and a slight, high-pitched whine let him know that the water was running in the toilet because of a recalcitrant float. He automatically walked to the bathroom and jiggled the handle on the toilet. The whine continued for about twenty seconds and then slowly changed pitch, and stopped. He walked out of the bathroom and into the living room, where he sat down on the couch.

What am I doing? I'm not a young kid. Hanging out, smoking pot, going to concerts.... Holy shit! What in the world is happening? Gloria gone with Sonny! The world's going crazy!

He put his elbows on his knees and bent his head into his hands. He stayed in that position for over a minute. Tears began to flow from behind his hands. "It's too fast. It's happening too fast!" he said in a low voice. He stayed on the couch for a full ten minutes, thinking about what he'd been through in the last day. He thought about possible courses of action. Gloria had gone off with Sonny, and claimed that she didn't love him. That was so weird, but it had had the ring of truth in it when she'd told him. As he sat there, he began to think that maybe it was for the best. They had spent many good years together, but the last several had found them growing further apart. He wondered if he really loved Gloria, or if he had just loved the safety of loving Gloria. It had meant that he hadn't had to do anything new. His days had been planned out all the way to the grave. *Work, home, tv, church, holidays, Summer, Winter, Spring, Fall....* A succession of thoughts, emotions, and actions that fit into the small box of one human's life.

Now, because of what had transpired, he'd been freed from that box. His next steps were unknown, unplanned. No longer half of a couple, he was alone. A feeling that he hadn't felt in many, many years began to swell in his chest. It was the feeling of unknown destiny, like he'd had when he'd been a young man. Who knew what lay around the next corner? His days no longer had to be mirror images. His life had changed, and, with it, his prospects.

He raised his head from his hands and looked towards the wedding picture on the mantle. There, he saw himself and Gloria in a younger, happier time. "Guess what, Gloria?" he called to the photograph. "Allen Toussaint has tickets waiting for me on the *President*."

He walked into the bedroom, opened up the closet door, grabbed a medium-sized, hardcover, gray and silver suitcase and began packing it with underwear, T-shirts, and socks from his dresser. Shirts, slacks, and jeans from the closet were then placed on top of the packed clothes. He looked in the back of his closet and found his tennis shoes, wrapped them in an old shirt, and packed them in, too. He got his dop kit out of the closet and went into the bathroom to fill it with razor, toothbrush, toothpaste, and other sundries. The bathroom mirror revealed his face a bit flushed and slightly worse for the wear of the last day, but he gave himself a grin and arched up his eyebrows as he shook his head at his image.

"Man, oh man.... What am I getting into?" he asked. Just for an instant, he could have sworn that the face in the mirror had Jim's wry smile. Shaking his head, he laughed out loud and headed back into the bedroom. He put the dop kit into the suitcase, closed and locked it, picked it up, and went back out into the living room. Here, he stopped and slowly looked around. Once again, he caught sight of the wedding picture. He put down the suitcase and walked up to the mantle, picking up the picture in his left hand. "Here's to better times ahead," he whispered as he laid the picture face-down on the mantle. He turned, picked up the suitcase, and walked out the front door and down the porch to his Mustang.

George left his house and drove back to the French Quarter. Turning onto St. Ann Street, he was surprised to find the same open parking spot where he'd parked earlier. He pulled the Mustang into the empty spot, turned off the ignition, and got out of the car. After grabbing his suitcase from the back seat, he walked around the block and went down the alley towards Astro's. Upon reaching Astro's doorway, he looked inside and saw JC standing behind the bar. There were two long-haired, bearded young men sitting on the bar stools in front of him. George waved and was about to continue down the alleyway when JC called out to him, "Hey, George, I want you to meet a couple of friends of mine!"

George stopped and walked into the bar, where JC continued, "George, this is Robert and Jimmy. Guys, this is my friend, George."

George shook their hands and could tell from their greetings that they were both Englishmen. Their fashion sense was certainly modern, too, with balloon-sleeved shirts and crushed velour pants, but they were friendly and inquisitive.

Robert, who had curly blond hair, asked, "Where are you from, George?"

"I was born and raised in New Orleans," George replied.

"Man, you are one lucky son of a bitch," said the dark-haired Jimmy. "If there's one place on the planet that I wish I'd been born in, it's New Orleans."

"Thanks," George said.

Jimmy continued, "And of all the places in New Orleans, this bar is the place that I love best!" Here, he raised his glass and toasted JC.

Robert chimed in with a "Hear, hear!" and raised his glass, as well.

"Well, that's mighty nice of y'all," JC replied with a beaming smile.

"If y'all will excuse me, I'm going to head back to the apartment," George said. "It was good to meet you."

"Yeah, and you, too, George," Robert replied. Jimmy chimed in, "Cheers, mate!"

"See ya, George," JC said with a smile.

George left Astro's and went into the courtyard, and then on to the door next to Mama Zulie's and opened it. He climbed an old-looking stairway that had a small landing halfway up, where the stairs made a right angle to save on space. When he got to the top of the stairs, he went down the hallway and opened the first door on the right. It was dark, but he reached his hand to the left of the door and found a light switch. He turned it on and saw that the room was spartanly furnished. There was a double bed which was made up, a bedside table next to it, and then a small, wooden table with two ladder-backed chairs, as well as a door that, upon examination, led to a small bathroom.

He put his suitcase down on the table, went to the bathroom, and then climbed into the bed. He felt exhausted as he lay there and thought about the last 24 hours. He was already getting drowsy when a thought occurred to him that made him feel instantly awake. *What am I going to do about a job?* George had been working since high school, and the thought of not having gainful employment left him with a hollow feeling in his stomach. This thought worried his mind for a long time before he slowly drifted to sleep.

9
APRIL FLOWERS

April 6, 1972

April Flowers had hated her name since she'd been a young girl. Her mother, in a fit of poetic fancy, had bestowed the name when she'd given birth to a girl after a long, brutal, Wisconsin winter. Growing up in Wisconsin as a youngster, April had been mercilessly teased. She remembered crying about the hurtful teasing and wishing her mother had named her Nancy, or Dorothy, or some other name that didn't cause her to stand out so.

Her family had moved to New Orleans in 1963, when April had been 16 years old. She'd grown to be a beautiful young woman, of medium height and build, with a pale complexion and long, curling dark hair. Her new home was decidedly different than northwestern Wisconsin in many ways, but in others, it was eerily similar. The climate was the polar opposite, trading cold for heat, and there was Spanish moss growing on many of the old trees, but, as in Wisconsin, there were many Catholics, and neighborhood bars abounded.

April's family lived in Metairie, a suburb of New Orleans that was filled with neat, ranch-style homes. The block she was on had 103 children, by actual count, who lived within the single block. Other blocks had slightly more or less children, but there must have been something in the water of Metairie that supported the old Biblical phrase, "Be fruitful and multiply." April had begun her sophomore year at River-dale High School, an all girls' school, and found, to her surprise, that her classmates didn't tease her about her name. In fact, most of the girls she'd met had thought her name was *cool*. She'd basked in her newfound status.

She'd graduated from high school in 1965 and enrolled as an art major, with a focus in photography, at the University of New Orleans. She worked at various jobs as she went to college, frequently going to school part-time. After seven years, when she was a senior, the university featured her photography in the senior art show. Her photographic subjects ranged from abstractions pulled from nature and man to more formal, dramatically posed photographs. Her favorite of the latter was one she'd taken of Ruthie, the so-called Duck Lady, on one of her photographic forays into the French Quarter.

At the exhibit, April stood near the display of her photographs and spoke quietly with a few different visitors as well as her fellow art majors. She was speaking with a classmate when an older man in a business suit came into the glass-fronted art center and, after nodding to April, began to look closely at her photographs. April found the man familiar, but couldn't place where or how she knew him. After spending several minutes examining her work, the man walked up to April and held out his hand.

"Hello, April. We haven't been introduced, but I've been following your work for the last year or so. I'm Benjamin Shelton, photo editor of the *Times-Picayune*."

When he spoke these words, April remembered where she'd seen the man. She'd sold several of her photographs to the newspaper, and now remembered seeing the man in a glass-enclosed office at one end of the press room. She shook his hand and said, "I'm sorry, Mr. Shelton, I should have recognized you."

He laughed an easy laugh and replied, "Don't worry yourself, April. I wanted to come down and see your show, and then speak to you about a job."

"A job! Why, Mr. Shelton, that sounds wonderful!"

"Well, April, don't get too excited. It's a beginning position with the paper as a photographer. The pay's not much, but it does come with some benefits."

April laughed. "That sounds good to me, Mr. Shelton. Life as a freelancer is not the ideal life for me. It's poor as a church mouse one month, and even poorer the next," she said with a smile.

"Well, the pay is $150.00 per week, health benefits included, and a pension plan," Shelton said as he returned April's smile. "You'll be working with the Human Interest desk—that's Marge Johnson, and she's a great person; you'll really like her. Mostly, you'll be taking photos of social gatherings, retirements, first communions, group meetings, things like that."

"Thank you, Mr. Shelton! That sounds great! When do you want me to start?"

"Let's say Monday, April. I'll see you in the press room at 8 a.m." Shelton shook April's hand again and, before turning to leave, said, "By the way, that's good work!" as he jerked his thumb towards April's photographs.

"Thanks, again, Mr. Shelton. See you soon!"

April watched as Shelton walked out the glass door and down the concrete sidewalk towards the parking lot. When he was obscured by the crepe myrtles planted around the art center, her friends gathered around her, congratulating her on getting the job. More than one was a little bit jealous, as their own job prospects at using their degrees were somewhere between slim and none, but they were a good lot and no one begrudged April's good fortune.

10
A JOB AND A STORY

April 7, 1972

George woke up bright and early the next morning. He could hear voices coming through the window overlooking the courtyard below. It sounded like Anna.

"I don't like what I'm seeing. There is a process afoot that bears a crushing weight!" said the female voice.

A male voice, though George couldn't tell whose it was, responded, "Yes, Inanna. The wheels are turning and all signs point to the Adversary. The grinding of the wheat begins anew, as ever...."

The voices diminished and disappeared.

Weird. Well, I guess it's time to get up, George thought, and he rose to begin the day.

When he went down the stairs and opened the door into the courtyard, he found it empty, but he was struck again by the growth of different trees, plants, and shrubs which gave a sweet scent to the air. There was one scent in particular that haunted him. It smelled strongly of banana. He cast his nose in the air and followed the scent until he found a large shrub with green leaves and small, cream-colored flowers; it was in the corner, near the brick building with the holes in the walls. The scent of banana was overpowering as he neared the shrub, and when he put his nose near one of the flowers, he found that the banana scent had the slightest edge of varnish to it. *Hmmm... he thought, a banana bush!*—coining a name for this unknown shrub. Then, pleased with his olfactory sleuthing, he left the courtyard. He walked onto Dumaine Street and moved towards Bourbon Street. He crossed Bourbon and turned right on Royal Street. The sidewalks were wet, following their cleaning by the various residents and business owners, and the air smelled of wet blacktop as the water evaporated from the warm street. More and more businesses, many of them antique shops, displayed their wares in the windows as he walked down Royal Street towards Canal.

He passed one such shop and stopped. A black and white "Help Wanted" sign was taped on the door. George looked more closely in the window. There were the usual sets of silverware in their velvet-lined, wooden cases, as well as antique vases, lamps, and jewelry on the display, but his eye was caught by something else. There, in the corner of the display, was a set of antique tarot cards. Three of the cards were overturned and visible, overtop the rest of the cards which were fanned out below. All of the figures on the cards were dressed in vintage costumes suggestive of 18th century fashions. He bent down and put his head near the window to look more closely. One of the cards showed a pair of young, male twins, laughing, each one with long, brown hair. Another card showed a woman, half-dressed with only a skirt on, standing next to a sheaf of wheat with a bunch of grapes in one hand and a silver spear in her other. The cards made him think of Anna and the twins, and he made a quiet exclamation as he stood up. He bent down to look again. The third card depicted a thin, desiccated man, slightly more than skin atop bones, with his legs looking ridiculously thin in their green stockings. His sunken chest was covered in a green doublet, with his arms held out and turned down, palms towards his back. His ancient face was wrinkled and the sparse hair on his head was swept up and back, giving him an otherworldly appearance. The sky seemed to darken as George looked at the eerie figure on the card, but it brightened as he stood erect.

On the spur of the moment, he decided to apply for the job, and grasped the door handle. When he turned and pulled, he saw immediately that the door was locked and that the shop was closed. He put his hands on the glass and pressed his face to his hands to look further back into the shop, but saw no one. When he turned to leave, though, he ran into a sprightly, elderly man who was just then turning into the doorway with a cup of coffee in one hand and a pastry in his other.

They both exclaimed, and the man threw up his hands to keep George from bumping his precious cargo. Luckily, there was a top on the Styrofoam coffee cup, and the pastry remained intact.

"Oh, excuse me!" George cried as they both regained their senses after the surprise. The elderly man was small and slight, with short and mostly gray hair. His eyes were intelligent and his face sensitive. He was dressed in a short-sleeved white shirt and dark brown, cotton slacks. George could see the old-fashioned, sleeveless undershirt the man wore through the thin white cotton of his shirt. His shoes were black, neatly tied, and he wore thin, black socks. George guessed that the man was in his 60s.

"Well, well, young man!" The old man looked over George. "What can I do for you now that you've almost made me ruin my breakfast?"

"I'm so sorry, " George replied, ducking his head. "I was looking at your display, and then I saw the 'Help Wanted' sign and tried to open the door." The adrenaline was still in his system from the surprise encounter, so he spoke quickly and added, "I guess I was disappointed that the door was locked and wasn't paying attention."

"Here, hold this!" The man gave George his coffee cup and reached into his pocket to pull out a large key ring that had at least a dozen keys on it. The keys jangled together as he searched with one hand for the proper key and, after he found it, inserted it into the keyhole, turned the doorknob, and beckoned George to come in after him. George followed dutifully, carrying the coffee cup.

The inside of the antique shop was even more appealing than the display. There was a large, ornate, plaster medallion in the center of the room's ceiling that served as the base of a crystal chandelier. Hanging from the ceiling were numerous lamps and chandeliers. The front room was filled with intricately carved, dark wooden furniture of all kinds, including tables, chairs, dressers, and buffets, most of which had lace cloths with rich ceramic and metal lamps resting on them. The walls were covered in oil paintings of various types. Landscapes, predominated, but there were many paintings of beautiful ladies in flowing gowns, as well as prosperous-looking gentlemen dressed in their best frocked coats. One of the latter paintings was of a smartly dressed Creole man who was painted as if he were looking at something off in the distance. Along the sides of the room were glass cases with shelves that were filled with antique jewelry, old silver and gold coins, exotic leather items, and other such small treasures.

The old man walked behind one of the counters and beckoned George to bring him his coffee. George walked up and placed the coffee on the glass countertop.

"So, you're looking for a job?" the man asked once he had his coffee in hand.

"Yes, sir," George replied. He stuck out his hand and said, "I'm George Santos, by the way."

The old man shook George's hand and replied, "G. Antonio Gentile, but I go by Tony."

Introductions having been finished, Tony leaned on the countertop—right above the paper sign taped to the top that said, "Please do not lean on the countertop"—and smiled at George. "Well, George, do you have any references?"

George thought for an instant, decided that honesty was the best policy, and replied, "Well, Tony, it's like this. I worked as a salesman for Forstahl Furniture—you know, over on Tulane—for just over 18 years. I got the job when I was 18, right after I got married. I was let go a couple of days ago because the new manager didn't like my low-pressure sales technique. I always felt like I'd like to sell the same way I would want to be treated by a salesman. To my way of thinking, it builds trust with the customer and helps with repeat business."

"Just so... just so..." Tony murmured. "Please continue."

"A few days ago, I got into an argument with Mr. Patrick, the new sales manager. He's a young guy who only thinks about the short-term, bottom line. When I tried to explain that customers like my approach to sales, he told me that I was full of shit. Well, I blew up and told him that he was full of shit, and he fired me. So, I don't think he would give me a good reference."

"I see," Tony said as he paused to scratch his head, "and do you know anything about antiques?"

"Not really. My wife, er... my ex-wife used to take me through some antique stores, particularly if we were on vacation. I used to do pretty well on guessing the age of things, and I do know the qualities of different species of wood, but that's about it."

"All right, George..." Tony looked around the room and pointed to a large, ornately carved love seat. "Tell me what you can about that."

George walked up to the love seat and examined it carefully. It was upholstered in a light green fabric with embossed, darker green vines with leaves. The back was carved in a sweeping curve from each arm to the middle of the seat, where there was a beautifully carved shell. The skirt of the loveseat was carved in a riotous scene of foliage and animals that continued down the slightly curved legs, which each widened to a foot in the shape of a claw placed atop a small ball. He turned towards Tony and said, "This is a loveseat. The wood used in construction, and which is intricately carved, is mahogany. It's been re-covered, I think a long time ago, in a chintz cloth. I would guess that the piece is originally from the 1700s or early 1800s."

Tony gave some small claps of applause and smiled. "Very good, George. That is a Chippendale love seat. It is indeed made from mahogany, from the West Indies. The curved legs that you see, that sit on top of the clawed feet, are called cabriole legs, and are typical of Chippendale. The upholstery is chintz, most likely from India, and the piece was re-covered sometime in the 19th century. The initial date of construction would be the latter half of the 18th century. So, you see, George, you did very well. You've got the job. The pay is $150 per week plus a 5 percent commission on sales. Now, for your first duty, please remove the sign from the shop window." And Tony then turned, opened the cash register, and bent down to open a small safe behind the counter.

George readily obeyed the order and then walked back to the counter. "May I ask a question, Tony?"

"Of course."

"Those tarot cards in your display—what's the story on them?"

"Ah, yes!" Tony absently scratched his cheek. "The tarot deck. That is a very interesting item, and it has a story that goes with it. That deck was given to me—or, left with me—by a woman many years ago..." his voice trailed off as his eyes lost a bit of focus.

"Go on," George encouraged him.

"Oh, yes, well.... It starts about 40 years ago, during the depression. I grew up near Lac Des Allemands, where my family had a farm that had been supplying New Orleans with vegetables for several generations. I was an impatient 25-year-old who didn't want to be a farmer. So, I got a job as an oilfield roustabout and spent five years travelling around South Louisiana, working on an oil rig for Unocal. It was a hard job, but a good job—long, hard hours, day or night, in all kinds of weather. Occasionally, there were accidents that cost someone a limb, or their life. Once, there was a blowout that left me with a burn on my back. I still wear the scar. Mostly, though, it was just hard, boring work. But, while many others were standing in bread lines, or working for the WPA or CCC, I was earning a good living.

"Since I stayed on site at the rig and worked most of the year, I didn't have much in the way of expenses, which meant that I could save most of my pay. I never was one for drinking much or spending my money on loose women—unlike many of my fellow roustabouts—so, after five years of work, I'd saved up a pretty penny. That Christmas, it so happened that we were between drilling jobs. All of the workers left to spend the holiday with their families. Both of my parents had died, and my brother—who'd inherited their farm—and I didn't get along very well, so I decided to rent a room in New Orleans and spend the holiday as a tourist.

"I'll never forget that! I rented a suite on the 12th floor of the Roosevelt Hotel. It was next door to the suite owned by Mr. Weiss, Huey Long's friend and the main owner of the hotel. Since I was alone for the holidays, and nobody knew I was just a farmer's boy from Des Allemands, I decided I would be a 'swell' for the length of my vacation."

"Excuse me, "George interrupted him, "what's a *swell*?"

"I'm sorry, George, I keep forgetting that time has passed and folks don't talk like they used to. A 'swell' is a person who dresses nicely, goes to all the right places to see and be seen, and who has a lot of money."

"Oh, I see," George said. "Please, go on."

"Where was I? Oh, yes. Well, I rented the suite on Christmas Eve. The lobby of the hotel was spectacular. It was a city block long, with polished marble floors and columns. There were extravagant decorations for Christmas—garlands, lights, flowers, and mistletoe, all along the lobby. I went to the 12th floor where my suite was. When I opened the door, it was the most elegant place I had ever stayed. There was a sitting room filled with antiques, lace over the tables, a crystal chandelier, and old oil paintings on the walls. The ceiling was about 12 feet high, and there were pocket doors between the sitting area and the bedroom, which were partly closed. The bed was an antique, four-poster bed with intricately carved, dark wood, and with a tester top of rich, red velvet. I remember sitting on that bed and bouncing up and down a little as I tested the softness of the mattress.

"I noticed that there was a silver bucket on one of the tables in the sitting area, with a bottle of champagne inside wearing a white, linen napkin like a coat. There were two champagne glasses on the table, as well. I thought about opening the bottle, but something stopped me, and I decided to go outside and go into the French Quarter.

"It was a typical, New Orleans Christmas Eve. The temperature was mild and there was a light mist falling from a cloudy sky. I made my way down Baronne Street, crossed Canal Street, and into the Quarter. It was late afternoon, and there were still a good many shoppers—mostly men on last-minute forays in the stores on Canal Street. The Quarter was fairly crowded, but the people had different missions. There were some who were on their way to, or heading home from, Christmas parties in this or that restaurant. Others were looking for Christmas cheer in one of the many bars. I walked down Dauphine Street for a ways, until I reached St. Ann. Then, I took a right and headed towards the Cathedral and Jackson Square. I was a just a couple of blocks from the Cathedral when I saw a small sign with a hand-painted on it. There was an eye in the center of the hand, and the sign read 'Madam Cassandra – Fortune Teller.' I've never been much of a believer in the occult, although my grandmother visited a palm reader frequently when I was a boy. The window had a curtain, so I couldn't see inside of the shop. Well, for some reason, I found myself turning into the alcove and opening the door to the shop.

"I walked in and smelled burning frankincense. I recognized it because I'd been an altar boy, and used to prepare the censer for High Mass. The room was dark and cluttered, with books and drawings lining the wall. There were a couple of small light sconces on the wall that provided the only light. I saw several tables and more chairs, with each tabletop containing some weird thing or another. I remember one of them had a crystal ball on a stand, and another had a stuffed crow mounted on a piece of driftwood. I stood there for a moment, looking, and had turned to leave when a voice came out of the back of the room.

"'Take a seat, please.' An older woman with silver-white hair drawn into a bun, and a long dress in the style of gypsies, was walking towards me. She pointed to a table. The top was empty, and she sat in one of the two chairs arranged on either side. I walked up to the table, but I remember that I felt very uncomfortable and tried to make an excuse. She waved away my excuse like it was cigarette smoke annoying her eyes and said again in a deep voice, 'Take a seat, please.'

"I sat down in the chair and, not knowing where to place my hands, put them on the table. I could see that she'd been beautiful when she was young, but now her face was wrinkled and the small hairs on her chin and cheeks seemed highlighted in the dark room. From somewhere I could not see, she produced a deck of cards and shuffled them. Then, she had me cut the cards and give them back to her. When I had finished, she began laying out the cards in a pattern that included rows and columns in a diamond shape, face-up. Several times, she placed cards on top of other cards she had already put down, but I couldn't figure out the rules for doing so. After she had gone through the deck, she began picking up a row here and a column there until she was left with three cards."

George interrupted again, "The three cards that are face up in the display?"

"Exactly!" Tony replied. "She picked up the three cards, and then set them down in the order you see in the display. She looked up at me and spoke again.

"'These cards represent your future.' She looked at me with an intense expression. I could see that she believed what she was saying, but I couldn't guarantee that she wasn't completely insane. She continued, 'You will meet a young woman very soon. She is very beautiful, and you will fall in love with her. You will be married to this woman before the Summer's heat chases away the Winter's chill.'

"The atmosphere was beginning to get to me, so I laughed and said, 'Now, that's a future that I like to hear about!'

"The look on her face was like a slap. I immediately looked down and listened while she continued, 'You will have children together. They will be twin boys. They will be active and intelligent.'

"I nodded, beginning to wonder how I was going to get out of this place without setting the old harridan off. Without looking at her, I asked—in what I hoped was a nonchalant tone—'What about him?'... and I pointed to the card with the insect-looking man.

"She actually hissed! 'That is your nemesis! The thief that steals in the night! The rat that spoils the food! He that takes! Remember that, in the end, all belongs to him. Now, go!' And, with that, the old woman got up from the table and began to walk back towards the rear of the shop.

"'Wait,' I called, 'I haven't paid you yet!'

"She turned, walked up to me, and placed the deck of cards in my hand. Then, she turned around and walked deliberately towards the rear. 'But... but...' I began. She responded with a dismissive wave of her hand and an indistinct mutter as she opened a door in the rear, walked through, and closed it."

"What did you do?" George whispered.

"I got up, left the shop, and walked to the nearest bar, where I had a couple of drams of scotch to settle my nerves. After a while, I left the bar and walked back to the Roosevelt. That night, I went to the Blue Room to listen to Glenn Miller and his orchestra. It was a beautiful place, with large columns that had their bottom halves painted in blue and white stripes and a beautiful, powder-blue ceiling, with tables placed around a central dance floor and the orchestra seating at the end of the room. Quite a bar, too! I got there before the orchestra was set, and walked up to the bar and ordered a Sazarac, just like I imagined the *swell* I was pretending to be would do. I looked to my left, and there was the most beautiful woman I had ever seen, dabbing her eyes with a cocktail napkin. I reached into my coat pocket, pulled out a clean handkerchief, leaned over, and said, 'Pardon me, but my handkerchief is clean and much more suited to touch such a beautiful face—and, may I say that the man who caused the tears is a cad.'

"The woman looked at me with a surprised glance, accepted my offered handkerchief, and finished drying her tears. Then, she gave back my handkerchief and said, 'Thank you, sir. You are a true gentleman.'

"We looked at each other and began to giggle, and that is how I met the love of my life, Martha. We had a whirlwind courtship, and were married the week after Easter. Martha's father had an antique shop on Royal—this very one you are standing in. Her mother had passed away when she was a child and her father had never remarried. He convinced me that it would be better, as a married man, for me to come home every evening rather than travelling around on a drilling rig. So, I came to work for him and, eventually, he left it to Martha and I."

"Wow!" George exclaimed. "Just like the gypsy woman had predicted! What about the twins?"

Tony continued, "We tried to have children for many years, and had almost given up on the possibility when Martha became pregnant in 1947. It was a difficult pregnancy, but she gave birth to two, beautiful twin boys, identical in every aspect except their personalities. We named them Eric and Freddie, and they were the joy of our life." Here, Tony looked down, and the expression on his face changed from one of smiling remembrance to overwhelming sadness.

George noticed, and try as he might, he couldn't help commenting, "Something happened to them, didn't it, Tony?"

"Yes, George. Our beautiful boys joined the Marines and went to fight the Communists in Vietnam. Eric was killed in 1967 during a patrol near the border with Cambodia, and Freddie was killed during the Tet offensive in 1968. Freddie got the Silver Star for bravery during the battle of Hue. I believe that a large part of him had died with Eric. The two were inseparable, and Eric's death greatly affected Freddie. After Freddie's death, Martha slowly... kind of disappeared. She went from being the bright, intelligent woman who I had married to a shadow of herself that lived only in the present. The doctor said it was *early onset dementia*, but I believe that she just lost the will to live. She died last year, three years after Freddie."

"Oh, my God!" George whispered. "That's so awful. I'm terribly sorry for having asked."

Tony reached into his back pocket and produced a handkerchief, with which he wiped his eyes and then blew his nose. He placed the handkerchief back in his pocket and reached out to pat George's hand where it lay on the counter.

"Not to worry, George. We all die—it's just that some die sooner than others. I fully expect to meet them in Heaven after I pass. I take comfort in that."

George waited in silence for several seconds, and then spoke. "Two of the things that the gypsy woman predicted came true. What about the third? The one she called your *nemesis*?"

Tony looked at George for a moment, and then said quietly, "I believe I've encountered him three times already." Then, he added, "Now, let's get to work cleaning this place up."

11

THE PRESIDENT

April 7, 1972

Tony closed up the shop at six o'clock that afternoon, and George had had a good day. He'd sold an 18th-century, small end table to one woman who'd been looking for an accent for her uptown home, and sold the Chippendale love seat to an eccentric-looking gentleman who owned an historic plantation in Natchez. Tony had complimented him on his sales technique as they'd closed for the day. "George," he'd said, "that was an excellent first day's work. Thank you for your efforts." George's chest had swelled with pride in reaction, and he'd thought to himself, *That little prick at Forstahl's made a mistake firing me.*

The day done, he shook Tony's hand and, once again, thanked him for the job, and then waved and headed back to his apartment. He walked back to Dumaine Street and turned down the alleyway. Passing Astro's, he saw JC behind the bar. No one else was inside. He stopped at the doorway and asked, "You sure you don't want to go with us to see Allen?"

JC laughed and held up his hands. "Thanks, but no thanks, George. Who would be here to take care of any customers?"

"I guess you're right, JC. It just seems a shame that you can't see your friend's concert tonight."

"You're right, George, but I've heard Allen play music for many years. Enjoy the concert!" With that, he went back to cleaning up the bar.

"OK, see you later." George left the bar and began walking to the end of the alleyway. When he reached the door, he found it to be unlocked. He turned the handle and walked into the lush courtyard. Once again, he was struck by the vibrancy of the green vegetation. It gave him the feeling of being in a lost world of abundant growth. *The land of giant houseplants*, he thought, a smile passing across his lips. He walked further into the courtyard, and when he reached the bench where he'd sat earlier that day, he saw the door near the pigeonnier open up and Mama Zulie step out. She wore a gaily colored dress that glowed in the flickering yellow gaslight from two sconces on the side of the brick pigeonnier. George smiled and greeted her, "Hello, Mama Zulie. Do you remember me? It's George Santos."

"Mais, oui, mon chere!" Mama Zulie said. "How could I forget such a handsome man who has eaten at my table? How are you, George?"

"I'm fine, Mama Zulie. I'm looking for Jim. We're supposed to be going to see Allen Toussaint on the *SS President* tonight."

"Ah, yes. I know Allen. A beautiful man, n'est ce pas? And his songs are so wonderful and full of life! Would you like some cakes, George? Or Champagne?"

"No thanks, Mama Zulie. I really need to find Jim so we can make it to the concert. Thank you anyway."

"Very well, George. I will not insist because I have somewhere to go now, but, remember, you are always welcome at the home of Mama Zulie!" She gave George a dazzling smile with her perfect, white teeth. "Adieu, mon amie!" she said as she walked to the courtyard door, opened it, and stepped out into the alleyway.

What an amazing woman, George thought to himself. *She has the knack for making a person feel right at home. She must have been a real beauty when she was young.* His thoughts were interrupted by the sound of someone clearing their throat. He turned around, and there was Jim in his wheelchair. Jim had changed out of his shorts and was wearing a pair of faded jeans. His T-shirt had been replaced by a plaid, snap-buttoned shirt like the ones worn by cowboys in the countryside.

"That Mama Zulie's something else, huh?" Jim asked.

"That's just what I was thinking. Do you know anything about her?"

"Like what?"

"I don't know. Like her life story. Where's she from?" George asked.

"Well, I know a little bit about her," Jim replied. "She comes from Haiti. That's why she speaks with the French accent. She's been here a lot longer than I have. I don't know how long. She and Anna seem to have known each other for ages. They're very much similar. Both of them are a kick to be around—full of life, easy to laugh with, but don't get on their bad side. That cat you saw the other day talking to Mama Zulie...."

"The tall, mean-looking dude?"

"Yeah, that guy. I've seen Mama Zulie go after him with the business end of a broom, and she wasn't playing, either. He was ducking and weaving with his hands over his head all the way out to the alley, with her yelling cuss words in French at him as she pounded him with the broom."

"Wow! What did the guy do?"

"I dunno. It sounded like he's been trying to pick her up for a long time, but she doesn't want anything to do with him. He is a persistent bastard, though. I've seen him here off and on since I came here three years ago."

"You ever spoke to him?"

"No, but he's told me to get out of his way a couple of times. And if looks could kill, I wouldn't be here today. He's a scary-looking dude!"

"Yeah, I agree. I wouldn't want to get cross-wise with him," George said. "You ready to head down to the boat?"

"Yeah, we'd better get going to Spanish Wharf if we want to make it on time. "

"OK, so my car or yours?"

"Let's take my car. It's easier for me to drive than to get into a passenger seat."

George got behind Jim's wheelchair and began pushing him out into the alleyway. Suddenly, though, he stopped and asked, "How about Anna? Have you seen her today?"

"Anna comes and goes by her own schedule," Jim said.

They called goodbye to JC as they passed Astro's doorway and headed out to Jim's car. George had quickly become an expert at helping Jim, and they got the car loaded up in no time. They were parking close to Spanish Wharf in just a few minutes.

The SS President had three decks, and their slight, rakish tilt towards both fore and aft reminded George of a giant, floating hot dog. She was a steamship with side paddlewheels, and had been a fixture in the New Orleans night scene since after the war. George remembered taking Gloria on a couple of dance dates on the *President*. One of them had featured Pete Fountain and his band, with Pete playing that smooth clarinet he was famous for. George couldn't remember who'd played on the other date cruise, but he did remember that he'd enjoyed the ambiance of the ship and had a great time each time he'd come.

There was a big crowd milling around the general admission gate near the ship. On Jim's advice, George pushed Jim's chair along a fence to a different gate where one of New Orleans' finest stood guard, next to a slightly bedraggled, older gentleman who was sitting in a folding chair.

"Hey, fellas, what's happening?" Jim asked jovially.

"Nothin' but the rent," said the bedraggled gentleman in a low, gruff voice. "What 'cha need?"

The policeman said nothing, just standing nearby with a disinterested look on his face.

"I think you've got our names on the list," George chimed in.

"What list they talkin' about, Jesse?" the policeman asked.

"The comp list, sir," Jim replied. "We're friends of Allen Toussaint, and he invited us to come watch him as his guests. He said that our names would be on a list."

Mollified, the cop looked at Jesse and asked, "What about it, Jesse? They on the list?"

"How would I know?!" Jesse replied, a bit put out. "I don't even know their names."

"I'm Jim Griffin and this is George Santos," Jim said helpfully.

Jesse got a notebook from underneath the folding chair. It was one of those with the yellow, shiny cover and a dull, cardboard back. He opened the notebook and flipped slowly through several pages, looking carefully at each one. George cast a glance at Jim, and saw that Jim was grinning from ear to ear, trying not to laugh. Jesse kept flipping pages in the notebook and moving his finger up and down the page. Finally, he stopped turning pages and said, "Okie dokie! Jim Griffin and George Santos. I've got y'all right here. Looks like they're on the list, Billy," he said to the cop.

"Well, then, let them in for Christ's sake!" Billy said in an exasperated tone of voice before he turned his attention back to the people heading for the general admission gate.

Jesse got up from the chair, walked a few paces, and unclipped a chain from across an opening in the wire mesh fence.

"Thank you, sirs!" George said as he wheeled Jim through the gate and towards the crowd going up the gangplank of the *SS President*.

"Yeah, yeah!" Jesse mumbled back.

George pushed Jim up to near the edge of the crowd and stopped. He and Jim waited until most of the people had made their way up the gangplank, and then George tipped the front wheels of the chair up and onto the gangplank. He lifted the handles of the chair when the rear wheels reached the lip of the gangplank and smoothly set the chair down as he began pushing it up.

"Not bad, not bad at all," Jim told him with a smile. "Smoothly done!" George smiled back and kept pushing until the chair was on the deck of the ship. He pushed it along a bulkhead until he reached a place where the deck widened out a bit and stopped, and then he stood there as men and women of various ages walked by. The smell of cigarette smoke hung thick in the air, and he and Jim both had to pay attention to keep people from brushing them with the lit end of their cigarettes. George leaned over the chair so Jim could hear him better and asked, "Where to from here?"

Jim replied, "Let's let the crowd thin out a bit more and then we can go into the central ballroom." They stayed on the deck until the crowd began to thin, at which point Jim said, "Bring me up to the staircase and let's see if we can get a little help."

George wheeled Jim to the stairs. In less than a minute, a long-haired, bearded fellow asked, "Do y'all need a hand?"

"Yeah, you right," Jim replied, "much obliged. If you'll take the foot of the chair, George here can handle the back."

"I got it, man," the bearded man said as he bent down and grabbed the chair's feet, and then backed up the stairway.

Halfway up, Jim said, "I feel like Ramah of the Jungle! Mush, boys, mush!"

"Yes, Sahib!" the bearded man said with a grin as he reached the upper deck.

"Thanks!" George and Jim said at the same time.

"No problem, y'all. Later." And the bearded man disappeared into the flow of people.

George wheeled Jim to the left of the door into the central ballroom, underneath a scene of palm trees and monkeys that was painted on the white wall. There, they began to hear the sweet sound of Irma Thomas coming through the door. *"It's raining, outside...."*

George told Jim, "Maybe we'd better go in."

"Let's go," Jim replied, and he began wheeling himself to the door. George opened it and the sound of the song enveloped them. The ballroom was large, with folding chairs set in rows facing the stage. A smaller balcony ringed the rectangular space. They made their way to the bar that ran along the side as Irma Thomas' sultry voice filled the room.

A bartender came up to them and asked, "What'll it be?"

"Two Dixies," George said, and he dug out his wallet as the barkeep got them their drinks.

They sat next to the bar and listened to Irma alternately belt out songs and croon in that wonderfully seductive voice of hers. When she was finished, they both cheered and clapped. Roadies came out on stage and cleared away the central mike, pushed a piano to the center of the stage before they disappeared. A minute later, someone shouted, *"Fess!!"* And, sure enough, Professor Longhair walked onto the stage and sat at the piano. Before he began to play, George noticed the thrumming of the big diesel engines that were powering the paddlewheels as the ship moved down the river. Then, Fess began to play the piano in his unique style as the beginning bars of "Tipitina" lifted the audience to new heights of musical adoration, with Fess' plaintive voice singing the New Orleans favorite.

In between songs, George leaned over to Jim and shouted over the crowd noise, "What a concert!"

Jim just grinned in response and nodded his head. The Professor began to whistle "Go to the Mardi Gras" as he pounded the ivories. As he finished this hit, he went straight into the trilling piano work of "Big Chief"... and the crowd pulsed. George could almost swear that the entire ship was moving and grooving to the rhythmic beat like a living being. He looked down the bar at the bartenders and saw they were dancing along with the rest of the people in attendance.

Fess played for about an hour, and by the end of the set, the audience was ecstatic. The applause as he finished with an encore of "Tipitina" was deafening, and punctuated with screams of "Fess! Fess!" It was hot in the room, so many folks in the audience began to go out to the deck to cool off as the roadies began to clear the stage for the next act.

George heard someone ask, "What have we here?", and he turned and saw Anna, Caz, and Paul standing next to himself and Jim. He had no idea how long they'd been there because he'd been so entranced with Professor Longhair's performance.

As they greeted each other, George noted that Caz and Paul were dressed in differently striped T-shirts and patched jeans. Anna wore a pair of faded jeans and a dark-colored crop top that tied in front. She looked stunning.

The audience began to make a buzz and George looked back towards the stage. The Meters were coming out and the audience knew that things were going to get funky. Preparations complete, Art Neville leaned into the mike and said, "One... two...." And the band broke into the homegrown funk of "Cissy Strut." The audience began to groove to the beat, and George couldn't stop his feet from moving to the music. He glanced down and saw that Jim had wheeled his wheelchair in front of Anna and the two were dancing with abandon—Anna moving her legs, arms, and body, and Jim wheeling his chair in rhythm with the beat and moving his head. George's heart filled at the sight of his friends' joy in the music.

When the song was over, Art spoke again: "Now, we'd like to bring out my little brother to sing a song for you."

A roar came up from the crowd as a large man walked up to the stage and took the microphone. The piano began the song with an arpeggio that led into the plaintive, "Tell it Like It Is." The crowd moved as Aaron

Neville, one of New Orleans' favorite sons, sang the popular favorite. The song ended, and the crowd clapped and whistled their approval.

Aaron nodded his thanks to the audience. "Now, I'd like to do something different for you. We love all types of music here in New Orleans. My brothers and I grew up with gospel and church music, and this song is among the very best." He turned and nodded to the band. They began to play a short, simple melody with single notes. It was obvious that this group of musicians could alter their style effortlessly, and the crowd was hushed with anticipation when Aaron's beautiful vibrato began "Ave Maria" by Shubert.

George felt tears brimming as the sweet devotional slowly soared to the heights of spiritual ecstasy. He closed his eyes and was transported to his childhood as an altar boy. When he opened his eyes again, he looked around at Anna, Jim, and the twins, and saw tears in their eyes, as well. Aaron Neville's voice lifted the assembled crowd with the soul and spirit with which he sang. When he finished, the crowd remained silent for several seconds, but then exploded into raucous applause.

George felt Anna put her arm around his shoulder and leaned down to hear what she was saying. "That was the voice of an angel," she huskily whispered into his ear. The band bowed to the audience and began to leave the stage.

Anna called out, "Hey, guys, why don't we go out on the deck and get some fresh air before Allen starts his set?"

"Sounds good to me," George replied. They all went out the door and headed to a different staircase that led to the top deck. Caz and Paul expertly carried Jim's chair to the top. There were many different groups of people at the railing around the upper deck. They themselves found an empty area, pushed Jim's chair up to the protective metal grate that ran along the edge, and leaned on the railing looking out over the city. The *President* had travelled downriver, and George could see the bright lights of the Chalmette Refinery. The twinkling lights of the different cracking towers and holding vessels lit up the night sky like a small city. George could see steam coming from the tallest tower and, like most New Orleanians, instinctively judged that there was a light, south wind blowing from the angle of the steam as it left the tower and climbed until it dissipated.

The warm, humid night was made a bit cooler from the speed of the ship as it made its way further south and into a much darker area of the river's edge. There were some stars evident in the clear night sky, but not many since the light pollution and humidity obscured most. George leaned on the railing, taking all of this in. In the periphery of his vision, he saw Jim reach into his pants and pull out the baggie of marijuana that had the small pipe in it. Jim packed it and then held it out to Anna. "Ladies first."

"Why, thank you, suh," she replied with a thick, Southern drawl, and they all laughed. Jim produced the lighter from his pocket and Anna lit the pipe and passed it along. After they'd each taken a couple of hits, Jim tapped the pipe on his chair to clean it, put it back in the bag, and put it all away down his pants.

12
THE VEIL LIFTS FURTHER

April 7, 1972

George was thinking that not much had been said by anyone as the boat glided on the smooth river with dark shorelines. He realized that it was not an uncomfortable, awkward silence, but rather the silence of good friends who were enjoying each other's company with no real need to speak. He smiled as he stared out over the river. Anna moved in next to him on the rail, leaned out to feel the breeze, and then turned and smiled her dazzling smile at him. "I guess you're feeling better tonight, eh, George?"

"Yes, thank you, Anna. I've decided that I'm gonna live for a while. I want to apologize for what I did last night", George ducked his head with embarrassment, "you know, getting sick."

Anna laughed heartlily. "'Twas nothing, George. Don't worry about it. I'm just glad you decided to give life another shot." She bumped him in the side with her shoulder. "Hey, Caz! Looking at this dark river shoreline makes me want to hear a story. You got one?"

"Sure thing, Anna. Let me think for a minute... ah, there.... I've got one."

"It was almost 250 years ago that a small ship that had come all the way across the Atlantic Ocean from France was making its slow way up the river. As evening turned to night, the ship hove to, dropping an anchor near this very spot to wait to make the last of its voyage in the next day's light. The Mississippi River, in those days, was not the tame river that we see today, neatly passing down to the Gulf of Mexico between its leveed banks, but was a wild thing. There were giant trees that were beached in shallows, waiting to snag the unsuspecting ship that passed too close. Whirlpools and shifting point bars made navigation in the dark an exercise somewhere between dangerous and foolhardy. The ship's captain, a Frenchman, went below and knocked on a door of the berth way. A nun, dressed in the black dress and white head-covering of her Ursuline order, opened the door and peered out.

"He said, 'Madam, we will put in for the night, and make for La Nouvelle Orleans tomorrow, at first light.'

"'Merci, mon Capitan. I will tell my charges. Bon nuit.' And she shut the door.

"The nun, whose name was Sister Jeanne Therese Eymard, turned to her charges. They were 28 young women from different parts of France who'd been recruited to journey to La Louisiane to marry the colonists. There were no prostitutes or fallen women amongst them. These were young women, orphans or poor, raised by the church's hand, who had few prospects in France, but did have the willingness to chance their fate in a new land. Each had been given a small chest filled with linens, clothes, and sundries that was to be their dowry. They were known, collectively, as 'La filles des cassettes,' after the small chests that they had been given for their dowries.

"Mother Jeanne Therese turned from the door and faced the inquisitive looks from the young women. 'Ma jeune filles. We will arrive in La Nouvelle Orleans tomorrow. We are at anchor in the great river. There is nothing to fear. Say your prayers, ask God to bless you in this endeavor, and go to bed.'

"'But, Mother, when we arrive in La Nouvelle Orleans, where will we go?' asked one of the young women.

"'I have orders to take you to the Convent of the Ursulines, which is built near the center of the town. There, you will remain, protected by the church, until you find your husbands.'

"'Will you be there with us, Mother?' another girl spoke up.

"'Mais, oui, ma Cherie, I will be with you. I am to be the new Mother Superior of the convent.'

"At this news, an excited buzzing of happy chatter came from the young women. Soon, they were all kneeling next to their bunks, as was Sister Jeanne Therese. When she had finished with her evening prayers, she extinguished the lantern and the berth room was dark.

"The next morning, Sister Jeanne Therese felt the ship begin to move in the earliest morning's light. She rose and roused the girls to perform their morning's ablutions. The girls were so excited that they refused breakfast and, instead, pleaded to go up to the ship's deck to see their new home. Sister Jeanne Therese found the captain, and he willingly agreed to have the women on the deck, after extracting a promise that none of them would get in the way of work that needed to be performed. The girls were talking excitedly amongst themselves as they left the bunkroom and climbed up the stairs to the deck of the ship. When they had climbed up to the deck, they went to the edge of the ship's rail and stood looking at the scene before them. The only sound was the sonorous call of orders to the sailors by the officers, to trim sails and guide the ship. The ship travelled close to the bank of the river, so as to avoid the strength of the current pushing the river's water down to the Gulf. There was forest as far as they could see, which was not very far, as the ground went slightly up from the river's banks and the great trees blocked the view of all behind them. Where they could get a glimpse of the area behind the trees of the natural levee, they saw only an endless succession of forest. Clouds of ducks flew in the air, startled into flight by the ship.

"The ship rounded a bend in the river and, there, on the right side of the river, lay the new-found city of La Nouvelle Orleans. They slowly approached the city. There were, perhaps, a hundred wooden structures that were laid out in a rectangular grid that had been surveyed by Monsieur La Tour. A few brick structures, small and simple in style, contained the government offices. At this rustic sight, Mother Jeanne Therese gathered her flock and hurried them below to prepare their belongings for leaving what had been their home for the last 40 days. The ship made its way to the quay, where it stopped. A gangplank was laid from the shore to the ship, and a customs official came aboard and greeted the captain. After discussing events and news, both local and from France, the captain turned and told his first mate to inform his passengers that they were allowed to disembark. The news of 'la filles des cassettes' had preceded their arrival, and there was a fairly large group of men who'd gathered to watch the parade of young women. Their arrival would nearly double the number of European women in the area.

"Standing a bit away from the local trappers, traders, and grandees who were waiting for the parade, was Father Doutreleau, a Jesuit priest who had travelled with the first group of Ursuline nuns. Sister Jeanne Therese led her charges onto the deck. The sight of the men gathered to watch them disembark made all but the most bold cast their eyes down as they were led down the gangplank to be met by Father Doutreleau.

"'Bienvenue, Sister Jeanne Therese! I am Father Doutreleau. Welcome to La Nouvelle Orleans, such as it is. We have all been eagerly awaiting you and give thanks to our Lord for your safe arrival!'

"'Merci bien, Father Doutreleau! It is a pleasure to leave the tight quarters of the ship and walk on ground that is not heaving under our feet. Girls, please say hello to Father Doutreleau.'

"At this, the young women all curtsied and said in unison, 'Bonjour, Father Doutreleau,' as they had practiced on the ship.

"'What charming young ladies! Bonjour, ma jeunes filles, and may God bless you in your lives in New France!' Saying so, he made the sign of the cross over the women. They crossed themselves, as did Sister Jeanne Therese.

"'Now, come with me to the new convent that we have been building. It is only a few blocks away.'

"The priest led the nun and her charges past the group of men who were milling on the levee. Most, but not all of the men doffed their hats or caps and bowed as they walked past. The young women cast sidelong glances as they passed the group, wondering which among them would be their betrothed. They walked down the levee and past the square that served as the center of town. There was a wooden church across from the central square. The church was flanked by two brick administrative buildings, all looking out over the Mississippi River. Sister Jeanne Therese looked at the wooden houses and was surprised to note that most of them were built on piers of bricks raised about three feet above the ground. She mentioned this to Father Doutreleau, and he replied that they were built so as to accommodate the occasional high water that came during the annual flooding of the river. The houses were built a short distance back from the street with outbuildings, kitchens, and barns placed further back on the rectangular lots.

"'If I may ask, Father, how large is La Nouvelle Orleans?' asked the sister.

"'At last count, we now have nearly 600 families who live in the city or nearby. There are an additional 300 native souls who live in the vicinity who have seen the light of our Savior and have been baptized. You will be of great assistance. We have established a hospital that is next to the convent, and your fellow Sisters of Ursuline have been ministering to the sick for the last year. It is a blessing,' he finished, and he crossed himself, as did the nun. 'Now, here we are!'

"Sister Therese looked at the large wooden structure that they had stopped on front of. At three stories tall, it was the largest building in the city, and occupied a lot with some outbuildings and a large garden. During their walk from the quay to the convent, and while the nun had been occupied in discussion with Father Doutreleau, the young women had been looking around and taking their stock of the new city. Now that that they had arrived at their new home, they began talking excitedly amongst themselves.

"'Bienvenue a la Convent d'Ursuline!' Father Doutreleau said, and walked up the path to the great wooden door. As he reached the door, it was opened by a nun in the typical Ursuline habit.

"'Bienvenue, Father! Sister! Jeunne filles!' said the nun with a booming voice. She bowed to the priest, and then walked up to Sister Jeanne Therese, grabbed her hand, and kissed it. 'Welcome, again, Mother Superior! We have been anxiously awaiting your arrival! I am Sister Marie.'

"Sister Jeanne Therese placed her right hand upon Sister Marie's head and bowed her head as she said a short prayer. Then, she raised her head and looked at Sister Marie with sparkling eyes. 'I am so glad to be here with my sisters. If you please, Sister Marie, could you assist me in showing our young charges where they will be staying?'

"She turned towards Father Doutreleau and bowed. 'Father, I thank you for your kind assistance and for taking the time to greet your humble servant. I await your orders as to how we may assist you in our heavenly duty to the souls in this new land.'

"Father Doutreleau raised his right hand and made the sign of the cross with two fingers upraised. All who were present crossed themselves. He said, 'We will talk soon, Mother Superior. Please make yourself and the girls comfortable in your new home.' With that, he turned and began walking down the path to the street.

"Sister Marie boomed, 'Come with me, ladies, and I will show you to your new home.'

"Sister Jeanne Therese smiled to herself and followed the group up the stairs. When they reached the third floor, Sister Marie opened the door to a large attic room. Huge, hand-hewn beams, with axe marks visible, served as the rafters to the convent house roof. The rafters were joined to central beams, forming the type of roof called *mansard*. Windows with shutters that could be opened for the cooling Summer breezes, or closed for the cold Winter winds, also provided some light for the interior. There were 28 beds set in orderly fashion along the walls. The windows were open at present, and Sister Jeanne Therese walked up to one of them and looked out over the back lot and towards the garden. She saw a young woman, obviously a native, who was dressed in a combination of leather skirt and cloth shirt, and who stood bent over a small table, working on something.

"She asked Sister Marie, 'Sister, who is that? And what is she doing?'

"Sister Marie walked to the window and looked out. 'That is just Clothilde. She is a native girl who is one of the servants of the convent. I'm not sure what she is doing.'

"Both nuns then turned to the young women and began to help them to settle into their new home.

"After several weeks, Sister Jeanne Therese began to feel at home in the convent, and in the new city. The unfamiliarity of a new place was giving way to the comfort of routine, day to day existence. One day, as she was walking around the garden, she encountered the young native girl, Clothilde, once again working on something at the small table next to the garden. She walked up silently and watched. Clothilde was taking clay, mixing it with sand, rubbing it between her palms into snakes, and coiling it around a flattened piece of clay that was to serve as the base of the vessel. Clothilde looked up and startled. 'No, my child, please continue' said Sister Jeanne Therese.

"Clothilde smiled and continued placing the coils of clay around the base. When she reached a height of a few inches above the base, she took a piece of smoothed bone and dipped it into a water vessel next to the pot. Then, she reached into the vessel with the bone and smeared the clay up the inside of the vessel, filling in the gaps between the coils.

When she finished with the interior of the vessel, she did the same with the outside of the vessel. Once done, she took the bone and flattened the topmost coil, and began to place her clay snakes in coils on the vessel. In the end, she had made a vessel which had begun from a base, flared outwards, and then become restricted around the mouth of the vessel. It was an altogether pleasing shape; however, it would be difficult to eat or drink from without spilling its contents. When she was done, Clothilde took the vessel in both hands and placed it on a bed of branches that she had stacked nearby for the purpose of drying her work. Sister Jeanne Therese spoke up, 'Do you understand me, Clothilde?'

"Clothilde looked at the nun and said, 'Yes, ma'am,' in a clear but heavily accented voice.

"'Why do you make the pot so?' the nun asked.

"Clothilde looked puzzled as she answered. 'It is the way pots are made.'

"'Could you make a different type of pot?' Sister Therese suggested.

"Clothilde's reply was silence, and she stepped back from the table.

"Sister Jeanne Therese looked around at the ground until she found a piece of charcoal which she bent and picked up. 'Here, let me show you,' she said, and she began to draw an open-mouthed bowl, of the type used in Europe, on the wood of the table. 'You see, you leave it open on top, so it is easier to get into and out of.'

"'It will not dry,' Clothilde said. 'The sides will fall.'

"'Perhaps we can use a hide sack filled with leaves to hold the sides while it dries,' suggested Sister Jeanne Therese, smiling her beautiful smile at Clothilde.

"'We will try,' Clothilde replied with a smile. It took several tries over the course of the next few days, but soon Clothilde was successful in creating the open-mouthed bowl. Over the course of the next few weeks, Sister Jeanne Therese would continue working with Clothilde in making plates, bowls, and cups for the convent. They were styled in the European fashion, yet fired in the native fashion by digging a small pit, placing the ceramic pieces in the pit, and covering it with brush and setting it afire. The pots, bowls, and plates that Clothilde created in this fashion soon became popular throughout the city. Over the course of the next few months, Clothilde became the first provider of serviceable, locally produced, European-style pottery for the new city."

George realized that the lights of the Mississippi River Bridge were passing overhead.

"Whoa! My God! How do you do that?" he sputtered, to the amusement of the rest of the group.

"He's got the knack," Anna said to the group's laughter. "We'd better go down to catch Allen's set now." And the group went back down the stairs to the ballroom.

When they got in, the same spot on the bar where they had been before was open for them. George was not particularly surprised after his experiences of the last day. He asked if anyone wanted something to drink and all answered in the affirmative, so he bought a round of Dixies for the group.

A beautifully polished, Steinway piano had been placed in the center of the stage, and, near it, a mike stand with a microphone. The back-up band was in place with drums, guitar, and a horn section. The audience was growing impatient, and the loud muddy noise that was the result of a thousand people talking loudly amongst themselves began to resolve into more coordinated chants of "Allen! Allen! Allen!" This went on for about three or four minutes more, and was interrupted by a tentative cheer and applause, which became cacophonous when Allen Toussaint walked onstage. Allen raised his hands, palms towards the audience, and waved them down to quiet the crowd. When the noise abated, he walked to the mike stand and removed the microphone. Then, he turned to face the crowd and spoke.

"Thank you, thank you, everybody! What a beautiful night for us to get together and enjoy our wonderful New Orleans music. Irma Thomas, Professor Longhair, and the Meters! Who'd a thunk we'd see them perform together on the same night? What a special night this is! And what a special city we have! Let's all give it up for our mother, New Orleans!" The crowd went nuts clapping, whistling, and yelling. Allen waved his hands to calm every one down, and the crowd got quiet again.

"It's such a very special night tonight, a southern night with warm breezes and something special in the air. It's so special to me, and I hope it is to you, as well. It's so special, in fact, that I have a surprise for you. An old friend called me tonight and asked if I would mind if he came along for tonight's cruise. I told him I would be honored if he joined us. So... it is my honor and privilege to introduce to you tonight, on our stage, the one... the only... FATS DOMINO!!!"

The crowd went wild as a short, stocky man in a suit and white captain's hat walked onto the stage in a purposeful manner. Allen shook his hand and walked back offstage, leaving Fats to bask for a moment in the crowd's adulation. Then, he turned towards the band and waved, walked up to the Steinway, sat at the bench, and immediately started rocking out to "A Whole Lot of Lovin'." The crowd was moving and grooving, and as soon as he finished, he went into "My Girl Josephine" and then "Blueberry Hill."

George looked at his friends and saw they were dancing in place to the music. He reached out and touched Anna on the shoulder. When she looked at him, he pantomimed dancing, and she smiled and nodded. He took her in his arms and danced to "Blueberry Hill"—and even though there wasn't much room to move, he was both happy and satisfied. Fats moved from one song to another, barely waiting for the applause to end before he began his next song. "I'm Walking," "Ain't It a Shame," "Blue Monday..." *bam, bam, bam.* Every song familiar, every song a hit. George felt a tug on his shirt. He looked down, and there was Jim, grinning like a fool. He leaned down and Jim said, "Gold, man... pure gold!"

"Yeah, you right!" George responded, and clinked the throat of his Dixie beer bottle to the one held in Jim's hand.

Fats finished his set with a rousing version of "Jambalaya," and the entire ship seemed to jump and move in beat to his piano playing. When this last song was finished, a roar went up from the crowd that must have been heard at Fats' house in the Ninth Ward. *"Encore, encore!"* sounded as the screams and whistles leaped above the ground swell of applause.

Fats looked at the band and nodded, and finally launched into "I'm Gonna be a Wheel Someday," quickly followed by "I'm Walkin' to New Orleans." When he finished, he stood, bowed, and waved to the crowd as he walked offstage. The crowd remained ecstatic.

Allen Toussaint walked slowly back out onto the stage. He was dressed in a long, multi-colored dashiki. The crowd roared. He waved and sat down at the piano bench, and then pulled the microphone over to him.

"Now, wasn't that something!" he said in his soft, mellow voice. "I told Fats that I hated to have to follow him, but I wouldn't miss the chance for anything in the world. He's a real New Orleans treasure." The crowd shouted their approval, and Allen nodded to the band and began playing "Java." George found himself singing along with the instrumental, like many in the audience. Everyone was in motion. When Allen finished, he looked at the band and said, "One... two..." and launched into "Brickyard Blues." This was followed by "Yes We Can," "A Certain Girl," and then "Working in the Coal Mine." Then, Allen stopped playing for a minute and spoke to the crowd.

"I don't know how many of you are local..." he trailed off, letting most of the audience let him know that they were locals, "but as I was saying, if you are local, then you know that New Orleans has never been far from the supernatural. From Voodoo to Gris Gris to fortune tellers, the veil between what we think of as reality... and a deeper existence... is very thin here. In fact, I wrote a song about this a while back...." And with that, he broke into "Fortune Teller." George could swear that Allen was looking directly at him and his new friends at the bar as he sang this song. He raised his beer in a salute to Allen, and was rewarded by a wink, a smile, and a nod from the singer. After the song was finished, Allen laughed and then broke into "Mother in Law," his song that had been so aptly covered by Ernie K-Doe.

The applause was raucous when he finished, and he waited a minute for it to die down before he leaned into the microphone again. As he did so, his hands moved deftly on the piano keys, playing a haunting melody. There were powerful bass notes, counterpointed by upper-range ripples that sounded almost oriental. He played softly at first and spoke as he played, "I told y'all that this was a special night. A night full of promise... of destiny... of love—" the music grew a bit louder, and he went on, "a night in a special place, and at a special time." He paused. "I don't know how many of you are musicians, and, if you are, how many of you have written songs, but I believe that they are given to us from elsewhere." He spoke slowly, softly and with feeling.

"There are times," he continued, "when they are given to us in pieces, as if we only get a glimpse of the divine, and there are other times when they are given to us whole. An entire song... melody... words... tempo, everything, presented to the fortunate songwriter as if it were a gift from above." The music grew louder, then faded into the background as he continued to speak into the microphone. "It's magical, really. The kind of magic you feel with your loving family or your friends. Instantly, everything just feels *right*. Like a perfect soap bubble hanging in the air and reflecting the universe of that moment in incredible detail. Now, songwriters don't get to choose when these perfect gifts are given. Oh, we can craft a song, and it might be a good song or even a great one, but those perfect songs always seem to come from elsewhere." Here, the music swelled again, and Allen stopped speaking as he played the haunting melody in silence for a minute. Then, he began to speak again.

"I visited an old, old friend today. One I hadn't seen in a while. Afterwards, I went back to the studio and sat at my piano." The music alternately grew louder and then quieter. "And then... I was given this...." And he began to sing.

"Southern nights...."

As Allen finished his song, the audience was so quiet that you could have heard a pin drop. George looked at Anna and saw tears running down her cheeks. He looked around at the people near him, including his friends, and saw several others tearing up. George wasn't surprised because he had tears in his eyes, as well. After a few seconds of awed silence, the crowd erupted. Allen stood up from the piano, bowed to the audience, and slowly walked offstage. At the same time, the ship's steam whistle gave a mighty blast, announcing to one and all that the ship had reached the dock. The crowd stayed put, though, showing their approval for five minutes more before they began to disperse down the stairs towards the gangplank.

Paul leaned over to George and said, "Man, that Allen is one talented dude!"

"I'll say," George replied, "that song was beautiful!"

"Perfect, I'd say!" Caz chimed in.

"I concur," Jim said. Anna kept looking towards the piano that stood on the stage.

"So, Anna, what did you think about that song?" Jim asked her.

She replied as she wiped the tears from her cheeks, "There are so few people in this world that can catch a glimpse of the divine and describe it to others. Allen is one of them."

The friends all nodded in agreement, and then Paul asked, "Well, y'all ready to go?"

"Yeah, we'd better head out. It was great to see y'all, Jim... George," Caz said.

"Yeah, there's still some stuff we have to do," Anna said, looking at George.

"Well, then, this was a lot of fun! Thanks for the story, Caz, and good to see you, Paul... Anna!" George said.

"Catch y'all on the flip side," Jim said with his smile. Anna and the twins gave him a thumbs-up and headed out of the ballroom. Jim and George followed, but stopped before the stairway to let the crowd thin out some. A few minutes later, who came up but the bearded guy who'd helped them earlier.

"Y'all need a hand?" he asked.

"My hero!" Jim joked as George nodded. "Tell me, friend, what did you think about this concert?"

The man responded, "That was, beyond a shadow of a doubt, the best music that I've ever heard in my life. If I die tonight, I'll die happy, knowing that I was here to listen to it."

"Amen," Jim replied.

By the time they'd disembarked and made their way to Jim's car, it was nearly 1 a.m. On the way down the alley Jim said, "That was fucking far out, George. I'm ready to go deaux deaux and dream sweet dreams."

"Me too, Jim. Thanks for everything!" George saw that the sign for Astro's was dark, and the bar's door was closed as they went past. In the courtyard, Jim wheeled his chair to a door that had a ramp built to go over the doorsill.

"Thanks again, Jim. You've been really great to me, and I want you to know that I appreciate it," George said.

"Don't worry about it, George, it was a ball! I had a good day, too. See you in the morning!" And, with that, Jim opened his door and wheeled himself inside, closing the door behind him.

George's suitcase was on top of his bed. He opened it, removed his dop kit, and went into the bathroom. Upon exiting the bathroom, he turned off the light, felt his way to the bed, removed his clothes, and got under the covers. He didn't notice the small bit of sand that fell from the cuff of his pants as he took them off. As he lay there in the dark, he thought about his day. It seemed like an age ago that he had been ready to commit suicide. The pain that he'd felt from Gloria and Sonny's betrayal now seemed like a memory from the distant past, and, as for his job, that asshole could have it. He thought about the new friends that he'd made, and his new job. The kindness of Tony, Jim with his wry sense of humor, Caz and Paul with their stories and boundless energy, JC with his calm and patience, and Anna.... Anna was so beautiful, George thought to himself that he was a little bit in love with her already.

"Don't be a fool," he chastised himself. He remembered the evening and thought, *I went on the* President *as Allen Toussaint's personal guest! And saw the best concert of my life!* And, thinking such pleasant thoughts, he drifted off to sleep sweet dreams.

13
THE FISH IN THE SEA

April 15, 1972

The rising sun cast bolts of golden light through the clouds and lit the marsh grass with a fiery glow. Standing at the center console of the boat was Fleming Babineaux, the fishing guide from Grand Isle whom Morgan had hired for the trip. He glanced at Morgan and the two other fishermen seated in the front of his boat, then returned his gaze to the water. The loud, continuous roar of the engine reverberated in Fleming's ear, the harmonics harkening back to childhood memories of fishing trips with his father and fantasies of hearing angels' hosannas.

Fleming was a short, stocky man with a swarthy complexion and massive forearms. His face bore the scars of an adolescent case of acne, and his quick, brown eyes betrayed a native intelligence. He scanned the horizon and all points between for telltale current marks indicating a submerged obstruction. As he scanned for problems, he also searched for diving gulls. These birds were excellent markers for schools of speckled trout who'd be feasting on huge schools of shrimp. As if on cue, Fleming spotted a group of ten or so gulls alternately diving and sitting on the water about a half-mile from the boat. He turned the boat in the direction of the diving birds and positioned it so that the combination of tide and the slight breeze would cause the boat to drift over the area. When he had them in the right position, he slowed and cut off the motor.

"Get ready, gentlemen!" he announced to the three fishermen.

They all grabbed fishing poles that were rigged with corks atop different colors of plastic baits, and cast their lines towards the diving birds. It took less than two seconds after the first cork hit the water for it to disappear as a fish took the bait. The pole arched as Harold, Morgan's friend from north Louisiana, set the hook and began to fight the fish. Bob, Morgan's cousin, and Morgan weren't far behind him as they set hooks and began to fight the fish on their poles, as well.

"This one feels pretty good," Morgan grunted as the drag whined and the fish took some line. The other men, focused on their own battles, agreed. After about three minutes of fighting the fish, Morgan got his close to the boat. As it neared the side and his pole bent near double, a string of slime appeared on his fishing line.

"Goddammit!" Morgan yelled. "A fucking gafftop!" He reeled up the fish and, indeed, the wriggling form of a 3-pound gafftopsail catfish showed at the bottom of a foot-long trail of slime on his line.

"Son of a bitch, man!" he said to Fleming. "I'm paying you to catch trout, not trash."

"No way I could tell, "Fleming responded as he bent to flip the fish off of Morgan's hook. He then did the same for the gafftops on the other fishermen's rods.

"Let's get the hell away from this school of turd hustlers!" Bob said.

"Yeah!" Harold replied, and with that, Fleming started the engine and began to work the boat deeper into the Barataria Bay estuary. As he did so, Morgan opened the ice chest on the front of the boat and got out beers for himself and the other two fishermen. He looked at Fleming and winked as he said, "None for you. You're driving."

Fleming smiled at him and shook his head. As he pointed the nose of the 23-ft. Carolina skiff to the north and throttled up the engine, Fleming thought to himself, *What a pack of assholes!* His reverie was interrupted by a bottlenose dolphin coming out of the water and riding the bow wave of the boat. The dolphin alternately sank and rose in the water column, casting a curious eye at the boat and its inhabitants as it enjoyed the free ride. Harold took a last swig of his beer, and then threw the bottle at the dolphin. The creature sank beneath the waves as the bottle sailed over the place where its head had been.

"That was almost 150 points!" Bob shouted over the engine noise.

"Yeah! The only thing that counts for more is a cripple in a wheelchair!" Morgan added.

Fleming's lips drew a straight line across his face as the three friends guffawed with laughter. Hearing them talk this way reminded him of the discussion he'd had with his father when he'd decided to get into the guiding business. He recalled his father's advice, given in an accent unique to South Louisiana—French mixed with country, and a bit of New Orleans Yat.

"*Fleming,*" his father had said, "*ya sure ya know what you're doin'? Ya gonna have to deal wit dose assholes from up da baya.... Loud-mouthed, selfish, and rude. Dey'll try an' cheat ya every chance dey get. It's a hard way to make a livin', cher.*"

Fleming remembered his response to his father, too: "*Not everybody's like dat, Daddy. An' mos' fishermen are pretty good guys.*"

He had been guiding for 20 years, and he had found that both he and his father had been right. Most of his customers were fun to be around, and appreciative of his skill and his easy personality. But, every now and then, he got the kind that his father had warned him about.

Looks like I'm gonna earn my money today, he thought to himself grimly. He could see a marsh island about a hundred yards ahead that formed a crescent in the open water. He eased back on the throttle, coming closer to the island, and killed the engine so they would drift within casting range.

"All right, gentlemen. We're here. Go ahead and make a few casts. Let's see if the reds are here today."

Morgan, Bob, and Harold stood up and grabbed their fishing poles. They cast towards the island expertly. Bob to the left, Morgan to the right, and Harold in the middle. As soon as the corks hit the water, they began popping the corks to make a noise to attract the fish. Suddenly, Harold's cork started moving towards the right slowly, and disappeared under the water like the conning tower of a submarine beginning to dive.

"There it is!" Fleming said in a low voice. "Let him take it under."

Harold waited until the cork was completely underwater before he reared back and set the hook. The pole was bent in a "C" over his head, and the water around where his cork had been suddenly boiled with the tail thrusts of a large redfish.

"Ho! Ho!" Harold cried. "Reel your bait up, Morgan! He's headed your way!"

The redfish was making the drag scream as it headed towards the right. Harold was an experienced fisherman, and he let the rod and the drag do the work. After about ten seconds of pulling the drag, the big redfish turned back and headed to the left. Harold reeled as fast as he could to keep the slack out of his line. When he caught back up to the fish, the reel began to scream again.

"Nice fish!" Fleming said. "Don't horse him. Let him tire out, and I'll net him for you."

"Don't worry. This ain't the first redfish I've caught," Harold responded. He kept pressure on the fish, using his rod and drag, and made up line when the fish gave him the opportunity. After about five minutes of battle, the redfish began to tire. The drag-screaming runs were shorter and shorter, and the fish got closer and closer to the boat. Finally, after nearly ten minutes of fighting the fish, it surfaced close enough to the boat that they could see the big red. The redfish also saw them and made one last drag-screaming run, but it quickly tired out.

Harold pumped his rod up and down and reeled the fish closer to the boat. It turned on its side as it reached the craft, and Fleming deftly netted the fish and raised it over the gunwale of the boat and onto the floor.

"Dat's a nice red," Fleming told Harold.

Morgan and Bob were patting a smiling Harold on the back as Fleming got down on his knees to take the hook out of the fish's mouth. He then lifted the fish by the gills and held it out to Harold, who took the fish and kissed it on the nose.

"Here! Take a picture!" Morgan shouted. He reached into his bag and handed his Kodak Instamatic camera to Fleming. Fleming obligingly took several pictures of Harold with his redfish, Morgan and Bob flanking him. Afterward, Fleming asked, "What do you want to do with it? It's a big female."

"What kind of question is that?" Bob replied. "We're going to eat this bitch! Put it in the ice chest!"

"Yeah! We're going to eat this bitch!" Morgan chimed in. Harold just grinned. Fleming opened up the 120-quart ice chest and threw the bronze-colored fish on the ice. Then, he shut the top of the ice chest.

"All right, gentlemen, let's see if there are any more out here," Fleming said, thinking that this was going to be a long day.

They cast again along the island, but to no avail. Shortly after that cast, Fleming started the engines and moved to another island in the marsh, where another large redfish was caught. They continued the pattern of "stick and move" (as Fleming's dad referred to it) throughout the rest of the morning, picking up a redfish here and a couple of speckled trout there. It was nearly 3 p.m. when Fleming asked the men, "You fellows ready to head back?"

"Yeah, it's time to get back to the camp," Morgan said as he took a sip from the endless supply of beers the men had brought, finished it, and threw it in the water. "You've got a lot of fish to clean!"

Fleming grinned back at Morgan and said, "Yes, sir!" He pointed the bow of the boat to the south and headed back towards Grand Isle.

When they reached the dock, Fleming expertly placed the boat next to the cleats, tied the boat off, and shut off the engine. The three friends climbed out of the boat and opened fresh beers as they compared their fishing prowess. Fleming gathered the trash from around the boat, hopped out, and put it in the trash can. Then, he climbed back into the boat and gathered the poles, which he placed on the dock next to the boat. He next turned his attention to the ice chest, full of ice and fish. "Would one of you please give me a hand getting this ice chest out of the boat?" he asked.

"Sure," Bob agreed, jumping back into the boat and grabbing the other side of the heavy 120-quart ice chest. They lifted it out of the boat and placed it on the dock. "Come on, you lazy bastards!" Bob chided Morgan and Howard. "Grab this ice chest and put it under the pavilion." With a modicum of bitching, the two friends complied as Bob climbed out of the boat, and Fleming continued with his post-trip procedures.

The three friends sat under a fan in the shade of the pavilion while Fleming finished cleaning his boat and filleted the fish they had caught. They drank cold beers as the breeze from the fan dried their sweat in the warm afternoon. As they drank, they continued the conversation which had begun out in the marsh. Their only annoyance was a small, biting fly which kept pestering them. Fleming couldn't help overhearing their conversation as he expertly began filleting the day's catch.

"So, tell me again, Morgan, this development deal in the Quarter that you're involved with will return 200 percent on investment? How's that going to work?"

"Well, it's like this, Harold. I've got an investor who's interested in buying an entire block of the French Quarter, knocking down those old, derelict buildings, and building a development with condos, shops, restaurants, and bars in the footprint. It's going to cost about five million to buy the properties, assuming we can keep the costs down. Demolition, site prep, and construction will cost approximately ten million. Now, here's the beauty part. I've found this investor who seems to be as crazy as he is rich. He's willing to fund the entire project himself for an 85% net. He's offered me 15% of net income to put the deal together and make it happen. He has a few crazy demands, but what's that when you're making money?"

"Crazy demands? What do you mean?" Bob asked as he slapped his arm where the fly was biting him.

"Well, for instance, he'll only do it if we place the development on this one specific block of the Quarter. Another demand of his is that no more or less than five condominiums be constructed, with four 5-story condos placed on the corners of the footprint, and a 10-story condominium placed in the exact center of the footprint. Other weird shit like that. No real big deal—just the whims of a really rich man."

"So, what's the rest of the money deal?" Harold asked.

"It's like this. I've got 15% of this deal that I can either keep or sell to anybody I want. Lucky for you, I'm such a good friend and cousin that I'm willing to cut y'all into the deal. Now, I've already got a partner for 7.5%, which leaves me 7.5% to play with. I want to keep 3.5% for myself, for my troubles, but I'm willing to let y'all in for 2% each. Goddamn fly!" Morgan slapped his calf.

"How does the money work?" Bob asked.

"Like this. There's going to be 180 condos that will sell for an average of $170,000 each. That's a gross of $30,600,000. Fifteen percent of that is almost 4.6 million dollars. That comes to $306,000 per gross percentage point. Y'all are my family, so I'm willing to sell you the two percentage points for $153,000 per point. That means that you'll double your money."

"Wait a minute," Harold interjected, "what's the risk that the condo's won't sell out? It seems to me that we don't double our money until they're sold."

"That's right, numb nuts, but these things will sell out in no time. Think about it. The economy is booming, and everything I hear from my oil and gas buddies says that things have nowhere to go but up. We probably won't have to wait two years for everything to sell out, and in addition to that, we'll lease out spaces for the restaurants and bars, which will provide almost six grand of yearly income per point. That means that the leases alone will pay for your initial investment in 25 years, even if no condo is ever sold."

"Holy shit! It sounds almost too good to be true," Bob said. "What about this mysterious investor? Who is he?"

"He's some Indian guy."

"Indian?" Harold asked, putting two fingers above his head like feathers.

"No, stupid, a dot-head Indian," Morgan replied, placing the tip of his pointing finger on the center of his forehead. "I've spoken with him once—a long-distance call. I guess he was calling from India because there were some strange sounds on his end of the line, but I could hear him clearly. Then, he sent over some people who met with me, an architect and a banker, both from New York. He also retained old man Michael Riley, from Riley, Watkins, and Lassiter. That's just about the most distinguished law firm in New Orleans. Mara paid over $300,000 up-front for his retainer, and Michael has seen enough proof of his bona fides that he assured me Mara's good for every bit of the proposal."

"Man, this is making me salivate! Can I buy more than two percent?"

"Don't be greedy, Harold! I want to make some money, too!" Morgan responded.

"I wish someone would convince this fly to stop being greedy. The little bastard has bit me twice already," Harold said.

"Here's to making money!" Morgan said, raising his beer in a toast. The others clinked their beers with his.

"And to crazy fucking Indians!" Bob chimed in as they hooted with laughter.

Fleming walked up to the cluster of friends under the pavilion. "Excuse me, fellas, I'm done cleaning up the fish. The bags of fillets are over there on the counter. If you don't mind, I'd like to get paid now so I can go home and clean up."

"Let's see," Morgan said, "the fee was a hundred dollars, wasn't it?"

Fleming felt his face redden. "No, sir, Mr. Sanborne. You know that my fee is two hundred dollars for parties of three."

"Yeah, I know," Morgan replied, "it just seems high to me." But he took out his wallet and counted out two hundred dollars. "At that price, don't expect a tip."

Fleming bit his tongue at the response that was on his lips, took the two hundred dollars, and said, "Thank you. Now, if you don't mind, I need to clean up this pavilion to get ready for tomorrow's clients. Thanks again for your business."

The three men got up from their chairs, leaving their empty beer bottles on the ground, and walked over to retrieve their bags of fish fillets and put them into an ice chest. Then, they carried the ice chest to their car and put it in the trunk.

Fleming could hear them continue talking as he cleaned up the pavilion.

"Brenda's coming over tonight and bringing a couple of her girlfriends."

"All right! Let's get them to dance on the tabletop."

"Yeah, I want to see some panties tonight!"

"Oh, yeah!"

And with that, they climbed into their Mercedes and, slinging shells, pulled out of the parking lot.

As they drove over the concrete bridge from the Cheniere to Grand Isle, they looked at the people fishing on the old wooden bridge that had been so severely damaged in Hurricane Betsy. They could see the tide was moving out through Caminada Pass into the Gulf of Mexico, and several dolphins were feeding in the fast-moving current.

"Look at those fish-stealing bastards!" Morgan said. "If it was up to me, I'd turn every one of them into dog food."

"Yeah," Bob replied, "Harold almost got one with that beer bottle."

"If I'd thrown it a little earlier, I'd have got him between the eyeballs, but I wanted to finish my beer!" Harold chimed in. They all howled with laughter.

They drove down Highway 1 on the island until they reached the camp they were staying in. It was a large fishing camp built up on wooden pilings about eight feet high, located on the beach side of the road. There was a low berm between the grassy part of the lot and a large, sand beach which fronted the Gulf. A brightly hand-painted sign that measured about three feet square was mounted on the front siding of the camp. A blue crab was painted on the sign, along with the name of the camp, "The Land Crab." The camp had a plain, rectangular shape with a shingled roof, and the siding was painted white, though it had been slightly dulled by dirt and mildew in the five years since it had been built. There was a red Camaro parked under the camp. Morgan parked the Mercedes in front of the camp, behind the Camaro, and the men got out of the car.

"Looks like Brenda and her girlfriends are already here," he chuckled to the others.

Just as he said this, the door to the camp opened up and a woman's hand waved out of the door with a large, ice-filled glass.

"That's my girl!" Morgan called out, and Brenda and her two girl-friends stepped out of the camp onto the porch. One of her friends was an attractive brunette, but the other was a stunning and statuesque blonde. Both appeared to be close in age to Brenda. The men climbed up the stairs to the porch, and Brenda walked up to Morgan and gave him a kiss on the lips.

"Why don't you introduce your friends, babe?" he asked her.

"Sure. This is my friend Debbie that I've told you about, and this is my cousin Janine."

"It's a pleasure to meet you both," Morgan said smoothly. Bob and Harold both made their introductions.

Bob commented, "I could use a quick shower and then a nice, cold drink."

Harold agreed, "Yeah, that sounds great. You use the master bathroom and I'll take a shower in the guest bathroom. Morgan, it looks like you'll have to entertain our guests, if you're up to it," he added, and gave Morgan an exaggerated wink.

Morgan and the ladies all laughed, and Morgan replied, "Oh, I'm up to it all right," and they all laughed again.

After everyone had bathed and had a few drinks, someone mentioned dinner and the men quickly began to prepare to fry up some of the fish that they'd caught that day. They formed an assembly line, with Harold dipping the fillets in a bowl filled with eggs, Bob taking the fillets and rolling them in Zatarain's fish fry, and Morgan dropping them into the pot filled with hot grease, taking heed of the time between dropping the fillets so that the grease didn't cool down too much and make the fried fish fillets greasy.

Morgan called Brenda over as he was frying the fish. "Brenda, do you remember that little job I asked you to do earlier?"

"The one in the Quarter?" she inquired.

"Yes, that one. I'd like you to go over there Saturday after next and see what you can find out. I want to move forward on this project as soon as possible, but there's still something I need to do before we start."

"Can I wear my peanut jeans?" she asked.

"I don't give a good goddamn what you wear!" he barked. "Just make sure you find out some dirt on our little friends there that will give me the lever I need to get them out of that place."

Brenda drew back, a little hurt by his tone.

Morgan pulled her to him, "Come on, babe. You know that this is important to me. I'm sorry I'm being grouchy." He reached out to her and brought her closer for a kiss. As he kissed her, though, he looked at her cousin Jeanine who was watching them with some interest, and gave her a wink. She smiled and winked back at him.

They had dinner and, afterwards, the ladies cleared the table. Harold fixed drinks for all while they were cleaning the dishes. The drink of the night had been bourbon, and he saw no need to change it. While Harold was making the drinks, Bob went to his bedroom. Morgan followed him in there and, a couple of minutes later, Bob came out with a record. He put it on the record player, so that the silky music of Barry White's "Can't Get Enough of Your Love" soon filled the camp. Bob walked up to Brenda and said, "Come on, Brenda. Dance with me."

Brenda, a bit puzzled, said, "Thanks, but I'd rather dance with Morgan."

Bob responded, "I think Morgan is busy right now," and motioned with his head over his shoulder. When Brenda looked, she saw Morgan whispering to Janine, who got up and began dancing with Morgan. Brenda's mouth fell open. She was confused about what was happening, and wanted to say something, but Bob took both her hands, lifted her from the chair and said, "Morgan said that you should dance with me tonight." She looked over to her friend Debbie, but she was dancing with Harold. Bob's insistence, coupled with whiskey and the nearly irresistible music of Barry White, was too much for Brenda's resistance, so she rose, drained the rest of her bourbon with one gulp, and began to dance with Bob.

The first things Brenda noticed when she woke up the following morning were the sound of snoring coming from the other side of the bed and the nasty taste of stale alcohol and cigarette smoke in her mouth. The next thing she noticed was that she was naked, and that the man who was snoring wasn't Morgan, but Bob. She started as she came to that realization. *Oh my God!* she thought to herself as jumbled memories of the drunken night shot through her mind like meteors on a dark night. The gorge rose in her throat.. She tried to get out of bed as quietly as possible, so as not to wake up Bob. After picking up her clothes, she went to the bathroom and put them on before sneaking back into the bedroom and out the door. She closed it quietly behind her. When she turned around, she saw that the porch door was slightly ajar. She walked to it and went out on the back porch, which over-looked the Gulf of Mexico. It was a bright, hot morning with a light south wind blowing ripples on the water's surface. She looked to the left side of the porch, and there was Morgan, drinking a cup of black coffee. He looked at her and smiled.

"Good morning, sunshine!" he said in a cheery voice. She stared back numbly in reply. "Come on, babe, what's the matter with you?" he asked, sounding concerned.

"You know what's the matter with me, Morgan!" she answered, her voice beginning to shake with anger.

"Oh, get off your high horse!" he said. "What's the matter with having a little fun in life?"

"Morgan, I thought I meant something to you! We've been together for almost two years! I mean, I know you're married, but I thought you might even love me a little," Brenda said. "Now, you're chasing my cousin and throwing me to your cheesy cousin!"

"Hold on, Brenda!" Morgan said sternly. "Nothing's changed between us. We just had a little fun last night. You're still my main squeeze!" He reached out to her and pulled her next in to him, then turned towards the Gulf and took a sip of his coffee with his arm around her waist.

"But," she said, "you slept with Janine! You've got to cut that out if you want to sleep with me."

"Sure, babe, sure, whatever you say," he replied, looking out over the blue water. "I tell you what, why don't we both take a bath and get out of Dodge? I'll give you a ride to your apartment. Bob and Harold can take your car and give the girls a ride back to wherever they need to get to, and then I'll go pick them up after they leave the car parked at Atlantis."

"That sounds OK," Brenda said, a bit uncertainly.

"All right, girl, then let's get to it!" Morgan slapped her lightly on the behind.

The trip back took them through a seemingly endless marsh, dotted here and there with small clusters of live oak trees that marked ancient Indian shell middens which had been built above the surrounding ground, and that, now, were the last dry land left. The endless marsh vistas gave way to neat farmsteads, and homes along Bayou Lafourche which had been settled by Acadians 200 years previously. Next came large fields of sugar cane growing in orderly rows, as had been the case since the advent of Europeans on the bayou. Here and there, they saw old sugar mills still actively processing the lucrative crop. The history of sugar cane in southeast Louisiana had been a history of boom and bust, but with the advent of government subsidies since World War 2, it had made a steady profit for those families fortunate enough to retain the land needed for farming it. Eventually, they came to Lac Des Allemands, initially a settlement of German farmers which had provided a steady supply of vegetables for the New Orleans market, and, after that, Paradis, with its acres of pastures for cattle. They also passed a goodly number of oil rigs drilling deep into the south Louisiana earth for both oil and natural gas. Brenda wondered why some of the oil and gas facilities seemed to be well maintained and clean, whereas others were dirty and seemed held together by rust.

A bit further on, they came to the Huey P. Long Bridge. This engineering marvel from the 1930s had two-way train tracks in the center of the bridge, and two-car lanes on either side of the tracks. It was famous for its narrow lanes with no shoulders—a nightmare for drivers who were afraid of heights, too, as the bridge climbed high over the

Mississippi River to allow for passage of the huge, ocean-going boats that plied the river. Brenda clutched the edges of her seat in her tightly fisted hands as Morgan sped over the bridge. She thought of the story of her grandmother, who had never learned how to drive, but who'd had to drive a car both ways across the bridge when her friend had frozen in fear partway up the structure. She smiled at the memory.

After crossing the bridge, it was a short, 10-minute ride to the Atlantis Apartments. Morgan, who'd been uncharacteristically quiet during the trip, leaned over and gave her a short, hard kiss on her mouth. "OK, babe, I'll see you in the office on Monday."

"OK, Morgan," she replied. She got out of the car and turned to wave, but by the time she'd turned around, Morgan had sped off.

"Bye…" she said quietly.

14

A CLEARER PATH

April 16, 1972

After dropping Brenda off at her apartment, Morgan backtracked his way to Bonnabel Blvd. and got on the interstate. He kept on I-10 towards New Orleans and eventually got off at the St. Charles Street exit. He drove down the street lined with old, beautiful oak trees until he passed Louisiana Avenue, and then pulled over and parked almost in front of his house. The house was a grand, 3-story, white-painted, Queen Ann Victorian mansion. It was set on almost a quarter acre of beautifully landscaped grounds, and had an enormous front porch with arsenic green-painted wicker furniture tastefully placed around the area.

He walked up the large steps and through the front door carrying a bag of fillets from his fishing trip. His daughter Florence was in the living room lying on the couch, watching a rerun of *Dark Shadows*.

"Hi, Daddy," she said in a distracted voice.

"Hi, Flo. Where's Mom and Danny?" he asked.

"Mom's in the kitchen and Danny went over to Preston's," she replied, not taking her eyes off of the TV.

Morgan walked into the newly renovated kitchen. His wife Sylva was mixing a marinade for the fajitas she was preparing for supper. He placed the bag of fillets on the counter, walked up to his wife, and gave her a kiss.

"Wow! Fajitas! My favorite!" he said approvingly.

"How was your fishing trip?" she asked.

"It was OK. Not great. But we caught enough to have supper!" He raised the bag of fillets.

The flesh-colored phone hanging on the kitchen wall next to the cabinet gave a shrill ring. Sylva walked to it and answered.

"Hello...? Yes... yes, just a moment, please." She turned towards Morgan and covered the mouthpiece with her palm. "Morgan, you just got home. You need to stay here with your family tonight!" she whispered fiercely.

Morgan shook his head with a wry smile on his face, took the phone, and turned his back towards Sylva. "Yes, this is Morgan."

"Mr. Sanborne, this is Robert Cochran."

"Go ahead."

"I need to see you as soon as possible. I think I've found a lever to help force the sale of that property we were speaking of."

"Oh, really? That would be very helpful."

"Yes, sir, but I'll need your help. It's too complicated to go through over the phone. Can you meet me at the Top of the Mart in thirty minutes?"

"Absolutely, I'll see you then." Morgan hung up the phone.

"Morgan, I told you—"

"Shut up, Sylva! This is business! Do you enjoy living in your garden district home? Do you enjoy going to teas with your friends? And having the kids go to private schools? I tell you, this is business... and I damn well will leave in order to support my family in the style which they have become accustomed to! Do you understand?!" Morgan glared at Sylva.

For a moment, she glared back at him, and he thought that she was going to engage, but then she looked down and away. "Go ahead, Morgan," she said with a sigh.

"Not until you apologize," he replied. "I don't give a good goddamn if you ever get a new dress or a new pair of shoes. I'm sick and tired of you questioning me... ME! I break my ass for you and the kids, and this is the thanks I get?!"

Sylva looked down at the floor, wiped her brow with her hand, and looked up at Morgan and said, "I'm sorry, Morgan."

Morgan's demeanor changed instantly. He got a broad grin on his face and said, "That's more like it. Now, I'll be back as soon as I can. I shouldn't be late. Bye!" And he kissed her cheek as he walked past her and towards the front door.

When he walked into the bar, he saw that it was relatively empty. He waved to a couple of acquaintances as he walked up to his usual table and sat down. The waiter walked up to him and asked, "The usual, Mr. Sanborne?"

"Yes, Henry, that would be fine," he replied.

Robert Cochran arrived the same time as the B&B. The waiter stood for a moment to see if the new arrival would have a drink, but Morgan waved him away. After he'd left, Morgan turned to the private investigator and asked, "So... Robert... you may have found a lever? Well, tell me about it."

Robert replied, "It's like this, Mr. Sanborne. I have an acquaintance that works for NOPD. He knows I'm a PI, but the fellow isn't the sharpest shovel in the shed, so after a couple of beers, he tends to talk a lot. Well, I saw him at the local bar where most of the 8th district cops go for a beer after their shifts. I drank a couple of beers with him and he opened up and started talking about a friend of his. It seems that this cop and his friend's wife have run off together, and the husband, or ex-husband, has taken to hanging out in the French Quarter. Now, guess where he's been hanging out?"

"Quit playing games, Cochran! Just give me the information!"

"Yes, sir. Well, this guy has been hanging out at Astro's bar and the property that's next to it. It seems that the cop was worried that his pal would commit suicide, and had gotten an undercover to look for him. After they found him, they followed him, and found out that he was hanging out with some hippies. They even got pictures of the guy smoking weed! Anyway, now they're going to start up an undercover investigation of drug activity there...."

Morgan picked up the story with ease. "And after they bust those druggies, I can get my fellow councilmen to support an effort to have the city condemn the property! Good work, Cochran! That's exactly what we needed!"

"Thank you, sir. Is there anything else I can do for you?"

"Just keep your ears close to the railroad track, Cochran. Let me know if anything changes, and keep me posted if the cops take action on those hippies. There are some things I need to do in the meantime."

"All right, Mr. Sanborne. Er... about my fee—"

"Shut up, Cochran! You'll get your fee when you're done with the job! Now, get out of here and let me think!" Morgan snapped.

"Yes, sir, Mr. Sanborne." Cochran stood and walked briskly out of the bar.

Morgan picked up his B&B and slowly sloshed his drink around and around as he looked into the colored liquor. Then, he took a long, slow sip of the drink and called the waiter over. When the waiter arrived, he said, "Bring me a telephone, please."

"Certainly, sir!" The waiter disappeared and returned shortly with a light blue Princess phone at the end of a long cord. He placed it on the table, nodded to Morgan, and left. Morgan reached into his back pocket and pulled out his wallet. From behind his driver's license, he removed a white slip of paper and placed it down on the table next to the phone. Then, he punched the "0" and spoke into the mouthpiece.

"Operator, I'd like to place a long distance, collect call to Bombay, India. Yes, the number is 33-456-33-12. My name is Morgan Sanborne.... Thank you."

He heard the operator enter the number, and then a woman answered, "Mara Industries." This was followed by the operator informing the person that a long distance, collect call was being placed, which caused a short delay on the other end.

Eventually, the person accepted the charges and the operator said, "Go ahead, sir," and got off the line.

"Hello," Morgan began, "this is Morgan Sanborne in New Orleans. I would like to speak with Mr. Mara, please."

"I am sorry, sir, but Mr. Mara is not taking phone calls at the moment," the woman replied, speaking English with a British-tinted Indian accent.

"I have some good news that Mr. Mara may wish to hear," Morgan continued in his most persuasive tone of voice. "It's about a business deal that he wishes to make in New Orleans, Louisiana, USA."

"I understand, sir," the woman replied. "I will give Mr. Mara the message. Would you please give me your telephone number in case Mr. Mara wishes to ring you?"

"I will only be here for the next 45 minutes. The number is 504-566-7889. Please inform him that, if he calls this number, he should ask to speak to Mr. Morgan Sanborne."

"Yes, sir, I will. Goodbye."

Morgan hung up the phone and picked up his drink, downed it, and then waved the empty glass at the waiter, signaling the need for another. The waiter returned with a fresh B&B in short order, and Morgan settled in to sipping his drink as he looked out over the New Orleans vista.

He was startled when the phone rang. It had been less than ten minutes. He put his drink down and picked up the phone headset. "Hello," he said.

A voice spoke in a slow, dry whisper. "Hello, Mr. Sanborne. I hear that you have some good news for me."

Morgan suddenly felt as if he were sweating. "Yes, sir, Mr. Mara. I believe that I have found the avenue by which to buy that property we've been having trouble acquiring."

"You *believe*, Mr. Sanborne?"

Morgan could taste dust in his mouth, and had to swallow before answering. "Ye... yes, sir. It shouldn't be very long now. I expect to have the property in hand within the month."

"Are you wasting my time, Mr. Sanborne?"

The whisper on the other end of the phone sounded eerily like the sound of a snake sliding on sandpaper. Morgan felt a sharp pain in his chest, and he raised his free hand to clutch his shirt. *Shit! I'm having a heart attack!* Then, just as soon as the pain had started, it was gone.

"No, Mr. Mara," he strangled out, "I would never waste your time. I thought you would like to know of the progress that I've been making."

"Very good, Mr. Sanborne. I hope for your sake that you are correct. You should know that I reward excellent work well. As for poor work....." the ancient voice let the sentence hang.

"Yes, sir, Mr. Mara." Morgan straightened up in his chair and continued, "You have been very generous in the terms of our deal, and I will do my best to—" he stopped, having heard a *click* followed by a dial tone. He'd been hung up on.

He pulled the phone handset away from his ear and looked at it with an unbelieving look. He mumbled, "Why...that old bastard!" Then, he looked at his watch, downed the rest of his drink in one gulp, and called to the waiter, "Put it on my tab, Henry!" He rose from the table and walked briskly to the elevators.

15
REALITY'S PRISM

April 8, 1972

George awoke the next morning with his stomach growling. He had to think for just a moment to figure out where he was, but the spare brick walls reminded him almost instantly. A dappled, early morning light came through the window on the wall opposite the door. The glass was clouded with at least a century of accumulated grime. He could see the wavy nature of the glass and remembered reading somewhere that glass was not a solid, but something between a solid and a liquid. Given enough time, a flat pane of glass would develop those wavy patterns. Now, in the dappled light, the wavy patterns of the windowpanes seemed to move like small waves on a pond.

Enough lying around, he thought to himself, and threw off the covers. He took a quick bath and dressed. Then, he went out the door, down the stairs, and through the door into the courtyard.

The sound of a mockingbird singing its long sequence of songs filled the air of the shady courtyard, announcing to one and all that morning had indeed arrived. He stood still and listened. It seemed that he could make out some of the calls. For instance, there was the call of a cardinal, and, after that, the call of a blue jay, and then he swore that the mockingbird was making the sound of a streetcar bell. The thought made him laugh out loud.

It seemed that all of the inhabitants of the building were either gone or asleep, so George decided to take a walk in the Quarter and find something to eat. Walking in the French Quarter early in the morning always made him feel connected with the history of New Orleans. The local businessmen and some residents were already at work with hoses and brooms, cleaning the sidewalks in front of their respective establishments and houses just as they had done for generations. He turned on Bourbon Street. This far down Bourbon, there were no bars or strip joints—just homes. He took a minute to appreciate the architecture of the various houses. The large, shuttered windows covered with what the locals called arsenic green paint, sidings colored with different pastel shades of yellow, blue, and red, and the slightly purple Welsh slate roofs. He went on until he reached Ursulines Street. When he reached Ursulines, he thought again of the story that Caz had told them last night, and could almost feel the presence of the casket girls on this street they'd once frequented. He took a right down Ursulines towards the river. He had to watch his step since the sidewalk was uneven, and in some places consisted of old ballast stones. When he reached the 500th block of Ursulines Street, he saw the sign that he had been looking for. *Angelo Brocato – Ice Cream and Pastries*. He quickened his pace and walked into one of New Orleans' locals' favorite establishments.

At the counter, he told the young man working that he wanted two cannoli and a cup of black coffee. In no time at all, he was sitting down at a wrought iron table with a tablecloth, eating his cannoli and drinking his coffee. He people-watched as he ate. There was a short, dark-skinned woman with an overweight son dressed in the khaki outfit of a Catholic schoolboy having some pastry at the table closest to the door, as well as an attractive couple having an early morning (or late, late night) slice of Brocatto's famous Spumoni ice cream—served in a saucer with a paper doily underneath—and a local priest reading the newspaper and having a cup of coffee. When the woman and her son had finished, they walked up to the priest and engaged him in a brief conversation, and then left the establishment. George finished his cannoli and coffee, and walked out of the door into the bright morning.

On a whim, he walked back to his car, climbed in, and began to drive. He drove, lost in thought, for a while and found himself in front of Delgado College, at the edge of City Park, then drove down Marconi Drive to Popp's Fountain—a large, abandoned fountain on the edge of the park that had been a favorite parking place for teenagers in his youth. He parked and got out of the Mustang, and walked down a sidewalk that wound its way through tall grass and scrub brush until he came upon the fountain. It had been built in the 1930s, as had many of the structures in City Park, by the Works Progress Administration, which had undertaken many monumental physical and cultural improvements in the country.

The structure was in the Greek Revival style, with a central basin surrounded by a broad, circular walkway that was edged by concrete, Doric-style columns. The columns at the entrance were semi-square, the edges planed in a fashion that created an octagonal shape, with molded, concrete caps. The central basin was empty, though there was a largish puddle that had yet to evaporate after the last rainstorm. Vines had overgrown the columns and intruded on the circular walkway and basin. There were cracks in the concrete where the vines had grown and expanded like living hands pushing aside the inanimate concrete. The worst culprits were clumps of Trumpet Vine and Virginia Creeper, with stems thicker than George's forearms that seemed to strive to pull down the columns and reclaim this place for nature. As usual, there was no one around, so George walked over to a bench in the warm sunlight and sat down. He watched as the honeybees flew from orange flower to orange flower on the Trumpet Vines, getting their fill of the sweet nectar within. Popp's Fountain had always been one of his favorite places to sit quietly and process the different things in his life. Sitting here in the sunlight, his troubles seemed less important. He thought about Gloria and Sonny. It was funny, but he felt as if he was studying them from a distance, as if his life of the last twenty years had been a dream and he had woken to reality.

He sat on the sunlit bench and thought. Shortly, he began to grow drowsy. The shadows seemed to move, first left and then right. His head felt heavy, and his eyes began to close. He began to imagine the fountain as it had looked when new, in the 1930s, when it had been a proud expression of New Orleans' struggle to beat the Great Depression. He could imagine the fountain jetting a column of water, with the cool mist delighting the young children who accompanied their parents there. His eyes slowly closed, and he began to dream....

Mardi Gras Day! Six-year-old Bobby Sommes had been looking forward to this day since Christmas. He leapt out of bed, glancing at the sunrise as it peeked over the rooftops and into his second-floor window. His big brother John, still mostly asleep in his bed in the corner of the room, rolled over and grunted at Bobby's excitement.

"Wake up, John! It's Mardi Gras Day!"

John gave another grunt and pulled the covers up over his head, even as Bobby jumped on his bed and began shaking him. Finally, he threw the covers off and grabbed Bobby in a hug.

"You miserable cretin! Let me sleep!" 'Cretin' was a word John had learned recently, being a precocious 9-year-old.

"But, John, it's Mardi Gras Day! We need to get dressed up in time to go see the parades!"

John thought about it for about two seconds, and then roughed up Bobby's hair and said, "You're right. Let's move."

He got out of bed and stretched. Then, he and Bobby made up their beds and went downstairs. The smell of bacon cooking on the stove reached their nostrils as they went down the stairs. When they reached the bottom, they saw that Aunt Sue and Uncle Ed, along with their young children, were already up and sitting on the couch in the living room. Their older cousin, Jake, a mature lad of 16, was also up along with his parents, Aunt C and Uncle Pete. The boys' father, Gaston Sommes, was one of the fortunate men in the city who still had a good job, as a steelworker. He sat in the living room talking to his relatives. The Depression had hit hard in New Orleans and the surrounding area. Gaston and his wife Maxine had been helping many family members over the course of the depression by providing a place to stay while they tried to get on their feet. Maxine was in the kitchen now—cooking a breakfast of eggs, bacon, grits, and biscuits. As was her wont, she refused anyone's help, saying that her kitchen was a "one-fanny kitchen."

The Sommes lived on Pauline Street, a few blocks from the river. The Mississippi River had been the focal point of New Orleans for over 200 years, and Bobby and John (and their neighborhood friends) spent a great deal of time along its banks, on the river batture and under the docks. But today was not the time for playing along the river. Mardi Gras was a holiday for both school and work in New Orleans. It was a day of merriment and costumes. The boys were going to dress up as clowns, this being the most common costume for Mardi Gras revelers. The parades had begun in the mid-19th century, and had gotten larger, and grander, with time. For the last several years, the float riders had begun throwing trinkets and beads to the assembled masses in a symbolic potlatch. The glass beads were considered treasures by New Orleans' young people. The most prized of the beads were known as "rice" beads, as they looked like drilled grains of rice strung on a silk thread and were wrapped in paper.

"Well, well, you've finally woken up," Gaston announced in a loud voice as the boys came into the room. Bobby ran up to him and jumped in his lap. Gaston gave him a hug with one of his arms and reached up and pulled John into a hug with the other. A chorus of "Good Mornings!" followed.

John then asked, "Daddy, can Bobby and I go to Canal Street early to watch the parades?"

"What? You don't want to wait for the rest of your family?" Gaston asked with a smile.

"It's not that, Daddy. We just don't want to miss anything."

Gaston and the other adults broke out into laughter. "If it's so important to you, then I guess it will be all right. But I expect you boys to meet us at 12 o'clock sharp on the corner of Carondelet and Canal."

"Yay! Yay!" Bobby jumped off of Gaston's lap and grabbed his brother's hands as they jumped up and down, shouting their happiness.

"Now, boys, I mean it. 12 o'clock sharp at the corner of Carondelet and Canal."

"Yes, sir!" the boys answered in unison.

"Bobby, John, come and help me set the table. Breakfast is ready!" Maxine called from the kitchen.

"Yes, ma'am!" The boys ran into the kitchen and began to bring out plates and silverware to put on the black-and-white, enameled dining table. Once they were done, they helped Maxine carry out the breakfast. Then, everyone gathered close together around the table, sitting on chairs and stools while Maxine said 'grace' before eating their breakfast.

When breakfast was done, Bobby was so excited that he couldn't keep still. He ran up into his room and got out the clown costume his mother had recently sewed for him and put it on over his pants. It was a one-piece, white coverall that ballooned out in the middle thanks to some cotton padding that his mother had sewn into the suit. The costume tied in the back and behind his neck, and was covered with large red, blue, and green colored circles. John's costume, identical to his, was lying over the chair in the far corner of the room. After putting on his costume, he put on his shoes and ran downstairs. When John saw his little brother dressed in his costume, he quickly finished his sentence and ran up to put his own costume on. In the meantime, Maxine walked back into her bedroom and came out with a tube of lipstick. She called Bobby over to her and had him sit still as she took the cover off the tube and turned the bottom to bring the bright red lipstick further out of the case. Then, she took her forefinger, dabbed it on the lipstick, and carefully placed a round, red circle on each of Bobby's cheeks. When she was finished, she put a dot of the bright red on the tip of Bobby's nose. By this time, John was standing behind Bobby and waiting for his mother to finish his costume, as well. Bobby ran into the bathroom and climbed on the small stool that was kept there to see himself in the mirror over the sink. When he saw himself costumed and painted, he laughed out loud. "That's the berries!" he said, looking at his image.

After Maxine had finished with John's costume, the boys hastily said goodbye and went out the front door onto the porch stoop. The houses on the block all looked similar, with small, open porch areas that stepped down to the sidewalk. They walked down to the corner of Burgundy and turned right, down Burgundy Street toward the French Quarter. As they walked, they saw other children as well as grown-ups, all dressed in various costumes. Many were dressed as clowns, but they also saw a young man with a black fright wig, a spear, and a kind of dress made of corn shucks. Curious, the boys asked him what his costume was. "I'm the wild man of Borneo!" the young man told them, shaking his spear. The boys giggled and continued walking. It was about 9 o'clock in the morning when they crossed Esplanade Avenue and entered the French Quarter. There were more people in the Quarter, many of them in costume. The boys were amazed to see a man in a wig and a dress walking nonchalantly down the street, accompanied by another man dressed as a 'swell' with cape, top hat, and cane. The boys' heads were on a swivel as they looked all around to see the different costumes worn by people walking through the French Quarter. They continued walking down Burgundy, heading towards Canal Street, where they wanted to be to see the parades.

When they reached Dumaine Street, Bobby looked to the left and saw a large black man dressed in a flowing, white Toga. He had a gleaming, golden crown on his head. The man appeared to Bobby to glow in the bright sunlight. He looked at Bobby with a large, brilliant smile, and waved. Bobby waved back, and then turned towards John and said, "I love Mardi Gras, don't you?"

"Sure! Other than Christmas, it's the best day of the year!" John replied.

They walked down the street looking at the people and at the old houses and brick buildings with decorative, wrought iron around the balconies. The closer they got to Canal Street, the larger the buildings became. Old, wooden houses, some of the kind that the adults called 'camelback,' gave way to two- and three-story brick buildings. The boys felt like they were in a canyon as they made their way the last several blocks. Then, they reached the corner of Canal Street and the world opened up to them. The spacious boulevard was already crowded with people, many in costume waiting for the parades. Families were everywhere, most with bags or picnic baskets of food to fortify themselves for the long day of celebration. Large, plate-glass store windows along Canal Street were decorated with bunting and Mardi Gras tableaus. Many of the decorations were in purple, green, and gold, the official colors of Mardi Gras.

The boys looked at the crowded spectacle around them and, unconsciously, Bobby's hand reached for his big brother's, who took the hand in his. The boys could see that there was something happening at the corner of Canal and Rampart. There was a stage that was set up on Rampart Street, near the intersection with Canal. A large crowd was gathered there, and the boys could hear a smattering of applause—and not a few catcalls. They walked up the street towards the stage and worked their way up into the crowd. When they got close to the stage, they could see a young woman doing a Betty Boop impression. She was attractive and did a pretty good job, and the audience liked her act and applauded her when she'd finished. Bobby tugged at the shirt sleeve of the man who was standing next to him and asked, "Hey, Mister. What's this all about?"

The man looked down at Bobby and said, "This is an amateur talent show. Some of the people are pretty good. Some of them are just awful."

"What's a talent show?" Bobby asked.

"It's where people get up and sing or dance or tell jokes in front of an audience. The winner is going to get that big turkey you see on the stool at the side of the stage there." Here, the man pointed to the largest dressed turkey that Bobby had ever seen. The drumsticks looked as big as Bobby's own legs. "Now, hush up, son, I want to hear this fellow sing."

There was an older man on the stage who was dressed as an Indian and trying to imitate Cab Calloway, singing "Minnie the Moocher." While he was slow-footing across the stage and "Hidey Ho-ing," John leaned down and spoke in Bobby's ear. "He's terrible. He doesn't sound anything like the radio!"

The audience agreed with John, and the catcalls and booing began—sparsely at first, then with gusto. The so-called Indian responded by waving a clenched fist and yelling at the crowd. The crowd loved this, and a brief but intense contest of loud abuse ensued, though it was easily won by the audience. The man slunk off of the stage, down the stairs, and out into the crowd walking down Canal Street. Bobby kept looking at the gigantic turkey, thinking about how his mother and father would be amazed if he brought the bird home. He looked up at his brother, who was busy watching the next act, and then left John and began to push his way towards the stairs at the end of the stage. He heard John call his name, but he was determined to win that turkey and be a hero. He continued pushing his way through the crowd and, looking back, could see John making his way after him, which made him redouble his efforts. He made his way to the stairs and had just started to climb up when a man with a large nose and dark, black hair grabbed him by the shoulder. "Whoa, there, little fellow. What do you think you're doing?" he asked, not unkindly.

"Please, mister, I want to win that turkey!" Bobby responded.

The man laughed out loud. "Well, well... you want to win that turkey." He looked at the people who were near the stairs and gave a broad wink. Some in the audience began to laugh, and there were smiles all around. "What exactly do you plan to do to win that turkey?"

Bobby thought about it for a second, and replied, "I'm going to sing."

This brought more laughter from the people closest to the stairs. Some more people were looking at what was going on near the stage, too, because the previous act had finished up. It had been a comedy skit imitating the 3 Stooges—always a crowd-pleaser—and had garnered a good bit of laughter and applause.

John reached the stairs by the stage and reached up to grab Bobby by the arm. "C'mon, Bobby. Let's get out of here," he said loudly.

The man with the long nose said, "Hold on, son. The little boy wants to sing, and I'm going to give him his chance to be a star. Now, what's your name, little boy?"

Bobby looked up at the man. "B-B-Bobby".

The man laughed again. "OK, B-B-Bobby. I'm going to go on stage and introduce you, and then you walk on and do your stuff." With that, the man walked onto the stage and announced, "Ladies and gentlemen. Our next contestant is a young man named B-B-Bobby, and he's going to sing for you!"

The audience responded with hoots of laughter as the man walked back to where Bobby stood at the top of the stairs.

"Go ahead, kid. Show 'em what you've got!" He pushed Bobby gently towards the center of the stage.

Bobby slowly walked to the center of the stage, looking at the large crowd. He could see individual faces—men and women, boys and girls, most of them with smiles on their faces and many of them laughing, some paying no attention to him. He reached the center of the stage and faced the audience. They were waiting expectantly. Bobby suddenly realized that he had no idea what he was going to sing. He stood there, working his mouth open and closed like a fish. Someone in the audience yelled, "What's the matter, boy? Cat got your tongue?" The audience laughed, and Bobby's cheeks began to burn and turn red with embarrassment. Tears began to well up in his eyes. Then, he remembered a song that his grandmother had taught him the year before. It was an old chestnut that she had learned from her mother. A tearjerker called "She's Only a Bird in a Gilded Cage." Bobby closed his eyes and began to sing in a high, piping voice....

"The ballroom was filled with fashion's throng,
It gleamed with a thousand lights.
And there was a lady who passed along,
The fairest of all the sights.
A girl to her lover then softly sighed,
'She has riches at her command.'
'But she married for wealth, not for love,'
He cried!
'Though she lives in a mansion grand.'
She's only a bird in a gilded cage,
A beautiful sight to see.
You may think she's happy and free from care,
She's not what she seems to be.
'Tis sad when you think of a wasted life
For youth cannot play with age,
And she sold her beauty for an old man's gold,
She's a bird in a gilded cage...."

Bobby had had his eyes tightly shut, but now he peered out into the audience. The audience had grown as quiet as a mouse. The song Bobby had chosen looked to have reminded many of them of grandmothers and grandfathers, and mothers and fathers, who had passed on. Popular in the gay '90s, the song was one that most of the audience had grown up listening to loved ones sing, and several of the audience had gotten to singing along with Bobby. He closed his eyes and continued, his piping voice growing stronger with confidence....

"I stood in the churchyard just at eve,
As sunset adorned the west,
And saw the people who'd come to grieve
For loved ones lain at rest.
A tall marble monument marked the grave
Of one who'd been fashion's queen;
And I thought, 'She's better there at rest,
Then to have people say when seen.'
She's only a bird in a gilded cage,
A beautiful sight to see.
You may think she's happy and free from care,
She's not what she seems to be.
'Tis sad when you think of a wasted life
For youth cannot play with age,
And she sold her beauty for an old man's gold,
She's a bird in a gilded cage."

When Bobby finished the song, he opened his eyes and looked out at the audience. It was dead silent for several seconds, and Bobby's knees turned to water. Then, a roar of approval washed over the crowd like a tsunami. People were yelling, clapping, and whistling. Bobby saw some of them dabbing at their eyes with a handkerchief. He felt so relieved that he burst into an impromptu jig, bringing even more happy noise from the audience.

Mr. Big Nose walked onto the stage clapping his hands and beaming a broad smile. He walked up to Bobby and put his hand on his shoulder. Then, he said loudly, "What do you think, folks? Do we have a winner?"

The crowd went wild. It was evident that they thought Bobby had won the talent show. Bobby was so elated, and scared, that he felt like he needed to go to the bathroom. Mr. Big Nose waved his hands in a downward motion towards the crowd. "Ladies and gentlemen, I present the grand prize, an 18-pound turkey, to the winner.... B-B-Bobby!"

The crowd went wild again. A teenage boy walked up onto the stage with some brown paper wrapping and carefully wrapped the turkey, taping it well. Then, he took the wrapped turkey and set it into Bobby's outstretched arms. Bobby could hardly hold the turkey, it weighed so much. He bowed to the crowd as best he could and walked to the stairs at the side of the stage where John was waiting. John took the turkey from his arms so that he could walk down the stairs. The boys then walked back through the slowly dispersing crowd as people roughed their hair and patted them on the back.

John said to Bobby, "That was something, Bobby! I can't believe that you did it!"

"Yeah, I know," Bobby replied. He was feeling kind of tired after the adrenaline rush of his performance. "Whadda'ya think, John? Should we go home now?"

"Yeah, we've got to, " John replied, "there's no way we can walk around carrying this big turkey around. So, the boys retraced their steps down Canal to Burgundy and began the long walk back to Pauline Street. They took turns carrying the bird, with John carrying it most of the time and resting every few blocks. It took them the better part of an hour to walk back to their house. When they climbed the stairs to the porch, John said, "Bobby, I want you to carry this turkey inside. You're the one who won it. I'll hold the door open for you." He then opened the door and hollered, "Everybody! Come see!"

Bobby walked into the living room. The entire family was there, just about to leave to celebrate Mardi Gras, when Bobby entered with the gigantic turkey. "What in the world?!" Maxine asked.

"Holy smokes!" Jake exclaimed. Then, the family crowded around the boys while Maxine took the turkey and put it into the ice box. The boys relived their morning's adventure, relishing in the telling.

Bobby sat on Gaston's lap and beamed as his father kept saying over and over again, "You little rascal. You won a turkey! I can't believe it!" After the tale had been told and the questions had been answered, the family gathered up and went out to celebrate the greatest Mardi Gras ever....

George woke with a start. He was confused by his surroundings for an instant, so real had the dream been. The sun had moved in the sky and the fountain was cast in the shadows of late afternoon. He sat up and gripped the bench on either side of him. The fog of confusion slowly lifted as he looked around Popp's Fountain. The slowly crumbling concrete looked dark in the shadows, and the large, twisting vines with their foliage moved slowly in the light breeze. The dream had been so real.

I wonder if this is what Jim told me about? he thought to himself. *It's almost like I was there watching it happen. I've got to tell him about this.*

He got up and, with one last glance around, made his way back to the Mustang. He reached into his pocket for the keys, felt something unusual, and pulled it out. It was something wrapped in a thin, tissue like paper. He unwrapped it and was astounded to see a delicate necklace with a gold colored, metal clasp. The necklace appeared to be made of white rice grains, drilled lengthwise, and threaded on a silk string.

Was the dream real? He steadied himself on the car door. *I need to see JC.* He wrapped the trinket back in the paper and placed it in his pocket. When he reached St. Ann Street, miracle of miracles, the same parking spot that had been there for him previously was available. He parallel-parked the Mustang with a smile at his good fortune, even as a thought passed through his mind that it might not be luck that made this particular spot available every time he came here. He got out of his car and walked around the corner to the alleyway. The door to Astro's was open, and he walked in to say hello to JC, who was polishing a glass behind the bar.

"Greetings, George. How's it going?"

"It's going as well as could be expected, JC. You know, I had something weird happen to me a little while ago."

"Really? What was that?"

George continued, "I went over to Popp's Fountain to sit and think for a while. While I was there, I fell asleep. Or, at least, I think I fell asleep. I had the most vivid dream about a young boy in New Orleans on Mardi Gras day during the Depression. It was so vivid... so real. When I woke up, I felt out of place, like I was adjusting to a different time. It was weird, but in a nice way."

"Anyway, I went to leave and found this in my pocket." He pulled out the tissue and unwrapped the dainty necklace.

"Ah," JC responded with his brilliant smile, "you are beginning to see the magic of this place, George, the connection between past and present that lies in this hot, humid speck of swampy ground. You know that, of the four known dimensions, time is the only one that is not physical in nature."

"Huh?" George questioned.

JC responded, "Well... the nature of time is to string together a stream of 'nows' so that we experience a coherent, directional path through this existence. Time is the thread that sews our experiences together. There are some places where the nature of time is more readily visible than others, and, in these places, some people are able to experience the glimmers of other 'nows' as either visions or dreams. New Orleans is one of those places, and this is what you've experienced."

George wasn't surprised to hear JC talk this way. His conversations with Jim had touched upon this subject and, after his recent experiences, he was not so quick to reject a world view that he would have laughed at a few days earlier.

"I think I understand what you mean, JC," George said. "It was so real. I thought it was a realistic dream, but after I found the necklace I was confused. I wonder if there's any way to tell if it really happened or if it was just a dream. "

"Think about it, George!" JC smiled. "History, the things that are written down and remembered, deal with great people and great times. But the overwhelmingly vast majority of human life and experience happens to regular people during uneventful times. No historian writes of these peoples' experiences—their trials, successes, joys, disasters, and sadness. I think that you may never know for sure whether it was a dream or a view into another 'now,' but if you think about it, it doesn't really matter. What matters is the glimpse into another's experience, the sharing of life's wonder, whether in this 'now' or others."

"Yeah, I guess you're right. I sure could feel the young boy's emotions as I went through the dream. Joy, anxiety, pride, love, wonder... they were all there."

"I'll give you another clue, George," JC continued. "Dreams are almost always disjointed. People and places morph into other people and other places. It's the rare dream that takes a linear, coherent path from start to finish. But, that being said, the experiences and emotions of a dream can give you valid insight into our shared connections. For instance, if you dream of being a rabbit that is hunted by a fox, the emotions that you feel in the dream may legitimately be the same as those that the rabbit would experience. It may not be able to tell you that it is experiencing fear, but it is, beyond the shadow of a doubt, fearful."

George looked at the necklace in his hand. Then he looked at JC as he stood behind the bar and began to understand the near reverence that everyone had for the black man. He asked, "How do you know so much, JC?"

"There are more things in heaven and earth, Horatio, than are dreamt of in your philosophy..." JC responded with a smile.

George grinned back at JC and held out his hand. JC grasped it in a soul-brother handshake and they both broke into laughter. George shook JC's hand and said, "I guess I'll go back and see if Jim's around. Have you seen him today?"

JC raised his eyebrows and said, "He left here not five minutes ago. You should find him in the courtyard."

"Thanks," George said with a smile as he wrapped the necklace in the tissue and put it back in his pocket. "See you later, JC!"

"Later, George," JC responded, and began to wipe down the bar.

George walked out of Astro's, took a left, and headed back to the courtyard entrance. He slowly opened the door and walked in. Jim was sitting in his chair under a large, smooth-barked crepe myrtle tree. George walked up to him and began to tell him about his so-called dream.

16
A LEVER AND A FULCRUM

April 17, 1972

The New Orleans City Council meeting room was off the main corridor of City Hall, just off the end of Tulane Avenue. The councilmen sat in comfortable leather swivel chairs around a raised, semi-circular dais that overlooked a large room full of empty chairs. The council was not yet in session, and the seven councilmen milled around behind the dais, chatting about matters both personal and governmental. The buzz of voices was punctuated here and there by chortles and guffaws as one councilman or another broke into back-slapping laughter.

Morgan Sanborne, as the city councilman for District A, spoke with his fellow councilmen. His impeccably tailored suit, purchased at Rubenstein's, made a subtle statement about the district he represented. District A was, by far, the richest district in New Orleans. It contained the wealthier part of Uptown and stretched all the way to Lake Pontchartrain and the western part of Lakeview. As such, District A supplied the lion's share of governmental revenue generated in the city. This gave Morgan a "first amongst equals" stature in the council—a privilege he used skillfully.

He held the arm of Bradley Rains, councilman for District D, as he spoke.

"Brad, I hope I have your support in my effort to get a grip around all these drug-crazed hippies in the Quarter. I believe my bill to force property owners to take some responsibility for what happens on their property will clean up the Quarter and make it the place it was when we were growing up. Have you seen the crime statistics lately?"

"Well, Morgan, I can't argue with the need to make the Quarter a better place for tourism, both local and out-of-towners, but I'm having a problem with the part that allows the city to seize property under eminent domain."

"Brad, that's only when it's been clearly proved that the property has been used for illegal drug activity. Surely, you don't believe that it's OK for these hippies to take over the Quarter so they can take God knows what?"

"Of course, I don't, Morgan. I'm as worried about the hippie problem as you. I've been pushing the chief of police to do something about it for the last five years. It's just—"

"Hold it right there, Brad," Morgan interrupted him. "If you really want to do something about the problem, then you have to get on board. I've spoken with the chief, and he thinks this is a great idea. I've met individually with each of the other councilmen, too, and have promises of support from each of them. We have an understanding that if one of us, or one of our family or friends, owns a property that falls within the purview of the bill, provisions will be made to ensure that the property is not seized. It's really aimed at the absentee landlords who don't give a shit about the city or care if it goes to pot. Literally!"

"I hear what you're saying, Morgan," Rains replied, "but I can't get past the seizure of private property in the case where a landlord has no idea what his tenants are up to. We both own rental properties. Can you swear that you know whether your tenants are up to illegal activities? I know I can't."

"Brad, I've already told you that we're covered. You will have say on whose property is seized. If there's anyone else you'd like to protect, you've got it. The same deal goes to every other councilman, as well as the mayor, the chief of police, and judges. I've been working hard on this for the last couple of months, and the time has come to either shit or get off of the pot. So, are you with us or against us, Brad?"

"Now, Morgan, don't go putting it like that. You know I'm not against you. I just can't, in good conscience, vote for a bill that takes people's property away even when they don't know what's happening. I hope you won't have any hard feelings."

Morgan looked at Rains with a cold, dispassionate look. He'd suspected that this councilman would be difficult to swing around, but he'd prepared for this eventuality. He stuck out his hand and said, "No hard feelings, Brad. Here's my hand on it."

Rains looked relieved as he took Morgan's hand and shook it warmly.

When they finished the handclasp, Morgan began to turn away, and then suddenly turned back. "Say, Brad. Speaking of hard feelings, how's that young man who you've been helping with his college tuition? His name is Tom, isn't it?"

Rains stood frozen as his face betrayed a sequence of revelations. First, stunned shock followed rapidly by embarrassment, and then anger, and finally fear. When he regained the ability to speak, he could only utter, "What?"

"You know what I mean, Brad. It's none of my business, but I'll bet that your wife and your constituents wouldn't understand how altruistic you're being, putting such a sweet young man through college."

Rains looked at Morgan with a mixture of fear, loathing, and understanding.

"I hope that I've got your support on the ordinance, Brad. No hard feelings, eh?" Morgan turned and walked towards his comfortable, leather seat.

Just then, the doors were opened to the public, and a few dedicated souls walked quietly into the room and found seats. As it was Morgan's turn to head the council meeting, he called the meeting into order.

Standard procedure was followed as the role was called, minutes from the last meeting were read, and some previous business was discussed and resolved. Then, Morgan called for new business.

The councilman from District B (covering the Warehouse District and parts of Uptown) raised his hand. When he was recognized, he said in a loud voice, "I'd like to propose an ordinance for the purpose of stopping the lawlessness that is increasingly happening in the Vieux Carre." Thus, Morgan's ordinance was introduced. Debate was brief and positive, as all council members agreed that things had gone too far in the French Quarter, and law and order was needed to stem the chaos which was on the rise. A vote was called, and Morgan watched as each city councilman raised his hand to vote *Aye*. When it became Brad Rains's turn to vote, Morgan gave him a cold smile. Rains stared at Morgan, and hesitated for just a second before he lowered his eyes and raised his hand.

Gotcha! Morgan thought victoriously. *Mr. Mara will be pleased.*

17
ALL THE COMFORTS OF HOME

April 28, 1972

G eorge quickly adapted to his new life. His routine began with rising early in the morning—he'd always been an early riser—and taking a walk around the Quarter. Some days, he went to Brocato's for canolli and coffee, and on others to Café Du Monde or Morning Call for beignets and coffee. Then, he would open the antique store, arriving well before Tony to get the shop ready for customers. He found the antique store stimulating, and was rapidly learning about the different periods and styles. He had an almost instinctive gift for being able to pair a customer with a specific style they'd gravitate towards, which made him an above-average salesman. Tony heaped praise upon his new employee, and spent most of his time between customers imparting his own knowledge to George, who soaked it up like a sponge.

After a couple of weeks, Tony said, "I think you are a natural at this, George. I've never met anyone who learned the business as fast as you."

George beamed at the compliment. "Thanks, Tony. I really do appreciate you giving me the chance to work, and learn. I'd be lying if I told you I didn't love it."

"That's exactly what it takes to excel in this business, George... a love of the history, craftsmanship, and styles that came before. Now, come with me into the back and I'll begin to teach you how to recognize forgeries from the real thing."

Tony and George closed up the shop at 5:30 every day. If a customer was in the shop, Tony would ask politely if they were interested in purchasing something or if they were just shopping. If the answer was the latter, Tony would request that they leave so he could close up and go home to supper. Once the shop was closed and made orderly for the next day, George would head back to his apartment. He inevitably found Jim waiting for him in the courtyard, and they'd venture out into the Quarter to find something to eat. His diet was varied, if not particularly healthy. Some days, they'd have a muffalotta from Central Grocery or Maspero's; other nights might find them picking up a Lucky Dog for dinner.

The evenings would always end with a visit to Astro's. George quickly grew to love JC's company. His recent experiences had shaken the foundations of his parochial system of beliefs, and JC, more than anyone else, provided the scaffolding on which his new appreciation of life and its realities grew. He found it profoundly interesting to discuss these things with JC and Jim. The night would always end with sitting on one of the courtyard benches, next to Jim's chair, while Jim pulled out his baggie and pipe. Some nights, Anna was there, and one night, Anna and the twins all smoked and visited until late into the night. George did notice that he never saw Mama Zulie out in the courtyard after night fell.

It had been almost a month since he'd first come to Astro's when, on a Friday night, George found a barbecue pit in an open area of the courtyard when he got home after closing up the shop. He went into his apartment to wash up, and by the time he came out, JC, Jim, Anna, and the twins were standing around the pit, which had a roaring flame over a large pyramid of charcoal briquettes. Jim, as usual, broke out his pipe and passed it around. George noticed that JC didn't join in the smoking, but had no apparent issue with it. The twins had brought a large ice chest full of Dixie beer and sausages.

They talked and laughed in the beautiful courtyard as dusk grew and the flames burned down to red, glowing embers of charcoal. The sausages went on the pit with a satisfying sizzle and soon the buns were broken out, to be smeared with creole mustard, and hot sausage sandwiches were enjoyed by all. George found himself a bit apart from the rest of the assembled crew as he finished his delicious sandwich. He watched their friendly faces and animated banter, and thought to himself, *I'm a lucky man to have these people as my friends.* Right as the thought passed through his mind, Anna called out to him, "George, JC tells me that you had a dream a few weeks ago. Why don't you tell us about it?" So, he stepped into the circle and told his friends about the uncannily real dream he'd had while sleeping at Popp's Fountain.

Caz commented, "George, you're beginning to open up. You are tuning in to New Orleans now." The others silently nodded their assent.

George felt pleased, and a feeling that he was experiencing some sort of unknown magic filled his chest. The party broke up soon afterwards as Anna and the twins left, and JC went back to Astro's. Jim and George were left alone in the courtyard.

"Well, amigo, I guess it's deaux deaux for me," Jim said sleepily. He held out his cupped hand.

George took it in a soul-brother handshake, which really was the most appropriate for Jim's disability, and said, "Thank you, Jim. Thanks for helping to make this a home for me."

Jim smiled up at George and said, "Think nothing of it, brother," and they both turned towards their respective apartments.

18

A CERTAIN GIRL

April 29, 1972

April Flowers began her new job with trepidation, but, in a very short time, she grew into it and was soon comfortable taking her photographs in many different social settings, from classrooms to Uptown soirees. On her days off, she enjoyed roaming through the streets of New Orleans and taking pictures of things that struck her fancy.

The cool, New Orleans Spring of 1972 began to warm as Summer neared. She went out on her daily assignments and dutifully took pictures of Ladies' Clubs, Cub Scouts, and Brownies, and even took some pictures of a group of "Pebble Pups"—a group of children whose parents belonged to the New Orleans Gem and Mineral Society, and who had built a replica of the World Trade Center on Canal Street; it was made entirely out of pieces of cut black and white marble. She enjoyed her work for the paper, but her favorite time was the weekends when she would walk around the city and photograph what she wished.

That bright, sunny Saturday morning, she was walking down Royal Street when she was suddenly taken by a reflection in the window of an antique gallery. The reflection picked up the wet sidewalk and street, as well as a large puddle which reflected silhouettes of the pastel-colored buildings across the street against a blue sky with puffy, white clouds.

She raised her camera, set the F stop and shutter speed to her desired settings, framed the picture, and pressed the shutter. At that instant, a man walked into the picture, fracturing the moment. April gave an exasperated gasp of disappointment which the man heard. He turned towards her and asked, "Excuse me, did I ruin your shot?"

April lowered her camera with one hand, and waved with the other and said, "It's OK," not really feeling it as that had been the last shot on the roll.

The man took several steps towards her and said, "No, really, I'm sorry to have messed up your shot. I was just going to open up, and wasn't paying proper attention." He held out his hand. "I'm George. George Santos."

April felt a bit trapped, but shook his hand and said, "April Flowers."

"Pleased to meet you, April. Won't you come into the shop and let me fix you a cup of coffee? It'll only take a minute."

April looked away for a moment and then replied, "No thanks, George. I really do have to get going." One hand was still on the camera.

George gave an easy laugh and said, "All right, April. It's been nice meeting you. I really am sorry to have stepped into your photograph. If you find yourself around here, do come on in and let me fix you a cup of coffee. I feel like I owe you one."

"Thanks again, George. I just might take you up on that." April smiled, and then gave a small wave and walked down Royal Street towards Esplanade, camera in hand.

George stood there for a moment and watched her as she left, but then turned and opened the door to the antique store. Before he stepped in, he turned the sign that hung on the door from "Closed" to "Open." In the store, he turned on the lights, walked behind the counter and unlocked the safe to get the cash for the register, and then busied himself with dusting the counters and antiques. As he dusted, he thought about the girl he had just met, and then his thoughts drifted to Anna. He and

Jim had spoken of her many times, and Jim had told him that Anna would come and go for various lengths of time. In his words: *"Anna is her own. She comes and goes. When she's here, things are nicer. It's like the cool shade of a cloud that holds back the pressing Summer sun."*

George had replied, *"Goddamn, Jim. I didn't know you were a poet!"*

And Jim had looked at him with an arched eyebrow, and said, *"I didn't know it, either."*

19

MATA HARI HEARS A STORY

April 29, 1972

Brenda had always treasured her free time on weekends. She woke up on this Saturday morning around 10 o'clock. She stretched languorously and began to contemplate her day. She also thought about what had happened in Grand Isle and felt depressed. *Gross!* she thought. *That goddamn Morgan. Why the fuck did I do that?!* She shut her eyes and shook her head, but finally got out of bed and ate breakfast. She then put on her bathing suit, a white bikini, and walked out of her apartment to the swimming pool. She left the pool around 12:30 and went back to her apartment.

While bathing, she began to think of what Morgan had asked her to do, and cheered up at the thought of playing detective. She finished and toweled herself dry. *This is going to be fun*, she thought as she pulled her faded peanut jeans out of her dresser and put them on. She found a brightly striped cotton shirt and put it on, as well. Like many young women, she wore no bra. She looked at herself in the mirror and brushed her hair, then put on a red hairband and examined the final product. Staring back at her was a young, attractive woman dressed up—well, actually dressed down—to the fashion of the time. She smiled and winked at herself in the mirror, then left the apartment and began walking towards Veterans Memorial Boulevard to catch the bus.

When she reached Veterans Boulevard, she had to walk for several blocks to get to a bus stop. It was approaching 2 p.m., and a typically hot late Spring day in New Orleans. When she reached the corner with the bus stop, she had to pee. The bus stop was in front of a small shopping strip that had a restaurant (closed), a small grocery store (busy), and a dry cleaner's which appeared to be nearly empty. The sign atop the cleaner's said "Number One Cleaners," and she smiled as she thought about the play on words. She walked across the concrete parking lot and saw through the plate glass that the dry cleaner's was empty, with the exception of a tall, thin young man with very long, black curly hair and large porkchop sideburns; he was sitting in a chair in the corner, behind the counter. The young man was reading a book, and hadn't noticed her. She walked into the open door and said, "Hello."

The place wasn't air conditioned, and the sound of a large fan in the rear of the building made a low-pitched, roaring background noise. It was hot and humid. The young man started, put down the book, and said, "Hello, can I help you?" He was wearing gold-rimmed, round glasses, but the arms of the glasses were missing and, in their place, were loops of strings that went around his ears. He was also barefoot. A small, box fan was placed near him, adding to the background noise.

"I've got to pee really bad. Can I use your restroom?" Brenda asked.

"Sure, let me show you where it is," he replied, and he led her into the back, past a large, modern, dry-cleaning machine and the presser's station with its different equipment for pressing clothes. The bathroom was in the rear of the building, and the young man showed her the door. "Excuse the smell," he said, and he walked back to the front.

What the hell? she thought as she opened the door. Then, the pungent smell of marijuana hit her. She gave a little laugh, shut the door, and sat on the toilet. When she was done, she headed back through the building to the front counter area. The young man was sitting down with his book in his hand.

"Everything come out OK?" he asked, smiling.

"Great," she answered, "but tell me something. Don't you worry that your customers are going to smell that pot and bust you?"

"I try not to think about it," he replied, still smiling.

"Well, good luck with that," she said, "and thanks a lot for letting me use your bathroom."

"Sure, have a good day!"

"OK, bye!" And, with that, she walked back out and to the bus stop. She was in luck, because the bus pulled up within less than a minute and she got on. The bus drove down Veterans, stopping at nearly every stop. When it reached the end of Veterans Boulevard, it turned right and got onto the Interstate for a few minutes, and then took the first exit towards Metairie Road. It drove down the I-10 service road, passing Lakelawn Cemetery and the spectacular Metairie Cemetery with its impressive tombs and mausoleums, and turned onto Metairie Road. After driving a short distance down Metairie Road, it reached the end of the line in front of Cypress Grove Cemetery, where everyone disembarked. Brenda walked with the others to the Canal Street bus stop. There was no open place to sit on the bench, so the people spread out to either side. Brenda looked for a place to sit, and saw some shade under a tree about thirty feet away, just to the side of the gate to the cemetery. She walked onto the grass and sat down in the shade, leaning back onto the whitewashed, stuccoed brick wall that bordered the cemetery. Looking back towards the bus stop, she saw two young men—twins with long, sandy hair—speaking earnestly to each other. One of them looked up in her direction, and she turned away so that he wouldn't think she was staring at him and his brother. The breeze in the shade was cooling, and she was feeling pretty tired. Brenda found her eyelids getting heavy with sleep as she looked at the shadows playing on the grass in front of the cemetery.

Maybe I'll just rest my eyes for a minute, she thought to herself. *I'll hear the bus when it comes....*

Suddenly, she was startled awake by a voice asking, "Mind if I wait for the bus here, too?"

She opened her eyes and saw the silhouette of a young man in front of her. She blinked a couple of times, and he came into focus. He was one of the twins. She made a quick decision and patted the ground next to her, saying, "Be my guest."

The young man sat down and said, "My name is Paul."

"Brenda," she replied.

"You from around here, Brenda?"

"Born and raised."

"Don't you love these cemeteries? You know, there isn't another place in this country that looks like this place where we're sitting."

"Really?" Brenda asked. She hadn't travelled very much outside of Louisiana, with the exception of a couple of beach trips to Pensacola and occasional trips to the Gulf Coast of Mississippi.

"Yeah," said Paul, "the history of these cemeteries is so closely tied to the history and development of New Orleans that I can't imagine the city without them. They've been here since the city was young. For instance, see that cemetery across the street?" Here, he pointed towards the old, slightly blackened Portland Cement-covered wall across Canal Street. Some places where the concrete had fallen off revealed old bricks that were greenish in color from algae that had grown in the moist environment.

"Sure," she said.

"Well, that one's called 'Odd Fellows Rest.' It was founded in 1847. The Odd Fellows was part secret society, and partly for mutual aid. In that time, various crises—both personal, like disease, fire, shipwreck, and things like that, and public, like wars or economic calamities—could affect the ability of a family to pay for the proper burial of their loved ones. Membership in the Odd Fellows provided a type of insurance where members would help one another deal with their crises, and to properly bury their loved ones.

"What do you mean 'properly' bury?" Brenda asked, intrigued.

"Think about it. Things were vastly different in New Orleans at that time. Streets and roads away from the city were little more than muddy ruts. Folks didn't want cemeteries close to where they lived for two fundamental reasons. First, people didn't want to be that close to disturbed spirits, and, second, they didn't want to be close to the smell of decaying bodies and disease that was associated with decay. Remember that here in New Orleans, you had two choices, burial in a shallow grave, which might be flooded and cause your casket to float to the surface, or burial in above-ground vaults. If you were buried in an above-ground vault, you could rest assured that your body wouldn't be exhumed by floods or—uh, sorry—eaten by dogs and rodents."

"That sounds just terrible!"

"Yeah, I'm sorry to mention it, but it was the reality of the time."

"How do you know so much about this, Paul?" Brenda asked.

"It's all around you if you only take the time to see it," he said as he looked out at the cars passing on Canal Street.

"I guess..." Brenda replied, "I just see a dirty street and a bunch of cars." She gave a little laugh.

"Would you like to hear a story about those times in New Orleans, Brenda?" Paul asked.

"Sure."

"OK. This story doesn't start here, but it ends very near here. When these cemeteries were first created, New Orleans was the third-largest city in the United States. It was over 130 years old. The city stretched along the levees of the Mississippi River, with the French Quarter being the oldest part of town. Eventually, the city began to grow towards Lake Pontchartrain, and the back levee swamps began to be drained by digging canals to take the water towards the lake. The land that you see around here, around the cemeteries, had been built up by an earlier Mississippi River levee, and the terrain between it and the bourgeoning city was low-lying and wet. Those were the years of terrible Yellow Fever epidemics. In some years, a significant portion of the city's inhabitants succumbed to the horrible disease...."

Brenda closed her eyes and listened.

Henri Delacourt walked down the street called Esplanade in the direction of Bayou St. Jean. It was a hot, muggy evening in 1853, and the buzzing of mosquitoes kept Henri's hands busy with brushing against his face and ears. A top hat covered the balding pate on his 46-year-old head, and long pantaloons and a frilled shirt with a frock coat protected the rest of his body from the ever-present cloud of annoying, biting insects. The Esplanade Ridge was an ancient Indian portage route between the Bayou St. Jean and the Mississippi River. As such, it drained fairly well after the typical summertime thunderstorms, unlike what could be seen down the intersecting streets this far from the river. The various and sundry puddles that lined the edge of the avenue coalesced into large, muddy pools on the central neutral ground—so named in this most territorial of cities because it was neither of one side or the other, but was, indeed, neutral—and the muddy side streets. A faint, miasmic smell of sewerage pervaded the air, occasionally pushed aside by pungent sweet olive or oleander.

Henri, a free man of color and a prosperous merchant, was walking down the banquette—what the city's residents called sidewalks—to visit his third cousin, Cecille, who had immigrated to La Nouvelle Orleans from France five years before. Cecille and her husband, Bernard, lived on Esplanade Avenue in the "back" of the city, a mile past Rampart Street, where the early inhabitants had built a rampart to protect the city. Henri prided himself on his physical fitness, and walked when he could have easily afforded a Hanson cab. The large mansions which had been built along the Esplanade in the first half of the 19th century were resplendent with gothic columns, large windows, and French doors which could be opened up to let the breezes blow the hot, musty air out and admit the cooler airs from outside. He thought about the message brought by a servant girl to his house earlier that morning. The message had read, in French:

"My dear Henri, if it would be possible and not too much of an imposition, would you please do us the honor of visiting our abode at 6 o'clock this evening? Your dear cousin Cecille has taken ill and I fear the worst. Your humble servant, Bernard St. Cyr"

If Bernard was right, it could only mean one thing., Yellow Fever, the Black Death, the 'Stranger's Disease.' Thousands had succumbed to the disease last year, and the plague had worsened that Summer, when even more thousands had perished. Great new cemeteries had been opened up at the back end of the city along the Metairie Ridge, where some dry ground existed to support the crypts. Indeed, there was talk of opening a new St. Louis cemetery near the end of the Esplanade, as the competition between the living and the dead took up all available dry land near the city. Henri crossed himself as he thought again about his cousin.

When he reached the home, he walked up to the door and saw that a wreath of muscadine vine was placed above the door knocker. Henri lifted the heavy brass ring and let it fall on the door. It made a startlingly loud sound. Some seconds later, the door opened a bit and he could see Bernard peering out through the opening.

"Hello, Bernard," Henri said, lifting his hat. "I have come."

"Ah, yes, Henri," Bernard said, opening the door with a sad smile on his face, "please come in."

Henri walked into the foyer and let Bernard take his hat, which he hung on the hat rack placed on the wall for that purpose. Henri smoothed his hair and offered his hand to Bernard, who reached out with both hands and shook it.

"I am so grateful, Henri. Cecille has been sick for two days. She has a very high fever, and has been vomiting and unable to eat. She is as weak as a kitten, and I worry for her."

"Let us go and see her, Bernard," Henri replied. Bernard led him to the stairwell. Dark mahogany railing with white stiles led up to the second floor, where the bedroom was to be found. When they reached the landing, they turned down the hall and stopped before a large door, also painted white.

"Wait here, Henri, and let me ensure that Cecille is prepared to receive her guest."

Bernard opened the door and walked into the room, closing the door behind him. Henri could hear some soft voices and, a few seconds later, the door opened and Bernard waved him into the room. The room was large, with a small settee to one side, two large chiffarobes placed on either side of the room, and a small, mirrored dressing table. The draperies were closed, and three candles in a silver candelabra were lit near the four-post tester bed.

"Mon cher, Henri!" came the whispered voice of Cecille. "Come closer."

Henri walked to the bed and knelt down at its side. Cecille was lying there propped up on pillows, wearing a simple cotton nightgown and with a coverlet on her lower half. Henri took Cecille's right hand in his and raised it to his lips. "Mon Cherie, cousine! What's this, I find you ill? You must get well soon and visit us in La Vieux Carre. I will send for Dr. Perrault. He will cure you." He could feel the heat of the fever in her hand and see that she was weak and very ill.

"No, Henri, I'm afraid that it is too late for that," Cecille said in a soft, weak voice. "I asked Bernard to reach out to you in hopes that you would be so kind as to assist him with my burial."

"No, no... don't speak of such things," Henri pleaded. Bernard, for his part, put his head in his hands and began to weep softly. "Let me have Dr. Perrault come. He can help you recover your health, mon Cherie."

"As you wish, Henri, but please give me your word that you will help us if the worst happens. I cannot bear the thought of being buried in this horrid, wet ground. A crypt in that beautiful cemetery on the Metairie Ridge in the back of the city will make me rest easier." Cecille's pale white face and bright, fevered eyes pleaded with Henri as she reached out and grasped his hand weakly. Henri could hear the low rumble of fluid in her lungs as she breathed. Tears began to stream down his face, and he bent his head to his cousin's hand.

"As you wish, mon Cherie. You will have the most beautiful crypt in the cemetery. As God is my witness, you will see from Heaven the finest marble crypt to rest your mortal remains, if that is to be your fate. But let me go now and fetch Dr. Perrault. He must begin to treat you soon or all hope will be lost."

Cecille was weeping as she slowly raised his hand to her cheek, and then to her lips. She said, "I love you, my cousin, and I thank you from the bottom of my heart." Then, a fit of coughing struck her. She released his hands and gave way to a bottomless cough that continued for almost a minute. Her face turned bright red with the effort of coughing. Bernard rushed to the bedside and gently pushed Henri aside as he grabbed a porcelain vessel that had been hidden under the bed. He raised Cecille from the pillows with his left hand and placed the vessel on her lap. Suddenly, she vomited a vile, black fluid into the vessel. Her eyes fluttered and her irises turned up, revealing only the white undersides of her eyes. Bernard slowly laid her back on the pillows. The only sound was her strained breathing.

Bernard set the vessel down next to the bed and said to Henri, "For the love of God, Henri. If you believe Dr. Perrault may help, I beseech you to have him come here quickly." He grasped Henri's hand and bowed over it. Henri waited until Bernard had let go of his hand, and then placed it gently on his shoulder. "I go now, my friend," he said in a low voice.

Henri and Bernard silently walked out of the bedroom. Neither could speak, so great was the knot in each of their throats. When they reached the foyer, Bernard reached up and took down Henri's hat. He turned and held the hat out to Henri with his left hand while reaching out his right hand. Henri took his hand and shook it. Both men had tears streaming down their faces. Henri said, in a strangled voice, "I will have Dr. Perrault come immediately. Good bye, my friend."

"We are forever in your debt, Henri," Bernard responded, grasping Henri's hand with both of his. Bernard then opened the door and stood aside as Henri walked out onto the porch, and placed his top hat on his head.

He turned to Bernard, made a short bow, and said, "I go."

Powerful emotions caused Henri to walk briskly along the banquette. He removed his handkerchief from his sleeve and dabbed at the tears flowing from his eyes. As he did so, he thought of Cecille and Bernard when they had arrived in the city in 1848. Cecille was 18 years his junior, while Bernard was only a decade younger than Henri. They had arrived from France full of life and hope. Cecille's family had been large plantation owners in Haiti, but had fled the country when the rebel, Toussaint L'Overture, had led the rebellion that pushed the French out of Haiti. They'd moved back to France, where Cecille had been born. She had married Bernard shortly after he'd come into his inheritance. He was an ambitious man, and had wanted to earn his fortune in the shipping industry. New Orleans' position as the greatest port in the United States, as well as its French heritage, had made it the logical choice for the French immigrants.

Shortly after coming to the city, and following Henri's advice, Bernard had purchased a barge and begun his business shipping goods—such as hides, bricks, and vegetables—from the north shore of Lake Pontchartrain to the city. The superior quality of the north shore bricks, made from a different type of clay than was to be found along the Mississippi River batture, made them highly prized for the construction of footings and the facings of buildings. The locally produced bricks became so soft that, after a few years, one could literally scratch a hole in them with one's fingernail. The north shore bricks also had a pleasing brown or tan color, as opposed to the bright orange of the River batture bricks. It had taken several years, but Bernard's business had recently begun to thrive. He was even contemplating the purchase of another barge. And now, this....

So engrossed was Henri in his thoughts that it seemed that no time had passed before he found himself in front of his house on Dauphine Street. He tipped his hat to Madame Crossier, his next door neighbor, who was leaving her house, and walked into the carriageway that led to his courtyard. As he walked into the courtyard, he spotted Samuel, his most trusted slave. He called him to his side and said, "I will have a message for you to bring to Dr. Perrault in a moment. Please come with me."

Samuel fell in by his side and they entered Henri's home. Henri walked to his desk, lifted the rolltop, and sat down to compose a note to Dr. Perrault. The note read: "My dear Dr. Perrault. My cousin, Mrs. Cecille St. Cyr, of 2021 Esplanade Avenue, has been taken terribly ill. I fear that it is yellow fever. If you would, at your earliest convenience, make haste to attend to her, I will be most grateful. Your humble servant, Henri Delacourt"

He gave the note to Samuel and said, "Go quickly, Samuel, and place this note in Dr. Perrault's hands."

"Oui, monsieur. Tres vites!" Samuel replied, and he walked out of the house.

Henri sat at his desk and placed his head in his hands. His wife Marie walked into his study with a quizzical look on her face. "What is it, my love?" she asked.

He reached out to her and pulled her to him, wrapping his arms around her waist and laying his head on her breast. "It is Cecille. She has yellow fever and is in mortal danger. She has asked for my help with her burial. Bernard is beside himself with grief."

"Oh, mon pauvre petit!" Marie exclaimed. "That is so horrible. We must pray!"

"Yes, my dear," Henri replied, and they both sank to their knees and began to pray for Cecille's recovery.

Before dawn the next morning, they were awakened by a pounding on their door. Henri, dressed in his nightshirt, walked down the stairs to see what was happening. When he reached the front hallway, he saw Samuel, with a candle, opening the door, and Bernard rushed in.

Henri said, "Bernard. What has happened?"

"Henri, all is lost! My beloved Cecille has gone to stay with the angels! Oh, all is lost!" He fell to his knees weeping.

Henri walked to Bernard and knelt next to him. He reached his arms around his friend and placed Bernard's head on his shoulder. In this position, the two men wept. After a few minutes, Henri stood and lifted his friend. Marie, who had watched the sad scene from the stairway, came down in her robe and said, "Come, let us go into the parlor. Samuel, would you please have the cook prepare some coffee?"

Once they heard Bernard's sad story of Cecille's last hours, Marie said, "I must go and prepare her body for burial. Henri, you must help Bernard make the arrangements. You must go to see Pierre Pointcarre for the funeral."

"Yes," said Henri, "I know him. His office is on Rue de la Bourbon."

Bernard looked up and spoke, "Yes, he provides the most beautiful funerals. Cecille would approve." And he broke down weeping.

Henri said, "I must go and speak with Father Manchault at the Cathedral." He rose and walked up the stairs to get dressed.

"Come, Bernard, let the cook prepare you some breakfast. You are going to need your strength. I will go now and prepare Cecille." Marie leaned down and kissed Bernard gently on the forehead. "Mon pauvre petit!" she whispered as he hung his head.

That evening, as they sat down to eat their supper, Henri told Marie about his discussions with both Father Manchault and Mssr. Pointcarre. "My dear," Henri said, "Father Manchault has assured me that we may hold Cecille's funeral services at Our Lady of Guadeloupe Chapel, next to the Cathedral. You are aware that funerals have been banned from the Cathedral for decades. There is some delicacy in the seating arrangements because of the cursed legislature, but the father has explained to me that, because of my position in the community, all will be overlooked. He is aware that I am the benefactor of my cousin and her husband and, even though they are white and we are of colour, propriety dictates that we be treated with honor at the funeral."

"That is good, mon cheri, and I am sure Bernard would agree."

"Yes, he is a good man, and so bowed with grief. I would be the same, my dear, if I were in his position." Henri held out his hand to his wife, and she grasped it and brought it to her lips.

"And I as well," she said. "What about Mr. Pointcarre?"

"Yes, it is all arranged, my dear. Their finest funeral hearse, drawn by a matched pair of striking black stallions, will arrive at their house at 6 o'clock tomorrow morning to bring Cecille to their establishment. They will put her in a fine casket, and will then take her to the chapel for her funeral mass, which will be held at 10. She will be buried in St. Patrick Cemetery. As I promised her, she will be buried in a fine, marble crypt that I have purchased through the kind assistance of Father Marchault."

"You are so kind, Henri! I love you!" Marie said.

Henri reached out to his wife and grasped her hand. "And I, you, my love."

The next morning dawned bright and hot. Henri and Marie rose, ate breakfast, and proceeded to dress for the funeral. At 9:30, they left the house and walked to Cathedral Square. There, they met other friends and acquaintances of Bernard and Cecille and, after exchanging pleasantries, walked into the small chapel next to the Cathedral. Cecille's casket was lying in front of the altar rail, with her head pointed towards the altar. The casket was made of cypress and had been painted a glossy black, with four embossed brass handles, two to each side. The casket had six sides, with the shoulder area being wider than either the head or foot—not too much different in shape than an Egyptian sarcophagus. The casket lid was closed, and a wreath of fragrant, white roses was tastefully arranged atop it. Bernard stood near the head of the casket, greeting and accepting the condolences of the few well-wishers. When he saw Marie and Henri, he stopped speaking mid-sentence and walked up to them.

"My dear family," he said, and embraced first Marie and then Henri. "I cannot thank you enough for your help with my poor Cecille. Please join me in the pew reserved for the immediate family."

They followed Bernard to the front pew of the chapel and sat next to him. At that time, a bell began to toll from the Cathedral tower, calling all in the city to pray for the newly departed soul. After the bell tolled twelve times, an altar boy dressed in a black and white cassock came out and began lighting the tall candles for the high mass that was to be the funeral service. Soon after that, Father Manchault exited the sacristy, dressed in his robes, and began the mass with the familiar intonation, "In Nominie Patrie, et Fillie, et Spriitu Sancti, amen." The ritual that had bound together the majority of the area's inhabitants for the last 150 years then began.

After mass had been said, four stout men dressed in somber black marched up to the casket and grasped the handles. They lifted the casket from its resting place and marched out to a black, glass-sided carriage with polished brass finishes. They were followed out of the church by Father Manchault, the two altar boys, and Bernard, and then the rest of the attendees followed at a respectful distance. The casket was placed into the funeral hearse and the wreath atop it for the ride to the cemetery. A second black carriage, with a matched pair of horses, pulled up. Bernard motioned Henri and Marie to enter this carriage with him. Other drivers and carriages waited in line to gather their respective occupants and make way to the cemetery. Henri couldn't help but notice that there was another funeral hearse behind the line of carriages, waiting for its turn to carry another victim of the plague. He crossed himself.

The funeral procession made its way through the Vieux Carre and onto Canal Street. There, it proceeded to head north towards the Metairie Ridge. The ground began to drop in elevation, and the live oak trees began to give way to cypress and tupelo gum trees in the recently drained area. As they moved down Canal Street towards the Metairie Ridge, the trees grew thicker and became heavily festooned with Spanish moss. Then, as they approached the back of the city and the high ground of the Metairie Ridge, traffic began to slow their progress. There were several funeral processions ahead of them that were causing the delay. Music and singing could be heard from at least two of them.

When they reached the ridge, they turned right towards St. Patrick's, but even before that, they'd begun to notice the smell of death in the air. They saw the source of the odor as they reached the end of Canal Street. There in front of them were some vendors selling different types of food, and behind them was the entrance to the Cypress Grove Number 2 Cemetery, where the poor were to be buried. The sight of dozens of caskets that had been raised from shallow burial, their tops bulging from the rotting corpses which were interred within, was complicated by groups of mourners placing freshly occupied coffins, side by side, in large trenches. Holes had been drilled into the coffins to try to keep them from rising out of the ground as the ground water rose during torrential rainstorms.

The horrible sight led Marie to lay her head against her husband's breast, and Bernard began to weep as he said, "God bless you both for helping my Cecille find her rest in a dry crypt."

Soon, the sounds and smells were bypassed and they reached the St. Patrick Cemetery. The neat rows of crypts, most whitewashed, were laid out with carriage paths around the sides. The hearse stopped, causing all of the following carriages to stop. The men opened up the back of the hearse and removed Cecille's casket. They carried the casket to the front of a large, white, marble crypt which stood open. They placed the casket on a wooden support in front of the crypt. Father Manchault then walked to the head of the casket and encouraged everyone to gather around near the foot of the casket. He made the sign of the cross over the casket. Everyone crossed themselves. He turned and blessed the crypt, sprinkling holy water while intoning the liturgy. Then, he turned and blessed Cecille. He began the "Pater Noster" and all joined in. Following this, he intoned the "Ave Maria" and was once again joined by all in attendance. When he was done, he turned and nodded to Bernard, who walked slowly up to the casket, tears streaming down his cheeks. He bent to kiss the top of the casket and his beloved Cecille one last time.

20
A FLY ON THE WALL

April 29, 1972

Brenda became aware that tears were falling down her cheeks. She reached into her purse, pulled out a tissue, and blew her nose. "Oh my God! That was so sad! It almost seemed true."

"That's because it was true," Paul replied. "Now, if you'll excuse me, there's my bus. See ya!" And, with that, he rose up and ran across the street to catch the Canal bus headed towards Lakeview.

Brenda watched the young man catch his bus, and sat against the cool, white stucco wall thinking about his powerful story. A couple of minutes later, she saw the Canal Street bus pulling up to the stop. She rose from her resting place and walked up to the line of people waiting to get on. A strangely sweet, unpleasant smell hung in the air as she stood in the line. *Somebody's not wearing deodorant.* When she boarded, she handed the driver her transfer and walked to the back half of the bus, where she took a seat on the passenger's side next to the window. She'd always loved looking at the changes in style of houses moving down Canal Street. With a pneumatic *ppsssshhhhh*, the bus door closed and the bus began its trek. It was one of the new, air-conditioned busses and was comfortably cool. She watched the houses and businesses as the bus rolled down the street. Every now and then, the bus would stop and someone would get on or off, and then the bus would make its way further down Canal. It took about fifteen minutes for the bus to reach Claiborne Avenue, the overpass serving as the unofficial boundary between homes and small businesses along the street, and the larger department stores and office buildings. She stayed on the bus for several blocks more and got off at Carondelet Street. It was further down the street than she needed to be, but she couldn't resist looking into the windows of Adler's Jewelers, one of her favorite places to window-shop.

After she exited the bus, she continued walking down Canal. She could see the antique clock that marked the storefront. When she saw the clock, she remembered the story that the young man had told her and wondered if it was from around the same time. She walked to the first window of the jewelry shop and stopped for several minutes to admire the display of sparkling diamonds, emeralds, sapphires, and rubies in the first window. After picking out several items that she would like to have, she began walking over to the second window. A young man coming out the door in a hurry bumped into her as she crossed in front of the door. The young man dropped several wrapped packages.

"Hey, watch where you're going!" the young man said as he bent to pick up the packages. He was short and swarthy, with dark hair, a goatee, and gold, wire-rimmed glasses. He looked a bit like a pirate.

"Sorry! I didn't mean to get in your way. You're in such a hurry," Brenda said, a bit miffed.

"Yeah, I'm sorry. I've got a couple of deliveries to make! Bye!" the young man replied, and then walked rapidly down the street to a yellow Volkswagen Beetle, which he got into and drove away.

Geez! Brenda thought to herself, and she walked over to the second window, where she spent ten minutes looking at each item on display and imagining herself wearing them.

After looking at the jewelry, she thought that she should get on with her task. She reached into her purse and pulled out a paper with an address that had been given to her by Morgan. She walked down Royal for several blocks, admiring the numerous antique shops with their displays. There were apartments in the upper floors of the buildings, with small balconies framed by wrought iron. Many of these balconies had potted plants and ferns on them, giving a sense of a living neighborhood. Making her way to Bourbon Street, she passed Al Hirt's club, the scene of several good times for her and Morgan, and Pete Fountain's club, which had been moved further up Bourbon just recently.

When she reached Dumaine Street, she dug out the note that she had in her purse and checked the address. The afternoon shadows were getting long, placing one side of the street in shadow and the other in sunshine. As she walked down the street, she could hear the *clop, clop, clop* of a mule's feet as it pulled a buggy of tourists who were craning their necks to look at the various landmarks pointed out to them by the driver. She crossed Dauphine Street and saw the sign for Astro's. She passed under the sign and looked down the narrow alleyway. *OK, here goes nothing*, she thought, and walked down the alley. When she reached the door to Astro's, though, she saw that it was closed. There was a handwritten sign taped up that said, "Back at 5:30."

Damn! It's probably only 4:30 right now. I'm going to have to wait somewhere for an hour. She thought for a moment and decided to go to Jackson Square. When she reached the square she stopped, taking in the scene. There were hundreds of tourists around the wrought-iron gates defining the square. Artists' paintings were hanging on the gate, and artists were at their easels painting other works or merely smoking a cigarette and conversing with passersby. She saw the dark red bricks of the twin Pontalba Buildings on either side of the square, these having been built in the mid-1800s by Baroness Pontalba. She walked on the sidewalk underneath the Pontalba's second-floor balcony, looking through the windows at the different shops. She saw a small group of people who were standing around listening to a young man play guitar and sing. She walked up just as the man finished a song and the crowd applauded. He was around 25 or so, with an intelligent, open face. He played several more tunes to the appreciation of the crowd, and Brenda thought, *This guy is good.* He looked at the crowd after finishing another song and asked, "Any requests? Tell me what you'd like to hear and I'll play it if I know it."

A woman in the back of the crowd called out, "Play 'Tennessee Stud!'"

The young man smiled and responded, "'Tennessee Stud.' That's a good' un. It was written by a man by the name of Morris who changed his name. You may know him as Jimmy Driftwood. Jimmy wrote a bunch of good songs, and 'Tennessee Stud' is one of them, but the version of the song I like to do is different. There's a man in North Carolina that I'm proud to know who recorded the song a couple years back. You may have heard of him. His name is Watson, Doc Watson." Here, several people clapped. "Well, I met Doc when I was a young teenager with a love of old-time folk music. He's a generous musician, both with his time and his advice. He showed me some of his favorite licks, and one of them is the lick that he used to kick off his recording of this song." He began to play the beginning lick of 'Tennessee Stud.'

Brenda knew who Doc Watson was because her grandmother was a transplanted North Carolinian who'd been born in Deep Gap, North Carolina. The same small town where Doc Watson had been born. Brenda remembered hearing her grandmother tell stories about the Watson family and Doc, the young boy who'd lost his eyesight and taught himself how to play the guitar so that he could fill in for a fiddle at the local dances. Given the family connection, Brenda was familiar with Doc's music and even had a couple of his albums. Brenda closed her eyes and listened to the young man play. His mastery of the acoustic guitar was incredible. Brenda could swear that it was Doc Watson himself playing the song. The notes rang true and clear, and there were times when it sounded like several guitars instead of only one. It was only when he sang the song that Brenda could tell that she wasn't listening to Doc. Not that the young man didn't have a pleasing voice, but it wasn't the rich baritone of Watson.

Brenda opened her eyes and clapped her approval along with the other people in the group. The young man bowed and pointed to a guitar case on the ground that had a few bills in it. "Tips are always appreciated," he said. A couple of people walked up and put some money in the case. Brenda dug out her wallet and pulled out a dollar bill. She walked up to the case and put the dollar in it as the crowd dispersed. "Thanks a lot," he said.

"You're welcome. That was a great rendition of Doc's 'Tennessee Stud!'" Brenda said with a smile.

"You know who Doc Watson is?"

"Sure, my granny grew up just down the road from the Watson's family in Deep Gap."

"Man! I'd love to have grown up close to Doc."

"She loved his music. Not only the songs he played, but the way he played them. She told me that when he was a young man, he was dirt-poor and made a little bit of money playing the guitar in a band. He could play faster and better than anybody."

"I'll say. Hey! If you like Doc Watson, you need to listen to a couple of other flatpickers. One by the name of Norman Blake, and the other one is a young kid that's fast as blazes. His name is Tony Rice. You'll like both of their styles, I guarantee." He smiled and held out his hand. "The name's Tom, by the way."

Brenda shook his hand and replied, "Brenda."

"Well, Brenda, I can tell by listening to you that you're from around here. What brings you to the Quarter to hear a poor musician sing for his living?"

"Oh, nothing special. I just felt like coming down today. There's this place that I want to check out. A friend told me about it. It's called Astro's."

"Astro's! I go there from time to time to talk to the bartender. He's a friend of mine. If you go there, tell JC hi for me!"

"All right, I'll do that. Well, I've got to get going. Nice meeting you."

"Nice to meet you, too, Brenda. Hope I'll see you around."

"Who knows? Later!" With that, Brenda walked back towards the Cathedral. She took a right on Chartres at the Spaghetti Factory, walked one block, and turned left on Dumaine. She spotted the sign for Astro's. Shadows darkened the alleyway as she turned towards the bar. She could see a cool, blue, neon light from above the open door on her left. When she reached the door, she looked in and saw the small bar. Her eyes adjusted to the dim light and she noticed the bartender, a black man with a huge Afro; he was wearing dark, wire-rimmed glasses. She put her hand on the doorframe as she walked through the door.

"What's happening?" the bartender asked, giving her a big smile.

"Uh, hi!," Brenda replied, a bit hesitantly. "Can I get a drink?"

"Absolutely! Come on in and sit down at the bar. What would you like?"

"I guess I'll have an Old Fashioned," Brenda said, ordering her favorite drink.

"One Old Fashioned coming right up. The name's JC, by the way."

"Wow! I just met somebody who told me to tell you hello."

"Really? Who was that?"

"A musician I just met. He was playing in Jackson Square. He's really good. Plays just like Doc Watson. His name was Tom."

"Oh, yeah! Tom, he's a good guy... hard-working, honest, decent, and very talented. He came to the city about four years ago and, like a lot of musicians, wound up sitting in that seat that you're sitting in. Like most musicians, he's an interesting fellow. I find that many musicians have this ability to look at people, and society, and suss out what's going on behind all of the social BS. Tom has that ability more than most. May I ask your name?"

"Oh, yeah, I'm Brenda. I'm not a musician or anything, but I do like to listen to music."

"Well, Brenda, if it wasn't for folks like you and me who enjoy listening to music, then the musicians would have to play for themselves—or the trees!" Here, JC gave out a loud, honest laugh. Brenda joined in. She instinctively liked JC, and felt comfortable in Astro's.

"I never thought of it that way, JC. If it wasn't for us, then musicians wouldn't have much of a purpose in life since they kind of exist to entertain."

"Exactly right, Brenda! There's a balance in life between the give and the take. Eastern religions call it the yin and the yang. One cannot exist without the other. The perceiver and the perceived. There's been a whole lot of philosophical energy spent dissecting the dual nature of our reality. Why, it's even been proven that the mere act of observing an experiment can have an effect on the results of that experiment."

"No kidding?" Brenda asked. "Like a watched pot never boils?"

JC broke into his laugh again. "Kind of, Brenda, kind of..." and they both laughed again.

"Excuse me, folks. I was wondering if I could get a drink at this establishment?" A young man popped a wheelie on his wheelchair to get over the door's threshold and made his way into the bar.

"Ho, Jim!" JC said, "This here's Brenda. She's not a musician, but she appreciates listening to music very much!" His broad smile included both Jim and Brenda.

"That's a trait that I can appreciate very much since I'm not much of a musician myself," Jim said as he held up his hands and looked at them. "How do you do, Brenda?"

"Hi, Jim, glad to meet'cha!" Brenda took his right hand in hers and pumped it up and down.

"What'll it be, Jim?"

"I'll take an ice-cold Dixie beer, please, JC."

"Coming right up!" JC bent down and pulled a Dixie out of the ice box behind the bar. "Would you like a glass with that?"

"Nope, the bottle's just fine!" Jim took a long pull on the cold beer. Then, he looked at Brenda and asked her, "Well, what brings you to Astro's bar, Brenda?"

"I don't know," she replied, "I've heard about it over time, and I wanted to come and see it. Then, I met this musician today named Tom, and he told me he comes here, too. So, I had to come down and have a drink."

"Yep, there's something about JC and musicians. You'd be surprised to find out who comes here from time to time. I've heard rumors that Bobby Dylan has sat in the same chair that you're sitting in, and I've seen Robert Plant and Jimmy Page drinking whiskey just down the bar from where you are now."

"Really?" Brenda asked, clearly impressed.

"Now, cut it out, Jim," JC protested, "I don't have any control over who comes into my bar, and I'm damned sure not going to turn down a paying customer!"

"Yeah, yeah... I know, but it's true, nevertheless."

"Wow!" Brenda exclaimed. "Bob Dylan, Robert Plant, and Jimmie Page? Were they here at the same time?"

Both JC and Jim laughed aloud. "No, no!" JC said. "They were here at very different times. I don't think Jimmy Page gets up before three in the afternoon, and Bobby likes being around the Quarter early in the morning—the 'jangling morning' as he told me once."

"Man," Brenda said, "this place is famous!" All three of them had to laugh at that.

JC began to wipe the bar with a towel and slowly moved away from Brenda and Jim. Jim took another pull from his Dixie and leaned towards Brenda. "Brenda," Jim whispered, "do you get high?"

Brenda perked up at the mention of drugs. This was going to be so *easy*! An unconscious look of guilt flashed across her face too quickly for Jim to notice. She responded, "Well, I've smoked a little pot. Why? Do you have some?"

"Come into my parlor," Jim replied with a smile, and then he called out again: "See you, JC!"

Brenda put two dollars on the bar and rose from her barstool to follow Jim, saying, "Yeah, it was nice to meet you, JC!"

"Bye, y'all," JC replied, stopping his wiping to beam a smile at the two of them.

Jim made his way out of Astro's with Brenda following. When he reached the door at the end of the alley, he leaned forward in his chair and turned the handle as he pushed the door open, and then wheeled himself into the courtyard. Brenda followed him, turning and closing the door behind them. When she turned back around, she was astounded at the lush foliage and colorful flowers that filled the courtyard. "Oh, my!" she said. "It's just beautiful here!"

"Welcome to my parlor!" Jim replied, smiling and raising his eyebrows.

"Cut it out, Jim!" Brenda laughed. "Really... it's beautiful here."

"Yeah, it's a little bit of paradise in the Crescent City. I've been here for several years, and still can't get over the tropical feel of this courtyard. Take a look at those Mandevilla and Bougainvilla vines. You won't find bigger or better ones anywhere," he said as he raised his hand towards the vines growing up the back brick wall of the courtyard, which was covered in a coat of pink and red blooms.

"Did you say something about getting high?" Brenda prompted him.

"Why, yes, I did!" Jim smiled and dug his hand into his shorts, coming up with a baggie and pipe. "Would you mind doing the honors?" he asked as he handed them to Brenda.

"Sure," she said, and she walked to a bench and sat down as she packed the pipe. He followed her and she handed it back to him.

He took the pipe and lit it in his expert manner, using a silver Zippo, and then he took a long hit and passed the pipe to Brenda. She took a small hit, making a snorking sound as she fought to keep it in for several seconds, and then let it out with a long exhale. They continued in this fashion until the pipe was finished. Then, Jim asked, "You want any more?"

"No, thanks," she replied, "I don't smoke too much, and a little bit goes a long way. That's some really good pot, by the way. What kind is it?"

"Primo Columbian buds," he replied, "and that's why it's so hard to keep it in. The best pot you can find in the city. Good sticky buds and not much shake."

"Far out! Where do you get it?" Brenda asked, a bit too eagerly.

"Whoa, girl! Don't you know it's impolite to ask a pothead where he gets his shit?" Jim asked, looking at her with a sideways look.

"Yeah, I'm sorry. I guess I'm just stoned!" Brenda laughed and brushed a lock of Jim's long hair out of his face. "You know, you're kind of cute."

Jim beamed at her. "I like you, too! Now that we've got that out of the way, Brenda, why don't you tell me something about yourself?"

Brenda was taken aback for a second, as she hadn't made up a cover story to tell, and so, instinctively, she decided to tell the truth. "Well, there's not much to tell. I was born and raised in New Orleans. When I was a kid, we lived in the Ninth Ward, really close to Parasol's Bar. You know, the one that has the big St. Patrick's Day celebration?"

"Of course."

"Well, I grew up there 'till I was 13, and then we moved out to Metairie Road, close to Bonnabel. I went to Riverdale High School and graduated in 1967. Then, I went to Delgado to learn secretarial skills like shorthand and typing. I got a job while I was in my first semester, and I've been working ever since."

"A secretary, huh? That's cool. Where do you work?"

Brenda paused for a second, and simply said, "I work for the city."

"Really? Where? City Hall?"

"Yeah, I work in the secretarial pool at City Hall," Brenda said glibly. "Now, why don't you tell me something about yourself? What's good for the goose is good for the gander."

"Yeah, yeah! There's really not much to tell. I grew up in Lakeview and was raised Catholic. Graduated from St. Aloysius High School in 1962. Trained as a welder, but you can see that's pretty much out of the picture." Here, Jim raised his cupped hands and gestured towards his chair. "Anyway, about six years ago, I was in a car wreck. Almost died. Spent a long time in Charity, and then in rehab. Anyway, I kind of gave up on life until I made my way here. That was about three years ago, and it's given me a new lease on life. You need to meet some of the folks around here. Particularly Anna. You'll really like her."

"Well, I sure liked JC. If Anna's anything like him, I'm sure I'll like her."

"Yeah, JC's great. There is something that I should warn you about, though, Brenda."

"What's that?"

"Well, you'll find that sometimes there are things that happen around here that are kind of unexplainable."

"What do you mean?"

"I can't really tell you. You'll just have to see for yourself, but just remember it's all for the good."

"OK?" Brenda replied, a bit puzzled.

21
THE MAGIC OF HISTORY

April 29, 1972

Jim saw the door to the alleyway open just then and Anna walked in with the twins. "Hello, everybody!" boomed Caz and Paul at the same time. Jim still had difficulty telling them apart.

"Hi, y'all!" Jim replied. "This is Brenda."

Brenda was staring at the twins. One of them walked up to her and stuck out his hand. "We've already met. Fancy meeting you here, Brenda."

In a bit of shock, she shook his hand and said, "Hi, Paul."

Caz elbowed his brother aside and said, "How about me? I'm Caz."

Brenda looked at Caz, and then at Anna, who grinned and shrugged, raising her palms up by her sides as if to say, *What can I do with these two goofballs?*

Brenda laughed out loud and shook Caz's hand. "Pleased to meet you, Caz. I met Paul earlier today by the cemeteries. He tells a mean story."

"That's just because you haven't heard one of mine," Caz said archly.

They all shared a laugh at this repartee, and then a voice interrupted, "Mon cheries, you are enjoying the evening, non?" Brenda turned and saw a beautiful, older black woman dressed in colorful clothes. She instantly noticed, and appreciated, the jewelry that the woman wore on her fingers, arms, and neck.

"Hi, Mama Zulie!" Jim waved her over. "Come and meet our new friend, Brenda."

Mama Zulie walked over to the group and held out her hand, which Brenda took. "It is a pleasure to meet you, Brenda!" she said in her strong, French accent.

"You, too, Mama Zulie," Brenda replied, "I just love your jewelry."

"Ah... a woman of taste... you like the finer things in life, Brenda?" Mama Zulie asked.

"Yes, ma'am... I mean, yes, Mama Zulie."

"Then, you must all come and have some cake and champagne in my apartment, mon cheries!" And, with this, Mama Zulie turned and walked back to the door she had emerged from, leaving the rest of them to follow.

They looked at each other, and Anna exclaimed, "How can we refuse that offer, Mama Zulie?!" They walked as a group and followed Mama Zulie into her apartment.

Brenda was amazed at the amount of color in the apartment. The walls were covered with art and masks, all gaily colored. The walls themselves were painted in various pastel shades. Jim interrupted her reverie by suggesting, "Why don't you sit here next to me, Brenda?" as he wheeled himself to an empty spot at the head of a beautiful, wooden table. Brenda did as she was told and sat in a chair next to Jim's wheelchair. Anna sat next to Brenda, and the twins occupied the two chairs on the other side. Mama Zulie appeared with a plate full of small cakes and set it down in the center of the table. She disappeared for a moment, returning with saucers that she placed in front of everyone. She disappeared once more before coming back with six champagne flutes which she ceremoniously placed in front of each place at the table. Then, after a moment, she brought out a magnum of champagne and placed it next to the plate of cakes.

"Monsieur Caz, would you please do us the honor of opening the champagne?"

Caz smiled. "With pleasure, Mama Zulie." He picked up the magnum and looked at the label. "Hmmm... 1959 Dom Perignon. Not bad, Mama Zulie, not bad at all." They all laughed at this, and he quickly peeled the foil and popped the cork before pouring generous portions into each champagne flute. After this was done, the cakes were passed around and they began to eat and drink. There was no conversation, as the cakes were so delicious and the champagne so cold and fresh. Brenda was amazed to see that there were more cakes on the plate after she and the others had finished their first, so she asked Jim to pass her another. He did so, and she continued eating cake and drinking champagne. When her flute was almost empty, Caz quickly filled it up again. The hum of conversation began to pick up as Anna spoke with Mama Zulie, the twins spoke to each other, and Jim kept Brenda entertained by telling stories of his wild youth.

Eventually, the cakes and champagne ran out, as did the conversation. They were sitting around the table in a contentedly full and slightly inebriated state. The silence was not awkward, but rather friendly and satisfied. Brenda felt a little sleepy, and almost started when Anna spoke.

"Caz, Brenda has heard Paul tell a story, so why don't you tell us one now?"

Caz looked around the table and gave a large, exaggerated, wolf-like smile. "Certainly, Anna. Now, tell me, Brenda, is there any particular type of story you'd like to hear?"

Brenda thought for a moment, and then said, "This courtyard is so beautiful. Can you tell me a story about it?"

Jim and the others chimed in with support of Brenda's suggestion.

Caz's smile turned from exaggerated to sincere. "Why, I'd love to tell you a story about this place, Brenda." He paused for several moments, as if he were listening. Then, he began to speak.

"You have to first understand that the buildings and walls you see here are not the first buildings on this lot. After the founding of the city, the streets were laid out in a square grid pattern and houses were built on the various lots. Some houses were built near the street; others were set back a ways. All of the houses had outbuildings of different types. Kitchens and storage buildings, barns, outhouses... any given lot could have several different structures on it. Most of these buildings were made of wood, although there were some brick buildings and walls. They made their bricks from the rich clay they dug from the Mississippi River batture...."

Charles Griffon Derneville awoke on March 21, 1788. He lay in his feather bed and, with his first conscious thought, grieved for Jeanne, his wife, who had died in childbirth a month earlier. Tears leaked from his eyes as he lay there. *Oh, Jeanne... if only you had lived....* The thought burned for the thousandth time in his mind. He lay there for several minutes, then wiped his eyes and steeled himself to face the day. There was much work to be done on the plantation. Spring had come early, and the Winter harvest of wax myrtle berries had been completed. The berries had been boiled in the large vats, the fragrant wax had been skimmed, and candles were being produced with the wax for local sale and export. He thought about the crop and felt a bit better. It was shaping up to be a successful year, at least as far as the wax production was concerned. Now, it was time to plant the second cash crop that Derneville grew on his plantation, the much-desired indigo plant. This plant produced the richest of blue dyes for fabrics and was the second largest export to France. Much prized by European aristocracy, the plant required a good deal of intensive effort in its planting, cultivation, and harvesting.

Derneville walked into the main room of his house. The house was built of rough planks of cypress wood. It consisted of four separate rooms—two bedrooms, a parlor, and a dining room. The house was built in the Caribbean style, raised on brick piers about six feet off of the ground, and there was a porch that extended on all sides. The entire structure was covered by a roof of cypress planks that shed rain effectively, keeping the inside of the home dry. The ceilings were twelve feet high, which helped during the long, hot, humid Summers. He walked into the parlor and opened the outside door. Exiting the house, he walked onto the porch and looked up and down the bayou road. There looked to be no one on the road stretching between La Nouvelle Orleans and the Bayou St. Jean, which had seen the earliest French occupation in the area. Seeing no one on the road, he urinated off the porch. He would never have done this, had Jeanne been alive, but now he thought, *What does it matter?*

His manservant, Claude, who had come from French Saint Domingue, came onto the porch and said, "Monsieur, would you like to have breakfast?" Claude was a dark-skinned black man. He was a free man, not a slave, who was indentured to Derneville for a period of seven years. Loyal service for the duration of his indenture was the price for the cost of his voyage. After this time passed, he'd be free to continue his services for a fee, or embark on an entrepreneurial enterprise of his own making.

Derneville replied, "No, Claude, today is a day of fasting. Please give me some water."

Claude went in, followed by Derneville. The servant retrieved a tankard from a large armoire that stood in the corner of the parlor, placed it on the table, and filled it from a pewter carafe. Derneville crossed himself and prayed over his glass of water. Today was Good Friday, the day of suffering and death of our Lord, Jesus Christ. "Lord God," Dernier prayed, "thank you for your sacrifice for me and all men. Make me worthy of you today, and for the rest of my life. In the name of the Father, the Son, and the Holy Spirit, amen." Dernier again crossed himself and drank the water. He then dressed in his church clothes and went outside to examine his plantation. His overseer, a man named Crespo, was already in the nearest field with a small but diverse assortment of French, Spanish, Negro, and Native American workers. None were slaves. They were finishing the planting of the indigo crop. Derneville had three of his eight arpents dedicated to indigo production. The rest were for wax production and gardens for food. Derneville walked the short distance to where Crespo was standing and asked, "How long do you think it will take to finish the planting?"

"About two more days, monsieur," Crespo responded as he kept a watchful eye on the workers.

"Remember, Crespo," Derneville admonished him, "it is Good Friday. The men are to cease their labors at noon."

"Oui, monsieur."

"Eh, bien. Merci, Crespo, je vais a l'eglaise." And, as if on cue, Derneville heard the bells of the Church of St. Louis calling people to mass. He took his leave and hurriedly began walking to the church. He crossed the small ditch and rough stockade that marked the edge of the city, very near his house, and then hurried down Ursulines Street to Chartres Street, where he turned right and walked up to the church. He arrived just before the mass began, and entered the church to pray with many other citizens. The first several pews in the center of the church were reserved for high-ranking Spanish officials and the wealthiest French planters. From his place in the middle of the church, he could see Governor Miro and his family, as well as La Freniere, several of the D'Estrehans, and the newly arrived Jean Etienne de Bore, who had recently married one of the beautiful D'Estrehan daughters and was attempting to grow sugar on his plantation several miles upriver from New Orleans. The somber mass, marking the crucifixion of Jesus, continued to its end. Then, Father Antonio de Sedella—known as Pere Antoine—led the congregants in the Stations of the Cross. Afterward, the crowd left the church around noon to go and, as Pere Antoine said, "contemplate this day and the sacrifice of our Lord, who gave his life so that we may live without the original sin, and enjoy the bounties of Heaven."

Derneville left the Church of St. Louis and strolled through the Plaza Des Armes to the Mississippi River's edge. A large galleon had arrived from Spain earlier in the week and he wished to get a closer look at it. The ship was a beautiful 3-master, about 130 feet long with high fore and aft castles and a low-slung mid. He could count 25 cannon ports on the starboard side, as the ship was anchored with her bow towards the current's flow. Her name was, *Nuestra Senora de la Concepcion*. He wondered over how many men she carried, and the different places the ship had visited. Lost in reverie for a while, he stood there watching the ship and the men that were still aboard perform those maintenance duties necessary for all ships. Eventually, his curiosity sated, he turned and began to walk towards his home.

He decided to take a different route, and began walking upriver along the quay, thence on the Route D'Allemends that connected the city with the small community of German farmers upriver. As he walked, he passed the intendant's house, and then the Maison de la Compagnie and the governor's office. When he reached the settled part of the city proper, he turned north on Custom House Street and walked past the powder magazine before turning right on Rue de Bourbon. He walked down Bourbon for three blocks and turned left on St. Louis Street. A short distance from Bourbon, he saw his childhood friend, Henri Latil, whose father had once owned the property that now belonged to Derneville.

Henri and his wife lived in a small, modest wooden house that was raised about three feet on brick piers. The house sat back about 75 feet from St. Louis Street. There were several other small outbuildings on the same lot, as was the case with the vast majority of the lots in

New Orleans. He visited with Henri for a while, and then continued his stroll. He passed by many other wooden structures, almost all of them raised against the yearly Spring floods. Levees had been constructed within a few years of occupation, and these levees kept the river from washing away the town. However, there was no defense against the backwaters of the swamp flooding the area from the north. These backwater floods usually stopped about one or two feet above ground level, but there had been some that had risen as much as eight feet, flooding many buildings.

New Orleans now had nearly 5,000 inhabitants, with the majority living within the confines of the streets initially laid out by Monsieur LaTour. They lived in narrow but deep lots that faced the city streets and their homes were in close proximity to each other. The homes were built of cypress wood, as it had been found to be both rot- and insect-resistant, and could take the occasional flooding without warping. Those portions of the lots that were not cultivated, or did not contain structures, were covered in elderberry and other shrubs which were turning green with small new leaves, while a veritable army of dried stalks of goldenrod stood tall among them. There was a large amount of dried, dead vegetation that was being supplanted by the vigorous new Spring growth.

He saw a few more friends on the way back to his house, and stopped briefly to visit with each of them. Derneville's friends came primarily from the French inhabitants of the city. Not that he wasn't friendly with some of the Spanish inhabitants—indeed, some of them were very good friends, but he and most of the French inhabitants still harbored some animus over the brutal way General Alexander O'Reilly had put down the rebellion of the city's French inhabitants when they'd been informed that La Louisiane had been transferred to Spanish ownership. The Spanish governor initially sent by the king to take possession of Louisiana, Senor Antonio de Ulloa, had been forced to leave the city and return to Spain with his pregnant bride, pushed to do so by a rebellion amongst many of the leading French citizens. The citizens had objected to restrictive Spanish trade practices, and claimed that it would strangle trade in the region. Gallic pride, which they would not admit to, had also played a part in their rebellion. When O'Reilly had returned with a fleet of 23 ships and 2,000 men in August of 1769, he had immediately rounded up the ringleaders of the rebellion. He'd had five of them killed in front of a firing squad, shortly after a trial for treason which had lasted nearly two months. Several others had been sent to prison in Cuba for various periods of time, but released after a couple of years. All properties of those deemed traitors had been seized, with the exception of dowries.

Derneville's father had taken a minor, peripheral role in the plot, but managed to avoid both execution and prison. Derneville remembered his father crying on the afternoon upon which he'd been required to take an oath of allegiance to the King of Spain. The Spaniards had, in short time, relaxed their strict trade barriers in a tacit admission of the realities involved in managing a huge colony on the periphery of the bourgeoning United States of America. Indeed, increasing numbers of Americans had been relocating to New Orleans to take advantage of its position on the Mississippi River.

Trade flowed down the rivers of North America, into the Mississippi, and then down to New Orleans to be shipped around the world. It didn't take a genius to see that New Orleans was placed in a position to become the premier trade center for most of the continent.

The day was unusually warm for late March, and a strong, southeasterly wind was blowing as he reached the boundary of his small plantation and climbed the steps to his house. Claude met him on the porch with a tankard of water, which he gratefully accepted. He stood there on the porch drinking his water, and watched a large wagon piled high with deer and buffalo hides make its slow progress towards the city on the bayou road. It had come from across Lake Pontchartrain, shipped from Mandeville by barge to the docks on Bayou St. Jean. He stood there looking at it, and caught the smell of smoke. There was nothing unusual in this, as fires were lit at all times of day and night for cooking, warmth, or to burn brush. He cast a last look at the white, puffy clouds moving from Southeast to Northwest in the blue sky, and walked inside to do some necessary paperwork. He was lost in his business book in short order, tallying costs of materials and projecting revenues from the sale of his products.

"Monsieur! Viens vite ici!" Claude called from the porch.

Derneville quickly rose from his chair and walked out. There stood Claude, pointing towards the city, where a cloud of black smoke billowed up in the distance. "There is a fire in the city, monsieur!"

Derneville acted in the same manner as most citizens of the time. He turned and ran into the house to get his coat while calling over his back, "Claude, get some buckets!"

Claude quickly complied, and they both ran out the front drive and toward the city. Derneville thought quickly and said, "We'll take Burgundy to St. Louis!" Alongside them, other people were running down the street towards the fire, most with buckets. They reached St. Louis Street and ran towards the river. The smoke from the fire was dark, acrid, and thick. They could go no further than Royal Street, and there witnessed a sight that shook Derneville to his core.

The buildings on both sides of the street were fully engulfed in flames which whirled like many tornados, with their upper ends twisting high in the sky, then running low almost to street level. As he watched, he saw a woman whose clothes were fully in flames, screaming as she ran down the street, and then stumbled and fell. Other poor souls were running as fast as they could away from the scorching fire. There was a line of men forming a bucket brigade to try to quell the fury, but Derneville realized that it was as futile as pissing on a forest fire. Nevertheless, he motioned to Claude and they brought their buckets, got into the line, and began passing full buckets of water up the line, and empty ones back down. Every couple of minutes, the men in the front of the line ran back, as they were getting scorched, and the next ones in line stepped up to throw the water. The crackling roar of the flames, coupled with the howling of the wind, made speech almost impossible. Other men came and began evacuating crying women and children from those buildings which had not yet been caught aflame. Embers as large as Derneville's hand were swirling everywhere. Some of these were starting secondary fires ahead of the main conflagration.

The line of the bucket brigade was pushed back further and further as the raging fire progressed.

Derneville had been fighting the fire for about an hour or so when he felt his arm being tugged. He looked and saw Colonel Maxent, a friendly acquaintance, who was one of the leading merchants of the city and rumored to be the richest man in Louisiana. Maxent leaned towards him and spoke loudly in his ear, "We need to abandon this area to the fire! The governor has ordered all men to the protection of the buildings along the river!"

"How has this happened, Colonel?" Derneville asked.

"The fire began at the home of Senor Nunez," Maxent replied, "and spread quickly because of the wind. The priests would not let us ring the church bells for alarm because it is Good Friday." Here, Maxent crossed himself. "Now, go!" Then, Maxent moved further up the line to inform others of the decision.

Derneville, sweat-streaked and soot-blackened, turned to Claude. "Come, Claude!" he yelled, and he grasped his arm as he turned and began running west towards the outskirts of the city. The fire had pushed them up St. Louis Street almost to Bourbon. Derneville and Claude ran back to Dauphine Street, and then turned left and ran to Customhouse Street before turning again towards the river. The air was clear here, being upwind of the fire. They ran back along the river to the Plaza de Armas where the military was organizing several parties to save what could be saved from the flames, as well as to organize several bucket brigades. Derneville saw a major who he was familiar with and ran to him. "Where do you need us, Senor?" he asked.

The major clasped him by the shoulder and said, "Governor Miro has asked me to save the prisoners in the jail. Come with me." Derneville nodded, and he and Claude ran towards the prison with the major.

For the rest of the afternoon, until well past dark, Derneville and Claude fought the flames. They passed buckets until their arms were dead weight, and then they continued passing buckets. At one point during the blaze, they assisted the treasurer (in whose house the conflagration had begun at an altar of devotion) in moving the king's treasure onto the river batture, under the watchful eye of the Guard. Their hearts were rent by the plight of those who had lost everything in the blaze. Many people were injured, mostly with burns. The weeping and wailing of men, women, and children who found themselves destitute rose as the crackling roar of the fire diminished. The fire had not consumed the entire city, yet almost every structure behind the first row of buildings along the river had been destroyed—between Conti and Dumaine Streets, and all the way back to Dauphine Street. Several other buildings in the city had burned from fires started by the flying embers, but these individual fires had not joined into the general conflagration. After seven long hours of toil and sweat, the great fire was controlled.

Derneville was exhausted. Claude, who had been by his side the entire time, was equally exhausted. Details could not be seen in the darkness. The area where the flames had consumed everything was pulsing with red, glowing embers in time to the diminishing gusts of wind. They had spent the last hour of the inferno assisting the priests in preserving the Ursulines Convent, pouring bucket after bucket on the roofs of the different structures to keep the embers from alighting and starting a new fire. Now, they stood on the street dumbfounded by their exhaustion and the tragedy that they had just witnessed. Derneville was standing there, arms by his side, when he saw his friend Henri walking towards him. Henri had his wife and two small children with him. He clutched a silver candelabra, which was the only possession he had been able to salvage from his house before it had been consumed. When Henri saw Derneville, he burst into tears and clutched his friend in a tight embrace.

"There, there, Henri. Do not cry," Derneville said gently. "Madam," he said, and Henri's wife's tear-streaked face nodded in return. "Do not worry, my friends. You will stay in my house until you are back on your feet."

"Merci, mon ami," Henri said with feeling, and then he turned and hugged his wife and children. "You see, my dears, I told you, God will provide."

Brenda blinked several times, and then she shook her head. Her arms were resting on the table with her hands held up at a 45-degree angle with her fingers extended. She looked around the table and saw everyone was looking at her with knowing smiles. She was confused.

"What... what happened?" Brenda asked nervously.

Jim laughed and said, "You got caught in Caz's story, Brenda. Both he and Paul tell some great stories!"

Brenda pushed her chair back from the table. "No... that's not right! I felt like I was there!" She stood up and brushed her hands down her shirt and jeans. Jim reached across the corner of the table towards her. The chair made a squawk, scraping across the brick floor as she backed up.

"Now, Brenda, calm down," Jim said soothingly. She looked at Jim, then around the table at Anna, Mama Zulie, and the twins.

"No, no... this isn't right!" she muttered loud enough for all of them to hear, but speaking to herself. She looked around the table again and said loudly, "I've got to go!" She turned and almost ran out of Mama Zulie's door. She hurried through the courtyard, down the alley, and towards Rampart Street to catch the bus. A slight smell of smoke followed her.

Jim was astounded, and he sat there with his extended arm tracking Brenda's movements as she ran out. "Wait...." His voice had almost been a whisper, but she was gone, anyway. They heard the gate to the alley slam closed. Jim looked at his friends around the table, and saw them looking at him.

Anna stood up, walked around the table to the side of Jim's chair, and put an arm around his thin shoulders. "Jim," she began, but he waved her away, backed his chair from the table, and wheeled himself out the door.

22

A LOOMING EVIL
AND A DATE

April 29, 1972

April returned to her apartment following her Saturday morning's photographic adventure. Her apartment was on the second floor of an old house on Marshall Foch Street, off of Canal Boulevard and near the interstate. The house had been a middle-class, single-family home when built in the early 1900s, with a tasteful bit of Victorian gingerbread, a small front porch, and a larger, screened-in, second-story porch. The glass-windowed front door opened into a small foyer, which included the entrance door for the downstairs apartment just to the right of a staircase. The staircase led to the door of April's upstairs apartment. When she got into her apartment, she set down her purse and immediately took her camera into the small bathroom that her friends had helped her convert into a makeshift darkroom. She set her camera down on top of the lavatory cabinet and walked back into her bedroom closet to gather the different trays for the chemicals. Back in the bathroom, she unscrewed the bare lightbulb from the simple fixture over the mirror, screwed in a red lightbulb, and turned on the switch. She closed the door and taped over the cracks, stuffing a towel under the door to block the light. She and her friends had already taped cardboard over the bathroom window to block the outside sunlight. She pulled her bottles of chemicals from the small linen closet.

She went back to the camera and rewound the film. When the tension of the rewinding eased and she knew the film was rewound into the canister, she opened the back of the camera and pulled it out. She'd shot a can of Kodak, black and white Tri-X 400. She grabbed the can opener, which was hanging on a lanyard over the towel rack, and opened one end of the film can. She wound the film on the reel after cutting off the tongue, and then she quickly placed the exposed film into the developing tank. She poured the developing chemical slowly into the canister. The smell of the developer was strong as she poured it. Then, she slowly agitated it for several minutes. When the developing time was done, she poured the developer out into the sink and poured the stop bath into the tank. She slowly agitated, once again making sure that all of the film had ample contact with the chemical. This step was followed by introducing the fixer chemical into the tank after pouring out the stop bath. Once this process was complete, she opened the tank, placed it in the sink, and ran cold water into it for several minutes. She then removed the reel and pulled the developed film out, making sure that her hands were wet and she touched only the end of the film. She hung the developed film from a line she had over the tub, and then turned and walked out of the bathroom to fix herself some lunch.

April had her lunch and then read a bit of a new book she'd started before venturing back into the bathroom. She replaced the lightbulb and took the film off of the line, holding it by the edge. She walked back into the living room and placed the film on top of a small, homemade light table which was placed in the corner of the room. She turned the light on, sat down, picked up a large magnifying glass which lay on the table, and began to examine her negatives. There were 36 exposures in the film roll. The first couple dozen had been done for a couple who'd hired her to take architectural photographs of their renovated home. She looked closely at the fine-grained negatives and was pleased with the subject matter, contrast, and focus. She made mental notes of which of the negatives she would enlarge and print. *The clients will be pleased*, she thought as she examined the negatives.

Once she'd finished close examination of the "business" negatives, she turned with pleasure to the last third of the roll, where she'd taken photos at her own pleasure during her morning in the French Quarter. The first several were pictures of people she'd found interesting during her stroll. These were followed by several abstract architectural features that she'd found interesting. One shot she particularly liked was a close-up of an ancient cypress door where the grains of the wood stood out in bas relief as they swirled around a knot. She spent several minutes looking at the details of this negative, quietly humming under her breath as she unconsciously sounded her pleasure with the photograph.

She moved on to the next negative and saw it was the photo of the puddle in the street, and the antique store window. Interested, she looked more closely with the glass at some of the details. There were the reflections of the buildings and the clouds in the puddle, and there, as she moved up the negative, there was the blurred image of the man who had walked into the picture from the right. She muttered under her breath as she moved her glass to the antique store window, and then gave a surprised grunt. She could see the blurred reflection of the man's face in the window, but looming above the man's reflection was an apparent reflection of a tall, thin, dark-skinned black man. The tall man's reflection was crystal clear. The malice in his face was palpable.

This is extraordinary! April thought. *That man wasn't there!* She looked at the negative again. She cold see the blurred image and reflection of the man who moved into her photograph, but only the reflection of the other man. *This doesn't make sense!*

That man who'd ruined her photograph had seemed like a nice fellow, albeit with a bad sense of timing about where he walked. *He even offered to make me a cup of coffee*, she thought with a bit of a smile. She felt strongly that there was something untoward in the photograph, and decided that she needed to enlarge and print the negative quickly.

She went to her bedroom to get the enlarger and rolled it into the bathroom. Once again, she prepared the bathroom for photographic work, this time placing plastic tanks in the tub, and commenced. When she'd finished printing the picture, she brought it out into the living room so she could examine it more closely. It was obvious that there was an extra reflection in the antique store window, and that this reflection was of a man dressed entirely in black. Unlike George's blurred face, he was crystal clear in the reflection. His sharp, dark, angular face was notable for the anger and malice that filled it as he loomed over the unaware pedestrian.

April was stunned. She didn't know what to make of the photograph. She was, of course, familiar with Kirlian photography, and the claims that had been made about photographing auras, but she'd never encountered anything like this. She put the photograph down and thought about it. The man—*George, that was his name*—had seemed nice, and she felt that she should go and show him the picture, but it was now later in the day and she didn't really feel like going back to the Quarter. "I'll go back there next week and show it to him," she said to herself, but, try as she might, she couldn't shake the feeling of danger that made the hairs on the back of her neck tingle.

Finally, she grabbed the print, put it into a manila folder, and walked out the door. She walked up to Canal Boulevard to catch the Canal Bus to the cemeteries, then down to the edge of the French Quarter. She carried a folder with the printed photograph. She had printed the photo on 8x10 paper so it was large enough to see details, but she'd also brought her large magnifying glass.

She thought about the photograph and continued to have apprehensive feelings about the unknown man looming over George. She arrived at the antique store on Royal just after 2 p.m. When she walked up to the door, she saw the "OPEN" sign, and she pushed her face against the door and cupped her hands around her eyes to see through the glass. A movement caught her eye, and she could see George with his back turned to her, messing with something behind the counter. April opened the door and saw George start, then turn. When he saw her, he broke into a beaming smile and walked quickly to the door. He opened the door, smiled at her, and said, "Well, hello, April!"

She smiled back and said, "Hi, George. You remembered my name!"

"Of course! What can I do for you?"

She looked down at the folder she was carrying. "I wanted to take you up on that cup of coffee that you mentioned... and to show you that picture I took."

George raised his eyebrows and pulled the door wide open. "Wonderful. Come on in." He walked around April, down the aisle and to the back of the store. In a few moments, he was walking back with two cups of coffee placed in saucers. He set the saucers down on a small table in between two wooden chairs and beckoned April over.

"Here, come and have a seat while you drink your coffee."

April sat and thanked George when he handed her a saucer with a coffee cup. She took a sip of the delicious, slightly bitter brew.

"Chicory?" she asked.

"New Orleans' finest, Café Du Monde coffee with Chicory. Do you know why we drink it with chicory here?"

"Not the foggiest," she replied.

"It comes from the Civil War times. New Orleans was captured early in the war. I think it was in 1862. Well, before the city fell to the Yankees, there'd been a naval blockade that stopped supplies from reaching the city. As their stock of coffee dwindled, the locals began to use other things to stretch the supply. They tried acorns and beets, but the best ingredient they found was chicory. It not only stretched the supply—some believed that it improved on the flavor of pure coffee. So, now we have a tradition of adding chicory to coffee." George picked up his own coffee and sipped.

"That's very interesting, George," April replied. She lifted the folder from her lap and handed it to George. She spoke a little faster as she began to explain, "I developed that picture that you walked into this morning."

"Again, I'm really sorry about that."

April waved her hand in a dismissive gesture and continued, "Well, I got home and developed the film. When I examined the negative, I saw something that I can't explain, so I printed it. I want to show it to you and see if you have any ideas. Go on, take a look."

George opened the folder and took out the 8x10 photo. He smiled as he saw his blurred image and shook his head a bit in embarrassment. The picture was in clear focus, with the exception of his blurred image as he walked towards the door. He raised his eyes to April, smiled, and said, "Is there anything in particular I should see... other than the fact that I ruined an otherwise beautiful photograph?"

April reached into her purse and pulled out the magnifying glass, handing it to George.

"Take a look at the reflections in the store window," she instructed him.

George took the glass and bent over the picture. Suddenly, he sat up straight in his chair, his eyes wide open. "Holy shit!" he exclaimed, and then he bent over the photo again. He looked at it intently for several moments, and then held out the magnifying glass to April. He looked at her and asked, "Did you see him?"

"That's just it. He wasn't there. Just you..." her voice trailed off a bit as she added, "I don't understand it."

George looked at her. "I've got an idea who it is," he said, "but I'm not sure what it is." He began to chew on a fingernail.

BY JOHN R. GREENE

April said forcefully, "Well, tell me who it is! Is it a ghost?"

George looked at her, momentarily confused, as she had broken his trail of thought. "A ghost? No... I don't think he's a ghost. I've seen him close up, and he's as real as you or me."

April was beginning to get upset. "That's nonsense. There's a clear reflection of someone who wasn't there... and that person's image is clear, as if he's standing still while you're moving. Now, what's going on?"

George looked at April and was silent for several seconds. Then, he said, "It's a long story."

"Well, go ahead," April urged him, "I'll sit quietly and listen."

George nodded and began to tell her of his experiences, starting with him losing his job. He didn't tell her every detail, but he covered the essentials. When he finished, he reached into his pocket and pulled out the tissue wrapped necklace. "This is the necklace I found in my pocket after dreaming of the boy on Mardi Gras day."

April's eyes widened as she looked at the small, delicate necklace. True to her word, she didn't interrupt him, but now she had to speak. "Don't get me wrong, but I don't know whether to believe you or not. There's something about you that makes me want to believe you, but this is a lot to take on."

He smiled at her and replied, "I swear that it's all true. I'm not sure what it means, but all of these things have happened. It's like the world has shifted on its axis. Things I thought I knew now don't seem to be important. Things that I didn't believe before are now as real to me as you. It's kind of like I'm surfing on a new wave of reality, if that makes any sense to you." Here, George gave a self-deprecating smile.

She couldn't resist smiling back at George. It felt like he was telling the truth, at least as far as he knew it. She took another sip from the cup and said, "OK, George. I guess I'll believe you. What I do know is that there is the reflection of a man who wasn't there in that widow. Now, tell me, do you think that the man in the window means to harm you? He certainly seems menacing."

"I don't really know, April," George replied. "I've seen that man around Mama Zulie. She won't have anything to do with him. If you had seen the way he looked at Jim and I, it wouldn't surprise me a bit if he wanted to hurt us. To tell you the truth, I'm kind of scared of him."

"Well, George, you'd better keep an eye out for this guy. Invisible or not, he doesn't look like someone to ignore. Do you have any explanation for how he can appear in the reflection and not be there?"

"Not really, April. No more than I can explain the way that those beads made their way into my pocket. When I ask Jim, or JC, they tell me that time in New Orleans is different than most other places on earth. That it can be touched, or experienced, as if it is present. I still think it's crazy, but I've felt it. I know it is unbelievable, but I'm forced to admit that there's something that's happening that doesn't fit with my understanding of the real world."

"You're right, George. My first thought is that you might be crazy, but I can't explain the man's reflection in the window. It's a fact in black and white. Do you know Sherlock Holmes' famous quote?"

"Not really. I read some of the stories,"

"I don't remember which of Doyle's stories it was, but the quote basically says that when you've eliminated all that is impossible, whatever remains must be the truth, even if it is improbable."

The door to the shop opened and a customer walked in. George rose and spent several minutes speaking with the customer, who was looking for a specific type of vintage Mont Blanc pen. After determining that there was no such pen in the shop, George directed the customer to another store down the street and returned to April.

"I'm sorry, April. "

"Think nothing of it, George. You're at work." She placed the empty coffee cup on the saucer and began to stand. "I wanted to come down and let you know about the man in the window. I never would have guessed at what you've told me. You're a decent guy, George. I wish you well. Thank you for the coffee, but I'd better be on my way." April sat the empty coffee cup on the saucer and began to stand.

"Wait, April!" George reached out to her and said, "I'm grateful to you for coming down and showing me the picture. Please forgive me if I'm being forward. I like talking to you. Would you consider going with me to La Petit Theater to catch the new play that's being performed tonight?"

April paused for a moment. He does seem like a nice guy. On impulse she replied, "Sure, George. That sounds like fun. We'll consider it reparation for ruining that picture," she added, and laughed a friendly, tinkling laugh that sounded like music to George's ears.

"Great!" George said. "It's a farce called The Amorous Adventures of Pamplemousse. It was written by Tennesse Williams."

April laughed again. "Perfect, George. What time does it start?"

"The curtain time is for 8. How about meeting me outside of the theater at 6:30 and we can go inside and have a drink before curtain time?"

"Sounds perfect, George, so I'll see you then. Now, I really do have to go." She stuck out her hand and George shook it, and then she turned and walked towards the door, which was suddenly opened by Tony. April startled as Tony stood there for a moment, but then he bowed and said, "Good afternoon, young lady."

George stepped up. "Tony, this is April Flowers. She's a friend of mine. April, this is Tony Gentile. He owns this store."

April stuck out her hand and they shook. "Pleased to meet you, Tony. Now, if you'll excuse me, I must be going." She smiled at Tony, and then looked at George and gave him a big grin. "See you tonight, George!" And then she walked out the door.

George and Tony watched her leave, and then Tony turned to George and said, "She's a very nice young lady, George, and a real beauty to boot."

George gave Tony a grin and a nod, and then he turned to continue his chores. He didn't realize that he was whistling as he worked.

George left the antique shop that afternoon at 4:30 so he could change clothes for the night. It was unusual for him to leave during business hours, but when he told Tony the reason, Tony insisted that he go home and get ready for his "big date." He went back to Dumaine Street and walked down the alley into the courtyard. Jim was sitting there reading a book. George walked up to him and asked, "What are you reading, Jim?"

Jim had been so engrossed in the work that he hadn't heard George open the gate and walk up to him. He looked up at George, and then smiled and held the book up with both hands so George could see the cover. On the cover, there was a picture of a pleasant-looking young man with long, dark hair and kindly eyes. The title of the book was *Autobiography of a Yogi*, and the young man, presumably the author, was named Paramhansa Yogananda.

Jim said, "You've got to read this book, George. It's fascinating. This guy is the real thing. It even helps explain some of the things that I've learned since moving here."

George laughed. "I'll be glad to read it when you're done, but right now, I've got to get dressed 'cuz I've got a date."

Jim opened his eyes wide. "Whoa! A date? Man, that's great! Who's the lucky girl?"

"Her name is April. I met her this morning when I ruined a picture she was taking. She came by the store this afternoon to show me the picture. It's weird! You can see everything clearly except me, 'cuz I walked right into the frame as she took it."

Jim interrupted him to ask, "What's weird about that?"

George continued, "That's not the weird part. There's a reflection in the window just above me that, I swear, shows that guy who pestered Mama Zulie . Tall, thin... he's a mean-looking man. It concerned April enough that she went out of her way to find me and show me the picture." George brightened and added, "She's really nice, Jim."

"Hmmmm... well, next time you see Anna or Mama Zulie, you'd better tell them about it. If there's one thing I've learned here, it's that there are no coincidences."

"Will do, amigo," George agreed. "Now, I've got to go and get dressed."

"OK. See you later," Jim said. George left him reading his book about the friendly young man from India who travelled to the United States to bring Eastern spiritual knowledge to the West.

23

PAMPLEMOUSSE

April 29, 1972

After George had finished taking a bath and getting dressed, he walked out into the courtyard, waved a quick goodbye to Jim—who was still engrossed in his book—walked by Astro's with a quick wave to JC, and made his way to Jackson Square. La Petit Theater was on St. Peter Street, across from the Cabildo and cattycorner from the square. It was housed in a beautiful, old, two-story, brick building with arched openings for doors, complete with handmade, antebellum hardware and an old, Spanish, wrought-iron balcony. There was an old streetlight on the corner where George stood, so that he'd be able to see April coming from any direction.

George spotted April as she walked towards him on Chartres Street, moving through the crowd of artists, young people, and tourists. She had on a flower-print sun dress and looked as nice as a cool breeze in Summer. He waved as she grew closer, and she responded with a smile and a wave before walking up to him. "Hi, George, been waiting long?"

"Not really, April. I got here about five minutes ago. Your timing is perfect. You feel like going in and getting a drink?"

"Why, certainly, sir!" April laughed.

He crooked his left arm, which she took in her right hand, and they turned and walked the short distance to the theater entrance. George bought two tickets at the box office, and he and April walked through the building to the small bar. He then turned to her and asked, "What's your pleasure?"

"I'll have a mimosa," she replied.

He turned to the bartender and said, "Two mimosas, please."

Drinks in hand, they wandered their way to the courtyard. While not as lush and beautiful as the courtyard that George's apartment looked out on, it was pleasantly green, with a small fountain in the center. Planters with benches around them, stand-alone benches, and some tables and chairs were placed tastefully around the courtyard. George and April found a planter bench that was empty and sat down. The courtyard wasn't very full yet, but had a few groups of people standing and sitting, talking and laughing. They each took a sip of their mimosa as they looked around the courtyard.

George nudged April and she turned towards him. "See that guy over there on the bench?" He gestured with the tip of his nose. She turned and saw an older man dressed in a white suit who was sitting alone on a bench. As she looked at him, two young men walked up to him. It was evident that an introduction was taking place. After a few moments, the older man held out his hand, and the young man who'd been introduced bowed over it and kissed the man's ring. April turned back to George. "That's Tennessee Williams?"

"Yes. JC says he keeps a place in the French Quarter. I've read that he says it's the only place in the United States that feels like home to him."

George leaned over and whispered, "Stella!" in April's ear. April's laugh was so pleasant that George had to keep himself from playing the fool just to hear it again.

They fell into an easy conversation, talking about their lives and experiences, and the time until curtain call passed quickly. They entered the theater, found good seats, and were entertained by the farce. The play was set in 18th-century France, and Pamplemousse, a simple-mind-ed stable boy, was repeatedly used and abused by a succession of older marchionesses and duchesses. The tremulous exclamations of "Oh, Pamplemousse!" in moments of passion never failed to bring laughter from the audience. On the whole, George found the play to be both silly and hilarious. April's wholehearted laughter convinced him that she agreed with him.

When the play finished, they walked out onto St. Peter Street and George asked April if she would like to get some beignets and coffee at Café Du Monde, to which she readily agreed. They sat outside on the patio and laughed as they sipped the rich coffee with chicory and covered themselves and their clothes in powdered sugar as they ate the tasty fried pastries. When they had finished, April said, "Well, George, I probably should be getting home."

"Did you take the Canal Bus?" he asked.

"Yeah."

"Then, I'll walk you to the stop and wait with you till you catch the bus."

"My, how chivalrous!" April laughed again.

They walked arm in arm down Decatur Street, passing several bars along the way. The sweet smell of oleander drifted on a slight, warm breeze as they walked towards Canal Street. They passed several groups of people walking their way. It seemed to George that the people they encountered were exceptionally happy. When they reached Canal Street, he crossed with April to the neutral ground and waited at the bus stop. All too quickly, a Canal Boulevard bus arrived and the door opened to accept passengers. April turned to George and said, "I really enjoyed the night, George."

"I did, too," he replied. "Maybe we can do something else sometime soon?"

She looked closely at him and said, "I'd like that. Give me a call." Then, she stood up on her tiptoes, kissed his cheek, and turned to get on the bus.

George stood dumbfounded for a moment, and then called out, "Hey, wait. I don't have your phone number."

She laughed, and George thought he heard the bells of heaven in the sound. "I'm in the phone book. Nobody else in this city with my name!" And, with that, she waved, the bus door closed, and the bus drove away. George stood there for another minute as a feeling of warmth and well-being coursed through his body. Then, he turned and began walking back to his apartment, whistling as he walked.

24

WEST GRUNCH ROAD

May 13, 1972

The next two weeks passed quickly. Both Jim and JC had told him that he was welcome to stay in the room above the courtyard for as long as he liked. When he'd asked how much the rent was, JC had waved the question away. George had tried to pursue it, but Jim had poked his arm and said, "Don't be impolite," so George had thanked JC and dropped the matter. He rose in the morning, went to work at Tony's shop, had his meals on the fly at different places ranging from Tujaque's, to the Central Grocery, to the Lucky Dog stand. In the evening, he and Jim would visit JC for a drink or two and some conversation, and he would end the evening with Jim, smoking a bit in the courtyard before he went to bed.

He had left the sale of the house to his cousin, a real estate agent. Gloria had agreed that the profit from the sale of the house would be split, after their divorce expenses were paid. George was fine with that. She'd also hired a lawyer and filed for an uncontested divorce, but the lawyer had informed her that Louisiana law required a reason for divorce, so she'd settled on charging George with abandonment. Once again, George was fine with that. When she'd asked what possessions he wanted from the house, he'd told her that he wasn't interested in anything except, perhaps, a couple of pictures. She had let him select the few photos that he wanted, and then promptly emptied the house.

He'd followed up his date with April by taking her to dinner the following weekend, and then, the following Wednesday, for an afternoon's excursion on the steamboat, *Natchez*. They'd both found that they enjoyed each other's company, and that conversation flowed easily between them. George appreciated the slow pace of their growing friendship. He'd resigned himself to the end of his relationship with Gloria. April, for her part, was happy to remain friends with George. She had no other romantic interests, and found him an interested and interesting companion.

The days were getting longer and longer, and there were a couple of hours of daylight left after George finished working at the antique store for the day. One afternoon, on returning from the store, George found Jim sitting in the courtyard and carefully examining a butterfly that was sipping nectar from a mandevilla bloom. The butterfly flew off as George approached, and Jim looked up.

Jim greeted him with, "What's happening, George?"

"Just got off of work, Jim. Sorry to have spooked your little friend!" George grinned.

"It's OK. I was just wondering what it would be like to fly around, light as the breeze." He raised both arms in a clumsy parody of butterfly wings.

George laughed and sat down on the bench next to Jim's chair. The last few weeks had reinvigorated George. Spending time with Jim, talking with JC, experiencing the slower pace of life in a French Quarter neighborhood, and working the new job had all combined to make him feel in control of his life once more. He gave Jim a grin and asked, "What would you like to do this afternoon?"

Jim cocked his head and looked up for a moment, and then asked, "You ever been to Grunch Road?"

George laughed. "You mean out by Little Woods? Sure, when I was dating."

Now, it was Jim's turn to laugh. "No, I mean West Grunch Road, out in Metairie by the lake."

"I've heard of it, but I've never really been out there," George said.

"Out a sight! Let's take a trip. There's a place I want to show you." With that, Jim began to wheel his chair towards the alley. George fell in behind him and began pushing the chair out of the gate, down the alley, and towards Jim's car. He had gotten used to what he called the "miracle of the parking place," so he knew where to wheel Jim's chair, and then he expertly helped Jim get into the car and stowed the chair in the back seat. He jumped into the passenger seat, and Jim started the engine and pulled out into the street.

George noticed two long-haired, bearded men who were standing across Dumaine Street. They didn't seem to be doing anything—just standing there looking around. George had noticed the pair a couple of other times in the preceding weeks, and thought they were some of the homeless hippies who'd taken up residence in the area. In his short experiences with the type, he found they were a bit of a nuisance with their panhandling, but represented no threat. One of the men looked directly at him as he and Jim drove away.

Jim quickly had the car onto the interstate and headed west towards Metairie. They saw the numerous crypts of the cemeteries near Metairie Road as they made their way towards the Bonnabel Boulevard exit. Jim turned north and drove towards the lake. When the pavement ended, a shell road crossed over the levee and ended in a small, shell parking lot that had a single, concrete, back-down boat ramp. There were some young boys, around twelve or so, fishing from the shore just west of the ramp. Jim parked the car and George hopped out and grabbed the wheelchair from the back seat, moving it into place next to the driver's seat after Jim opened the car door. Jim hopped onto the chair and said, "Good Claudius, pray, drive this chariot onto yon pavement!" He pointed clumsily in the direction of the abandoned blacktop of the Old Hammond Highway.

George smiled. "Hail Caesar, your wish is my command!" He pushed the chair over the bumpy shell parking lot and onto the slightly less bumpy blacktop, heading east. Scrub trees soon hid the parking lot as well as the levee to their right. They could still see the lake and its shoreline of concrete rip-rap to their left through the scrub growth. As they continued along the blacktop, the shoreline moved farther away and they soon came to a flat area of shells, with the scrub growth mostly cleared and some small trees spaced around it. Jim asked George to stop, which he did, and he turned the chair towards the small park-like area. It was a pleasing view—a thick shell bed with pleasantly spaced, small trees, all cleaned of paper, bottles, plastic, rope, and other debris, and leading down to the rip-rap where the small lake waves lapped. George looked around and noticed that there were a few decorative touches. Net floats wrapped in cordage hung from a few branches, and there was a small bench facing the water to catch the lake breeze.

George was amazed. "How did this get here, Jim?" he asked. "And how did you find out about it?"

Jim was quiet for a moment. He replied in a soft voice, "After my accident, when I was able to get around in my chair, I was a mess. I wanted to die, but my body wouldn't let me. So, I was determined to get just as fucked up as I could on whatever drugs I could find. Uppers, downers, psychedelics... I still didn't die. One day, I scored a big bag of brown smack—you know, heroin. I was determined to do it. I was going to inject the whole bag and OD. It seemed like the only way out of the hell that I was in."

George gave his head a small turn and a sympathetic, "mmmhhh," encouraging Jim to continue.

Jim continued, "Well, I got in my car and drove down to the Bonnabel boat launch. I thought I would sit in my car looking at the lake and do it. When I got there, there were some kids fishing, like I used to do when I was a kid. I sat and watched them catch a couple of hardheads and croakers, and decided I didn't want the kids to find me 'cuz it would probably scar them for life. So, I wrangled my chair out of the front passenger seat, onto the ground, and got in. It wasn't easy, but I wheeled myself over the shell parking lot and onto the blacktop. It was easier going then, so I kept rolling myself along for a ways, and then I ran into this." Here, Jim raised his curled hand and waved his arm towards the small park.

He continued, "I saw this, and thought that it was the perfect place to end it. It seemed so peaceful with the shade, the shells, and the blue water of the lake. I was getting ready to reach down into my pants and pull out my paraphernalia when I heard someone say hello. It scared the shit out of me. I looked over there, to the bench behind that tree."

George looked where Jim was pointing and noticed a second small bench, a short distance away.

"Anyway, there was an old guy walking up to me. He'd been sitting on the bench when I pulled up. He introduced himself as Gaston. I was mad at first, 'cuz he'd ruined my plan, but he was a nice, old guy—short, kind of stocky, with white hair that was a little too long. He wore an old, stained orange, zippered jumpsuit, and wiped his head with an old, blue handkerchief. We got to talking and I asked him about this park. He told me that he'd done it by himself. His wife Maxine had passed away several years before, and he found that time hung heavy on his hands. Both of them had grown up in New Orleans, and he said that his wife had particularly loved Lake Pontchartrain. They lived a few blocks from the lake, and used to come to this spot to look out over the water and talk. After she passed, he would find himself coming out here and wishing he could speak with her. As time went on, he began to clean up bits and pieces of the area here with all the shells. He cut down some brush and some trees, and slowly began cleaning up the area. He called it Maxine's Park. He put some of the flotsam that he found up in trees, and made a couple of small, wooden benches and put them here. So, he made this beautiful place, out of his grief for the love of his life. He saved my life that day, and I didn't even tell him. I came back a few times, and saw and spoke to Gaston a couple more times, but I haven't seen him for at least two years. Don't know if he's still around."

"Jim, do you remember the dream I told you that I had at Pop's Fountain?"

"Sure."

"The boy's father was named Gaston, and his mother's name was Maxine! That's too much of a coincidence. I wonder if..."

"There are no coincidences, George," Jim said solemnly.

"I'm glad he stopped you. Thank you for telling me." George said. "That's sad and happy at the same time! Did he bring in the shells?"

Jim laughed and looked around the ground for a minute, and then responded, "See that brownish-black thing on the shells there?"

George looked and saw the item that Jim was pointing towards. "Yeah, sure."

"Grab it and bring it to me."

George walked several steps onto the shell bed, bent over, and picked up the item. He turned it over in his hand. It was black, but had small, brownish-yellow and reddish blebs in it. It had obviously been wave-worn because there were no sharp edges. "Tar?" he guessed as he handed it to Jim.

Jim laughed again. "Nope, Indian pottery. I thought the same thing you did until Gaston set me straight. He told me that, when he was young, he used to ride the streetcar out to near here with his little boy. I think his name was Bobby..."

George interrupted, "That was the name of the little boy in my dream!"

Jim looked at George archly and said, "I told you, George, there are no coincidences. Anyway the natives had some mounds here. They became known as the Bonnabel Mounds. That was before they built the levee. The mounds disappeared when they built the levees and used the dirt in levee construction. Gaston said that the mounds were around 1500 years old. You see all these clam shells?"

"Yes."

"The shells are the remains of a *midden*, or garbage dump, that the Indians left. The lake is full of clams, and the Indians ate the shit out of them," Jim continued. "The shells last forever, or at least a long time, so you see that they ate them a lot."

"Wow! I never would have thought about pottery or an Indian site," George said. "There must be a million shells here. I wonder how long it took to get this many shells."

Jim smiled and replied, "I have no idea. Gaston told me about this place, and he never mentioned how long people lived here."

George suddenly felt a cold breeze and looked up. He was surprised to see a large, ominous black cloud directly overhead. The air smelled like rain and ozone. He grabbed the handles of the wheelchair and leaned down. "We'd better get out of here. It looks like a storm is coming." The wind began to pick up and the water took on a black color. George started pushing Jim back along the old, blacktopped road towards the parking lot. The wind got stronger and the scrub trees began to whip around. They were close to the point where they should have begun to see the parking lot when there was a sizzling *SNAP* of a lightning bolt, followed immediately by a thunderclap that both men could feel in their chests.

George let out a bellow and began to push the wheelchair at a jog. There came another *Snap—Boom*, and George stopped as a lightning bolt hit the blacktop ahead of them no more than fifty feet away. The lightning was so powerful that pieces of macadam were tossed into the air. Jim screamed at George over the sound of the wind, "Go back to the park!"

George whirled the chair around and began pushing in earnest, running as fast as he could go over the bumpy road. There was another bolt and boom, and a tree that was behind them, just off of the road, burst into flames. George kept running. The terror he felt combined with the exertion of pushing the wheelchair made his breath whistle with each inhale. The bolts came faster, and closer, as they neared the park. George pushed for all he was worth.

When they reached the shell glade, he turned the chair towards the lake. A gigantic bolt of lightning hit nearly at his feet and he was lifted into the air, his hands still on the wheelchair handles. The chair tipped, and he and Jim flew a dozen feet, landing on the shells within the grove. George kept his face down in the shells and put his hands over his ears. He was amazed he hadn't been electrocuted. He didn't bother to see how Jim was because he was so terrified of this unearthly barrage.

The lightning bolts sizzled and struck on the road, in the water—and everywhere, strangely, but within the small confines of Maxine's Park. The air was thick with the smell of ozone, and the wind whipped and howled. Large waves broke against the concrete rip-rap. George twisted his body and raised his face upwards to look. The trees whipped back and forth, presenting brief glimpses of the sky. George saw black clouds moving quickly in a circular motion around an even darker void, and had the impression of a huge, black mouth vomiting bolts of deadly lightning. He lowered his face to the shells and closed his eyes again as the cacophony continued, and then, as suddenly as it had begun, the crackle of lightning and booms of thunder ceased.

George raised his head and looked over to where Jim lay on the ground near his overturned wheelchair. He got up on his hands and knees, and gingerly crawled over the shells to Jim. Jim's face was turned away from George, but when he called out to him, Jim halfway raised himself with his arms and turned his head to look at George.

"Goddamit, Jim! You all right? What the hell was that?"

Jim's face was white with shock. "I skinned my hands, but otherwise I think I'm OK. I don't know what that was, George. I've never seen anything like that. It was almost as if that storm wanted to kill us."

George felt exactly the same way. He looked up into the sky, and saw that the dark cloud had almost completely disappeared. As he watched, the last remnants transformed into a fluffy, white cloud that gave no hint of the tempest that had just occurred. He got up, brushed himself off, and walked over to Jim's wheelchair. Righting it, he wheeled it over to Jim and locked the wheels. Then, he carefully moved in front of Jim, who had raised his upper body in a half push-up, and he passed his hands under Jim's arms until his elbows were snug against Jim's armpits, and raised Jim in one, smooth motion onto the chair. Once in the chair, Jim used his arms to position himself properly, and then he unzipped his pants. George was surprised to see that Jim had a catheter and urine bag, and turned away to afford Jim some privacy.

Jim gave an ironic laugh and said, "Don't worry, George. Anyone in my condition has given up all sense of decorum."

George looked down and something caught his eye. He bent over and picked up the thing that he'd seen in the shells. When he stood back up, he held it up and examined it. It was a thin, quartz crystal, about two inches long and a quarter of an inch in diameter. Clear and perfectly formed. He marveled at finding it and remembered the story that Caz had told that day at the lakefront. He turned and held it out to Jim, who had resolved his issues. Jim held out his hand and George dropped the crystal into his cupped palm. Jim bent over it and gave a whistle. "Son of a bitch! A quartz crystal! I guarantee that this didn't come from around here."

"You remember the story Caz told us that day at the lakefront?" George asked.

Jim looked up at him, smiled, and said, "You don't think that this is the same quartz crystal, do you?"

"I don't know what to think, Jim!" George replied. "There's been so many strange things happening to me since Gloria left that I'm not sure about anything."

Jim looked quizzically at George, and then held out his hand with the crystal. "You're not kidding, kiddo!" Jim said. "I think we should leave this here. What do you think?"

George took the crystal from Jim's cupped palm and dropped it near where he'd first seen it. Jim watched, said nothing, and then motioned with his head towards the old, abandoned, blacktop road. George got behind the wheelchair and carefully backed it out of the shells. It took some effort as the thin wheels sank into the shells, forcing George to lift the back of the chair to make any headway, but they finally reached the blacktop. Once on the road, he retraced their path towards the shell parking lot where the car had been left. When they arrived, they saw the young boys just getting out of Jim's car. The boys waved and walked up to the pair. One of the boys explained, "We're sorry, but that was a scary storm and we thought that your car would be the safest place for us to wait it out. We didn't take anything, I promise." The other boys nodded, serious expressions on their faces.

"Don't worry about it, boys. There isn't anything of value in old Nellie, so I know y'all didn't take anything. And, you're right, that was the best place for y'all to ride out that storm. Did you ever see so much lightning?" Jim asked as he smiled at the young boys.

"Jeesum, no, mister!" one of them replied. "That was the weirdest storm we've ever seen, and we come out here a lot!"

"Well," George said, "it's over now, and the lake should calm down in a little bit. Gonna be muddy, though, which makes the fishing tough."

The boy replied, "That's OK, mister. We've got some crab nets and some hardheads and croakers to bait them with. The rough water makes the crabs run." With that, the boys shouted their thanks as they ran back to their gear, which had been stacked close to the rip-rap.

George looked at Jim and chuckled. "Reminds me of me when I was their age."

Jim laughed and agreed, and George helped Jim back into his car, after which they left the lake and headed back to the French Quarter.

Jim drove them back to the Quarter, and George wasn't surprised to see the usual parking place open, waiting for their return. He helped Jim with the chair and then wheeled it up the alleyway. The door to Astro's was open, and JC stood there behind the bar polishing some glasses. George wheeled Jim up to the bar and grabbed a seat. By the time he'd sat down, Jim was telling JC about their experience on West Grunch Road.

"Jesus, JC! It's like the storm wanted to kill us. I've never seen so much lightning, and it was hitting all around us!"

"Yeah," George pitched in, "I looked up at one point and saw a dark black vortex spitting out lightning bolts!"

JC listened with a concerned look on his face. Then, he spoke, "Jim, George, this is very troubling. I'm afraid that you are both in danger."

"Danger!" George exclaimed. "From what?!"

"From something you don't fully understand," JC replied. "I want you both to promise me that you will tell me if anything else happens to you. I don't care how small a thing it is. If you feel threatened by anything, come and tell me." He reached out both his hands and placed them on Jim and George's shoulders. George felt his anxiety lesson at the touch.

"Sure thing, JC," they both promised.

"Now, how about a Dixie on the house?" JC gave them a gleaming smile.

"Now ya talkin'!" Jim replied in his best Yat accent, and two ice cold Dixie bottles were soon on the bar. George and Jim sat talking with JC for the better part of two hours, and, after the pink and blue sky darkened to black, they left, saying their goodbyes. They went into the courtyard, where Jim reached in his pants and pulled out the bag of weed and the small pipe; each took a couple of hits, and then they said good night and went into their respective apartments. Neither had thought to tell JC about the man in April's photograph.

25
THE BUST

May 14, 1972

A loud pounding on the door woke George up with a start. He wondered for an instant if he'd been dreaming, but then the insistent pounding began anew.

"Open up, it's the police!" a loud voice bellowed.

Outside, he could hear more pounding and other voices yelling. He swung his feet off the bed and bent over to grab his pants and put them on. Suddenly, the door flew open and several policemen burst in. George looked up, frozen bent over, noticing two men in suits and three others in uniform. "Up against the wall! Feet back and spread 'em!" one of the uniformed officers screamed at him. The suited men ran up to George before he could move, grabbed him by the elbows, and roughly threw him against the wall. As he stood there in his underwear, one uniformed policeman began going through the pockets in his pants while the other two began rifling through the room, throwing covers and mattress over as they performed a search.

The two suited policemen stood on either side of George. The one on his right spoke loudly to him, asking, "What's your name?"

George's throat was so dry from fear that he could hardly croak out, "George Santos, officer."

He'd turned to look at the officer as he responded, and the one on his left side roughly grabbed him by the neck and said, "Look at the wall, motherfucker. Don't move a muscle unless we tell you to."

He was frisked, which took no time at all since he was standing in his underwear, and then he just stood there facing the wall as the policemen tore up the room, clearly looking for something they were destined not to find. Outside, he could hear more commotion, and he heard Jim's voice clearly over the noise.

"Hey, you sons-a-bitches, I'm paralyzed. Get me my fucking wheelch..." The last word was swallowed in a loud *smack*. Then, George's attention was drawn back to his own situation as one of the suits grabbed him by the hair and pulled his head back.

"So, tell me, George Santos, where are the drugs?"

George swallowed. "I don't have any drugs!"

"Come on, asshole! We know there are drugs here. You'd better tell us where they are or you're going to be in a world of trouble."

"I told you, officer, I don't have any drugs!"

The suit looked up at the uniformed cops who were still tearing up the room. "Find anything?" he asked.

"No sir, not yet," grunted one of the cops as he pulled open the door to the large chiffarobe with the carved grapes and wheat stalks, and began searching the inside.

The search of the room took another ten minutes. When it was done, the policemen stood in a semicircle around George, who was still standing with his hands on the wall and staring straight ahead, in his underwear.

"Nothing, sir. We've been through the room with a fine-toothed comb. There are no drugs here," one of the uniformed cops reported.

The suit on George's right side said, "Very good. That's enough for now. Go out there and see if anyone needs help." Then, he told George, "All right, George, put on your clothes. We're going to take you to the station for questioning."

"Can I ask why, officer?" George asked as he walked to the side of the bed frame, given that the mattress and box spring were across the room, where the policemen had thrown them, and he grabbed his pants and put them on.

"Why do you think, smart ass?" the other suit demanded. "Suspicion of dealing drugs. Just 'cuz we didn't find any in your room doesn't mean you're not responsible for drugs we find elsewhere on this property."

For the first time since the loud pounding on his door, George had the time to think about the others. He felt sick to the stomach, and he paused as he reached down to pick up his shirt off the floor. Jim, Mama Zulie, JC, and Anna... what if...? *God,* he thought, *please, don't let anything happen to them.* He put his shirt on, slipped his feet into his shoes, and told the policemen, "I'm ready."

The nicer of the two policemen told him, "Turn around, George. We're going to have to cuff you." George complied as his hands were drawn behind his back and handcuffs were placed around his wrists. He was grateful they weren't placed too tightly.

"Come on, let's go," said the gruff officer as he grabbed George by his elbow and guided him to the door and down the stairs. When they opened the door to the courtyard and stepped out, George was blinded by flashlight beams directed at his face. There were about a dozen policemen, most in uniform, standing around the courtyard. "Goddamn it. Drop the lights, you're blinding me," the gruff detective said. The lights dropped down, and George could see that several of the policemen were standing around something that lay on the courtyard.

"Jim?!" George strangled out, and he took a step towards the motionless figure on the ground.

"Freeze!" the detective ordered him, grabbing George by both elbows and holding him tightly.

"What happened here?" asked the nicer of the two detectives.

"He tried to run away, and slipped and fell," said a uniformed cop from the shadows.

"He's paralyzed!" George shouted, only to have the detective let go of one elbow and grab him by his hair and push his chin down on his chest.

"Shut up, motherfucker, or it's going to be you lying on the ground," the detective said from between clenched teeth. The nicer of the two walked up to Jim's motionless figure, knelt on the ground, and placed two fingers on Jim's neck. He looked up at the uniformed policemen and said, "Call an ambulance. Now!"

George looked on helplessly. "Is he dead?" he asked. The kneeling dectective stood up and replied, "No, but he needs an ambulance."

The gruff detective grabbed George by the elbow and said, "Now, let's go!" He pushed George towards the courtyard door.

George stumbled and walked towards the door to the alleyway. As he walked, he heard one of the policemen behind him say, "These two were the only ones here. We searched all of the other rooms, but they don't look like they've been lived in for years." He had no idea what they were talking about.

The street outside the alleyway was blocked by several police cars with their lights flashing. George saw a pale face peering from behind some curtains in the second story of a building across the street. There were a couple of young men, who'd obviously been partying based on the unsteady way they stood, midway down the block. They stared at the scene, illuminated by the eerie, blue, flashing lights. The gruff detective steered George by his elbows towards a new, white Ford Galaxy 500. The car had a blue, flashing light set on its hood, above the driver's side. The nicer detective walked up to them and opened the rear door of the car, pushing George's head down as he got into the car so that he wouldn't bump it going in. Then, he shut the door. George sat on the seat gingerly, leaning forward so as not to hurt his hands and arms, which were behind him. His thoughts were whirling.... *How was Jim?*

Where were the others? What did that policeman mean, saying that the other apartments hadn't been lived in for a long time? What in the world is going to happen to me?

Both front doors opened at the same time, and the two plain-clothes detectives got into the front seat. The driver, the gruff detective, reached out the window and brought down the portable flashing light, turning it off in the process. The other detective turned half-around in his seat and threw his arm on the back of the other seat. He looked at George and asked, "Well, George, is there anything you want to tell us now?"

"I don't know what you mean, officer. What do you want me to tell you?" George responded.

"How about telling us who supplies the drugs?" the gruff detective demanded.

"Yeah, George, we can make it easy on you if you give us the information we want."

"What drugs?" George asked.

"Cut the crap, George," said the nicer one. "We've had someone in there who saw marijuana being smoked, and God knows what else. If you don't tell us what's going on, we'll throw the book at you. You're looking at a long time in Angola. The penalty for dealing marijuana is five to ten years. That's a long time to be cutting cane."

George leaned back in the seat carefully and closed his eyes. *Oh, shit*, he thought, *I'm in a lot of trouble.*

He suddenly sat up straight as he thought of Jim. "What happened to Jim?" he asked. "Is he OK?"

"He got what he deserved, if you ask me," said the gruff one.

This was followed by the other detective saying in a gentler tone, "They've called an ambulance. They'll take him to Charity. He was still breathing, and may just be knocked out."

"He shouldn't have resisted," said the first detective. Then, silence filled the car as it made its way to Parish Prison.

26

ABANDON HOPE

May 14, 1972

Parish Prison was a sprawling, darkly stained complex of concrete buildings next to the court building on the corner of Tulane Avenue and Broad Street. George's mind was spinning as the car entered a garage and stopped. The detectives opened the rear door and George got out. He hardly noticed as he was guided by his elbows down a series of corridors until they stopped at a door. When it opened, the room revealed was almost as small as a closet, with one chair behind a desk and another chair in front of the desk. They had George turn in front of them and then released him from the handcuffs. He immediately rubbed his wrists. When they told him to sit in the chair in front of the desk, he complied, and they both left the room and closed the door. Questions were racing in his mind as events of the last couple of hours flashed in his memory. He sat in silence for fifteen minutes. He took the time to survey the small room with the spartan desk. The top of the desk was bare, and there was a bit of veneer flaking off of one corner. George saw that someone had written graffiti on the edge of the desk closest to him. *"Abandon hope..."* was what it said.

The door opened and the nicer of the two detectives came in. He walked around the desk and sat behind it. Opening a drawer, he pulled out a pad and pen, and placed them in front of him. Then, he looked at

George. "George, I'm Detective Mark Hastert. I work in the narcotics division. I don't have to tell you that narcotics are a big problem in this city. It's coming in on boats, planes, trucks, and automobiles. The city is drowning in drugs. If you don't believe me, just take a look at the emergency room at Charity. People are overdosing left and right, most of them kids. Losing their lives for some cheap thrill 'cuz they're bored or feel they've got nothing better to do. LSD, PCP, Mescaline, uppers, downers, heroin... it's a fucking disaster!

"But you know better. You're 36 years old. You've got a job and a wife, or at least you used to. I've looked you up, and you've never been in any kind of trouble outside of a parking ticket. Now, you're mixed up with some drug gang and you're in a lot of trouble. My advice to you is to tell me everything you know, slowly and carefully. I'll keep your name out of it. You don't have to worry about being a rat or suffering any retribution."

There was a knock on the door, which opened to let a large, uniformed policeman come into the room. He looked at George and then walked to the other side of the desk. He bent and whispered something into Hastert's ear, which George couldn't make out. Hastert looked surprised, and lifted both hands as if to say, *"Well, then, OK."* He gave George a look, shook his head slightly, got up, and walked around the desk and headed out the door, to be followed by the uniformed cop.

George wondered what was happening. He didn't have long to wait, though, because the door opened. Sonny Lacoure walked into the room and closed the door behind him. George jumped up. "Sonny!" He reached out his hand, which Sonny took, and the two men shook.

"Jesus, George!" Sonny said after they'd both sat down. "What the shit have you gotten yourself into?"

"What do you mean, Sonny?" George asked.

"What do you mean, 'What do I mean?' Drugs, George, drugs. You've got yourself mixed up with some seriously big shit. These people you've been hanging out with have got the attention of some high-powered big-wigs. They're out to get rid of them. The chief is chompin' at the bit to throw the book at 'em and put 'em under the jail. I haven't seen him this worked up, ever. I don't know who's behind this, but they must be some powerful people to get the chief this worked up."

"Sonny, you've got this all wrong! Yeah, they smoke a little pot, but I haven't seen any other drugs. And, for that matter, not a whole lot of pot, either. These are some decent young people. I've been around them enough to see that they're not criminals. And Jim... my new friend that's in a wheelchair.... When they came and arrested us, they hurt him. I think they hurt him badly. I'm telling you, Sonny, they're wrong about these people!"

"Bullshit, George! You just haven't seen everything! You've only known these people for a few weeks. How can you know all about them?"

"I know about them just like I knew about you the first time I met you, Sonny," George said, looking straight at Sonny. "I'm telling you, they're decent people!"

"Then, what about the drugs?" Sonny asked, his eyebrows arching.

"I'm telling you, Sonny. The only thing I saw was some pot smoking. No other drugs. Nothing! I don't know what you're hearing, but if it's about hard drugs, than it's wrong!"

"The word is that they're a major heroin-smuggling operation. They may be responsible for all of the smack that's out on the street."

"I'm telling you, Sonny," George said earnestly, "that's bullshit! These people have nothing to do with it. Shit, I've been around them for long enough to tell if they're decent or not, and I'm telling you that they are."

Sonny looked at George for a full five seconds. Then, he dropped his gaze and looked at his own hands for a moment before looking George in the eye. "OK, George. I've known you since Christ was a corporal, and I've never known you to lie. Not knowingly. And, for that matter, you've always been a pretty good judge of character... so, if you say these people are small-time druggies, I have to believe you. But why would the chief have such a hard-on for them?"

George felt some relief for the first time since he'd been woken. "I have no idea, Sonny. Now, what's going to happen to me?"

Sonny replied, "You need to tell the detective everything that you know about these people. Just tell the truth. If they really are just small-time potheads, then you've got nothing to worry about. I spoke with some of my uniformed buddies and they told me that the crippled guy had about a quarter-ounce of pot in his room, and nothing else was found. That's simple possession, and it's also his problem, not yours. You should be out of here by early morning."

"Have you heard anything about Jim? That's his name. He really is a good guy, Sonny. You'd like him. Just a Yat who got hurt driving too fast. Not really any different than you or me."

"Umpf," Sonny grunted. "Well, I heard they were bringing him to Charity. I don't know how badly he's hurt. Won't do nobody any good if he's hurt bad. Well, I've got to go now, George. I'll tell Gloria that you're OK." And, with that, Sonny held out his hand and said, "Oh... and, George.... No hard feelings, eh?"

George looked at Sonny, then down at his outstretched hand before raising his hand to shake. "Naw, Sonny. I can't say that I was very happy about it, but you're my best friend, and... I guess, if Gloria had to leave me for somebody else, I'd rather it was you."

They shook hands, and Sonny walked out of the small room.

A minute or so later, Mark Hastert walked back into the room and sat down behind the desk. He opened a drawer and took out a yellow notebook, and then reached into his shirt pocket and grabbed a ballpoint pen. George could see that it was advertising Fitzgerald's, a seafood restaurant built on pilings over Lake Pontchartrain down at the West

End. He opened the notebook to a blank sheet of paper and poised the point of the pen over the blank sheet. Looking up at George, he asked, "How long have you known Sonny?"

"We've been best friends since we were kids."

"Well, you're lucky to have him for a friend. He's a good cop. A really good cop... and he's vouched for you as a good guy. So, now, George, why don't you tell me about the people that you've been associating with?"

George replied, "It's like this, detective. I've seen a little bit of marijuana being smoked there, but no hard drugs. I swear."

"Un huh," Hastert grunted as he wrote, "and who have you seen with the marijuana?"

"Mostly Jim. In fact, just Jim. I haven't seen Anna or the twins, Caz and Paul, with any pot there. Not JC, either. I've only seen him behind the bar—you know, at Astro's. And I don't even think that Mama Zulie smokes pot."

"Whoa there!" Hastert exclaimed. "Take it easy! Let's go through this one piece at a time. Now, tell me who lives in the apartments around the courtyard."

George told him about Mama Zulie, Jim, and Anna, and then about the twins and JC. He told the detective almost everything that he could remember about his experiences over the last few weeks, leaving out those parts that he thought would be unbelievable. He was thinking quickly, as the adrenaline was still strong in his system, and decided that the experiences that he'd thought supernatural wouldn't help either him or his friends.

After an hour or so of questioning, the detective leaned back in his chair, looked at George, and said, "So, that's the story, George? Three other people—Anna, Jim, and this Mama Zulie—live in the apartments around the courtyard?"

"That's right, detective."

"And the only drugs you've seen are small amounts of marijuana?"

"Yes, sir."

"Well, I've got to tell you that I don't think you're telling me the whole story," the detective said as he leaned forward and looked hard at George.

"I promise, that's the whole story," George replied.

"Well, George, then tell me why we only found signs of two apartments being occupied—yours and Jim's. All of the other apartments were empty, dilapidated and covered in years' worth of dust."

George was incredulous. "That can't be. Jim and I had breakfast with Mama Zulie in her apartment yesterday morning. There was furniture and art all over the place."

"It's the truth, George. So, can you see why I have to believe that you're lying to me?"

George stared at the detective and shook his head. "I'm telling you the truth. I swear it."

The detective looked at George for a moment, and then he lowered his eyes to write something in the notebook. When he was done writing, he looked up and said, "I can't figure you out, George. I feel like you're telling me the truth, but I saw those apartments with my own two eyes, so I know you're not. All I can figure is that you were hallucinating, which means that there were some hard drugs on the premises. You've gotten yourself in over your head, George. I think you're heading down a bad path, but since we didn't find any drugs on or near you, and since your pal Sonny has vouched for you, we're going to let you go. Let me give you some advice, though. If I were you, I'd stay away from those people, George. There are some very powerful people who are going to see to it that these people are caught and punished. You don't want to be around when that happens. Now, sit tight and you'll be able to leave as soon as your paperwork is processed."

George cleared his throat and asked, "Excuse me, can you tell me how Jim is?"

Hastert had gotten up from the desk. Now, he paused as he looked down at George, and said, "He's at Charity. I don't know anything else."

"Thank you, detective," George said as the detective opened and then walked out the door.

It took an hour, but finally George found himself outside of Parish Prison and on the street. They'd given him back his wallet, and he'd looked inside of it and seen that what money he'd had remained. The street was dark, and there were halos of insects flittering and hovering around every street light, as if they were attempting to darken the lights through sheer strength of numbers. He began walking down Tulane Avenue towards downtown. It didn't take very long before he found himself outside of Forstahl Furniture, his old place of employment. As he walked under the neon sign that he thought was so pretty, he looked in at the furniture inside. Even though he knew every inch of the place, he felt as if he was separated from it by a gulf rather than a window. He thought of his former boss. *Little prick*, he thought with a grimace, and continued walking down Tulane towards Charity Hospital.

The night seemed to get darker as he walked. George began to feel a little nervous, and he looked around. The cars parked along the sides of the street seemed to just be dark shadows, and the light of the streetlights struggled to pierce the darkness. Each streetlight was clouded by myriad flying insects, and George could hear a low-pitched, buzzing noise as he continued walking. He noticed that there were no cars travelling down Tulane. He hunched his shoulders and put his hands in his pockets as he quickened his pace, mentally chiding himself for being nervous. He walked by a particularly dark business entrance nearly equidistant between two streetlights, and was startled to sense, rather than see, movement in the blackness. He unconsciously took his hands out of his pockets and began to raise them, palms out, as if to fend off something as he turned his head towards the entrance. The buzzing noise got louder as a figure emerged from the blackness into the dark, shadowed street. George stopped, frozen with a kind of fascinated terror. He couldn't see the person clearly as they slowly shuffled towards him. The buzzing noise increased, and in a deep, interior part of his lizard brain, he identified it as the sound of uncounted, chitinous insect parts rubbing together.

The indistinct figure shambled closer, and George understood why he was unable to clearly view the person. What he'd thought of as a human being, a robber, he could now see was a writhing mass of insects—constantly moving, wings buzzing, with their carapaces sliding across each other. The mass had an amorphous, humanoid form, which moved and flowed like water as the squirming multitude shambled closer to him. George almost fell as adrenaline surged through his system, fighting with the paralysis that gripped him.

Hssssssrrrrrzzzzz.... The sound emanated from the roiling mass. The gorge rose in his throat as the mass slowly flowed closer to him. He closed his eyes....

The sound of a car's horn broke his paralysis. He opened his eyes and watched as the flowing mass of insects disbanded into a cloud that broke apart to fly in all directions. A large, flying cockroach landed on the bridge of his nose and he swiped it away and down with his right hand. The horn honked a second time and George turned towards the street. He saw his Mustang pulled up to the curb. The light was on inside, and Anna was beckoning to him from the driver's seat.

George made a guttural sound and lunged to open the passenger door. He jumped inside and closed the door and yelled, "Go, GO!"

Anna reached over and put her hand on his shoulder. The touch of her hand felt warm through his shirt.

"It's over, George. It's all right. You're safe now," she said.

George was breathing heavily, but her touch and calm words brought him back from the madness of the last few minutes. He leaned back in the seat as Anna pulled out into the street. A quiet mist had begun to settle down in the still night. They drove slowly down Tulane. George calmed as they drove on in silence. He turned and looked at Anna. She had a visible golden aura glowing around her, making her look slightly blurry. He saw no other cars moving on Tulane in either direction and, turning around in the seat, saw no cars behind them, either. He looked at Anna and said, "Thank you, Anna. Can you tell me what just happened?"

She pulled up at a stoplight and turned towards him. The golden aura gleamed stronger. She touched his arm and said, "I can't explain it to you, George, because you wouldn't understand. Or, you wouldn't believe it."

"Try me," he said as he looked at Anna. "Please."

She gave a slight shake of her head and said, "George, Jim has been badly injured. He's in the hospital now. Would you like to come see him with me?"

The memories of the night came back into George's mind with the intensity of a bursting dam. The police, Jim, Sonny, the story of the empty apartments... it all rushed into his mind at once.

"Oh my God! Jim! They said he's at Charity and no one could tell me how he was. They said that no one else lived there! Jesus Christ! What's happening?" George put his head in his hands and rubbed his eyes hard. Anna remained quiet. In a moment, George raised his head from his hands and told her, "Yes, Anna. I'd like to see Jim."

She reached out and patted his arm before she spoke. "I thought you'd like to." They had reached the front of Charity Hospital now. The large cluster of block-like buildings loomed a short distance back from the street. Light from many windows made halos in the mist that had settled over the night. Anna drove around the block and parked in a spot near the emergency room entrance.

They got out of the Mustang into the misty night and George noticed that Anna's golden aura had diminished until it was barely noticeable. They walked up to the emergency room door, opened it, and walked in. The light was harsh and white. A stained, tile walkway led to a large waiting room containing about twenty people. Some of the people were holding bloody cloths to arms or faces. Others held their head in their hands with their elbows on their knees. In the corner, two small children were sleeping on the floor.

Anna took George's hand and walked through a double door in the back of the waiting room. A nurse who was sitting at a desk nearby paid no attention to them. They walked down a corridor and, as they walked, they passed by several gurneys that held people who were mostly men and mostly black. They also paid no attention to George and Anna. One gurney held an old black man who moaned as he clutched his chest. When they passed his gurney, he looked at Anna and said, "Help me... please."

Anna stopped. She let go of George's hand and stood over the gurney, and laid her hand on the man's chest, over his hand. She took her other hand and laid it on the man's forehead. The man stopped moaning, and his breathing slowed. He looked into Anna's eyes, first with wide-eyed amazement and then with a kind of familiarity. His eyelids slowly lowered until his eyes were closed and his breathing became regular. He appeared to be asleep. Anna leaned over and brushed her lips over the man's forehead.

She turned back to George and took his hand. "Come on, we don't have much time," she said, and continued walking down the corridor until they came to a bank of elevators. One of the elevator doors opened as they arrived and they walked right in. Anna pressed the button for the 7th floor. They arrived at the floor and turned right out of the elevator and walked past the nurses' station. Three nurses and two short-coated interns were looking at charts and talking to one another. No one paid any attention to George and Anna. They walked up to another double door. Above the door was a sign that read, *CCU*. They opened the door and walked in.

The room smelled of disinfectant and, just slightly, of urine. There were curved metal bars hanging from the ceiling. Curtains hung from these bars, delineating spaces where patients were lying in their beds. Signs warning of fire danger from oxygen use were posted in several places. Most of the curtains were drawn closed on the individual spaces, but some were open, and they could see empty hospital beds and associated IV stands and heart monitors.

There were several nurses and orderlies moving in and out of different 'rooms' as they took care of the needs of the critically ill patients. Once again, like earlier, no one took notice of George and Anna. After his recent experience, it didn't occur to George to question their stealthy entrance. Anna took George's hand and led him to the end of the room, where a gray-painted, metal door stood closed. She opened the door and they both walked in.

The room was very small, about 8 by 10 feet. There was a hospital bed centered on the far wall with the railings up. George heard a clear, pneumatic hiss followed by a low, muffled *tic, toc* which was, in turn, followed by the pneumatic hiss. George heard all of this, but his mind was solely focused on what his eyes beheld. There on the bed, dressed in a hospital gown and covered with a thin, blue blanket, lay Jim. He lay on his back and his eyes were held closed with clear tape. His thin arms were outside of the blanket, lying motionless by his sides. There was an IV line going into his right arm and a series of wire leads coming from the top of his hospital gown to a cardiac monitor, whose screen was black with a glowing green line that showed an irregular series of peaks and valleys. George saw all of this, but what held his immediate focus was the tube coming from an incision at the bottom of Jim's throat, and which was attached to a bulky machine next to the head of the bed.

George's eyes filled with tears and he felt a lump growing in his throat. He looked down at his hand, still holding Anna's. When he looked up, he turned his gaze towards Anna and saw her looking at him with a gentle and loving smile. The tears brimmed over and began trailing down his cheeks. He swallowed and found his voice, asking, "Can you help him?"

"Poor George," Anna said gently. "Your love for your friend proves the spark that I saw in you that night in Astro's." She turned her head and looked at Jim. The machine kept making the regular *hiss... tic, toc....* She let go of George's hand and reached down to the foot of the bed, where Jim's feet lay under the thin blanket. She stroked Jim's right foot gently for several seconds. George looked up to the cardiac monitor with its irregular, green line. He heard Anna begin to sing softly in some language that he had never heard before. She sang a beautiful, lilting melody full of hope and sadness. The room began to fade, and George's senses became confused. He could hear green forests and snow-covered mountain peaks. He could see the sweet scent of wildflowers in a valley. The touch of white clouds tasted slightly of earth, and the taste of a clear stream sounded like trumpets blown from far away. Lastly, and most strongly, the smell of love lightly caressed his cheek.

George was brought back to the room by a piercing whine coming from the cardiac monitor. He looked up and saw that the glowing green line with the irregular peaks and valleys had become stark and flat. He couldn't move for a moment, and then Anna took his hand and led him to a corner of the room. She held his left hand in hers, and wrapped her right arm around his shoulders as George's tears began to flow again.

The door burst open and a nurse ran into the room, followed by an intern pushing a machine on a cart. George watched as they threw off the blanket and pulled off Jim's hospital gown. The intern rubbed two paddles together and called *"Clear!"* before placing them on Jim's chest. The charge went through Jim's body. His legs raised into the air. George looked at the monitor. The nurse had shut off the alarm, but the line remained flat.

"Again!" the intern said. "Clear!" Another jolt to Jim's body got the same effect, to no avail.

"Again! Clear!" And a third jolt was administered. The line remained flat. All the while, the pneumatic *hisss... tic, toc* continued and Jim's chest raised and lowered. "That's enough," the intern said finally, setting the paddles back on the machine. "Let's call it." The intern reached over and turned off the ventilator, and then took the stethoscope that he'd been wearing around his neck and listened for a heartbeat.

"Sarah, please make a note. Time of death was..." here, he looked at a wristwatch that he was wearing, "4:55 a.m." The nurse walked to the foot of the bed and picked up a chart that was kept there. She took a pen and wrote on the chart, and then replaced it. While she did this, the intern took the blanket and placed it over Jim's emaciated body, drawing it up to his chin. Then, he and the nurse stood at the foot of the bed.

"Poor guy," the intern said.

"What happened?" the nurse asked.

"I'm not sure. The police brought him in like this. One of them said he was resisting arrest, but I don't see how somebody that was in his shape could put up much resistance."

"Poor guy," the nurse rejoined, and then they both walked out of the room.

George and Anna stood in the corner, unseen. George had sobbed, unheard, through the episode. He'd gotten control of his grief now and was wiping his eyes with his hands as more tears fell to his cheeks.

Anna let go of George and walked up to Jim. She bent over his body and placed a long, slow kiss on his forehead. George heard her whisper some words, but couldn't make out what she said. She was still leaning over his body when she waved George over to her. George walked up and looked down at Jim's face. His features had relaxed, but missing was that ineffable something that spoke of life. "He looks different," George whispered to Anna.

"The spark has moved on," she replied, brushing Jim's golden locks back from his forehead. "His spark burned so brightly that the loss of it is more evident than in many."

Then, she straightened up and looked at George. "It's time for us to go." He took one last look at his friend, wiped away a tear, and turned to follow her. They retraced their steps through the CCU and the hospital just like before, with no one paying them any mind. When they arrived outside of the emergency room, the mist had settled even more thickly. They climbed into the Mustang and pulled out onto the street. Anna was again surrounded by the golden glow. She said, "I'm going to take you where you can spend the night in safety."

He replied, "I don't know when I'll be able to get to sleep." He looked out the windshield at the deepening fog. The lights were points within large, fuzzy halos, like a Van Gogh painting, and everything else was indistinct. George wondered how Anna could see well enough to drive.

He looked at her, and she said, "You need to go to sleep now, George."

Before he could tell her again that too much had happened for him to sleep, he felt his eyelids closing and a yawn escaped his lips. His last thought was, *I'm not sleepy....*

27
NOT WHERE, BUT WHEN

May 14, 12,072 B.C.

When George awoke, he opened his eyes to faint light. He saw he was in a dimly lit area. The walls were made of interwoven branches with some sort of mortar filling in the spaces. He looked up and saw that the ceiling of the structure was thatch, carefully placed over branches which went from the top of the wall to a hole in the center of the ceiling. There was a shaft of bright sunlight that came from the hole in the roof and, following it down, terminated in a small fire pit with some smoldering embers. He watched the wisps of smoke snake up the bright beam of sunlight and out of the roof, and realized that he was lying on some furs, under some sort of fur cover, naked. He looked to his side and saw a woman's bare shoulder and back. The strawberry-blonde hair told him it was Anna. He could hear a low, distant roar that he couldn't identify. He lay there quietly, and tried to remember the events of the past night. His breath caught at the lump in his throat as he thought of Jim. Tears welled up in his eyes, and he reached up to wipe them away. He could recall everything up to the moment he and Anna had left Charity Hospital. Try as he might, he couldn't recall how he'd ended up here, wherever it was, with Anna.

He felt Anna turn towards him, and moved his head to look at her. She was beautiful, greeting his attention with a tender smile. He reached up and moved a lock of her strawberry-blonde hair away from her eyes.

"Good morning, George," she said.

"Morning.... Jim's gone, isn't he, Anna?"

"Yes, George, he's gone."

Tears spilled from George's eyes. He reached up to wipe them away and fought the lump in his throat to ask, "Where are we, Anna?"

"Not so much where, George... as when," she replied. "Go ahead, take a look around."

He pushed off the cover, stood, and walked to an opening in the wall that was covered by a large piece of soft, tan leather. He pulled the leather aside and looked outside. The structure was in a clearing of the forest. There were other small structures like the one he and Anna were in. Enormous trees lined the edges of the clearing, and an early morning mist softened the ground. He turned to Anna and asked, "What do you mean 'when'?"

She sat up, and the dark fur cover fell off of her and gathered at her lap. George felt his breath catch at her golden beauty. "We're near the place that you know as Houma, George, but about 12,000 years before you were born. I had to bring you to a place of safety. You can only stay for a short time."

"So it's real. The glimpses I've been getting of different times, they've all been real."

He looked at her for another moment, and then turned back towards the opening. As he watched, a large man with bronzed skin and long, dark hair held back by a leather string wrapped around his head walked from of the other structures. He looked at George and placed a hand to his heart by way of greeting before walking through the small village into the forest. George responded to the man with a brief wave, and then watched the man disappear into the forest before he turned and let the leather covering fall back down. When he turned back towards the bed, Anna had risen and was nearly fully clothed. She held his clothes in her hand and raised them towards him, as a clear suggestion that it was time to get dressed. He took the clothes from her and put them on slowly. When he was finished, he looked up at her and asked, "What's next?"

She sat next to him and took his hand in hers. "You cannot stay here, George. We must go back to your time, and soon."

"Can I take a look around before we leave?" he asked.

A look of mild annoyance crossed her face, but it was quickly replaced by a kind smile. "Sure, George, it's not every day that a guy can see how the world looked in the past. Come with me."

Anna walked past George and out of the opening. He followed quickly. It was early morning, and there was no one to be seen stirring. George could now see that there were a total of five small structures. Smoke rose from all of them, suggesting that morning fires had already been stoked. Anna took George's hand and walked with him. A fairly clear trail led into the forest, and they followed it. It was a crisp, cool morning, feeling more like Fall than late Spring. George remarked on this to Anna, to which she responded, "There are glaciers all the way down to Illinois at this time, George. It doesn't get nearly as hot now as it will during your time."

They continued walking down the trail. George was astounded at the size of the trees they walked amongst. Their topmost branches were lost to sight, and the canopy made a covering of the entire area like some green cathedral. The forest floor was lit with diffuse light. There was not a great deal of brush, with the exception of an occasional area where one of the forest giants had fallen and allowed the sunlight to penetrate to the forest floor. These areas were a vibrant green with growth. As they walked, the roar that George had noticed in the village became louder. They suddenly came upon an area where the large trees stopped and George looked out on a scene that was alien to his eyes. Before him was a gigantic river's floodplain. Braided streams of rushing water filled his vision. The spaces between the braided streams were filled with cobbles and pebbles, some as big as his fist. It seemed to him that the braided riverbed was at least two miles across, and he could see hundreds of large, rushing rivulets in the bed.

He turned to Anna and asked, "What is this? And what are all of these rocks? There aren't any rocks south of Lake Pontchartrain!"

Anna laughed a clear, happy laugh. "George, George," she said after she had stopped laughing, "this is the course of the ancestral Mississippi River. During this time, the level of the Gulf of Mexico is 150 feet lower than it is in your time. That means that the coastline is further away from here than it is from the north shore of Lake Pontchartrain during your time. This time is a little dryer than your time, and some of the Mississippi River's water is still captured by what you know as the Sabine River. In fact, the band that built the village where we stayed are from that area. They traveled here over the course of several years. They hunt the mastodon, giant sloth, and camel, and as the large game became scarcer they moved further east. Here, there are still some of the large game left." And with that statement, she directed George's attention upriver. He looked, and was amazed to see a large, hairy elephant with long, slightly curved tusks about 500 yards away. The mastodon was amazingly light on its feet as it picked its way around and through the various braided streams on its way across the wide floodplain.

George could feel that his mouth had dropped open, and he quickly closed it. He turned to Anna and said, "It's magnificent!"

"Yes, George. It is magnificent!"

"How do they hunt them, Anna?" George felt he had to ask.

"With spears tipped with intricately knapped, stone spearheads. Here, let me show you." Anna reached into the air, and suddenly she held a large spear point in her hand. She gave it to George, who held it in his own hand. It was about five inches long, made of a honey-colored chert. George held it up and could see that the chert was translucent along the edges of the spear point. It had been very finely knapped, making it perfectly symmetrical, with numerous flake scars being evident on both sides. The edges had been retouched, creating a fine series of very small flake scars around the entire outer edge of the point. The outer edge of the point extended a short way further down than the center of the point, making a slightly concave base. Lastly, on both sides of the point, a small, central channel was flaked off for about an inch from the base.

George gave the point back to Anna and said, "That is beautifully done. I can see that whoever made it knew what they were doing, and took their time doing it."

Anna laughed again. "Yes, George, there are very great artists among these people, both in working with stone and in other forms. Now, it is time for us to leave." She took his hand.

"OK," he replied, lifting her hand and kissing it, "whatever you say."

She smiled at him. "I need you to lie down on the ground."

He cocked his head quizzically. "On the ground?"

Her laugh was musical. "You're the worst! Just lie down and close your eyes."

He did as he was told, and soon heard Anna singing in a soft, beautiful voice. He couldn't understand the words, if words they were, but the lilting tune and her beautiful, throaty voice lifted him like a leaf on a Spring breeze. He could feel the cool touch of a waterfall's mist and smell the rich earth in her voice. Time ceased to have meaning as his consciousness was fully captured by her voice. It lifted and moved him in tempo with the song as it grew faster and then slower until, finally, it trailed off in a minor key.

28
GRIEF, AND
AN EXPLANATION

May 14, 1972

G eorge opened his eyes and saw that he was back in his room above the courtyard in the French Quarter. He lay on the bed under the cover, and all signs of the night's disturbance had been erased. Everything was in its place. He looked around for Anna, but there was no sign of her. When he sat up in bed, he found that he was fully clothed, and when he looked to the side of the bed, he saw that his shoes were neatly placed where he could get to them on arising.

"Anna?" he called. There was no answer. He got out of the bed and walked to the bathroom. No sign of Anna there. He walked back to the bed and put on his shoes. He looked out of the window into the courtyard. There was no sign of anyone around. He thought, "Was it a dream? No... it can't have been." Once again, the thought of Jim's passing brought tears to his eyes and a lump to his throat.

He walked down the stairs and opened the door to the courtyard. The lush green plants and the colorful flowers reminded him of the place that he'd been with Anna what felt like a short time before, and he felt very confused. The light suggested that it was either early morning or late afternoon, but the warmth made him fairly confident that it was afternoon. He looked across the courtyard at the door to

Jim's room, and brought his hand up to his forehead in an unconscious salute. Then, he walked across the courtyard to the gate and opened it. When he did, he could see that Astro's door was open. He walked to the door and looked in. JC was standing behind the bar, cleaning a glass and looking in his direction.

"Come in, George," he said gently.

"JC! Jim..." George began.

"I know all about it, George. Here, sit down." And he patted the bar in front of a stool across from where he stood cleaning.

George sat down and looked at JC. His eyes were hidden by the dark sunglasses, but his smile was gentle and understanding. George put his elbows on the bar, placed his head in his hands, and began to weep. JC stood there for a moment, and then said, "Go ahead and cry for your friend, George. He was worth crying over." He reached over the bar and squeezed George's shoulder.

George wept, his body wracked by silent sobs, for several minutes. When he raised his eyes from his hands, he saw that JC had placed a cold Dixie beer in front of him. He looked at JC through his tears, whispered a quick thanks, and took a long sip from the cold brew.

"It's unreal, JC," George sighed.

"I know, George," JC replied, "it's a lot to happen in a very short period of time, but I need to give you a warning." George looked up quizzically. JC continued, "There are powers at work here that you do not understand... powers not of this universe. They fill in the spaces between. Doing so, they operate despite the best intentions of others. You must assume that they control authority. They will not hesitate to kill you, should they find you in their way."

"But, JC, what are they after? Why kill Jim? He didn't do anything to anyone. It's not fair. IT'S NOT FAIR!

"This is a struggle that has been going on for a long, long time. Before the pyramids, before America was populated, and for that matter, before North America was a recognizable continent or earth was a recognizable planet."

"What? Before earth?! Please, JC. I don't understand. Somehow you all can move through time. I get that, but I don't understand how, or even what you are. Are you gods?"

"No, George, we are not gods. Nor are we people. We exist between the realities. George, I'll do my best to explain it to you, at Anna's request. Listen to me. In this universe, there are two basic, opposing principles. Let's call them, for the sake of argument, the principles of creation and destruction. The two principles are intrinsically opposed to each other. One builds up; the other tears down. One creates; the other destroys. One celebrates life; the other revels in death. It goes on and on, and may best be understood as two sides of the same hand. Humans have understood these principals instinctively since their earliest days of cognition. Gods and demons, light and dark, yang and yin, God and Satan, good and evil... there are many examples. By having one, you define the other.

"These fundamental principles manifest themselves in many ways, and it is far too complicated to express in words. Suffice it to say that the dynamic interplay between these opposing forces is a defining condition of this universe, and all universes."

"I'm not sure that I understand you, JC," George said as he scratched his head.

"Let me try another way." JC smiled at George and went on, "Consider the difference of scale when looking at the stars versus looking at the earth."

"OK."

"Now, consider looking at areas on the earth and the differences there. There's a large difference in the details of observation when comparing, say, a city block to a planet."

"Yeah... I agree," George said, a little quizzically.

"Now, look at a single house in that block. People, pets, plants, bugs, furniture, pictures, et cetera. Smaller details come into clearer focus because of the closer focus of the investigation."

"Uh, OK," George said, though he didn't sound convinced.

"Keep following me, George." JC leaned over the counter. "Now, take a spot on the countertop in the kitchen of that house. Examine it under a microscope. What seems like a smooth surface is shown to be rugged, filled with tiny organisms of varying sizes that are invisible to the naked eye."

George now put his hands on either side of his head.

"Almost there, George." JC gave a short laugh. "Now, take the most powerful electron microscope and focus on a small part of the microscopic scene. The scale is getting larger and larger as we look at smaller and smaller things. Now, move into the atomic scale, and complexity is still with us. Even smaller, into the subatomic scale, and there is still an inescapable complexity of particles interacting with each other."

George interjected here, "Enough, JC, I'm getting a headache thinking about this stuff."

JC laughed again. "OK, George. Now, here's the punch line. What do you suppose is the one thing that links everything together, from the stars to the smallest subatomic particle?"

George took a big swallow of his beer and said in a small voice, "I give... what?"

JC slapped the bar with the flat of his hand and said, "Interaction! Everything in this material universe, and every other universe, interacts with everything else. And this interaction occurs in a number of different ways. Gravity, space, time—they're all meaningless without the interaction of all parts of all of the universes. Here and there, now and then, are meaningless without interaction. The primal force is interaction, from which all other properties derive meaning. That is our playground. We aren't gods. We just are. No different from you in that sense."

George looked at JC, and then laid his head on the bar, covering it with a small cocktail napkin.

JC gave a deep, bass chuckle, and then spoke again. "Well, George, Anna asked me to explain things to you. Have I done so?"

George sat back up, cocktail napkin falling from his head onto the floor. He got up from his seat, bent down, and picked up the napkin and put it on the bar. Then, he said, "Let's see if I get this right, JC. Without interaction, nothing exists. When I stood up, the napkin fell off, interacting with gravity, I guess, and falling to the floor. But none of that—neither the napkin, gravity, nor the floor, nor me, or you—exist without the interaction of everything in the universe?"

JC beamed. "That'll do, George, that'll do."

"But, wait, what does that have to do with Jim, or Anna, and the danger that you say I'm in?"

JC got a serious look and leaned back over the bar. "George, you'll have to trust me on this. You are in danger, through no fault of your own. The forces that are in play are larger than you can understand, but that doesn't minimize the possible consequences to you."

George took a sip from his beer, slightly lowered the bottle, looked at JC, and said softly, "Like the insect man I saw last night?"

"Yes, George. Amongst other dangers." And JC went back to polishing the bar with his rag.

"What do you think I should do, JC?" George asked.

JC stopped polishing the bar, looked up at George, and beamed his beautiful smile before answering, "It's simple, George. Live your life with joy! Now, if you'll excuse me, there's something I need to do."

George took the last sip from his Dixie, wiped his mouth with his hand, and stood up. "OK, JC. Thanks for the beer and the conversation."

JC beamed his smile again and said, "Anytime, my friend!"

George left Astro's and began walking towards the Mississippi River. He made his way down to Decatur and turned left. The smells of the French Market—slightly overripe fruit and fresh vegetables—meshed with the sounds of the vendors hawking their produce and made for a tableau that could have happened anytime in the last 150 years. He walked under the open, flat-roofed, barn-like building and saw the many boxes filled with tomatoes, beans, and squash. Other boxes contained more exotic fare like mangos and pineapples. Several vendors had burlap sacks full of unshucked corn. As George walked past the stalls, moving in the direction of Esplanade Avenue, he began to feel a level of... not contentment, but more like acceptance, and peaceful resignation that replaced the angst and grief that had been his primary emotions for the past twelve hours or so.

He spent a half-hour wandering around the French Market, and at the end of the stalls, ran into a small flea market that was populated by young people, most of them hippies, who were selling various items like candles, tie-dyed shirts and dresses, and incense. He stopped in front of one table that had some carved wooden items. There were bowls, carved fruits, and boxes which had been carved with a crude representation of the Last Supper with Jesus and his disciples painted in bright colors. Behind the table stood a young man who was thin with long, curly black hair and glasses held to his face by string wrapped around his ears. Next to the young man was an older man, also with long, curly black hair who was in a wheelchair. George looked at the merchandise, and reached down and picked up one of the boxes. The young man ventured, "They are hand-carved in El Salvadore." George raised the box to his nose, and the smell of cured, tropical wood touched the back of his throat. "We're normally asking ten dollars for the boxes," the young man offered, "but things have been kind of slow, so you can have it for eight if you want."

George reached into his back pocket and pulled out his wallet. "I appreciate that," he said as he pulled out a $10 bill, "but I think this box is worth every bit of ten dollars." The older man in the wheelchair opened up a cigar box on the table and took the bill from George. George could see that the man, like Jim, was a quadriplegic, in the limited way he used his hands and arms.

The man looked up at George and said, "Thanks, brother."

George smiled back and, tucking the box under his arm, began walking back to his apartment. When he reached the alley, he saw that Astro's was closed. He opened the door to the courtyard and found that it was also empty. He'd hoped that he would find JC or Anna or Mama Zulie there to talk to, but it was not to be. He sat alone on the bench and felt the emptiness of the courtyard in his chest as he thought of Jim.

29

THE BEST LAID PLANS

May 14, 1972

Morgan Sanborne woke up feeling good about the world. The first thought that passed through his mind when he opened his eyes was a memory of the phone call he'd had with the chief of police the afternoon before. The chief had told him that the operation would be going down overnight. That meant that the last obstacle which had stood in his way would soon be brushed aside, and he could finalize the purchase of the remaining part of the property for Mr. Mara. He hummed a tune as he finished getting dressed.

After breakfast, he kissed his wife and children goodbye and climbed into his Mercedes to go to the office. Upon arriving at City Hall, he smiled a greeting at Brenda before walking up to her desk. She looked up at him quizzically and he put his finger up to his lip before whispering, "You did good work, Brenda. The cops busted the place last night."

A concerned look passed across her face for a moment, only to be replaced with a smile. "Thanks, Morgan."

He patted her shoulder as he walked past her into his office. Once inside, he took off his coat and hung it on the coat tree before walking around his desk and sitting down. Then, he reached for his telephone, punched a button, leaned back in his chair, and put his feet on his desk. "Get me the chief of police," he said into the mouthpiece. He was thinking about what he was going to do with his commission for the project when he heard the chief's rough voice.

"Anderson here."

Morgan responded, "Hello, Chief Anderson. This is Morgan Sanborne. I won't waste your time. I'm calling to get an update on the drug bust you carried out last night. How did it go?"

"How did it go? Let me tell you, Sanborne. I don't know what kind of bullshit you've been feeding me, but I'm goddamned pissed off."

"Wh...what?!" Morgan stammered. He took his feet off the desk and sat up in his chair, listening.

"You know what, Mr. City Councilman, nobody lives there except a middle-aged man and a poor, crippled hippie... or, used to live there."

"Wait a minute, Chief," Morgan said, speaking faster, "what about the drugs? My spy saw drugs being taken by several people. All of them were living there."

"Oh, yeah, drugs.... Well, Mr. City Councilman, you're right. There were some drugs. My officers found a total of a quarter-ounce of marijuana, all of it in possession of the cripple. Not enough to make a case for attempted distribution, even—just simple possession."

"That can't be..." Morgan strangled out. "What about the others?"

"You're not listening to me, Mr. City Councilman," the police chief spoke with disgust. "There were no others. We searched the entire property! No one has lived in there for years. There was dust an inch thick in all of the rooms except for the two that were occupied by the men I told you about. My officers did a thorough search. Not only were the other rooms unoccupied, but there were no indications that anyone other than these two men had lived on the property remotely recently. Nothing. No power, no phone, no garbage, nothing. I don't know what kind of game you're playing, but you've got us involved in a real shit show! One of the men was accidentally injured during his arrest, and he's died of his injuries. The press has begun asking questions."

"What?" Morgan yelled into the phone.

"That's right! It was the cripple. He resisted arrest and one of my officers had to restrain him. Unfortunately, he restrained him by hitting him on the side of his head with his billy. I questioned him. In a normal person, it would have knocked them silly and given them a headache to remember it by, but this fellow had broken his neck and it resulted in a reactivation of the earlier injury. We brought him to Charity, but there was nothing they could do for him and he died this morning."

"Oh, my god!" Morgan exclaimed as he cast about in his mind for some way to salvage his objective. "Well, what about seizing the property because it was used for drug activity?"

"Are you stupid or something?!" the chief yelled into the phone. "I already told you that there weren't enough drugs to prove anything other than simple possession of marijuana! That doesn't cross the threshold for property seizure! No matter how much you want the property!"

Morgan heard the chief slam the phone down, and the connection was broken.

He put the phone down in its cradle, set his elbows on his desk, and placed his forehead on his palms. He remained in this position for several minutes as his mind raced to find a solution to his dilemma. Finally, he reached out and punched the button on the intercom. "Brenda, could you come in here, please?"

The door opened and Brenda walked in. She closed the door after entering, and walked up to his desk. "Hi, Morgan, how are you today?" She gave him a warm smile and leaned over his desk.

"What the fuck is going on, Brenda?!" Morgan growled.

Brenda straightened up, the warm smile replaced with a look of surprise. "What are you talking about, Morgan?"

"You know what I'm talking about. The police went to the compound last night. They claim that there wasn't a nest of hippies living there... just two guys, one of them a cripple."

"That's Jim," Brenda said, still not understanding exactly what Morgan was getting at.

"Whatever the fuck his name is, the police say that those two guys are the only ones who have lived in that place for a long time. There was no sign of the other people you told me about."

"Well, they're wrong!" Brenda said defensively. "Jim told me that Anna, Mama Zulie, and the other guy live there. We had cake and champagne at Mama Zulie's apartment—"

Morgan slammed his hand on his desk with a noise so loud that Brenda jumped and shut up.

In a low, menacing tone, every word pronounced with hard edges, Morgan said, "Brenda, if you're lying to me...."

Brenda backed up two steps. "I'm not! I'm not lying to you, Morgan, I swear it!"

Morgan looked at her disgustedly and replied, "Get the fuck out of here."

Brenda sniffed, wiped a tear from the corner of her eye, and turned and walked out of the office.

When she was gone, Morgan again placed his forehead in his palms and began to think about how to salvage his plan. He didn't believe that Brenda was lying. *Shit*, he thought, *she's too stupid to lie. There's no way she made that shit up.* So, she had seen those people at the compound. That left the question of what the police had found. The chief was adamant that there'd been no signs of any other people in the compound, though, and Morgan couldn't make sense out of the two bits of conflicting evidence. He rubbed his eyes, and then a thought struck him. He reached out and punched the intercom button again.

"Brenda, could you come here, please?"

A few seconds later, the door opened, this time a bit tentatively, and Brenda stuck her head into the office. Morgan could tell by the smudged mascara that she'd been crying.

"Come in, Brenda, and close the door." She complied and walked up to his desk like a small child waiting to be spanked. "I'm sorry for flying off the handle at you, Brenda," Morgan began. "It's just that this is a very important project and I can't afford to have it go wrong."

Brenda began to cry, wiping her eyes with a Kleenex she clutched in her right hand. "I know, Morgan," she pleaded, "but I promise! I wasn't lying to you. Those people were there and everything happened just like I said it did!"

Morgan stood up, walked around the desk, and put his arms around Brenda. "There, there, Brenda. That's enough. Don't cry. I believe you."

She pulled back from him and looked up into his face. "You do?"

"Of course, I do. Now, let's take it again... slowly. What are the names of the people who live there?"

Brenda put her finger on her cheek as she collected her thoughts, and replied, "Well, there was Jim. He's the guy in the wheelchair... and George.... Jim said he hasn't been there for long. He moved in after his wife left him. He wasn't there, but he lives there."

"Is he a middle-aged guy?" Morgan asked.

"Yeah, I guess so. Jim said that he's not a kid," Brenda said, looking earnestly at Morgan.

"Good. Now, who else lived there?" Morgan asked, encouraging Brenda to continue.

"Anna and the twins. She looks like she's in her late 20s or early 30s. She has strawberry-blonde hair and is very pretty. The twins are tall, dark young men with long, sandy hair. Very handsome...."

"What are their names again, Brenda?"

"Well, one is Caz and the other is Paul, but I'll be damned if I could tell them apart. Caz was the one that told the story when I went on that weird trip I told you about."

Morgan got a more focused look on his face and said, "I remember. Now, Brenda, this is very important. You told me that you went on some kind of a trip. Do you remember if they gave you anything to take?"

"No, Morgan, I swear! The only thing I did was drink an Old Fashioned at Astro's, smoke some pot with Jim, and then we had some cake and champagne in Mama Zulie's apartment."

"Oh, yes, Mama Zulie. Tell me about her, Brenda."

"She's a beautiful, older black woman." Brenda squinted her eyes in an attempt to recall, and added, "I guess she was about 60. Her skin was more the color of café au lait. She had beautiful jewelry and she was very nice to me. I liked her."

"You liked her... now, tell me who was with you at Mama Zulie's," Morgan prodded her.

"Everybody. They were all there... uh, except George. It was very festive, like a party. I had fun," Brenda said, glancing downward.

"And then, afterward...."

"Well, after we had the cake and champagne, Anna asked Caz to tell a story. And that's when I went on the trip I told you about. It was as if I was in a different time and place. Not scary, but not unscary, either. When it was over, I came to and was sitting at the table in Mama Zulie's apartment with everyone else."

"Un huh!" Morgan exclaimed. "Now, Brenda, tell me about Mama Zulie's apartment."

Brenda screwed her face up again to remember and replied, "It was very colorful. The walls were painted different colors. There were lots of wooden masks and religious things like crucifixes hung on the wall. Some of the masks were painted, and some of the crucifixes were, too. There was a big table with chairs, and some other chairs in the room. Some colorful blankets.... That's all I can remember, Morgan. I promise." Brenda looked as if she expected Morgan to yell at her.

"Don't worry, Brenda, I'm not going to yell at you," Morgan said, as if he could read her mind. "Now, tell me what happened afterward."

Brenda answered, slightly offended, "Why, nothing happened, Morgan! I got scared and left. I walked to Canal Street, caught the bus to the cemeteries, then the Veterans Bus, got off at the Tolmas Street stop, and walked back to my apartment. That's everything!"

Morgan said nothing, seemingly lost in thought for several moments. Finally, he took Brenda's hand in his and gave it a pat before walking back around his desk and sitting down. Brenda stayed put for a moment, and then turned and walked out of the office, closing the door behind her. Morgan looked up at the closed door for a second. He shook his head, leaned back in his chair, and closed his eyes as he tried to make sense of the conflicting information. He was sure now that Brenda was telling the truth, and yet, the chief of police was no fool. His information had to be correct. So, something was going on at that compound that was being skillfully covered up. It *had* to be a sophisticated operation to fool experienced police officers.

All of the evidence pointed to drugs, and that was his ticket to acquiring the property. His mind made up, he opened his eyes and sat up in his chair. He reached for the phone and, once again, said, "Connect me with the chief of police."

After a moment, the chief's secretary came on the line and asked him to wait a second. Then, the chief's booming voice sounded again. "Well, what is it, Councilman Sanborne? I'm up to my ass in alligators right now and don't have much time."

"That's fine, Chief," Morgan responded, "I won't take up much of your time. I just wanted to ask if you could tell me a little about the other man that your men found living at the compound. You know, the middle-aged one who isn't a cripple?"

The chief replied, "Him? He wasn't any help... claimed that there were no hard drugs on the premises and that he'd never seen any hard drugs. He did say that he saw marijuana being smoked, which fits with what we found in the cripple's apartment. It's funny, though—"

Morgan interjected, "What's funny, Chief?"

The chief continued, "My investigator said that the guy insisted that there were several other people living in the compound. He pushed him on this, and the guy insisted, but all of the evidence suggests that nobody else has lived there for a long time. The investigator had a hunch that there might have been some hard drugs involved, but there was zero evidence."

"That's very interesting, Chief, because my informant indicated that there may have been some LSD or something that causes a *trip*, like LSD, in the place. Tell you what, Chief, can you get me the name of this guy? I'd like to see what I can dig up on him."

"What? Oh, sure, I'll have my secretary find out and get that info to you later today. But let me warn you, Councilman, I'm already having to deal with a shit storm as a result of the crip dying. Don't bring any more crap down on me, or I'll dump twice as much crap on you. Is that clear?"

"As a bell, Chief, as a bell. Sorry to bother you. Next time I see you, the drinks are on me."

"They better be!" the chief boomed before hanging up.

Morgan put the receiver back in the cradle. *He's the one who knows what's happening*, he thought before turning his attention to his appointment book and seeing what was on his schedule that day. He hummed tunelessly as he checked on his appointments and meetings. He was looking forward to finding out what this man knew.

30

A FRIEND IN NEED

May 14, 1972

George sat in the courtyard for over an hour hoping that someone would come. He desperately wanted company. He needed to talk about what had happened, but no one came. He finally decided to call April and see if she was free. He rose from the bench and walked to a payphone he knew of on the corner of St. Ann and Bourbon. The payphone was inside a metal pedestal with a bell-like finial on top. It rose from the street like some greenish-black, metallic mushroom. Graffiti was scribbled inside of the nook that sheltered the payphone. The phone rang three times before she picked up.

"Hello?"

"Uh, hi, April, this is George."

"Hi, George, what a pleasant surprise. What's happening?"

George swallowed. "April, something has happened. A good friend... you remember me telling you about Jim? Well, he died this morning, and I need to talk.... I just don't want to be alone right now. Do you.... Would you mind talking to me for a bit?"

He heard the concern in her voice as she answered, "Oh my god, George! You poor thing! Of course, I'll talk to you. Do you want to come over to my place?"

"Yes, April," George spoke as if he were in a dream, "that would be nice. Bye."

"Wait! George, you don't have my address."

"Oh...yeah, sorry. What is it?"

"I live at the corner of Marshall Foch and Brooks streets, in Lakeview. Just take the Canal bus and get off at the stop just past the I-610 overpass. That's Brooks Street. Walk down four blocks and I'm on the lake-side corner. It's a two-story, white house. Come in the door, and I'm in the upstairs apartment."

"OK, I've got it. I'll be there in about an hour. And... thanks, April."

George hung up the phone and walked towards Canal Street. He was lucky and didn't have to wait long for the right bus, so he reached the corner of Canal Boulevard and Brooks Street within forty minutes. He walked down the tree-lined street and thought how picturesque it was. Many of the houses were two-story wooden structures built in the teens and twenties, in a style somewhere between Greek Revival and Federalist. A few were late Victorian in style. Many of the two-story houses had screened-in porches on their second story. The sun was beginning to set as he approached the corner of Brooks and Marshall Foch. He followed April's instructions, walked up to the front door, up the stairs, and knocked. April opened the door with a concerned look on her face.

"Come in, George. Here, sit down on the couch." George walked to the couch, which was small and comfortable, with a faded, red and white checkered cloth cover. April came and sat next to him. She took his hand and said, "Now. Tell me what happened."

George stiffened a bit, but then he relaxed. He looked at April and saw she was concerned for him. It was almost like a switch had been thrown. Tears began to flow as he described the events of the last night. April stayed silent and listened as he spoke. He withheld nothing, not caring if she thought he was crazy. His tears had stopped before he finished talking. When he finished, he added, "Thank you..." but she shushed him, reached over, and pulled his head onto her breast, cradling it.

"I'm so sorry, George. I'm so sorry."

He hugged her as she cradled him, and was grateful for the comfort. He raised his head, looked into her eyes, and said, "You do believe me, don't you, April?"

She held his eyes with hers and replied, "George, after seeing that frightening man in the reflection when no one was there, I do believe you. I don't understand it, and it frightens me, but I do believe what you're telling me." He laid his head back down, and they stayed like that for several minutes.

April broke the silence by asking George if he would like some tea. He sat up, rubbed his face with his hands, and said, "I'd love some. Can I help?"

"Sure, follow me."

He followed her into the kitchen, where she handed him a kettle and asked him to fill it from the sink. He did so and placed it on the old, white, porcelain gas stove. She pointed out the kitchen matches, and he used one to light the burner while she pulled out a box of Constant Comment Tea from the cabinet. The kitchen was small, and George tried to keep out of April's way as she moved to get some honey from another cabinet, but their hands brushed as she moved by. She looked at him and gave him an easy smile, and then continued. The kettle whistled, and April poured the water into the cups she'd put the teabags in. She told George to go back and sit, and she would bring the tea. He went back into the living room and looked around as he waited. There was a light table in the corner, a couple of unmatched, cloth chairs, an end table next to one of the chairs, and a built-in bookcase along one wall. There was a paperback book with an orange cover on the table. He walked over, picked it up to see what it was, and was surprised to see that it was the same book that Jim had been reading, *Autobiography of a Yogi*. April walked into the room with the tea, and George turned towards her with the book in his hand.

"Jim was reading this book! He said that it explained some of the experiences that we've been having." April looked thoughtful as she replied, "It's a very interesting book, George. A good read... maybe you should read it."

He brought the book with him to the couch and sat next to April. Thanking her, he took his cup in one hand and held the book in his other. "What is the book about?" he asked.

April smiled, and replied, "It's exactly what the title says. It's an autobiography of an Indian yogi who came to the United States in the 1930s, meaning to explain Eastern religion and mysticism to the West. It's filled with his stories about miracles that he witnessed... miracles that aren't considered possible in today's world. I don't know how much you know about Eastern religions...."

"Not much at all," George admitted.

"Well, it's a basic, underlying belief in the Eastern religions like Buddhism and Hinduism that what we perceive as reality isn't really real. In fact, the Greek philosopher Plato argued that our perceptions of reality aren't really real. He likened our perceptions of reality to a person being chained in a cave and watching shadows thrown on the wall, thinking those shadows are real because the person can't see anything more. Plato argued that reality is something different from our perceptions of it. Really, that's the same fundamental belief as that of the Eastern religions."

George chimed in, "Wait! I thought Plato was a Western philosopher."

April jabbed him with her elbow, "He was. I guess there's been a fundamental change in Western beliefs since Plato's days. Here's another interesting fact. Did you know that many physicists who were involved in the development of the atomic bomb became fascinated with the perspectives of the Eastern mystics? One of them, I think it was a guy named Neils Bohr, said that the fact that religions have spoken in images, parables, and paradoxes just means that there's no other way to grasp the reality they refer to, but it doesn't mean that that reality isn't genuine. Also, have you heard of Robert Oppenheimer?"

"The guy who ran the Manhattan Project? Sure!"

"Well, he was also interested in Eastern philosophies. When they tested the first atomic bomb, he used a quote from the Baghavad-Gita to describe the result."

"Baghavad what?" George interjected.

"Bhagavad-Gita... it's like the Bible for most Hindus."

"Can I ask you a question, April?"

"Of course."

"How do you know so much about this?"

"Well, I minored in Philosophy at UNO, and took a couple of classes on comparative religion. As for the physics part, I dated a physicist for a while, and I guess some of it rubbed off. It's been an interest of mine since I started college. I was raised Catholic, but quit going to church when I was a teenager. I wasn't comfortable with the whole *mystery* thing. Any time I had a hard question, like, 'Why do little children get leukemia?', or, 'If God loves us so much, why does he send some of us to hell to suffer for all eternity?', the priests would just answer that it was a mystery, and that we couldn't understand or judge God's motives. It seemed like a cop-out to me, so I began looking into other religions. The ones that felt most comfortable to me were the Eastern religions, particularly Buddhism."

George looked at April with new-found respect. This young woman had depths that he had been unaware of. He asked, "If you don't mind my asking, how old are you, April?"

She laughed her easy laugh and said, "I don't mind George. I made 25 my last birthday. Now, since I told you, how old are you?"

"Shit, April." George shrugged and replied, "I'm an old man. Made 36 my last birthday."

"That's not old, George. Don't you know that women mature earlier than men? I mean, technically, you're barely out of your teenage years." Here, she laughed uproariously and poked George in the ribs, to which he responded by grasping her hands in his and joining in the laughter.

"OK, OK... you win!" he finally strangled out. "I'm still wet behind the ears! God knows with everything that's happened lately, I can hardly tell what's real and what's not."

They both stopped laughing, and April looked into George's eyes, took his face in her hands, and said, "George, I haven't felt like this in a long time. I don't know what it is about you, but I feel that I can trust you. Is that real?"

George looked deep into April's blue eyes. He felt like he was drowning in them for an instant, and pulled his head slightly back to get her face back into focus. "It is from my perspective," he answered. Then, he leaned towards her and gave her a slow kiss on the lips. She kept her hands on his face and responded, both of them closing their eyes as the kiss grew deeper. Their arms instinctively wrapped around each other, and the kiss eventually resolved into a long, slow hug.

April sighed and gave a comfortable, 'mmmmm... sound. George slowly pulled back from the hug, their arms still around each other, and looked into her eyes. His heart beat faster at what he saw. He caressed her face tenderly and said, "I don't know if I should say this, but I think I'm in love with you, April." His heart swelled as she responded with a languorous smile. She raised her hand and began to caress his fingers. She took his hand and began to slowly kiss his fingers.

They both leaned their heads on the back of the couch as they sat facing each other, and then George said, "I'll go as slow or as fast as you want, April. You know that I'm still married. It's going to take a year for my divorce from Gloria to be finalized. That gives us plenty of time to get to know each other better."

"That's what I find funny about this, George!" April smiled at him sweetly. "I feel like I've known you for a long time."

George leaned in to kiss her again, and said, "I feel the same way, April." This kiss was different from the first one. If the first kiss had had the sweetness of Spring and green, growing things, this kiss had the heat of Summer and sweat. Their passion grew as they kissed and hugged each other, until April said, "George, let's go to bed."

"I'd love to, April," he murmured, "but I don't want this feeling to stop for the time it takes to get there."

"I know what you mean," she whispered. They slowly rose from the couch and, hand in hand, made their way to the bedroom.

31

CELEBRATION OF A LIFE

May 15, 1972

It was early the next morning when George woke up to the repetitive song of a mockingbird in the tree next to April's bedroom window. He lay there in the early light of dawn and looked towards April, who was sleeping on her side with her back to him. They'd spooned as they'd slept, and George had felt perfectly comfortable. The hum of the window air conditioner changed as the compressor kicked in, and he reached out and pulled the cover over her bare shoulder. She sighed and backed up slightly towards him. He put his arm around her, resting it on her hip with his hand resting on her thigh as he lay there, thinking about the events of the past few days. He thought about Jim, Anna, JC, and the twins, and then, curiously, his mind turned to his discussion with April about the nature of reality. April gave her shoulders a slow shrug and turned towards him. He looked at her sleeping face and felt at peace. Her eyes opened and she gave him a smile as she put her arm around him. He rolled onto his back and she laid her head on his shoulder.

"Good morning," she said softly.

"Morning, April," he said as he gently kissed her head. "It's Monday, so you know what that means."

"Yep, gotta get ready to go to work," she replied.

"Yeah, but I'd give everything I own to just stay like this." He kissed her head again. She raised it and kissed his lips. "What time to you have to be at work?"

"I need to leave here no later than 7:30," she said.

"Well, then, I need to be getting back home." He got out of the bed, gathered his clothes, and sat back down to put them on. April lay on her back with the covers up to her neck, watching him. The mockingbird, which had continued to repeat its greeting to the morning, finally fell silent. When George had finished getting dressed, he leaned back down and gave April a long, slow kiss. "Would you like to come to my place tonight?"

"I'd love to, George. I'll get off of work at 5, and then I need to come home to get some things. How about I get there around 6:30?"

"That'll be perfect. I'll meet you in front of the alleyway leading to my place. We'll go get something to eat." He gave her directions to the building, and then leaned down and gave her a quick kiss. "Bye, April. Thank you for everything. I can't wait to see you again."

She took his hand and replied, "Thank you, George. I'll see you this evening," and then she brushed the back of his hand with her lips.

George laughed and said, "If you do that anymore, I'm not going to be able to leave, and our whole day will be shot!"

April laughed and let go of his hand. "Bye, George."

"Bye."

He left April's apartment and began walking back to Canal Boulevard. The air was cool in the early morning, and the trees were full of calling birds and squirrels chasing each other around. He made it back to his apartment, took a bath, got dressed, and made his way to the antique store, stopping along the way for some cannolli at Angelo Brocato's.

When Tony arrived at the store, and before any customers entered, George told him about his weekend. He left nothing out and told the

BY JOHN R. GREENE

entire story. Tony didn't interrupt a single time—just sat and listened. George wept again when he described the scene in the hospital, and Tony reached out and patted his hand. He finished by telling him about April and their burgeoning romance. When he was done, he just sat there, spent.

Tony scratched his head and looked at George. "I'm sorry for your loss, George. I know how hard it is to lose someone you care for. The circumstances make it even worse."

"Yes, Tony, you would have liked him. He was a good, decent, New Orleans boy... kind and gentle and smart. I've learned that, just because a person smokes pot, that doesn't make them bad. They're still the same person that they were."

"You don't have to convince me, George. My boys joined the Marines because they were caught with the butt of a marijuana cigarette. They were given the choice of two years at Angola Prison or joining the armed services. The way they were, the only service they wanted to join was the Marines, so they enlisted." Tony's voice choked, and it was George's turn to pat Tony's hand.

A customer walked in the door and stopped the discussion. Tony rose quickly and walked into the back of the store while George went to take care of the customer. She wanted to look at some silverware, and George led her to the silverware section. As he did, he glanced over as Tony went through the back door and into the workshop, shoulders stooped.

The day continued apace, and both Tony and George's moods improved as they handled customers and worked on some restorations. The busyness made for a short day and closing time came quickly. George left Tony at the door locking up, saying "See you tomorrow, Tony," and hurried back to his apartment. When he walked down the alleyway, he could see that JC had Astro's open, so he turned into the door.

JC, as usual, was behind the bar cleaning. He gave George a big smile and said, "Good to see you, my man! How are you doing?"

George sat on a bar stool and replied, "I'm better, JC—still sad, but better."

"That's good, George. Jim wouldn't want to see you sad. He lived his life to the fullest, and in a very real way, he's here right now." JC looked intensely at George.

"I know, JC. It's just that I can't talk to him, or tease him, or even smoke with him."

"Just keep trying, George. You'll be surprised what you can do."

George started with surprise, but then said, "Wow, I almost forgot. I've got someone I'd like you to meet tonight. Her name is April. She's a new friend of mine—a very special friend. She's coming over tonight and we're going to get some dinner, if you'd like to join us."

JC laughed a big, booming laugh. "No thanks, George! I wouldn't want to intrude on y'all's dinner. I'll just stay here and take care of any customers that drop in. I'd love to meet her, though, if you want to bring her by to say hello."

George smiled and said, "Will do, JC. Thanks! See you later."

He went back through the gate into the courtyard, which was empty. He climbed the stairs up to his apartment and took a quick bath, then put on clean clothes and walked back down the alley to wait for April on the street.

He hadn't had to wait for more than five minutes when he saw her walking towards him down Dumaine Street from Rampart Street.

He walked up to her and gave her a big hug and a kiss. "It's so good to see you again, April."

"Yeah, and you, too, George." She took his hand in hers. "I'm starving. Where do you want to go eat?"

"Well, it's a Monday, and you know what that means in New Orleans."

"Sure, it's wash day, so you've gotta eat red beans and rice!"

"Exactly! How about we go to Buster Holmes for some good red beans? It's just around the corner."

April clapped her hands and agreed, "That's a great idea! I've been wanting to go there for the longest time." She gave George a quick hug, and then they walked, hand in hand, to Burgundy Street and took a left. Buster Holmes' restaurant was just a block away on the corner of Orleans. It was a nondescript building, painted pink with green, cypress board doors and windows. The shutter in front of the door was open, and displayed a large Barq's Root Beer sign. There was a stand mounted sign in front that said, "Buster's Soul Food Restaurant Now Open – Soft Drinks Good Served." They walked into the restaurant and sat at the counter. The waitress approached and George held up his hand with two fingers raised. Without a word, the waitress turned and yelled, "Two beans!" before asking what they wanted to drink. They both ordered a Barq's and, before long, two steaming bowls of delicious red beans and rice were placed in front of them. They were silent as they ate their meal, both engrossed in the mix of flavors that made Buster's the best place in the city for red beans.

When they finally came up for air, April told George, "That was delicious. The best red beans and rice I've ever had. Do you come here often, George?"

"Truth be told, April, I came here with Jim last week for the first time. They do make the best restaurant red beans that I've ever had, though."

"Yeah, I hear you," she replied, "the best food in New Orleans is at people's houses, not in restaurants."

George laughed. "Spoken like a native, April. Spoken like a native." They left Buster's and walked slowly back towards Dumaine Street. George asked, "Would you like to go out to the lakefront, April?"

She stopped, cocking her head to look at him. "You're not trying to take me to the submarine races, are you, George?"

George stopped and laughed so hard that he doubled over. "My God, April! It didn't even occur to me. I'm so sorry…" he strangled out.

April, who was laughing as hard as George, said, "No, no, George. I'm just teasing you. I'd love to go to the lakefront with you… submarine races or not."

George finally got his breath back. "Shit, April, I almost peed myself." Then, he broke down and started laughing again. She grabbed his arm, laughing with him, and he finally settled down.

"Come on, George. Let's just go before you start laughing again!"

He led her to his Mustang, opened the passenger door for her, walked around and climbed into the driver's seat, and they left.

They made their way to Esplanade Avenue, then down towards City Park. When they reached Wisner Boulevard, they took a right, driving alongside Bayou St. Jean to Robert E. Lee Boulevard. They crossed, and George told April to look to her right. There, in front of the levee, were some old, brick foundations. "That's the remains of an old Spanish Fort. There's been a fort here since the settlement of New Orleans. I think there was an Indian site here, too, or at least, I heard a story about one."

"Wow! I never knew," April replied. George kept driving, and then pointed out a cannon in someone's front yard. "That is Mayor Schiro's house. You know, the last mayor."

"Sure, I know who Mayor Schiro is," April said.

"I heard that the cannon comes from the old fort."

"Wow, imagine having a cannon in your front yard!" They both laughed.

When they reached the end of Spanish Fort Boulevard, they took a left and drove down the lakefront for a bit. It was sunset, and there was a light breeze blowing from the lake. They could see people fishing and crabbing from the seawall. George found an area with fewer people and pulled into a parking space. They got out of the car, walked up to a white and green concrete and wood bench, and sat. The breeze blew the hair back from April's face, framing her face so that she looked like Botticelli's *Spring*. George could hardly keep his eyes off of her.

"What? What are you staring at, George?" she asked.

"You, April. You're so beautiful!"

"Stop it. You're embarrassing me," she ordered him. "So, tell me, George, you grew up around here, didn't you?"

"Yeah, I did."

"Did you guys come out to the lakefront when you were a kid?"

"Sure!" George sat back on the bench and put his arm around the back of the bench, and April leaned back on it.

"When I was little, about 5 or 6, we would come out here almost every weekend with my paw paw and uncle. My dad and uncle would go out early in the morning, before work, to the undeveloped part of the lake and collect clams by walking around in the water barefooted, feeling with their feet, and picking the clams up with their toes. They would fill several coffee cans full of clams for bait. After work, we would eat supper, and then we'd all ride to the seawall on Lakeshore Drive. I used to love those trips. My dad, uncle, and paw paw would take their shirts and shoes off. I can still see them in those thin, sleeveless T-shirts, with their dark blue, cotton workpants rolled up past their knees and their feet covered by black socks. They wore socks because the bottom steps that are in the water are covered with algae, and very slippery. The socks gave them better footing on the algae covered steps. Anyway, as the sun went down, they would light a couple of Coleman lanterns—you know what they are?"

"Sure, we used to go camping every now and then," she said.

"Well, they would light those and put them down on the last dry step of the seawall. My job was to take the clams, one at a time, out of the coffee cans, and break them open with a hammer. I learned really fast how to hit the clam and not my fingers. So, when I had seven or eight clams cracked open, one of the men would come get them, walk back down to the bottom dry step, and throw them in the lake. They would wait about five or ten minutes, and then throw a big cast net over the area they had thrown the clams. When they pulled the net back in, it would have shrimp, croakers, pinfish, catfish, and maybe a mullet or two in it. They had a bushel basket that they would put the bottom of the net into, then lift up the round net opener and shake out what they'd caught into the basket. I would keep cracking clams and putting them into an empty coffee can. When I had the can full, I would get a shrimp from the basket, bait a hook, and cast out my little fishing rod. We would stay out there until 10 or 11 o'clock at night, catching shrimp and fish. If I caught a catfish, I would have to have one of the men take it off since these saltwater catfish—we called them 'hardheads'—have sharp fins with some sort of poison or something that can really hurt you."

"Wow! Did you catch a lot?"

"We did, April, we did. I remember, many times, coming home with an ice chest full of speckled trout, white trout, and croakers. We didn't catch too many redfish. And they used to catch a bushel basket of shrimp easy, nearly every time we went out."

"That's amazing, George. We moved here when I was sixteen, and never came out to the lakefront to fish. We had a few picnics under the pavilions, and I used to come out with friends in high school and goof off, but we never fished or crabbed."

"Just goes to show you what you were missing," George said with a laugh. He indicated, with a nod of his head, a young family—a mom, dad, and two little ones who were walking up to the seawall nearby with some fishing poles. In short order, each had a bait in the water, and it didn't take long for the father to hook a fish. It looked like the fish was fairly big, too, judging by the bend in the pole. When he reeled it up the last little bit, he pulled it out of the water and towards his out-stretched hand. It was a large, wriggling eel. He pulled his hand back, avoiding the eel while his kids and wife squealed in disgust. He carefully maneuvered the eel to the top step, unhooked it using a rag, and threw it back in the water.

"Yuck!" April said. "That makes me glad I didn't go fishing here."

"We rarely caught eels here, April. I mean, we caught a few, but they were rare. How about we go back to my place and get a drink at Astro's now? I'd like you to meet JC. He's a really great guy."

She took his arm and said, "OK, George. Lead the way."

They walked back to the Mustang, and George drove back to the French Quarter. He'd grown to expect his usual parking place to be available, and it was. He mentioned this to April as he parked and she agreed that it was very unusual.

They got out and walked to Dumaine Street. It was dark, and the blue from the Astro's sign filled the alleyway with an otherworldly glow. When they reached the open door, George let April enter before him. He was surprised to see Anna and the twins on the first three barstools, Dixie beers in front of them. JC was, as usual, wiping the bar with a towel.

"Hi, everybody! This is April," George announced. Anna and the twins stood up and greeted them.

Caz or Paul—George could never be sure who was who—said, "Man, George. Is she as smart as she is beautiful?"

"Shut up, Caz!" Anna piped in. "Don't let that knucklehead worry you, April. He's harmless."

April laughed, and replied, "Well, I don't know about beautiful, but I think I can hold my own in a conversation."

Paul elbowed his twin brother out of the way and said, "Well put, my lady," and then bowed.

JC gave a booming laugh and said, "Welcome, April. Any friend of George's is a friend of ours. What's your pleasure?"

April looked at the bar and said, "It looks like everyone is having a Dixie, so I'll have one, too."

"Make that two, please, JC," George said.

"Two ice cold Dixies coming right up!" JC bent down and pulled two bottles out of the ice cooler behind the bar. He opened them and set them down next to the already open bottles on the bar. Anna and the twins got back on their barstools, and April and George sat on the next two. April was the first to speak.

"George has told me a lot about you guys. I just want to say that I'm sorry about the loss of your friend, Jim."

They were all silent, their heads bowed, for a count of about three, and then Anna looked up at April and said, "Thank you, April. Jim was a special soul, and we were lucky to know him. His spirit continues to shine and will contribute to the light of the universe forever."

Everyone raised their beer except JC, who raised an open hand. George took a swallow of his cold Dixie, and wiped the tears from his eyes. Suddenly, a thought occurred to him. "Wait!" he exclaimed, "what about Jim's body? We need to go get it so we can hold his funeral!"

Anna, who was sitting next to April, leaned over and touched George on the arm. "We can't, George. None of us are family. They'll have held his body for his next of kin. He told me that he had a sister who lives in Metairie. I'm sure that she's made all of the necessary arrangements. Given what happened, it may cause the family more grief if we go to his funeral. It's best that we remember Jim as the bright light that he was, and let his family process their grief in their own way."

George sat silently for a moment, hunched over, and April reached over and put her arm around his shoulders. Then, he spoke out, "I guess you're right, Anna. I'm being selfish. Who's to say that my grief for my friend is greater than that of his family? And, you're right... the family might think that I was, at least partly, responsible for what happened, and that would make his funeral even harder for them." He took another sip of his beer as April wound her right arm through his left, and laid her head on his shoulder. He leaned over and touched his cheek to the top of her head, then sat up and said, "I do know one thing.

Jim wouldn't want us to mope over his passing. I can almost hear him saying, 'Come on, y'all, that's enough sadness. Let's have some fun!'"

JC spoke up, "You're exactly right, George. That is what Jim wants us to do—celebrate his life, not mourn it."

"I know," Caz spoke up, "Dr. John is playing at the Warehouse tonight. His set won't start till 9 or 9:30. We've got enough time to make it if y'all want."

George thought about work, and then about Jim, and decided he was in, but he needed to make sure that it was something April would want. He asked everyone to excuse them and walked April out into the alleyway. "Would you like to go to the Warehouse, April? I know it's a work night, and it's OK if you need to get home and go to bed."

"Ordinarily, that's exactly what I would do, George, but this is kind of like a funeral celebration for your friend. I know you cared for him a lot, and I'm sorry that I never got the chance to meet him, but the least I can do is to be there at the celebration of his life. Besides, I *love* Dr. John. A good friend of mine from high school had a big brother who knew him when he was just Mac Rebennack, a kid at Jesuit High School. She told me that her brother said that Dr. John was kicked out of Jesuit because he wouldn't stop playing music in nightclubs!"

"Man, I didn't know that," George said in surprise. "Let's go back in and tell everyone that we're in."

They walked back into Astro's and George was astonished to see JC on their side of the bar. He walked up and said, "You're coming with us?" JC nodded and opened his arms wide for a hug. George gave him a big bear hug and said, "April and I are in. How do y'all want to go?"

Paul said, "We've got Sunshine parked down the street. Why don't we all pile into her and I'll drive us?" This was met with general agreement, and they walked down the alleyway and down the street to where the gaily painted, wood-paneled station wagon was parked. They made their way to the Warehouse on Tchoupitoulas Street. The venue was exactly what the name indicated—an old, brick warehouse that was nondescript on the outside, and even less impressive on the inside, yet the home of some great music. They arrived after the doors had opened, and there were just a few people standing around outside, most smoking cigarettes and some smoking pot. Two men—both large, one black and one white—sat on stools in front of the entrance. George and April were walking in front of the group and, when they reached the front, one of the men said, "Tickets" in a flat tone.

JC, Anna, and the twins walked up behind George and April. JC said, "Hey, Louie! King! What's happenin', y'all?"

Both men looked at JC and broke into wide grins, one of whom greeted him with "JC! Man! It's great to see ya! How've ya been?"

They hugged JC in greeting, who then said, "Guys, these are my friends. We came to see Mac perform tonight. Y'all got room for us?"

One of the men replied, "Any friend of yours is a friend of ours, JC. We've always got room for you. Y'all come on in!" And with that, the men waved them through the doors. They walked in and found a place to spread out on the old, stained carpet near the speakers by the stage. It was hot and humid, and the air smelled of cigarette smoke, patchouli oil, incense, and pot. The stage was set up with drums and other instruments. Their group had been there for less than five minutes when they heard the sound of rattles and tambourines. The crowd began to clap and whistle as Dr. John and his band walked up to the stage. He was dressed in a colorful outfit sewn with beads and mirrors, and he wore a striped hat topped with feathers. The group danced their way around the stage as the drummer sat first and began to beat a rhythm, and then the rest of the group walked to their instruments and began to play.

Dr. John, guitar in hand, walked up to the microphone and began to sing, "They call me Dr. John, known as the night tripper. A satchel of gris-gris in my hands...." The song, "Gris Gris and Gumbo Ya Ya," settled into a funky groove, and the entire Warehouse started rocking to the same beat. George was standing behind April with his hands on her waist as they moved to the beat. He looked around and saw by the smiles on everyone's faces and the moving of their bodies that JC, Anna, and the twins were enjoying the music, as well. The first song morphed into a funky, slow, bluesy number with a call and response chorus between Dr. John and two female back-up singers. When the song finished, Dr. John spoke into the mike. "How y'all doin', tonight? Y'all feelin' bluesy? Or y'all wantin' to get down? Whatta y'all want tonight?"

The crowd roared back, but George was damned if he could tell what they were saying.

"All right... all right... y'all wanna get down tonight. Get some funk in ya minds. Yeah, we're gonna pitch one tonight. Yeah, you heard it right, you said it right. Dr. John is gonna put down his guitar right now and play some piano right now!" He lifted the strap from his shoulders and set his guitar up on a stand. Then, he moved over to the piano that was on stage, sat down, and adjusted the microphone. "All right, all right.... Let me tell ya now, ya see, what it is.... Ya know, life go on like a river, you know what I mean, it ain't got no beginning, ain't got no end—it just go on, ya know what I'm tryin' to tell ya. And what it is when ya been in a place ya ain't never been before in ya life, but ya say, 'I've been here before.' A funny feelin', ya cain't explain it. What it is, I don't know, but I'm gonna try and tell ya what I think it is." Here, he broke into "Familiar Reality"—a funky piano number filled with piano riffs and plaintive echoes of the back-up singers' high-pitched refrain of *"Familiar Re-al-i-ty"* that settled down into a funky refrain before ramping back up to a keys-pounding chorus. George came to realize that he and April were moving in time to the music along with the entire Warehouse. He turned and caught JC's eye, and returned his beaming smile. Anna was dancing with Caz and Paul, and George could swear he saw a glow around the three of them like a golden bubble.

The song came to an end, and the whole Warehouse was in a hot, sweaty ecstasy. Dr. John grabbed a towel from the top of his piano, wiped his face, and began to play a rollicking rock and roll song on his piano. The crowd began to move as one again. When the song was done, he said, "This next one is from our new album. I'm not gonna tell ya its name, 'cuz if ya can't figure it out after ya hear it, I dunno...." Then, he broke into a syncopated beat that settled into "Let the Good Times Roll." Once again, the crowd moved like waves on the ocean.

The piano was staged at about a 45-degree angle towards the center of the stage. George and his friends were to the side and slightly behind Dr. John as he sat and played. After he finished the song, Dr. John turned on the piano stool and looked directly at JC. He moved his right hand, palm down, out and then up. JC returned the gesture. Dr. John nodded at JC, then spoke into the microphone: "Y'all think ya know what's happenin'. Right? But, I wanna tell ya' that ya seein' shadows. Thas' right. Good and evil are real, y'all. I know. I seen it. I felt it. I lived it.... There's this cat I met once. Tall, thin man. Bad dude. Bad dude... scared me right outa my mind. Not scary like *I'm gonna kill ya*. Scary like *I'm gonna take ya soul...take ya soul*.... An' da funny thing about it is that I saw him in an alley that leads to the closest place ya can get to Heaven in N'yawlins.... Good and evil.... Good... and evil...." He nodded to his bass player and a heavy bass line began to play before he added, "I went straight home and wrote this song after I met that dude."

Dr. John gave a growl from deep in his chest, his face contorted as if possessed by some evil spirit. The base line sounded like doom, punctuated by the *shhhhhhhhh* of cymbals. Then, he began to sing "Gilded Splinters."

April was mesmerized by the sing-song, chanting and eerie quality of this song. She could feel the powerful menace described and, when she looked away from the stage and at the audience, she saw that they were still, held in a spell by the power of the song. She turned and looked over her shoulder at George, and saw that he was staring at the stage with an expression that was almost fearful. She turned and saw Anna looking at the crowd. The expression on her face was one of almost angelic concern, as if she wanted to hold each person and comfort them. The twins and JC were watching the stage calmly. She wondered at the power of the song, and was jolted back to the present by the syncopated piano riffs of "Iko Iko," and the crowd began moving again in time to the music.

When the song reached its end, Dr. John said, "We wanna thank ya' for comin' out tonight. We love ya, N'yawlins!" And he and the band walked off of the stage to raucous applause. The applause continued along with whistling and stamping for a couple of minutes, and then Dr. John walked back out with the band. He settled behind the piano, pulled the microphone towards him, and said, "Thank ya, thank ya... allright," before he broke into "Little Liza Jane." The crowd began moving again to the funky beat. When the song was over, they went straight into "Wang Dang Doodle," which went on for ten minutes. George, April, and the rest of their group moved along with the rest of the audience. George leaned down and spoke into her ear, "Jim would have loved this." She turned and gave him a brilliant smile, then kissed him and pulled his arms around her as they swayed in time to the music. When the song ended, Dr. John and the band all stood in front of the instruments and microphones, wrapped their arms around each other, and bowed to the audience. The applause was deafening, and then it died down into a buzz of conversations as the tired, sweaty audience piled out of the Warehouse.

Once they were in Sunshine, April said, "That was a great concert, but that song about gilded splinters creeped me out."

Anna, who was sitting between the twins in the front seat, looked back and said, "You're right to be creeped out, April. That was a powerful song. Mac has been interested in Voodoo since he was in high school, and the song he wrote is about its evil aspect."

April replied, "It really had an effect on the crowd, too. I was looking around and everyone was standing still. They were really moving for all of the other songs."

JC came into the conversation and said, "Songs of power are recognized in all cultures. They are powerful for different reasons, but that doesn't make them any less powerful. Think about it... when you hear "The Star Spangled Banner," doesn't it put goosebumps on you?"

"Well, yes, it does," April said.

"That's a powerful song that derives its power from a strong feeling of national pride. Now, think about the most beautiful love song you know."

"That's easy. For me, it's "Unchained Melody." Never fails—it gives me goosebumps every time I hear it."

"The power of that song," JC said, "is the human need for love. The connection between both powerful songs is a human yearning for connection, for interaction. John Donne said long ago, "No man is an island, entire of itself; every man is a piece of the continent, a part of the main...." That need for connection, interaction, is as human a trait as the opposable thumb."

George chimed in, "Interaction. You said that it was what linked the entire universe together."

JC gave a booming laugh and said, "You're a quick study, George. That's exactly right. In all things, great and small, animate and inanimate, personal and impersonal, it is interaction that drives the universes."

Caz spoke up, "Well, folks, we're here." They all piled out of Sunshine and walked the few steps to the alley.

JC stopped at the door to Astro's and spoke, "This night was for Jim, my friends."

"Yes, for my sweet Jim," Anna said, "whose spirit is still with us, held in our hearts. Come, let's have a group hug and send Jim our love."

They all moved their heads together, put their arms around each other, and hugged.

George spoke up, "Well, I think April and I will head up to my apartment now. Thank you all for the evening, and for being my friends."

"Yes," April added, "thank you all so much. You've been very kind to me, and I'm grateful."

One of the twins said, "Awwww... y'all are good kids," and everyone had a good laugh before saying goodnight. George led April through the courtyard and up the stairs to his apartment. Later, as they lay in bed, intertwined and falling asleep, he brushed his lips on April's forehead and said, "I love you, April."

She replied, "I love you, too, George," and sleep overtook both of them.

32
THE EVIL EXPOSED

May 15, 1972

Morgan knew he was in trouble, but he wasn't terribly worried. He'd always been able to talk, scheme, or buy his way out of trouble. It helped, of course, to be a descendant of the blue-blooded elites of New Orleans, and to have all of the important connections that arose from that lineage.

First things first, he thought as he looked in the mirror while brushing his teeth, *I've got to get a hold of this guy, and find out what's really happening in that den of hippies. Once I get him to talk, then I can motivate the chief to do what I need and get that goddamned piece of property.* He grinned at his reflection. *Then, I'll make more money than I can spend. Maybe I'll give Brenda a nice necklace, and take Sylva and the kids to Disneyworld.* He spat and rinsed, gave his reflection a wolf's smile, and walked downstairs to the kitchen.

Sylva was cleaning the kitchen after preparing breakfast. The children had left for school, and his breakfast—two eggs, bacon, grits, and toast, along with a glass of orange juice—was sitting on the kitchen table. The phone rang, and Sylva answered, "Hello... yes, this is the Sanborne residence. ... Well...." She held the phone out to Morgan and said, "It's long distance from Bombay, India. They said to hold on for Mr. Mara."

Morgan stepped quickly to the phone and took it from Sylva's hand. He put the phone to his ear and heard nothing but some slight static. He shook the receiver and put it to his ear again. Once again, nothing but static came at first, but then he heard a click, and an old, dry voice spoke to him.

"Mr. Sanborne?"

As before, an unreasoning fear began to clutch at Morgan's chest. "Y-Yes, sir, Mr. Mara. This is Morgan Sanborne. How may I help you?"

"I am not a fool, Mr. Sanborne. And I am not misinformed. You have not performed as promised..." the voice hissed, with a dry paper sound.

"But, Mr. Mara—" Morgan began.

"Shut up, Mr. Sanborne!" the voice commanded. Morgan fell silent and, unconsciously, began to worry the top of his buttoned shirt. "You told me that you were about to acquire the property. Now, I hear from other sources that nothing could be further from the truth. I have been generous with the commissions you will receive from carrying out my instructions—very generous indeed, Mr. Sanborne. You, however, have performed less than satisfactorily. I must remind you, Mr. Sanborne, that I will not abide failure. Do I make myself clear?"

Morgan felt a bead of sweat trickle down his forehead and into the corner of his eye. He wiped it away and choked out a reply. "Yes, sir."

"I don't believe you truly understand me, Mr. Sanborne," Mara hissed.

Suddenly, Sylva, who'd been standing by the kitchen sink with one hand on the counter, listening to Morgan's side of the conversation, gave a low moan, *Uuoooo,* and clutched her chest. She looked, wide-eyed, at Morgan with her hand on her chest. Her eyelids fluttered, and he watched as her eyes rolled to the back of her head and she collapsed on the floor, hitting the back of her head on the Formica countertop on her way down. He screamed, *"Sylva!"* and dropped the phone, running over to her prone body. Blood was leaking out of her right nostril.

Morgan called her name again as he bent over her. Her eyelids began to flutter, and then opened. She looked blankly at him for a moment, and then closed her eyes for a second. When she opened them again, she focused on his face.

"Morgan! What happened? What's this? Blood! What happened?!"

He raised her head and shoulders, sat down on the floor, and held her in that position with her head resting on his chest. He said not a word, just rocking slowly back and forth. The trickle of blood from Sylva's nose quickly stopped, and she reached her hand up to grab his hands. He carefully lay her back down on the floor, got up, and grabbed a kitchen towel that was lying over the oven handle. Then, he sat back down and put Sylva's head on his lap, using the towel to clean up the blood that had trickled down her face. They sat there for several minutes, and finally Sylva said, "I think I can get up, Morgan."

"OK," he said, and he helped her get to her feet and onto a chair around the kitchen table, which still held his breakfast. Morgan began to sit in the chair next to Sylva, and then he suddenly jumped up, shouting, "Mr. Mara!"

He ran to the phone receiver, which was dangling by its coiled cord and picked it up. "Mr. Mara?" he spoke into the receiver. "Mr. Mara?" But all he heard was static. He hung up the receiver.

Morgan walked back to the table and sat down. He put his elbows on the table and laid his head on his palms. Sylva reached out to him and asked, "Morgan, what's wrong?"

"Be quiet, Sylva! Let me think!" Then, remembering himself, he asked, "How are you feeling?"

"I feel OK, Morgan," she replied. "I don't know what happened. All of a sudden, I couldn't catch my breath, and it felt like a giant's hand was squeezing my chest. The next thing I knew, you were holding me on the floor. Do you think it was a heart attack?" Sylva asked in a worried tone.

"I think you need to call and get Dr. Mason to see you today, Sylva," Morgan replied.

"Will you take me?"

"No, I can't. There's something very important that I have to do today. I'm sorry, but it can't wait. You'll have to call your sister and get her to take you," Morgan said flatly. He stood up, grabbed the phone, and handed it to Sylva. "Here, call your sister now. I'm going to eat my breakfast, and when she gets here, I've got to go."

Sylva did as she was told. Morgan ate his cold breakfast in silence as he tried to think of a way out of his predicament. He was in too deep. He knew for a certainty that he couldn't walk away from Mr. Mara's project. He thought about his experiences with Mr. Mara and with the baron, and the feelings of breathlessness he got, almost like a heart attack, when Mr. Mara was displeased. The way the baron had menaced him at Jefferson Downs, and seemed to grow to gigantic proportions. Morgan had put all that down to coincidence... weird chance. Now, it was clear that this Mr. Mara was something outside of Morgan's experience. He was much more dangerous than anyone, or anything, which Morgan had experienced before.

Sylva's sister arrived in less than ten minutes. She had to be told the story of what had happened as she sat at the table and held Sylva's hand. As soon as the recounting was finished, Morgan stood up, walked quickly over to Sylva, knelt by her side, and kissed her cheek. Then, he asked, "Are you both going to be all right?" while looking at Sylva's sister.

Her sister, who looked a great deal like Sylva, only heavier, replied, "We'll be just fine, Morgan."

He looked questioningly at Sylva, and she waved her hand at him, "Shoo. Marlene will take me to see Dr. Mason. I'll be fine. Go ahead to your meeting, Morgan." Morgan rose, and walked out of the house and got into his Mercedes. He ordered his thoughts as he drove to his office.

First, I've got to get the guy's name from the chief.... Then, I've got to find him and, somehow, convince him to tell me what's going on in that place. His course of action plotted, he put his foot down harder on the gas pedal and cursed the young woman on the bicycle who was slowing him down as he drove down St. Charles Street.

When he arrived at City Hall, he walked through the front door, into the elevator, and up to his office. He stuck his head into the secretarial pool and saw Brenda sitting at her desk typing something. He walked up to her and asked, "Brenda, could you come see me in my office, please?" Brenda gathered her notepad and pen, and followed Morgan to his office. Once inside, he went to his desk, sat down, and asked, "Did the chief send anything for me?"

Brenda thought for a moment, and then brightened. "Yes! He sent you a messenger envelope. It's on my desk, so I'll go get it quick." She turned and walked back out of the door. A few moments later, she returned with a tan messenger envelope that had obviously been used many times before, judging by the amount of names that had been scratched out. The last name, unscratched, was his. He took the envelope from her, unwound the red thread from the two red, riveted, cardboard washers that bound the flap, and reached inside. There was a single sheet of paper which he took out and read aloud.

"George Santos. White male. 36 years old. Separated. Worked as a furniture salesman for Forstahl Furniture before being fired. Currently works at Gentile Antiques on Royal Street. Brought a young woman, April Flowers, to a play the night of the raid. No arrests, no police problems with the single exception of a parking ticket. Well, well, Mr. Santos. You're a very clever man. Managed to stay below the radar for a long time...." Morgan looked at Brenda and said, "Thank you, Brenda. That's all for now." A quick look of relief passed across Brenda's face as she turned and left his office.

Morgan leaned back in his chair, put his feet on his desk, and looked at the sheet of paper the chief had sent him. He muttered to himself. "Hmmmm.... How am I going to get this guy to talk?"

His thoughts turned back to Mr. Mara, and then to the baron. Suddenly, an idea struck him and he sat up. *Mr. Mara has other sources of information about what's going on. That was obvious by what happened this morning. I wonder if the baron is his source? The baron is local, and more likely to have access to information around here. Maybe I can get the baron's help squeezing this Santos guy?*

Morgan opened the top drawer of his desk and found the small sheet of paper that the baron had given him that day at Jefferson Downs. The paper had a local telephone number. The number began with 586, and this told him that the telephone was somewhere in the French Quarter. Morgan dialed the number. He heard the *brrrrrrr...* sound of the phone ringing on the other end. It rang a number of times and, just as he was getting ready to hang up, someone picked it up on the other end. He swallowed involuntarily, and heard a deep bass voice on the other end say, "Yes, Mr. Sanborne?"

"Er, hello, Baron."

"Get on with it, Mr. Sanborne," the voice commanded.

"Well... er... you told me to call you if there was something I needed, and I need your help."

"I'm listening," the baron replied, and Morgan began telling him about his efforts to change the confiscatory laws of the city, the report from Brenda about drug use at the compound, the police raid, and the finding of only two persons living in the building. He spoke quickly, as he was nervous, and the baron told him to slow down twice in the telling. When Morgan was finished talking he waited, but there was silence on the other end of the phone.

The baron finally replied, "We are aware of your plan, Mr. Sanborne, and we are also aware of how pitifully inadequate it is. Mr. Mara is displeased with your efforts. It was my opinion that you would be inadequate for the task, and I attempted to dissuade Mr. Mara from his decision to hire you. You have proven me right. Unfortunately, circumstances are such that the die is cast, and you are the sole person with whom we can work to achieve our goal at present time. So, I will assist you, Mr. Sanborne, but mark my words. If you fail us, for any reason, your life will be forfeit. Do I make myself clear?"

Morgan was sweating as he listened to the baron. Now, he felt the need to pee. He answered, "Yes, sir."

The baron replied, "Not sir, Mr. Sanborne—Baron!"

"Yes, sir... I mean, Baron!" Morgan choked out through his tightened throat.

"Now, Mr. Sanborne, I would like you to meet me tonight."

"Yes, Baron, I can do that."

"I will meet with you at 9 o'clock. Come to 152 St. Ann Street. You will ring the bell that is next to the wrought-iron gate covering the carriageway. Someone will let you in. Do you understand me?"

"Y-yes, Baron," Morgan said.

"Goodbye, Mr. Sanborne."

Before Morgan could reply, the connection was broken. He was too shaken up to even bother with the rudeness. "My God! What have I gotten myself into." He put his elbows on his desk and laid his hands on his palms. "Who are these people? These things?" He sat like that for several minutes, then straightened up in his chair. "I have no choice," he thought. "I'm dead if I quit. I'm dead if I fail. So, I'm not going to fail. The baron will have a plan that will work. Maybe I can work out a deal with him. I might not make as much as I could have, but if I make something, that's better than nothing, especially if the baron can help me pull it off." He didn't think about his promised portion to his cousin and Harold. They were the least of his worries now.

33
BARON SAMEDI

May 15, 1972

That night, after dinner, Morgan left his house in the dusky evening and drove the Mercedes to the French Quarter. He parked at the Royal Orleans Hotel, his usual parking choice when he went to the Quarter. He walked up the steps from the parking garage to the hotel, and walked through the hallway, past several offices with their doors closed and onto a marble staircase. In the lobby of the hotel, he strode confidently past the concierge stand, then the Rib Room, and exited out onto Royal Street. When he exited the hotel door on Royal, he saw that along with the darkness had come a heavy mist, or light rain. He turned right out the door and noticed the streetlights were cloaked in mist, creating halos of yellow around the lights. The street was mostly dark, with the exception of the areas immediately adjacent to the streetlights, as he moved towards St. Ann Street. When he reached St. Ann, he saw that Number 152 was on the corner. He walked along the building and came on an arched carriageway that, presumably, led into a courtyard. There was an ornate, black, wrought-iron gate across the carriageway, and an electric doorbell next to it. The carriageway was barely lit by a couple of dim, yellow lights which looked for all the world like candles, coming out of the right-side wall just over head-height. He straightened, gave himself a wry grimace, and pushed the button. He didn't hear a sound, but about thirty seconds later, a shadow moved towards him in the carriageway, and he could hear the sound of shoes on the brick floor.

He stood back and, to his surprise, an attractive young woman with dark skin opened the gate and beckoned him in. She was dressed in some sort of satiny, flowing garment and had a cloth wrapped around her head. She said not a word. He followed her, and the gate clanged shut with a locking *clunk*. They walked down the carriageway and out into a courtyard. The courtyard was dark, lit once again only by a few yellow lights that barely penetrated the black night. Morgan could see a couple of gnarled trees, branches twisted and knotted, with few leaves, and the flagstone-covered ground was uneven with weeds growing in the cracks between the stones. The young woman walked to the right side of the courtyard, up to a two-story brick building that was separated from the main structure facing the street. She walked up to a darkly painted door and opened it. She stood aside, and motioned for him to walk into the dimly lit room ahead of her. He nodded as he passed and stepped over the elevated threshold.

He looked around the room after his eyes had adjusted to the dim lighting. The first thing he noticed was that the light was, indeed, coming from several lit candles strategically placed around the room, which itself was small and crowded with furniture. There was a large, round table in the middle of the room, with several smaller tables placed haphazardly in other areas. He could see a total of five wooden chairs, three of which were equidistant around the table. Two others were placed near small tables. Each table contained a bottle of some sort of spirit and various, crudely made statues. He looked at the statues and noticed that many of them had grinning skulls for heads. Most were dressed in clothes with feathers and beads decorating them. Morgan heard the woman clear her throat, and he looked up at her. She motioned him to sit in one of the chairs placed around the large table.

He sat down and looked at a statue placed in the center of the table. This statue was much better made than the others he'd seen. It looked like a statue of the Virgin Mary, but in place of her face, there was a grinning skull. A black, lit candle was placed on top of the statue's head, and the wax slowly dripped down the sides of the candle onto the statue. The statue held what appeared to be a rosary in her right hand, but on closer examination, each bead of the rosary was an intricately carved skull. Morgan was so engrossed in looking at the details of the statue that he jumped and turned when a door creaked open. Another woman walked through the door and into the room. She was almost a twin of the young woman who had let him in. Fine wrinkles around her mouth indicated that she was older than the first woman, but that was the only indication. She, like the younger woman, was dressed in satin, with a satin wrap around her hair.

She walked up to the table, sat down in a chair, and motioned to the younger woman. "Come sit, Marie. We will make the trilogy that is needed to summon the baron." The young woman replied, "Yes, maman," and sat in the other empty chair. A bottle of rum stood next to the statue of the skulled Mary. The older woman took the bottle and tipped it up to her mouth. Then, she pursed her lips and blew the rum onto the candle. The flame flared up as the alcohol ignited, and, as it did so, both women began to chant in a patois that was unintelligible to Morgan. Their united voices rose and fell in a hypnotic rhythm, punctuated every few minutes with another mouthful of rum blown on the candle. The women's voices began to rise, and Morgan could see that their eyes were beginning to roll to the back of their heads as they continued chanting. Their bodies began to jerk and shake in some sort of weirdly syncopated, seated dance. Flecks of foam began to collect in the corners of their mouths. Morgan was beginning to sweat, and the hairs rose on his arms and the back his neck. The chanting continued, and now Morgan could swear that he heard more people speaking than the voices of the two women. Their jerky motions increased, and Morgan could feel his own body jerking involuntarily. The light from the candles seemed to dim, and Morgan felt as if he was looking at the room through the small end of a funnel. The tension became nearly unbearable when both women suddenly screamed, and the candle flame grew large and blindingly bright. Morgan threw both arms over his face protectively.

The room was suddenly silent, and Morgan could see through his covering arms that the light had resumed its previous dim aspect. He slowly lowered his arms, and was astounded to see the tall, dark form of the baron standing against the wall on the other side of the table from him. Both women had laid their heads down on the table and appeared unconscious. The baron glared at Morgan and spoke. "So, we meet again, Mr. Sanborne."

Morgan swallowed hard. "Y-yes, Baron."

The baron continued, "And now you recognize that your plan was insufficient and seek my assistance?"

Morgan felt nearly paralyzed. "Yes, Baron."

The baron walked around the table and grabbed Morgan's chin, turning his face up and towards him. Morgan looked silently up at the tall, dark man. "I will assist you, Mr. Sanborne, but be aware my assistance comes with a price. Are you willing to pay the price?" Morgan was released from his paralysis enough to barely nod his assent. The baron released Morgan's chin and looked down at him. He said in a deep voice, "Listen... and obey!"

Morgan was released from his paralysis. He nodded and again said, "Yes, Baron."

"Your plan was doomed to fail from the start, because you do not know what you are fighting. You believe that you are powerful, but you are, in fact, a child. Grabbing and kicking... striking out when you cannot gain what you wish. Those are the actions of a child, and will be of no avail in the battle to come. You will do as I say. You will be disciplined. If you do this, we will not fail. If you do not...." Here, the baron leaned down until his nose was level with Morgan's. Morgan could smell his breath, a foul smell of decay, and pulled back involuntarily. The baron smiled, and his teeth were now sharp, white rat's teeth. A groan escaped from Morgan's lips.

The baron stood up straight and said, "Now, Mr. Sanborne. This is what you must do. There is a man living at the house on Dumaine Street. He is newly arrived, and has been taken up by our enemies."

Morgan felt the blood return to his face. He nodded. "George Santos. I learned his name today."

The baron waved his hand to cut off any further speech. "Listen, Mr. Sanborne. You will find this man... this George Santos... and you will take him to Grand Terre Island. Are you familiar with it?"

Morgan nodded again. "Yes, Baron. The island next to Grand Isle. It's where Jean Lafitte lived with his pirates. I'm familiar with it."

"Good. There are usually people who stay on the island... scientists who have a research station there. They will not be there when you arrive. You must bring this Santos to the island tomorrow evening. I will be there, with others. This Santos will become the tip of our spear into the hearts of our enemies. You will bring him to the inner yard of the fort and I will take him from you there. Do you understand?" The baron looked down on Morgan with a deadly look.

"Y-yes, Baron, I understand. I will take Santos to Grand Terre tomorrow evening and deliver him to you, but... how will I convince him to come with me?"

"That detail is left for you, Mr. Sanborne. Remember, if you fail, your life is forfeit."

Morgan swallowed and said, "Yes, Baron."

"Now, go!" The baron waved dismissively.

Morgan didn't hesitate. He rose from the table with hardly a glance at the two unconscious women and made haste to leave the room, going back through the courtyard and the carriageway. When he reached the gate, he pushed on it and it opened onto the street. He staggered out onto the street and the gate clanged shut behind him. There, he leaned against the damp wall of the building, breathing hard. The events of the evening had so unsettled him that it took him a moment to orient himself. Then, he began walking. The night was still and the mists hung over the French Quarter like a blanket of spiderwebs as Morgan walked back to the Royal Orleans, got his Mercedes from the parking lot, and drove home.

Inside, he found the house quiet. He walked up the stairs to the bedroom he shared with his wife and found her asleep. In the bathroom, he brushed his teeth, and then he slipped quietly into the bed next to Sylva. He lay there awake, thinking of the evening and of how he was going to get George Santos to agree to go with him to Grand Terre Island. The beginning of an idea was forming in his mind. He thought, *That girl is the lever I need to get Santos to Grand Terre. I need to talk to Brenda tomorrow morning, and I need to get in touch with Fleming Babineaux and arrange to rent his boat....*

34
A TRAP IS SET

May 16, 1972

April woke to the loud, repetitive call of a mockingbird. She lay there on her side with George's arm thrown across her. The bird's call was softly punctuated by George's regular breathing. She began counting to herself as she listened to the bird, to see if she could determine how long the song sequence was. There was one particular call that sounded like a streetcar bell, which made her smile. She used this particular call to begin the timing. She thought, *One, and two, and three…*, and reached 43 before she heard that particular call again. She couldn't help letting out a small chuckle. *Smart mockingbird.*

George heard April's chuckle as he lay in a state between sleep and wakefulness. He felt completely at peace lying next to April. He moved his arm and she turned towards him, smiling.

"Good morning, sleepyhead!"

"Mmm… morning." He smiled back, then raised his hand and rubbed the sleep out of his eyes. "I guess we need to get up to get ready for work."

"Unfortunately, I think you're right, but let's just lie here for a minute." She took his arm and put it back around her.

"Perfect…" he murmured as he kissed the back of her neck.

They lay like this for a short time, and then she said, "OK, George. It's time." She moved his arm and sat up. He whined like a puppy, and she laughed and bent over and gave him a kiss. "Really, George, if we don't get up, I'll never make it to work on time."

"OK," he replied with a reluctant smile, and got up.

After they were dressed, he asked April if she would like to get something to eat for breakfast. "That sounds great. Why don't we go get some beignets at Café Du Monde?"

He replied, "That's good with me," and they left his apartment and walked down the stairs to the courtyard.

There was no sign of anyone in the courtyard, and April looked around and said, "I just love this courtyard. It's so green and full of flowers. I would imagine the Garden of Eden to look like this."

"It certainly is a beautiful place, April, but time's a'wastin'. We need to get a move on if either of us is going to get to work on time."

It was a little early for the tourist trade at Café du Monde, so they had no problem getting a table. They had their powdered beignets and rich café' au lait in short order. After they'd finished their breakfast, George walked with April to Canal Street so she could catch the bus. The bus pulled up as soon as they reached the bus stop. April gave George a quick kiss, and wiped a smudge of powdered sugar from the corner of his mouth. "Bye, George."

"Bye, April. I'll give you a call when I get off work."

"OK. See you later!" She got on the bus, paid her fare, and found a seat.

George waved as the bus pulled off, and then turned and walked back to the antique store on Royal Street.

When he reached the store, he unlocked the door and began his morning's preparations. Ten minutes or so later, Tony walked in carrying two cups of coffee.

"Good morning, George!" he said cheerfully. "I've brought you some caffeine."

George laughed and thanked Tony as he took the Styrofoam cup and pried the plastic lid off. "Ah, just the way I like it!"

He took a sip, then set the cup down on a doily and continued getting ready. In short order, the shop was ready for business, and George went to the door and turned the sign from "Closed" to "Open." Tony asked for his help in removing an old moth-eaten, chintz, chair cover in preparation for re-covering.

The morning passed quickly, with a smattering of customers punctuating Tony and George's efforts to restore some old pieces. Around noon, they were both in the back working on an old chest with one broken hinge when the tinkling of a bell called from the front of the store. "I'll get it, Tony," George said, and left the back to take care of the customer. As he walked from the back of the store, he could see that the customer was a tall, thin, well-dressed, dark-haired man. He walked up to him and said, "Good afternoon. I'm George. How may I help you?"

A look of surprise passed across the man's face for an instant, but was replaced with a smile. "Hello, George. My name is Morgan Sanborne. Perhaps you've heard of me?"

35

AN UNUSUAL ASSIGNMENT

May 16, 1972

April arrived at the *Times Picayune* city room, which was filled with desks and the bustle of people talking to each other or on the phone, along with the clack of electric and manual typewriters. She smiled a hello to several of the people she passed who were sitting at different desks. When she reached her desk, she put down her purse and camera case. Then, she saw a sheet of paper on her chair. She picked it up and read, "April, please come see me. Ben." She put the paper down on her desk and walked over to the glass-enclosed office at the end of the large room. Noise followed her into the office, and then subsided when she closed the door.

Ben Shelton was sitting behind his desk, which was littered with paper. He had a cigarette between his lips and was listening to someone on his telephone. He waved April towards a chair on the other side of his desk. She had to move a stack of papers from the chair to the floor in order to sit, and she heard him say, "That's fine with me. Talk to you later. Bye." He took a puff from the cigarette and put it in the full ashtray that was on the corner of his desk. "Hi, April, how are you today?"

"Fine, Ben. What's up?"

He replied, "I got a call from one of our city councilmen this morning, asking specifically for your efforts as a photographer."

April laughed. "Gee, I must be getting famous."

Shelton snorted a laugh and continued, "Yeah, you must be. Anyway, Councilman Sanborne's secretary called me and said that he's going to be taking a tour of Fort Livingston, down close to Grand Isle, and he wants you to go with him down there to document the trip. He wants to meet you at 4 o'clock. She says he has someone who'll write a PR piece about the trip, so we wouldn't need to send our Human Interest reporter. I told her that it was a bit of an unusual request, and that I retained editorial responsibility on anything that was written. She said the councilman would agree to that, so here we are. I've already set it up so you can use a car from the car pool."

April smiled, "That sounds like fun, only I'd better get some bug dope. I've been to Grand Isle once before and got eaten alive by mosquitoes."

Shelton laughed again. "Don't be a wimp, April. The mosquitoes don't really get bad till evening. It's those biting, green-head flies that you have to watch out for."

April winced and replied, "Proves my point, Ben. I need to get some bug spray before I go down there. Where am I supposed to meet this guy?"

"He gave me some directions... here, let me see." Ben rooted around the papers on the top of his desk. "Aha! Here it is. The Law of Superposition never fails!" He handed April a sheet of yellow, lined paper.

She took the paper and asked, "Superwhat? What's that?"

"The best thing I got from my undergraduate geology class. The Law of Superposition was first proposed by a guy named Steno. It simply states that if there is no disturbance, older stuff is below younger stuff. It's an integral part of the science of geology."

April chuckled, "Ben, I didn't know you were a geologist!"

Ben smiled and said, "I almost flunked the course, but I've always remembered the Law of Superposition. It's what I use to keep order here," he added, waving to the stacks of paper scattered around his office.

April looked at the sheet of yellow paper in her hand, rose from the chair, and said, "OK, Ben. I'll get on this. If I have to meet the guy down in Grand Isle by four o'clock, I'll need to leave New Orleans by 2 or so. I'll swing by K&B and get whatever I need. My guess is that I'll be late getting back, so I need to call my boyfriend and let him know."

Ben raised his eyebrows. "I didn't know you were dating someone."

April smiled. "It's been kind of sudden, but I like it. He's a nice guy."

"That's the girl!" Ben said in an avuncular way. "Pick the nice guys, not the cool guys. You'll be happier." Then, he waved her out of his office as he turned back to the telephone and began dialing.

April smiled and nodded, and then walked back to her desk. She glanced at the clock hanging over the door leading out of the room and saw that it was 9:30. She sat at her desk and reviewed her scheduled assignments. Luckily, there were none that day, so she began a cursory review of some of the negatives from photographs she had taken and developed the previous week. She did this by looking at the negatives through a large magnifying glass while holding them up to the row of fluorescent lights that passed over her desk. She made some notes of which ones she wanted to examine more closely. When she looked at the clock again, she was surprised to see that it was already 11:50. She collected her purse and camera case, checking to make sure she had plenty of film—both black and white and color.

She walked down to the car pool and was assigned a cream-colored, 1968 Ford Falcon. April got into the car, after sliding her purse and camera case to the passenger end of the vinyl bench seat, and was pleased to discover that it had an automatic transmission. She waved goodbye to the carpool employee who had brought the car to her and left the parking lot. She drove towards her house so that she could change clothes. When she reached Canal Boulevard, just past the cemeteries, she pulled into the parking lot of a K&B drugstore to get some bug spray. She looked up at the big, purple sign that announced the name of the drugstore and smiled as she thought of the jingle that accompanied their television ads. Inside, she picked up a couple of cheese crackers and Slim Jims for snacks, a Coca Cola, and a honeybun. She walked back to the sporting goods section and soon found what she was looking for—a small, plastic bottle of 6-12 Insect Repellent with the "Convenient Pump Spray" that would fit in the top pocket of the shirt she was planning to wear. After paying for her items, she left the store and drove home.

Once home, she tried to call George at the store, but Tony told her that he'd left for the day. She left just before 2 o'clock, hopped onto the I-610, and got off at the Clearview exit heading south. The sky was dark, and a thunderstorm struck just as she was getting onto the Huey P. Long Bridge. The lanes were very narrow, and her knuckles whitened as she tightened her grip on the steering wheel. The rain fell so hard that it became difficult to see, even with the windshield wipers on maximum. A large 18-wheeler pulled alongside her as she reached the peak of the bridge, and she felt squeezed between the side of the truck and the bridge guard rail. She lifted her foot from the gas pedal and the car slowed, allowing the truck to pass. Once it passed her, she moved her car so that it straddled the mid-line and followed the truck off of the bridge. The rest of her trip was uneventful, and she enjoyed seeing the small houses with neat yards and gardens as she drove down Bayou Lafourche.

She passed Golden Meadow and began driving down that portion of LA-1 that followed the ever-larger Bayou Lafourche. Shrimp boats were docked along the side of the bayou, and small camps and houses were built on small stilts across the highway from the boats. There were several hand-painted signs advertising fresh shrimp or oysters for sale.

She was approaching Grand Isle when she noticed a large cluster of cumulus clouds that floated over the Gulf of Mexico to her right. She kept glancing to her right as the cluster seemed to grow. She looked again, and noticed that one cloud seemed clearer than the others; it even began to take on a shape that looked like JC with his large afro. The blare of a horn snapped her back into awareness and she pulled back into her lane as a pickup truck passed in the opposite lane, the driver shaking his fist angrily. She shook her head and paid more attention to her driving.

April arrived at the pavilion just after 4 o'clock, and pulled into the shell-covered parking area. The pavilion was located in what the locals called the "Cheniere"—French for "oak"—before the bridge that led to Grand Isle. April knew this because, the one time she had been to Grand Isle, her family had rented one of the camps on the Cheniere. There were two people sitting in chairs under the shade of the pavilion. The contrast between the bright sunlight reflecting off of the white shell parking lot and the shade made it difficult for her to see clearly. She waved as she walked up, and called out, "Councilman Sanborne?" When she reached the shade, she stopped with surprise. George was sitting in one of the chairs with a big grin on his face.

"What?! George, what are you doing here?!"

The other man answered, "You must be Miss Flowers. Please excuse me—I'm Morgan Sanborne. Mr. Santos is here at my invitation." The man rose and walked up to April with his hand extended. She shook his hand, but kept looking at George.

George rose, walked up to April, and gave her a hug.

"It's an amazing coincidence, April," he began. "The councilman came into the shop today looking for an armoire, and as we talked, he told me that he was coming down here to tour Grand Terre Island, and that you were supposed to meet him to take pictures for the newspaper. When I told him that I knew you, he invited me to come along."

April shook her head, puzzled, but said, "Uh, OK." She saw the beginning of a crestfallen look on George's face, and added with a smile, "I'm glad you're here, George," before she turned to the councilman, "I'm here, Mr. Sanborne. Can you tell me a bit about the job?"

"Please call me Morgan, April. We're all informal here. We'll be using this boat to take the short hop to Grand Terre, where we'll meet the others. Then, we'll tour Fort Livingston, listen to a brief lecture, and climb back aboard and return here before dark. Will that be all right with you?" He smiled sweetly.

April looked at George, then back at Morgan. "Sure, Morgan. That will be fine. Would it be all right if George and I ride back together?"

Morgan waved his hand. "Absolutely. I expected it when I invited him to come along. Now, if you will, we'd better be getting over to the island... wouldn't want our other guests to wait too long for us." Morgan led them to a small slip with a boat tied up. He said as he stepped in, "I arranged for this boat. I love to fish, and I'm very familiar with the waters around Grand Isle, so please don't be concerned." He held out his hand to help April in. She sat in the seat in front of the center console. George got in last and waited until Morgan had started the engine before he untied the bow rope from the dock cleat. Then, he pushed the bow of the boat out towards the narrow canal that led to Caminada Bay. He stood on one side of the console holding onto a chrome handle that ran from the bottom of the windshield to the floor.

36
PASSING THROUGH
THE VEIL

May 16, 1972

Once out of the canal and into the bay, Morgan said, "OK, hold on!" He pushed the throttle up. The bow of the boat reared up for a moment and then settled on a plane, and Morgan headed northeast, paralleling the Cheniere. They were shortly at an opening where they could see the concrete pilings of the new Grand Isle bridge, which had been built after Hurricane Betsy had damaged the previous bridge. The old bridge had been constructed of creosote pilings. The local government had demolished the central portion of the old wooden bridge and left two thirds of the bridge intact, one third on either side of Caminada Pass for fishermen to use as a pier.

April looked at George and saw that he had a huge smile on his face. George looked back at her, leaned over, and yelled over the motor's noise, "It's been four years since I was on a boat! Isn't it great?!" April smiled back, as she felt it was too noisy to speak. They passed along the back side of Grand Isle, looking at the camps both large and small, some raised to great heights and others sitting nearly on the ground. April noticed something funny about the sky as she looked across the island towards the Gulf of Mexico. She had noticed the large, cumulus clouds as she'd driven the last part of Highway 1 down towards Grand

Isle. Now, all she saw was a grayish white sky. The boat continued to parallel the Island, dodging a few, small marsh islands that dotted the bay. Just as they reached Barataria Pass that ran between Grand Isle and Grand Terre islands, the fog bank reached them. Morgan had to throttle down the boat to nearly a crawl as visibility sank. They could see no more than twenty feet in front of the boat. April looked around at George and saw beads of water forming on his face as the thick fog rolled in. George smiled and shrugged his shoulders. The noise having lessened, he leaned down and said, "It's like taking a bath."

Morgan had taken a bearing just before the fog bank rolled in, and he followed the bearing on the gimbaled compass that was mounted on the console behind the steering wheel. He steered by this bearing, motoring at a walking pace for several minutes. It was between tides, so the water was calm. The sudden *Whoosh!* of an exhaled breath made them all start. April turned and said, "Oh, Look! A dolphin!" The dolphin submerged again, only to reappear on the other side of the boat, again with a loud *Whoosh!*

"Get outta here!" Morgan snarled, and he made as if to throw something at the dolphin. The creature sank beneath the waves and did not return. George and April looked a question at each other. Morgan turned his attention back to navigating the boat through the thick fog. The engine rumbled at a steady pace as the boat slowly inched forward.

George pointed to something dark in the fog ahead and called out to Morgan, "Look out!" Morgan put the boat into neutral and glided up to a dilapidated pier that rose about three feet above the water level. George stood up, walked to the front of the boat, and grasped the wooden planking of the pier. He then bent over and picked up the bow rope. He climbed on top of the pier and tied it fast to the top of the nearest piling.

Morgan cut the engine of the boat, and the silence was deafening. If there was any sound coming from the island, it was completely muffled by the thick fog. Morgan turned, grabbed a rope that was tied to the back cleat of the boat, and tied it fast to a piling. The boat was now tied fore and aft, and floated next to the pier.

April stood up and, with George's help, climbed onto the pier. Morgan followed. The fog was so thick that the shore was lost in a blanket of white wisps. They carefully walked along the planks, and the brushy shoreline was soon evident. They walked off of the pier and looked around. The fog shrouded everything, but they could see the shore was covered in low brush, and that there were some larger trees looming just inland.

George spoke first, "Well, we're here, Morgan. Where's everyone else?"

"I'm not sure," Morgan replied, "but I guess they'll be here soon enough."

They saw a narrow path that led through the brush. Morgan said, "Let's follow that path. It probably leads to the fort, and that's where the others should be." He took the lead and began walking. April followed with George bringing up the rear. The path wound its way through the brush, then through a copse of gnarled, live oak trees. The trees dripped water on them as the fog condensed on the Spanish moss-covered branches.

They had walked for less than ten minutes when someone in the mist shouted, "Halt!"

They stopped in their tracks. The voice called out again, "Who goes there?"

Morgan called back, "It's Morgan Sanborne! The baron told me to meet him here."

Morgan began to say something else, but was interrupted by a rather small, thin man wearing homespun gray clothing and a red sash around his waist, who appeared through the misty fog. He was carrying a large-barreled gun and had it pointed towards the three of them. He walked warily towards them and stopped when he was about ten feet away.

"Ye say ye are a Sanborne? Methinks ye are a spy. Now, move on ahead of me, and I'm warnin' ye, don't try any tricks. We'll see what the captain says. Now, March!"

37
NEZ COUPÉ

September 16, 1814

George was bewildered. He began to ask what was going on, but as soon as a sound escaped his throat, the small man prodded him with his gun and said, "Shut up!"

April couldn't stop herself from chiding the man, "What do you think you're doing?"

"Be quiet, Missy," he replied, and motioned with the barrel of his gun. "Just start walking and don't try anything funny."

They continued walking down the path, which grew wider. The oaks grew sparse and were replaced by grass and a few scrub trees. After a short walk, a building loomed in their view. There were two windows in the small, single-story, wooden structure. It was raised on brick piers and the windows spilled a yellow light haloed by the fog. The man called, "Ahoy! Look smart! I've captured some spies!"

April looked at George and whispered, "This doesn't make sense. Do you know what's happening?"

George looked around quickly and whispered back, "April, we're not in our time. I..."

"Be quiet!" the small man said harshly, poking George with the point of his gun again.

The door to the building opened and two men strode out. The first was tall and dark-haired, and wore a tall, dark, worn felt hat with a white feather on the side. April drew in a breath as the second man walked up. He was bare-headed, dressed in dark clothes with a black, cloth jacket, and was horribly disfigured. He had no nose—just a hole in his ruddy face where his nose should have been. He spoke first, and his words had an eerie sibilance as air escaped from the hole. He spoke English, but with an Italian accent.

"What have you brought us, Henry?"

"I believe they are spies, Nez," the small man replied, keeping his gun in such a position as to cover his so-called captives.

Morgan spoke up angrily, "Now, look here! I don't know what kind of dress-up games you're playing here, but you're messing with the wrong man! I'm a New Orleans city councilman! I'm supposed to meet the baron here. You'd better get me to him, or there'll be hell to pay!"

The noseless man, Nez by name, snorted a laugh, and some mucus flew from the hole in his face. George saw April flinch. Nez walked up to Morgan, raised a cutlass, and laid it on Morgan's shoulder. George watched as he moved the blade closer to Morgan's neck. He saw Morgan begin to shake, but was surprised to see that the man stood his ground.

Nez kept the cutlass against Morgan's neck for a count of three, and then he shrugged and dropped the cutlass to his side. "You say you are the baron's man. Very well. I will take you at your word for now. We will soon find out if you are spies, either from the British or the Americans."

The small man piped up, "He said his name be Sanborne."

The tip of the cutlass raised as Nez cocked his head. "Sanborne? You may well be a spy, then."

"I told you, I'm not a spy! I'm Morgan Sanborne. I'm the New Orleans City Councilman for District A!" Morgan's voice didn't have quite the emphasis it had held a few moments ago, and had taken on a plaintive tone.

Nez turned away from Morgan, towards George and April. "And are you also a New Orleans City Councilman?" he asked George.

"No, sir, I'm George Santos. Just a regular person. This is April Flowers. She's a photographer for the *Times Picayune*."

"Photo grav... eh? What is that?"

April spoke up, "I take pictures to publish in the newspaper."

He nodded. "Oh, so you are an artist. Very well. My name is Nez Coupe´ for obvious reasons." He pointed to the hole in his face. "You are my captives. Henry, search them."

Henry searched George and Morgan and collected their wallets. He took April's purse and camera bag, but did not search her person. The camera caused the greatest excitement as the privateers struggled to figure it out. This went on for a couple of minutes when Nez Coupe´ announced, "Dominique, take their belongings inside and examine them. Be prepared to give the results to le Capitaine. Now, all of you... follow me. Henry, go back to your guard duty." He then spoke to his so-called captives again, adding, "There is nowhere for you to go on this island, so do not try to escape."

Nez Coupe´ turned and headed back towards the building. The path widened as they neared the structure, and buildings began to appear out of the fog. Nez Coupe´ walked past the building they had first seen as the path widened into a sandy street. The man called Dominique turned and went inside the building. George could now see that there were buildings on both sides of the street. All were made of wood and most of them were raised on brick piers. They loomed ghostlike in the thick fog, and only the facades were clearly evident. The small group made their way down the street until they came to a large, raised house. The first floor was made of brick, solid and thick. The second story was wooden with a covered porch that wrapped all around the house. There was a wooden stairwell that provided entrance to the upper porch. Nez Coupe´ walked up the stairs, followed by Morgan, April, and George. He opened the door, turned, bowed, and motioned the captives to enter the house before him.

It took a moment for George's eyes to adjust to the candlelight, but when he could see, he was amazed. The room was large, with a candlelit, crystal chandelier hanging from the tall ceiling over an ornately carved, wooden table. There were eight cloth-covered, wooden-backed chairs set around the table. George instantly recognized them as Chippendale. Each place was set with settings made entirely of silver. Plates, glasses, saucers, and cups were all made of the precious metal, as were the knives, forks, and spoons. April looked around the room and saw several paintings on the walls. She was struck, in particular, by a painting of a beautiful, Spanish woman in a red dress with black lace mantilla and a fan. There were other pieces of furniture around the room, and the mantle over the fireplace held a pair of exquisite Chinese vases.

Nez Coupe´ walked through the door and announced, "Welcome to my humble abode. Please, you may be my captives, but there is no reason not to enjoy your captivity. May I offer you some fine Madeira wine?" He motioned the three to sit at the table.

"William!" he called.

A tall black man walked into the room and answered, "Yes, sir."

"Bring us some Madeira."

William walked up to a cabinet, opened a carved door, and pulled out a carafe. He brought the carafe to the table and filled a silver glass of wine for each of the guests. He then walked to the head of the table and poured a glass for Nez. When finished, he returned the carafe to the cabinet and asked, "Is there anything more you require, Master?"

Nex shook his hand dismissively. He grasped his glass and raised it, saying, "To victory over the British!"

George and April looked at each other and raised their glasses, echoing Nez Coupe´'s toast. Morgan sat there with an astonished look on his face. "What the hell is going on here?" he demanded.

Nez Coupe´ put down his glass and stared at Morgan. "Monsieur Sanborne. If you cannot be a civil guest, perhaps you would prefer to be placed in the calaboose?"

Morgan paled. "No... no, I apologize.... I meant no offense. I'm just having a hard time understanding what is happening."

Nez Coupe´ took a sip of his Madeira, and then delicately used a cloth handkerchief to dab at the hole in his face. Again, he looked at Morgan. "Well, Mr. Sanborne, what is happening is that you are my captives—no, my guests, until the captain arrives and decides what to do with you."

Morgan said, in a more conciliatory tone, "The captain. Who is this captain? All I know is that the baron told me that I was to meet him here today. Is the baron here?"

Nez Coupe´ smiled and gave a slight shrug of his shoulders. "Who do you think is the Captain of Grand Terre, Mr. Sanborne? Why, Monsieur Jean Lafitte, of course. Everyone knows that. As for the baron, he comes and goes as he will. I can no more control the baron then I can the hurricane's wind."

April asked, "Where is Monsieur Lafitte now?"

Nez Coupe´ turned towards her and replied, "Direct, and to the point. That is a trait that you share, mademoiselle, with my late wife." He pointed towards the painting of the beautiful Spanish woman. "I will answer your question. The captain left for New Orleans several days ago to discuss a recent visit to Grand Terre by the English who left the area this very morning. You are, no doubt, aware of the current state of affairs between the English and Les Americains. They presented several letters to the captain in an attempt to gain our assistance for an attack on New Orleans—" he turned towards Morgan, "where you are a *councilman*. The captain is an honorable man, not a traitor. He will inform the alcalde—the mayor, that is—of the British offer. In return, he only asks that we may be allowed to continue our poor efforts at enterprise here...."

Nez Coupe´'s story was interrupted by someone walking in the front door. It was a man, pale-faced with ruddy cheeks and black hair. His hat was large and turned up in front, and he had the bearing of a man used to giving orders. When he saw the man, Nez Coupe´ immediately rose up. George, April, and Morgan sat for a moment more, but then they stood up, as well.

The man surveyed the assembly and asked in French-accented English, "What goes on here, Nez?"

"Capitaine!" Nez announced, "These guests arrived unannounced on the bayside of the island. Henry was standing guard and found them coming towards the village. I have brought them here to await your orders."

Jean Lafitte stood silent, looking at the three 'guests' for a moment. He doffed his hat and bowed. "Bonjour, madmoiselle, et monsieurs. I am Jean Lafite. May I know your names?"

Morgan rapidly replied, "I am New Orleans City Councilman Morgan Sanborne, of District A, and I demand—" Morgan instinctively stopped talking as he saw the look on Lafitte's face change from polite blandness to intense anger.

"Sanborne! Sanborne! Fils de putain!" He walked up to Morgan, grabbed him by the shoulders, and threw him to the ground.

"Stop! Stop! It wasn't supposed to be this way!" Morgan lay on the floor with his hands covering his face. His chair had toppled with him as he'd gone down and now lay over his legs.

"Capitain! What has happened!" Nez asked with alarm.

Lafitte got control of his temper and backed away from Morgan. "Fils de putain! They were very solicitous of me when I gave them the English letters. 'Thank you, Monsieur Lafitte! You are a true patriot, Monsieur Lafitte! Bah! I spoke with my attorney, Livingston, just before I departed New Orleans, and he informed me that Governor Claiborne's lackey, Sanborne—" here, he paused and kicked the prone Morgan, who yelled and curled up into a ball, "that sac de merde, has already ordered the invasion of Barataria by American troops. We must make provisions to leave immediately, before their ships arrive. But, first... take these three, tie their hands, and put them in the calaboose. Then, send for Dominique. Bring him to my house. We must make a plan. I have an idea, but it will involve sacrifice." Lafitte turned and walked out the door without another glance at the captive guests.

<h1>38</h1>

THE CALABOOSE AND A REVELATION

September 16, 1814

Nez Coupe´ called for William to bring him some rope. After he had complied, Nez told William to find Dominique and bring him back. William made ready to leave, and Nez stopped him and ordered, "Send one of the guards here before you go to Dominique." William left, and Nez spoke again, "If you would, please stand next to each other and turn around with your hands behind you."

Morgan looked up from the ground as if he were getting ready to refuse when Nez pulled a knife from somewhere on his person and laid it on the table, almost daring Morgan to do something. Morgan slowly stood and turned with his hands behind his back.

George could feel his heart pounding. He glanced at April and saw fear in her eyes. He looked at Nez and said, "Mr. Coupe´, we are your guests, and we expect to be treated well."

"I will do what I can, Monsieur," Nez Coupe´ responded. "I ask you, on your word of honor, do any of you have any weapons upon your person?"

George replied in what he hoped was a confident tone, "On my word of honor, we do not." He nodded to April, and then both stood up and walked over to Morgan. They turned with their hands behind their backs.

Nez Coupe´ proceeded to tie the rope first around Morgan's waist, and then to tie his hands behind him, before going on to April and doing the same. Before he began to tie her hands, he said, "I am very sorry to have to do this, mademoiselle." Then, he went on to George. When he had finished tying George, he had the three of them tied in a line, their hands useless. He said, "I will return in a moment, and then I will lead you to the calaboose, and I warn you, do not try to escape." He left the room, and returned in a moment with a lit torch. "Please follow me," he said politely as he stepped out the door.

He walked out the front door at a deliberate pace, and Morgan, April, and George followed. The guard was waiting outside. They saw that evening had come and the fog was thicker than before. It would have been difficult for George to see Nez in the foggy evening's faint light if he hadn't had the torch held high as he walked ahead of the bound trio. They walked down the stairs, being careful to coordinate their motions, and then down the street. The guard followed just behind them. The houses on the street loomed dark. Many had windows that were lit with a warm, yellow glow which was haloed by the thick fog. They walked for several minutes before arriving at a low, brick building built on the ground.

Nez stopped in front of the door, reached into a pocket of his jacket, and pulled out a key that he used to open the door. He then stepped aside, and waved his prisoners into a small, dark room before ordering the guard to stay outside. There was just enough light for George to see that the room was sparsely furnished, with only a small table and one chair. Nez followed them into the room with the torch. He used it to light a torch mounted on the wall. He admonished them not to try anything before untying them. When he had freed them of their bonds, he turned, without a word, and walked out of the door. They heard the *click* of the lock as he turned the key, and his orders to the man to stand guard at the door. Then, his muffled footsteps slowly faded as he walked away into the evening.

Morgan sat down in the chair, leaving George and April on their feet. George looked down at him and said, "Hey, Morgan, why don't you let April sit down?"

George was surprised by the look of hatred on Morgan's face. "I don't know what kind of charade is being played on us, but it's all your fault!" he snarled.

It was George's turn to be perplexed. "What are you talking about, Morgan? Are you crazy? What have I done to you?"

Morgan looked half out of his mind with fear and anger. He ignored George and put his head in his hands.

George was beginning to get angry. "Hey, Morgan, I said for you to let April—" he quieted as April grabbed his arm and shook her head.

She turned towards Morgan and said in a calm voice, "Why don't you tell us what's going on, Morgan?"

Somehow, her voice reached through the tumult in Morgan's mind. He looked at her with a blank face for a moment, and then his face hardened. "It's all your boyfriend's fault! He's involved in a drug ring that's peddling the stuff out of that compound in the Quarter."

George was taken aback. "That's not true!" he exclaimed.

Once again, April put her hand on his arm to quiet him. In the same calm voice as before, she asked, "Why do you say that, Morgan?"

Morgan laughed and said scornfully, "I say that because I sent my secretary there as a spy. She was given some kind of drug, a hallucinogen that frightened her so badly she ran out. I told the cops and they raided the place looking for the drugs, but this asshole outsmarted them!"

"What!?" George shouted. "*You're* the reason the police raided the place? You're the reason Jim died? There were no drugs, you son of a bitch!" Something snapped inside George, and he grabbed Morgan out of the chair and began pummeling him. Morgan screamed and fought back, grabbing George and throwing him against the brick wall. George leapt back, grabbed Morgan again, and both men fell to the ground fighting. April jumped out of the way and backed up to the nearest wall.

She watched the two men roll on the ground for several seconds before she screamed, "Stop it! Stop it! You're not doing us any good!" She looked around for something to throw on the pair, but saw nothing. Then, she noticed the torch. She ran to the wall, grabbed the torch out of its holder, and swung the flaming brand over the wrestling men. The zipping sound of the swirling flame passing close over them, coupled with the heat of the torch, made them stop fighting. Both were breathing heavily. April swung the torch over them again for good measure and said sternly, "Stop it! Now!"

George and Morgan pushed away from each other and slowly got to their feet. The guard began pounding on the door. "What's going on in there?" he demanded.

April lowered her voice and hissed at the two men, "We're trapped in this prison, in a place and time that we're not supposed to be in! God knows what's going to happen to us. We need to work together and try to get out of here. Fight some other time!"

George hung his head sheepishly. "I'm sorry, April. I lost my head. It's just—"

"I'm not done with you," Morgan interrupted him with a snarl, "but she's right. I was supposed to meet the baron here, and he was going to fix everything, but he's not here and everything has gone to shit! I don't know who's running this lunatic asylum, but these people are fucking dangerous!"

George listened to Morgan rant and then said, "I agree. We're in danger here, and we need to work together to get away." He fixed his gaze on Morgan until he nodded, then turned to April. "OK, April, we'll all work together to get out of here. Now, does anyone have any ideas?"

April walked back to the chair and sat down. She absentmindedly raised her hand and smoothed her hair. When she brought her hand back down, she brushed against something in the top pocket of her shirt. She got a puzzled look on her face, and then reached in her pocket and pulled out the small, plastic bottle of insect repellent. The heavy fog had kept the mosquitoes from flying, and she'd forgotten all about the repellent. An idea began to form in her mind.

She whispered, "We need to get the guard to open the door."

George looked at her, then at Morgan, and nodded. He quietly said, "Morgan, get down on the floor." Morgan gave him a defiant look. George whispered, "I've got an idea to get the guard to open the door, but you need to lie on the floor." Morgan gave him a sullen look, but complied. George walked over to the chair in the flickering light, grabbed it by the back, and then, like the mighty Casey at bat, he swung the chair at the brick wall with all the force he could muster. He screamed as he swung, "I'm going to kill you, you son of a bitch!" The sound of the chair splintering, coupled with George's screams, was too much for the guard. He inserted the key in the door and opened it, coming in with a dagger in his right hand.

"What's going—" But before he could say anything else, April began squirting the insect repellent into his eyes. He screamed, dropping the dagger as his hands rose to his blinded eyes. Morgan grabbed the dagger from off the floor as George took the man and ran him, head-first, into the brick wall. The guard dropped like a limb from a tree.

The three looked at each other. George spoke first, "Quick! Let's get out of here and get back to the boat. It's our only chance."

39

ESCAPE INTO DANGER

May 16, 1972

They ran out the door and into the dark, foggy night. The fog had grown even thicker, and they could barely see the yellow lights of windows in the buildings across the street. George led them to the left, into the brush behind the structures. The branches of the small wax myrtles scratched them and they made slow progress. They could hear no sign of pursuit, but the muffling effect of the fog greatly reduced the distance that any sound would travel. George led the group through the brush and finally onto the shoreline, which was marked by a thin line of sucking mud and waist-high marsh grass. George led them through this, as well, and then out into the shallow water where their progress became easier. He turned right and followed the line of marsh grass, with the others wading behind him.

After what seemed like thirty minutes, but was probably closer to ten, George walked right into the wooden plank of a pier, opening a small gash on his forehead. He cursed quietly and whispered a warning to April and Morgan. They felt their way under the pier to the other side, and found Fleming Babineaux's boat tied where they had left it. Morgan clambered aboard as George helped April into the boat, where she sat down in front of the center console. George climbed aboard and loosed the bow rope as Morgan did the same for the stern. George tried to push the bow of the boat away from the pier, and did so with difficulty since the tide was now going out and the force of the water were pushing the boat against the pilings.

Morgan found the key in the ignition, just where it had been left. He pushed it in to choke the motor and turned the key. The loud whine of the starter made them all jump. The motor didn't start. Morgan repeated the procedure, and was gratified to hear the motor catch with a throaty growl. He pulled the throttle back into reverse and the boat pulled away from the pier. Just then, they heard shouts from the shoreline, invisible through the fog, followed by a volley of shots. April heard the *zzzzip* of several bullets flying nearby. It was impossible to tell how close they had come, but the noise terrified her. Morgan pushed the throttle forward to max thrust and the boat leaped away from Grand Terre, into Barataria Pass.

George stood next to the console and tried to peer through the dark night and fog. Suddenly, the boat passed out of the fog like it was climbing out of a snowbank. The night sky was bright with a full moon. George looked back and saw the thick wall of fog reflecting the silver moonlight. The strong tide made the water's surface choppy, and the moonlight reflecting off of the waves made long, dancing shadows on the water's surface.

Morgan suddenly pulled the throttle back, slowing the boat and putting it into neutral, making George lose his balance and lurch towards the bow. He caught himself on the handrail at the side of the console. When he looked at Morgan, he could see the dagger in Morgan's hand. It was pointed at him. The boat slowly turned as the current pushed it out towards the open Gulf of Mexico.

"Get up in the bow! I don't want you standing close to me!" Morgan ordered him, and motioned with the dagger. George raised both hands and complied, sitting on the elevated deck in the bow of the boat with his back towards the bow, facing the center console. Morgan continued, speaking above the putting sound of the motor, "I'm not done with you yet! Either of you! Don't make me use this! Now come here, April, and steer the boat!"

April hesitated and George saw Morgan wave the dagger. She slowly moved behind the console and grasped the steering wheel. George watched helplessly as Morgan stood beside April, dagger in his left hand, and said, "It's just like driving a car, only less responsive."

I'm going to have to jump him and get that knife, but I have to wait for him to be distracted. I can't let him hurt April.

Morgan pushed the throttle forward, and pointed with the dagger for April to steer the boat towards the back side of Grand Isle. They flew across the water's surface in the bright moonlight. The electric lights of camps on Grand Isle were plainly visible to their left as they skimmed through the silver and shadow of the water.

Morgan had been formulating a plan during their escape, and he was now ready to carry it out. He thought, *I'll get back to Babineaux's pavilion and get these two in the car. I'll make April drive and George ride shotgun. That way, I can keep this dagger on him and stop any monkey business. I'll take them straight to the house on St. Ann Street. I'll bring them to the baron. He can do with them as he pleases.* He felt exhilarated as April piloted the speeding boat on the bay side of Grand Isle. He reached down and pushed the throttle to full bore.

It was calm behind the island, and the moonlight was sufficient for him to recognize the few small marsh islands and guide April to avoid them. When he reached Caminada Pass, the outgoing tide once again made the water choppy and made long shadows dance between the reflecting, silvery waves. The boat barreled through the chop with the spray rising on both sides of the gunnels.

George sat on the bow deck and waited for an opportunity.

40
THE PILING

May 16, 1972

The piling had been there since the 1950s. The crew that had been paid to remove the cribbing from the well head had pulled all of the pilings but one. It was late in the evening, and the orange sun was sinking into the endless tract of Spartina marsh to their west, when the crew made ready to pull the last piling. There was a loud, grinding noise, and smoke rose from the crane motor. "What da fuck, Bobby! Shut 'er down!" the crew boss hollered. The smoke slowly subsided, and they were soon able to see that the crane was disabled.

"What'cha wanna do, boss?" one of the hands asked.

The crew boss thought about it for a second, and then looked at Grand Isle, a small collection of camps, shacks, and small homes that had been battered by storms for centuries. Decision made, he said, "Fuck it! Unwrap that piling and let's get the fuck outta here!" He was already beginning to fill out the job completion sheet, ignoring the remaining piling.

Over the years, the piling had served as a marker for fishermen, a tie-off point for boats, a lookout spot for thousands of sea gulls, and, once, as the home of an osprey's nest. The sides of the piling were covered with white guano, like a spotty whitewash thrown against it. This night, in the moonlight filled with shadows and silver reflections, it was perfectly camouflaged. Morgan was smiling to himself with satisfaction at his plan to deal with George and April. A piling standing stout in the water was the last thing on his mind as the boat, at 35 miles an hour, ran dead into the center of the obstruction.

41

AN UNLIKELY RESCUE

May 16, 1972

The impact drove the nose of the boat down into the water, raising the propeller up into the air and filling the air with a vibrating scream that punctuated the violence of the collision. The impact threw all three passengers out of the boat.

George flew out backward and into the water. He didn't have time to think as he flew out of the boat. He struck his right shoulder on the chrome bow rail and found that he was in the deep water. He didn't lose consciousness, but was completely disoriented, and choked and sputtered since he had taken water into his lungs on the instant of hitting the water. He tried to keep afloat, but his shoulder was badly damaged and hurt terribly. His right arm was of no use as he tried to keep his head above the choppy water. He could feel the current trying to suck him down, and fought to keep his head up. He caught a breath and screamed, "April!", and then sucked in some water and coughed uncontrollably. He could hear nothing but the sound of his struggles in the water. The current, like some dark hand, pulled him underwater with the relentless rush of the tide. He fought his way to the surface again and caught another breath right before the current pulled him back under. His struggles began to weaken, and he heard a crackling, almost insect-like *hisss* in his ears as he tried to reach the surface again. His head broke water, and he tried to make some headway, but he couldn't fight the pull of the current.

George could feel the strength leaving him, and time seemed to slow. A part of him was aware that this was the end, even as he continued to try to keep his head above water. It was almost as if he was watching a movie of himself drowning. The panic he felt was replaced by a peaceful feeling of resignation. His struggles became less frantic and his head began to go down for the last time. He could see the silver sparkles of moonlight and had time to appreciate the beauty of the scene.

Just before his head slipped beneath the waves, he saw a large fin in the water. *Shark!* The thought panicked him and he began to struggle again. He felt something large rub against him. He tried to scream, but it made him breathe more water and he had a spasm of coughing. He slipped back underwater and began to sink, resigned to his fate, until something pushed between his left arm and his body and lifted him up so that his head was above the water.

He gulped in air and looked down. There, jutting out from beneath his arm, was a dolphin's snout. He looked behind his arm and saw the dolphin's dark eye, and felt the strong strokes of the animal's flukes. He thought he might be dreaming and that he was really drowning under the waves, but a splash of water in his face every now and then convinced him of the reality of his situation. He moved his left arm over the broad head of the creature and grasped the dorsal fin with his hand. The dolphin seemed to appreciate the gesture, and picked up its pace a bit. George's right shoulder hurt like hell, but he hung onto the dolphin's fin with his good left hand as he felt the power of the animal's rhythmic progression through the water.

He heard a voice in his mind. He thought it was coming from the dolphin, but it was Jim's voice. "Don't worry about a thing, George. I've got you."

George was sure he was in shock and hallucinating, but he murmured, "Thanks, pal," and let the dolphin take him where it would.

Soon, they were in a calmer section of water, and the standing waves of tidal current diminished along with the undertow. The dolphin glided easier, with less powerful strokes of its tail. Every so often, the dolphin would breathe, making a whooshing noise. George wondered where the dolphin was taking him. He started as he remembered April, and shouted her name aloud, almost losing his grip on the dorsal fin.

Jim's voice replied in his mind, "Don't worry, amigo. She's fine." George looked the dolphin in the eye. Once again, he heard Jim's voice in his mind, "Well, who else is around here to talk to you?"

George began to laugh, first in fits and then with hysterical giggles. "Who's going to believe me? A talking dolphin?!"

Jim's voice again: "Hey! Don't look a gift dolphin in the mouth! Here.... I'm going to submerge for a moment. Look across my body."

The dolphin fully submerged for the first time since it had lifted George with its snout. He looked forward in the silvery moonlight and saw another dolphin a short distance away. He could see there was a person holding onto the dolphin's fin. "April!" he yelled. No reaction from the person. He yelled for her again, and saw the white flash of a smile in response.

The dolphin reemerged and continued with long, slow strokes of its powerful tail. For the second time that night, George resigned himself to his fate, but this time with a glad heart.

After an indeterminate amount of time, the dolphin slowed its pace and George's legs, which had been parallel to the dolphin's body, began to sink. His feet touched a muddy bottom about four feet down, and the dolphin stopped and floated there. He released the dorsal fin, found his footing, and stood up straight, or as straight as he could with a damaged shoulder. He saw April standing several feet away. The dolphin that had saved her was also floating silently a few feet away. He moved to her and put his left arm around her.

"April! Are you all right?"

"I'm fine, George," she replied, shivering, "but I was drowning and it saved my life." She was looking at the dolphin. He cradled his bad arm in front of his body and the two lovers stood staring at the dark forms of the dolphins in the silver moonlight. The dolphins floated motionless in front of them.

George was overcome with emotion, and spoke, "Thank you, Jim. Thank you for everything. For teaching me to open my eyes, for the friendship, the adventures, for saving April's life, for saving my life. I love you, my friend."

The dolphins stayed still, looking at the two humans. April's dolphin turned and slowly swam away. Then, George's dolphin rose from the water, powered by short, strong, movements of its tail flukes. It was a large creature, and its white underside gleamed in the silver moonlight. It rose at least eight feet out of the water and remained still, tail working, both flippers out to its side, with its eyes looking directly at George and April. George was struck by the resemblance of the pose to Christ on the cross. He felt he was receiving a benediction, and was profoundly moved as he began to weep. He pulled April closer, and felt her body shaking from sobs, as well.

The dolphin stayed in that pose, motionless except for its powerful tail, for a count of three, and then slowly descended back into the water. It turned and gave a slap on the water with its tail, splashing George and April. They both began to laugh, and with a final slap of its tail, the dolphin disappeared into the moonlit waters.

42

SAFE ASHORE

May 16, 1972

G eorge's shoulder throbbed with pain, and a moan escaped his lips. April said with concern, "You're hurt, George. We need to get to shore," and began to lead him towards the bayside shoreline of Grand Isle, her arm around his waist.

He stopped, and asked, "Are you hurt, April?"

"No. It's a miracle, but I'm not hurt. I was disoriented when I flew into the water, and that current... it's so strong. I'm not a good swimmer, and I couldn't fight it. It felt like something was pulling me down no matter how hard I tried to keep my head above water. Then... then, I felt something big push me up. When I broke the surface, I saw the dolphin. I grabbed its flipper. It saved my life." She stopped talking and began to sob, "I thought you were dead!" They clung together just off of the shoreline for another minute. George took his good hand and brushed the hair away from April's face, and then bent down and gave her a long, slow kiss. They broke apart and, together, made their way to land.

They made their way through the thin line of marsh grass and onto the brush-covered shoreline. Moving was difficult with George favoring his right shoulder and April helping him walk by keeping her arm around his waist. After several minutes of wending their way through the brush, they found themselves at the end of a shell-covered street. They walked down the street towards a small house that had a porch light on. As they walked into the circle of yellow light in front of the house, they were surprised to see that each of them was bloodied from cuts and scratches, mostly as a result of the accident.

They walked up the low stairs to the porch, and April knocked at the door. It was opened by a short, plump, dark-haired woman in a bathrobe. "Mais, what's going on here?" she asked sternly.

"Please help us," April said. "There's been an accident."

The woman sprang into action and hurried onto the porch. "You poor things! Quick, come inside before the mosquitoes eat you alive! Jacques! Come here now! Vites!" Jacques, the woman's husband, ran out onto the porch, looked at what was happening for a moment, and then helped George into the warmly lit house as the woman assisted April. Now that the adrenaline of the recent event was beginning to subside, both of them began to shiver. The woman, Marie by name, walked out of the living room and came back quickly with two blankets that she arranged around the two of them.

"Run, Jacques! Call the chief of police!" Marie ordered him. Jacques left the room.

"Come, sit down, mon pauvre petits!" Marie murmured. George remembered Mama Zulie using that phrase to Jim, and his eyes welled up with tears. They let Marie lead them to an old, comfortable couch.

April stopped before sitting and said, "But we're all wet."

"Shush now! Sit!" Marie ordered, and they both complied. George sat with his right arm in front of him, cradled to his stomach, and his left hand grasping his right elbow. His shoulder throbbed with pain. Marie looked at his gray face and said, "You need to go to the hospital, ma chere. Don't worry, the chief will be here soon and he'll call for an ambulance."

George smiled wanly and thanked Marie. Then, he turned towards April and tightened his mouth for an instant. She understood what he meant instantly. In a few minutes, the door opened and Jacques returned with a man dressed in blue, cotton workpants and a checkered shirt. He nodded at Marie, and then walked up to George and April, and said with a gentle tone, "I'm Logan Dufrene, Chief of Police for Grand Isle. Tell me what happened."

Marie interrupted, "They'll tell you what happened, Logan, but first call for an ambulance. Can't you see that this man is hurt?"

The chief looked at George, nodded, and walked back outside to his car to call for an ambulance on the radio. When he was done, he came back inside and said, "OK, Marie. I've done what you want. Now—" he turned to George and April, "tell me what happened."

George and April both started talking at once, beginning at different parts of the story. The chief threw up his hands. "Whoa! One at a time. We'll get the whole story. Tell me first, how did you get hurt?"

George looked at April and she nodded for him to tell the tale. He began, "I'm George... George Santos. This is April Flowers. We were in a boat coming back from Grand Terre Island. There were three us. We hit something in the water. Hard. I hurt my shoulder and couldn't swim very well, but I made my way to shore. When I got there, I found April. She helped me walk up here to these kind people, and they called for you."

The chief looked at April and she nodded. "That's what happened, sir."

"There's somebody else out there?" the chief asked.

They both answered, "Yes, sir."

The chief looked at Jacques. "Jacques, go find Fleming and the other volunteer firemen and get them to look for someone on this end of the island, quick! I'm going to call for another ambulance." Jacques and the chief walked out of the door together. The chief came back in after a couple of minutes, sat in an overstuffed chair next to the couch, and asked, "Who is it we're looking for?"

April spoke first, "His name is Morgan Sanborne. He's a New Orleans City Councilman. He was holding us at knifepoint."

"Holy shit!" the chief let out a low whistle. "At knifepoint! A New Orleans City Councilman!" He shook his head and then stood up. "The ambulances will be here in about twenty minutes. They're coming from Golden Meadow. I've got to go and look for Mr. Sanborne." He started walking to the door, but stopped, turned, looked back at them, and said, "We'll talk more about this later." Then, he walked out the door.

George was feeling woozy with the pain from his arm and shoulder. Marie could see this and went back into the kitchen. She shortly returned with two cups of hot café' au lait. George and April gratefully took the cups and George felt better as he sipped the hot, sweet beverage.

There was soon a knock on the door. George could have sworn that it had been no more than ten minutes since the chief had called for an ambulance, but there was the medic. He came in and asked some questions. He began to examine George as his partner cleaned up some of April's cuts and scratches. After cutting George's shirt off, he determined that George had broken his collarbone. He wrapped George's arm in a sling. His partner, who had finished doctoring April's wounds, said, "I'll go get the gurney."

"Wait," George interjected. "I can walk. If you'll help me, I can get into the ambulance."

The medic patted George's good shoulder. "That's not how it works, friend. It's onto the gurney you go." In a minute, the gurney arrived, and George walked to it and gingerly laid down.

April said, "I'm going to go with him."

"That's fine, ma'am," the medic replied, "all I ask is that you stay out of my way if there's something I need to do."

"Of course, I will," April replied. The two men then began to wheel the gurney out of the house. April said, "Wait!" and they stopped. She walked to Marie and gave her a hug. "Thank you so much for helping us, Marie."

"Now, hush, cherie!" Marie responded, embarrassed. "You go with your young man and take care of yourself!" George waved his thanks to Marie as they wheeled him out the front door onto the porch.

The men carried the gurney down the steps and then began wheeling George to the ambulance, which stood in the street with its lights flashing. George could see that some people in the neighborhood had come outside to see what was happening. They opened the back door of the ambulance, positioned the gurney, and pushed it into the well-lit back. April and the medic climbed in beside him, one on either side. The medic quickly pulled out a bag of lactated ringers, searched for and found a vein in George's good arm, and got a fluid line started. The radio crackled to life as he was starting the line and they heard a voice announce that Morgan Sanborne had been found, and that he was injured but alive. Finished, the medic announced to his partner, "Line started. Let's go!" The partner put the ambulance into gear and, with lights flashing, began to make their way up the bayou road to the hospital.

43
NO ESCAPE

May 16, 1972

When the boat had struck the piling, Morgan had been thrown through the plexiglass windshield, which had shattered on impact. A large piece of the plexiglass had pierced his abdomen, and he'd been thrown into the water. The pain and shock had paralyzed him for several moments, and caused him to breathe in some water. This had brought him to his senses, and survival mode had kicked in. Morgan had always been a good swimmer, and he'd begun to swim instinctively. The pain in his abdomen had made it impossible to slip into his normal freestyle, so he'd quickly adopted a sideways crawl. Seeing the lights of Grand Isle to his left, he'd felt the current dragging him towards the Gulf of Mexico.

He assessed his situation as he swam towards the shoreline, and felt confident that he could swim to shore, but the pain in his gut grew as he exerted himself, and he felt himself tiring rapidly. The water's choppy surface frequently caused him to breathe in water, stopping his progress as he coughed and retched. The current's eddies and whirlpools began to affect him and pull him underwater, forcing him to expend more energy to keep his head above the surface.

He tried to look for the lights of shore, and saw that he hadn't made much progress. The tide was moving out and carrying him towards the bridge between the Cheniere and Grand Isle. He kept swimming, but the pain in his gut made it more and more difficult. His head slipped beneath the water for a moment and he choked again. He wasn't going to make it. Morgan began to weep with fury as he tried to continue swimming, but the injury was too great, and the adrenaline rush was losing to growing fatigue. The current pushed him inexorably towards the Gulf, and he soon saw the dark form of the concrete bridge pilings ahead. His arms could hardly move to keep his head above water, and he'd stopped kicking his feet by the time he passed underneath the bridge. He could see bright lights just above the water's surface, and re-alized it was Coleman lanterns that had been lowered from the old cre-osote bridge by fishermen. He could no longer keep his arms moving. He was tired and badly hurt. He ceased to weep and became resigned to his fate, so that, when his head slipped beneath the water for the final time, his thoughts were composed. He saw Sylva and his children in his mind's eye, and wondered what would happen to them. He saw his cousin, and his friends, and wondered how they would react to news of his death. His eyes were open underwater, and he saw the light of a Coleman lantern to his right as it cast its yellow circle onto the clear Gulf water.

He heard the baron's voice clearly. "No, Mr. Sanborne. No easy death for you. You have failed, and you belong to us." Morgan lost hope and consciousness at the same time.

On the fishing bridge, a young man who worked as a fireman in New Orleans had been fishing for speckled trout since early evening. He'd hung a lantern to attract smaller fish and shrimp, which were soon followed by the trout. The water was clear and he was watch-ing trout come up and eat the bait, trying to select the larger trout to cast towards. He suddenly saw a large shadow streak past his lantern's light. Before he could say anything, a dolphin jumped out of the water close to his lantern. It landed with a splash that just missed putting out his light. The young man had fished off of the bridge many times before, but he'd never seen a dolphin act this way. He was transfixed, and watching closely for any other show when he saw a man just under the water slowly float by. The water was clear enough for him to see that the man's eyes were open. He yelled, "There's a man down there. Help!" This attracted the attention of fellow fishermen and women on the bridge who hurried towards him. He threw down his fishing pole and kicked off his tennis shoes, climbed onto the bridge railing, and leapt to the water fifteen feet below. He hit the water with a large splash, then emerged and swam towards where he thought the current had taken Morgan. He found him at the edge of the circle of light cast by the lantern. Morgan was unconscious. The fireman wrapped one arm around Morgan's torso, raising his head above water, and began side-stroking towards the shore. The crowd on the bridge shouted advice and ran along the bridge towards the shore, following his progress.

After several minutes of swimming, he was able to touch the seabed, and he floated Morgan in his arms, like a baby, into shallower water. When he had maneuvered Morgan into the shallow water, several onlookers jumped in and carried Morgan to shore. Another person moved their car and turned on the lights for illumination. A woman identified herself as a nurse and knelt next to Morgan, holding his head to the side. The young fisherman bent over to see the man better just as Morgan began coughing and vomiting up water. Morgan moaned, and then the fisherman and nurse both noticed the large piece of plexiglass jutting out of his abdomen.

"Look at that!" the fisherman exclaimed.

The nurse responded by saying in a commanding tone, "Everyone back. Give him some room." Morgan was alternately coughing and retching, his legs rising off the ground with the violence of the spasms. These spasms soon slowed, then stopped. Morgan lay there, unconscious and breathing shallowly. The nurse called out, "I need a knife!" One of the onlookers gave her a sharp pocketknife. She cut away Morgan's shirt, pushing it aside to see the location of the puncture wound.

She spoke to the young man, saying, "It's in his intestines. We can't take it out now. It will make it worse. We have to leave it in until he gets to surgery. We need an ambulance!"

The young man turned to the onlookers and yelled, "Somebody get the police! We need an ambulance!"

It took less than ten minutes for two police cars to arrive with their lights flashing. A uniformed officer stepped out of one vehicle, and a man dressed in work pants and a checkered shirt stepped out of the other. The plain-clothes man quickly walked up to where Morgan lay on the shoreline. The nurse spoke first. "He's alive, but he's badly hurt. He has a piece of glass in his abdomen—probably pierced his intestines. We can't remove it. He needs surgery!"

Chief Dufrene knelt next to Morgan and responded, "I'm Police Chief Logan Dufrene. There's an ambulance on the way. It should be here in ten minutes. Tell me what happened."

The young fisherman told his story to Chief Dufrene. Morgan began to move his head and tried to speak. The chief leaned down close to Morgan's mouth to hear what he was saying. He stayed like this for more than a minute, just listening. Then he looked up.

The nurse asked, "What is he saying?"

"He's not making any sense at all," the chief responded. "He just keeps repeating 'Save me from the baron. Save me from the baron,' over and over." They heard the distant wail of an ambulance siren getting louder. The siren turned off before it reached the shell parking lot at the base of the fishing bridge, but its lights kept flashing. The two paramedics quickly brought the gurney down to the shoreline and, after speaking to the nurse and examining Morgan, loaded him onto the gurney and into the ambulance. The siren began to wail as the ambulance took off from the parking lot on its way to the hospital in Golden Meadow.

The young fisherman looked at the nurse and asked, "I wonder what he meant, by 'Save me from the baron'?"

"God knows," the nurse replied, "But congratulations on catching him. You may have saved his life."

The young man smiled and said, "You, too." He stuck out his hand, and they shook.

44

A BRIGHT MORNING

May 18, 1972

George experienced the next day as a blur. The doctors at the hospital had treated him for his broken collarbone and also for a fractured humerus. They'd cast his arm and put it in a sling that night. The following morning, they'd insisted that he remain in the hospital since he'd developed a slight fever. They'd kept him well-sedated with pain medications. The combination of the stress, injuries, and pain meds had resulted in George sleeping most of that day and night.

He awoke the next morning to find April sitting in a chair next to his hospital bed. His arm and shoulder were sore, but the throbbing pain had diminished. He gave April a smile and asked, "How long have you been sitting there?"

She shrugged and replied, "Maybe an hour."

"What time is it?"

"Eight-thirty. You slept most of yesterday and all night."

He gave her a grin. "That must be why I'm feeling rested." He looked down at his right arm, which was in a cast and held in a sling held against his chest. "Lucky I'm left-handed. I don't know what I would do if I broke my left arm." He threw the covers off of himself and slid his feet off the bed, turning himself as he did so to sit up. He grimaced as his shoulder pained him during the maneuver, but as soon as he'd reached a stable sitting position on the side of the bed, the pain in his shoulder quieted. He looked at April with concern and asked, "How are you doing, April?"

Surprised, she smiled and answered, "Me? I'm fine. Just a few scratches." Here, she pointed to some small scratches on her forehead, cheek, and the bridge of her nose. "You were the one who got hurt... and Morgan." She frowned.

George drew in a breath. "Morgan! I forgot about him. I guess he made it. How is he?"

April pulled her chair closer to George. She spoke in a low voice. "They think he's going to make it. He had a puncture wound in his gut and had to have surgery. He's in the intensive care unit here in the hospital. The nurse told me that they're afraid he may have peritonitis. He's not out of the woods."

George gave a low whistle, shook his head, and growled, "What the hell is going on with him? I thought he was a good guy. Now, I know better. He's the one who got Jim killed. He was up to something last night...." He waved April's correction away. "Night before last, I mean. The way he reacted to Nez. It's like he was expecting something to happen to us and not him. Remember? He kept asking about some baron. Then, after we escaped, he had a dagger and said that he was going to use it on us if we didn't follow his instructions."

April leaned towards George and put a hand on his knee. "Listen, George," she said, "the chief of police questioned me yesterday about what happened. I told him that we were all going to Grand Terre, on Morgan's suggestion. Some people were supposed to give us a tour and I was there to take pictures. My boss at the *Times Picayune* verified my story. I told the chief that Morgan invited you personally. Can Tony verify that Morgan invited you to come to Grand Terre?"

"Of course," George said, "he was there when Morgan invited me, and told me to take the afternoon off and have fun."

"Good." April continued, "I told him that when we arrived, Morgan began acting strangely, and we couldn't find the people who were supposed to give us the tour."

"But—"George tried to interrupt.

"Shush!" April admonished him, "Listen! I told the chief that Morgan appeared to have some sort of breakdown. That he threatened us and held us captive. He asked if Morgan had hurt us, or me, particularly, and I told him no. I didn't mention Nez, or Jean Lafitte, or any of the weird stuff that happened last night. Just that Morgan had some sort of breakdown."

George looked at April and nodded. He asked, "What did the chief say?"

April replied, "It's funny. He seemed to expect it! After I told him my story about what had happened, he told me that when they rescued Morgan from the water, he kept repeating, "Save me from the baron." The chief was convinced that Morgan had suffered some sort of breakdown before I even told him about it.

"Thank you, April," he said as he picked up her hand and kissed it. "You are so smart, and brave, and kind..."

She laughed and slapped his knee. "Yeah, I know, I'm the best!"

He grabbed her hand again and held it. "Yes, you are the best. Now, how can a fellow get breakfast in this joint?"

April pointed to a string that was hanging above the bed. "If you pull that string, a nurse will answer. Maybe you should ask her?" They both laughed.

45

THE BILL COMES DUE

May 18, 1972

Morgan was in a fevered dream. He was walking along a rocky path in a cave. His way was lit by a red glow, as if the ground was glass and that glass lay over a lava lake. It was hot. The path was barely wide enough for him to walk, and the sharp rocks were too low for him to walk upright. His back ached, for it had been hours since he'd been able to stand up straight. Sweat poured down his forehead and into the corners of his eyes, making them burn. He wanted something to wipe his eyes. He looked down and saw that he was completely naked. He used the back of his knuckles to wipe at the sweat, but it only worked for a moment, and his eyes felt as if they were filled with sharp sand. He had to keep moving.

He was thirsty... incredibly thirsty. *I need to find some water*, he thought to himself as he walked deeper into the cave. The path twisted, and in the low, red light, he could see a rock wall ahead as the path turned towards the right.

"It's only a little bit farther," he encouraged himself, "and I'll find some water." He continued walking. Time felt different in the cave. He could have walked for five minutes or thirty. The path turned to the left, and he thought he heard the sound of falling water. He picked up his pace, repeatedly wiping the burning sweat from his eyes as he labored along the rough path. The sound of water became more distinct. He picked up his pace again, stumbling every now and then with a curse. Water was close, and he had never been thirstier in his life. He could smell water now, and began to trot. The path turned to the right and he came to a stop. There in front of him was a beautiful, tropical oasis. Lush and green, different types of fruit trees, date palms, and colorful flowers surrounded a deep, dark pool of water that lay at the bottom of a tall waterfall. He laughed out loud.

He realized that everything was getting blurry, and a bright light seemed to fill the spaces around him. He wanted to scream, "Stop!"— but found that he couldn't speak. His mouth was so dry. He saw a blurry shape, and as his eyes began to focus, he recognized it as a nurse clad in blue scrubs, with a white, cloth mask covering the lower part of her face. He realized that he was lying down and the nurse was standing over him. He was in a room in a hospital! He heard her say, "He's coming around, doctor," and looked down towards his feet as he lay in the hospital bed. He could see there was a tall man, dressed in a white lab coat at the foot of the bed. The man's back was turned towards him. Morgan realized this was the doctor that the nurse was speaking to.

He looked back up at the nurse, and saw that she had blonde hair and nice, kind eyes. He had an instant's thought of what it would be like to take her mask off and see her lips and chin. She looked down at him. He saw something move on the ceiling above her masked face. He squinted his eyes to focus, and saw it was a large, crawling cockroach. A shiver passed through his body.

He felt the doctor come up to the other side of his bed as he focused back on the nurse's face. It suddenly began to melt, as if it were made of wax. A grunt came unbidden from his throat. The melting wax face of the nurse seemed to separate into thousands of distinct, small shapes. He turned towards the doctor as he leaned over the bed and looked down at Morgan. He was dark, and the contrast made by his skin and the bright, ceiling lights above him made Morgan blink his eyes to try to gain focus on the man's face. The doctor seemed to recognize the difficulty that Morgan was having focusing, and he moved his head to block the light at the same time that he removed the cloth mask he wore.

Morgan's eyes widened with horror. The face smiled, sharp white rat's teeth gleaming in the light. The cruel eyes of the baron danced as a slow, deep chuckle escaped his lips. Morgan turned away from the baron and looked back towards the nurse. He saw a grotesque caricature of a man composed of thousands of sharp, spiny insects. He could feel his gorge rising and heard the rustle of dry wings as the man leaned down towards him. A desiccated parody of a human voice that he recognized as Mr. Mara spoke, "Well, well, Mr. Sanborne. You have failed, and now you will pay that which you owe."

The screams rose from the balls of Morgan's feet through his legs and loins, his gut and chest, and escaped his throat with the hopelessness of a trapped animal.

46
SUMMER'S JOY

June 4, 1972

The mockingbird's call slowly woke George up to a cool, gray dawn. He lay in bed with April. She was still sleeping on her side, knees drawn up, with her back to him. He lay and listened to the mockingbird, and wondered if it was the same one he had heard before—the one with the call that sounded like a streetcar bell. The bird seemed to be listening to his thoughts as its call progressed to the *clang, clang, clang* of a streetcar's bell. *Smart bird*, he thought, smiling.

It had been over two weeks since the encounter with Morgan. George had thought about that experience a lot in the past days. He had satisfied Logan Dufrene as to why and how he had been there that day, and how the accident had occurred. Moreover, when he'd returned to New Orleans and been questioned by the NOPD, he'd found out that Sonny had caused the opening of an inquiry into Morgan and his influence with the chief. They'd questioned Brenda and she'd told them of Morgan's plan to force the sale of the property on Dumaine Street. On questioning, the chief had dropped Morgan like a hot potato, and provided testimony that Morgan had been involved in a property scheme for ill-gotten gains, as well as that, in doing so, he had illegally used the influence of his position as a city councilman. The chief's contention was that he'd been playing out rope to ensnare Morgan in a sting operation. The investigators had been satisfied with the chief's explanation.

Morgan, for his part, had suffered a complete mental breakdown and, when released from the hospital in Golden Meadow, had been committed to Southeast Louisiana Hospital in Mandeville. This was a state mental institution. He responded to no external stimuli, and no one could tell what was going on inside his mind. The only clue was a look of perpetual horror on his face.

April stirred and turned towards him. She opened her eyes and smiled sleepily. "Good morning," she said as she rubbed sleep from her eyes.

"Morning, sweetheart."

"Have you been awake long?"

"Not really. I was just lying here listening to the mockingbird. I really do think he's imitating a streetcar bell."

April laughed out loud. Then, she put her head close to him and kissed his cheek. He responded by tickling her. April squealed, and began to tickle George.

"Stop! Stop! My arm! Ow!" he yelled.

April stopped immediately, with a look of concern on her face, and, once again, he reached up and tickled her. They tussled for a minute and then stopped. April said, "I'm hungry. How about you?"

"I could eat an alligator from the tail up!" he replied. "Let's get dressed and get some beignets and coffee."

"Yummy!" she said, licking her lips.

They came back after the coffee and beignets. The sun was shining, and the air was warm with the promise of Summer's heat and humidity. They walked down the alleyway, past the closed door of Astro's and through the door leading to the courtyard. George was always amazed at the lush and fragrant garden. Today was even better than usual. The smell of bananas wafted in the air, mixed with sweet honeysuckle. Mandevilla and Bougainvilla displayed their gaudy blooms as the vines grew along the brick walls. The citrus trees had finished blooming and sported small green fruit amongst their glossy leaves, and the smooth bark of the crepe myrtle invited hands to feel their cool texture.

They stood in the courtyard, speechless for a moment. A door opened, and Mama Zulie stepped out of her apartment. She was dressed beautifully, as always, and walked up to the lovers.

She spoke in her thick, French accent. "Bonjour, mon cheries! It is wonderful to see you on this beautiful morning!"

"Good morning, Mama Zulie!" they chimed in unison. April had been staying with George since Grand Terre, and she had already gone to Mama Zulie's and eaten cake and champagne.

"I must go perform some errands, mon cheries, but perhaps some cake and champagne later?"

April replied, "That sounds wonderful, Mama Zulie!"

And, with a breezy, "A tout a l'heure!" Mama Zulie left.

Almost immediately, JC and Anna walked through the door into the courtyard. They cheerily greeted George and April, then walked up and gave hugs all around. JC said, "Now, what are you two lovebirds up to today?"

George replied, "We don't have any plans, really. We just went to the Café du Monde. How about you?"

"You know me," JC replied. "I'll stick around here and get ready to open Astro's. You never know who's going to walk in the door, and I like to be ready when they do."

April asked, "What about you, Anna? Got any plans?"

Anna reached out and grabbed April's hand. "Well, yes, April. The twins invited me to the lakefront to join them and a group of their friends. If you and George would like to come, I'm sure they'd love it."

George looked at Anna with his head cocked to the side and asked, "Is it what I think it is?"

She winked back at him, smiled, nodded, and said, "Yes. Death soccer".

George whooped and grabbed April's hand. "You're going to love this, April. Come on, Anna, let's go!"

The mockingbird began to sing as they walked out of the courtyard.

47

EPILOGUE

June 4, 1972

JC watched Anna, George, and April leave the courtyard. He followed them as they turned at the end of the alleyway. The open door of Astro's beckoned to him, but he made no effort to enter. He just stood in the alley outside the door. He did not have long to wait.

The tall, thin form of the baron turned into the alley from Dumaine Street. He strode to JC and stood just two feet away. His dark, granite face was carved into a scowl. JC retained his usual peaceful countenance.

The baron spoke first. "You think saving these miserable humans is success? Your meddling in our plans will come to naught, I tell you. You are as insignificant as a mosquito in the face of the dark force that is moving. Mara has sent me to explain the futility of your present course, and to invite you to join in the preparations for the dark time that is to come. If you continue, you may serve to delay that time for a short period, but you, Anna, and your friends will inevitably be crushed. The great wheel is, at last, turning, and you will either choose to help with the grinding or be ground yourself. What is your choice?"

JC had listened to the baron's diatribe patiently. His face had remained passive throughout. He slowly brought his arms up, palms outward, until they were raised halfway, as if showing that he meant no harm. He spoke slowly and calmly, "Why don't you come into the bar and have a drink, Baron?" He then turned, and walked into the open door of Astro's.

The Baron stood there motionless as his scowl grew even more pronounced. "You have chosen unwisely," he said as he turned and marched out of the alley and onto the street.

It started as a low growl, and grew higher in timber and voice as it progressed through a howl into the upper registers of a full-throated scream. It was bloodcurdling, or would have been if anyone had been around to hear it on the 55th floor of the Mara Building. The frustration and hate that filled the scream was palpable enough to send the pigeons that had been roosting on the cornice of the roof into flight, dodging with their wings folded as if being pursued by a falcon. They felt the danger in that scream, and something else that pushed them to fly faster. A promise... a promise of action that would come as surely as a dark night followed the bright light of day.

THE END
12:49 PM
OCTOBER 7, 2020

Made in the USA
Columbia, SC
04 April 2024

34007499R00240

ABOUT
THE AUTHOR

John R. Greene was born and raised in New Orleans. He attended the University of New Orleans (UNO), off and on, and graduated with a BA in Anthropology in 1979. He worked his way through college as a dry cleaner, cemetery caretaker, and as a student worker at the Archaeological and Cultural Research Program (ACRP) of UNO. He worked as a professional archaeologist for the ACRP, focusing on both the historic and prehistoric archaeology of southeastern Louisiana, from 1980-88. During his time at the ACRP, he completed all course work for a BS and MS in Geology from UNO. Following that, he worked as a marine archaeologist and social scientist for the Minerals Management Service, Department of the Interior, until 1998. After leaving the Department of the Interior, he began a new career as an exploration geologist and worked for the next two decades as an independent geologist. He has an abiding love for the history, culture, geology, and geography of New Orleans and southeastern Louisiana matched by a passion for music. He lives on a small farm on the North Shore of Lake Pontchartrain with his wife, Patti, their dog, Elly, and two horses.

Follow John R. Greene on social media
twitter.com/@jrgreeneauthor
Instagram: @frenchquartersaints
Website: johnrgreene.net

musicians. Having grown up in New Orleans I was lucky enough to see many of them perform. Indeed, one of my earliest memories is of an impromptu trip with my family to see Fats Domino's house in the Ninth Ward after watching a movie at the old Skyvue drive-in. I have tried to describe New Orleans' musicians as I see them, forces of light in a difficult world. They have brought a great deal of joy to my life.

I hope that I've provided some entertainment to those who have read the novel and that my readers find a glimpse of the love I hold for the city of my birth. It is also my sincere hope that my readers gain some knowledge of that most European of American cities, New Orleans. I owe much to my family, friends, and mentors. I owe much to New Orleans. I am sincerely grateful.

careful remembrance. I've also tried to be true to the placement and description of these places. All the historical vignettes are, to some extent, true to the City's history. I've taken liberty with characters, etc. but the underlying facts are real. For instance, excavations at the Hermann-Grima house in the 1980's uncovered some pieces of pottery which had been locally made and fired in the manner of the indigenous inhabitants of the area. This pottery appeared to have been closer in style to European types of plates and bowls.

Another example, I spent the better part of two years working on archaeological investigations of Cypress Grove No. 2 cemetery, much of which is still underneath the road and neutral ground (median) of Canal Boulevard near the intersection of Metairie Road. This was the "potter's field" for the city during the worst of the Yellow Fever epidemics of the mid Nineteenth century and the final resting place for about 40,000 souls. The description of the cemetery in the vignette of the Yellow Fever epidemic is accurate.

Yet another example is the tale of Bobby on Mardi Gras day. This is a fictionalization of my family's history. My father won a talent show on Canal Street during the Depression when he was about 8 years old. He sang "She's Only a Bird in a Gilded Cage" and, after being declared the winner, did an impromptu jig. His prize was a large turkey which he and his brother took turns carrying home.

While I have tried to be true to New Orleans' history and geography, all the major characters in my novel are entirely fictitious. Any similarity between these characters and real persons is completely coincidental. Novels typically have protagonists and antagonists, and this novel is no different. All these characters' attributes, both good and bad, sprang, like Athena, from my brow. One of the entertaining things about writing fiction is that you get to play God with your characters.

My readers may notice that I have an almost reverential attitude towards musicians in general, and, specifically, towards New Orleans

AFTERWORD

This novel is a work of fiction. It is set in New Orleans as it was in 1972. Those of you who were around New Orleans back then know that it was a tumultuous time. Old ways were being challenged and some new, different mores were being developed. To paraphrase Bob Dylan, the times they were a'changin'.

It is interesting to note that the changes that were occurring, particularly among the young people of the nation (and world), reflected a reality that had, to some extent, been existing in the French Quarter of New Orleans for a generation. The laissez-faire attitude towards race, sexuality, drugs, spiritualism, and other practices which had been noted in the Quarter in the 40's and 50's spread throughout the nation, and the world.

Rock n' Roll was the exuberant expression of this dynamic change, and New Orleans was at the forefront of this new type of music. John Lennon once said that without Fats Domino there would have been no Beatles. I believe that without New Orleans, there would have been no Fats Domino. Not that Fats, or any other New Orleans musician, approved of every trend that has been associated with Rock n' Roll. Rather that the true spirit of New Orleans is one of inclusion, and not of exclusion, and that our musicians have an instinctive understanding of this.

I've taken pains to write about real places that existed in the New ⌒ leans of 1972. This involved a fair amount of research and some